HIGh ЦАКИ

Mark Law is a former feature writer and commissioning editor for *The Times*, the *Mail on Sunday* and the *Daily* and *Sunday Telegraph*. He was the founding editor of the online news magazine *The First Post*, now *theweek.co.uk*, and is the author of *The Pyjama Game, A Journey into Judo*, for which he was named Best New Writer in the British Sports Book Awards.

HIGH
HARM

MARK LAW

First published 2016 by
Ravelin Books

www.highharm.com

Publisher: Graham Coster
Cover design: Jamie Keenan, www.keenandesign.com

The author would like to acknowledge the kind help of Robert Cowan, Pearson Phillips, Nicolas Soames, François von Hurter, Tom Coveney, John Lobrano, Peter Blewett, Ben Soames

A catalogue record for this book is available from the British Library.

Typeset in Minion and GoBold by SX Composing DTP, Rayleigh, Essex
Printed and bound in the UK by Amazon CreateSpace

To Joan

The following events are true but some of them have not yet occurred.

Prof. Glyn Owen

PROLOGUE

Wake up, dead man! It's time to move. Spring is here and the big show in the valley is about to begin. The people from the damp grey cities in the plains will soon be arriving and they're coming here to play. This is their idea of heaven – but it's not the sort of heaven where people like you just lie around doing nothing. Not that you qualify for entry. Anyway, this is no place for you now. These people don't like dead bodies: you lower the tone – particularly one in your state. God! Your face! What did they do to you? It's like a smile that's gone badly wrong. But it isn't just the sight of you that is unhelpful, even talk of corpses creates negative attitudes around here. Monsieur le Maire and Monsieur le Chef de Publicité would surely be hurrying to the Mairie as soon as they have heard the news. Monsieur le Maire striding across the square cursing this unfortunate corpse situation, while Hector Beluzon, his PR man, head turned deferentially towards his master as he talks, scurries along beside him trying to calm him by listing some damage-limitation options.

So, dead man, now they have found you they will want to ask you some questions. 'What happened? How did you die?' You are not obliged to say anything, but you will. Corpses always do. In fact some can be quite chatty. Although you will be talkative, you may not be too informative. How they will wonder what to make of you. They will also wonder who did that to your face.

It will have been someone on foot who found you, but the gendarmerie would have come by helicopter, landing some distance away where the ground is level. The engine cowling ticks like a tin clock as the metal cools and contracts; the gendarmes pant and sweat as they climb the slope in the sunshine. There will be birdsong because the finches have come back for the summer.

It will be so warm that it will be hard to believe how cold it was when you died.

Died?

ACT ONE

1

'This is the bit but you need to look very carefully,' said Tyler. 'It's only a moment.'

The four of them huddled closer to the screen as the head-cam bounced around, crashing through the low snow-covered branches. Sometimes the camera flicked up so that the sky was momentarily visible between the tops of the trees; mostly it ducked down to show the tips of the cameraman's skis as they cut through the lumpy pillows of the forest terrain.

'There! Look,' said Tyler in an excited half-whisper, his finger stabbing involuntarily at the screen. 'Can you see him?'

'Well possibly . . . but not really,' said Mike, who could see nothing more than a faint blur of a moving shape caught by the camera as it hurtled past on its wobbly course. Almost instantly it was gone.

'Billy, can we have that again please,' he asked.

The picture quality was lousy but on the second viewing there was no doubt about it. First they saw the path ahead jumping from side to side and then, a few metres down the slope in the trees beside the track, what at first looked like a snow-covered boulder rose up and unfolded into a human figure clad entirely in white from head to toe. Tyler said he thought the man was very small, but couldn't be sure; he seemed to be carrying some sort of cylinder swathed in white cloth, but when Billy replayed it for them frame by frame they all agreed it looked more like a powerful telescopic camera lens.

2

Fear. Owen had always felt anxious about this enterprise but, understandably, his anxiety had now turned to fear. It had first manifested itself three months earlier with some spasmodic appearances; these had grown ever more frequent until now – now this fear was always with him. Sometimes it was a cold stone lodged in his head; sometimes a great soggy weight clamped around his whole frame.

No one in the audience, flicking glances at him while the Director did her introduction, could have guessed his mental state as he sat there silently, exuding a warm undiscriminating 'hello' to one and all, and nor did they realise how carefully he was scanning their faces. New intake, mostly early twenties, raw, he thought. A couple of lookers in there too.

'. . . he is the author of numerous books and papers – you will have heard of *The Marketplace Bombers, a Coming Threat,* which has had a profound influence in intelligence circles around the world . . .'

The Director was a bit of a looker herself in a trim forty-plus kind of way. Owen was certainly enjoying her flattering introduction.

'. . . a distinguished commentator on irregular warfare. Gadfly of the military establishment . . .'

Gadfly or madfly?

'. . . but certainly one of our most original thinkers . . . a true controversialist . . .' *Controversialist? You haven't heard the half of it yet, darling.*

'. . . whose ideas constantly surprise . . .' *What was it he found so sexy about women who were fascinated by war?* '. . . so please join me in giving a warm welcome to Professor Glyn Owen.'

Owen stood up, responded to the applause with a couple of perfunctory nods and gave them his self-deprecating, I'm-just-a-humble-academic smile.

Here we go then. He stepped onto the dais and tapped the

start key on the laptop. The large screen behind him went black for a few moments before the title faded in: five words in white on black in a chunky matter-of-fact font: TRIUMPH OF THE GANGSTER STATE.

3

> True freedom is working for somebody else.
>
> *Reginald Peplow*

Pity the soul who has never stood in an Alpine dawn. The mountains begin to wake with the first signs of light and as the darkness grows pale you can see these silent creatures stretch, yawn and breathe a little faster. Mike liked to study their faces in the light of the new day to see what sort of mood they were in. He usually rose early when he was here in Val de Ligne – often when it was still dark – for the early morning was when he could work best; life's problems were less inclined to intrude in those precious, optimistic early hours. As soon as the sun began to seep into the sky he would make a shot of coffee to take out onto the wooden balcony where he watched the town wake up.

Mike Warne from Harpenden, Herts had been coming to this French ski resort almost every winter for twenty years, since his teens, and the little place was the scene of some of the happiest days of his life. His situation was very different from his first visit as a young man, unattached, with a bunch of university friends. Now that he had a family, skiing was a less casual affair. But this was his time – three whole weeks in Val while his wife and son were with the in-laws – thanks to a backlog of leave from Olympia Engineering. Mike did love his skiing.

4

Ski resorts operate on a brilliant business model. For centuries the Alpine population had clung to a precarious life in its valleys by milking, eating, and trading cattle fattened on summer pastures. Then, about one hundred and twenty years ago, adventurous travellers from faraway lands arrived to explore the mountains. They gave their fellow countrymen such rhapsodic accounts of the benefits to health conferred by the Alpine climate that the locals were soon prospering from a brisk trade in accommodation, food and transport.

The mountain folk had no sooner congratulated themselves on being able to sell their air when they discovered they had another treasure that was almost as plentiful. Snow! The tyrant who appeared each winter, trapping them in their houses for half their lives, suddenly became a precious asset. Observing the locals move around on skis, the visitors copied them and were so entranced by the experience that they encouraged others to try it. Others brought others and so on until the mountains received an annual deluge of visitors who saw skiing not as a utilitarian solution to a logistical problem, but a sublime pleasure. If these eccentric enthusiasts had made a mistake with their travel arrangements and ended up in Shanghai instead of Wengen, they would probably have turned rickshaw-pulling into a popular leisure pastime, one that would in time evolve into a multi-billion-dollar global industry and a major Olympic sport.

The exquisite pleasure of the skiing, the scenery, the pure low-oxygen air, combined with the tempting arrays of food and drink laid out by the locals, caused visitors to loosen their grasp on their wallets and excrete piles of currency all over the place. The once impoverished inhabitants now possessed an alchemy that could turn frozen water into gold.

To lure more prey, the locals learned how to festoon their mountains with webs spun from steel thread to carry moving cabins and chairs. Cattle were soon a minor element of the economy of the little towns and villages, which had now become fabulous clanking, whirring bio-mechanical money-machines.

5

As the words TRIUMPH OF THE GANGSTER STATE faded into black, Owen began to speak. *Be different from the others.*

> 'Before we address our subject perhaps you'd all like to join me in offering up our profound gratitude for the illegal trade in drugs. We sometimes spend too much time being negative – for instance, we obsess about the victims whose lives are ruined by this commerce – but pay scant attention to those who prosper from it.'

The delivery was cheerful and smiley; Owen's voice had that sonorous Welsh polished-wood quality which seemed constantly on the edge of song. Shortish and somewhere between stocky and comfortable, he had a full head of slightly wayward brown hair; his face, pale and heavily lined, appeared nonetheless to be in a state of constant amusement. The colleague who gave the eulogy at his funeral a few weeks later said that if you saw Owen without a smile on his face it was because one had only just left and another one was due in shortly.

> 'Millions benefit from regular or part-time employment in the illicit drugs industry. Small farmers' lives have been transformed by the cultivation of the opium poppy and the coca leaf; customs officers can enhance their pay by taking bribes, prison officers can make some extra cash by bringing drugs into the workplace for their charges. Then there are the mules – the couriers – who get free holidays in exotic places,

the dealers, their bodyguards, the chemists and, of course, the whole army of those who deal with the human remains – doctors and nurses and the rest of the addiction industry.'

Owen was pleased to see some of his audience shifting in their seats, adjusting their posture to cope with this unexpected intrusion of poor taste. *I have unsettled them.*

'And then, we must not forget, us! Where would *we* all be without "the trade"? Well for a start, we wouldn't be here this afternoon in the glorious countryside of Hedley Coram. The trade has brought us together here, us well-paid foot soldiers in the war on drugs.

'Oh what a lovely war!'

6

Although, of course, Mike did not realise it at the time, he would say afterwards it all began to go pear-shaped for him one afternoon in his second week when he tried to dodge a snowboarder on the bumps at the top of Farandole; he caught an edge and went flying. Legs left to their own devices will sort themselves out; it's when you strap boots and skis on them that the trouble starts. Joints can get horribly bent and twisted so a cruciate or a medial goes *rrrrippp* or *snap,* and your kneecap is left feeling like a bowl of writhing linguine. This one wasn't too bad, thank God, but certainly something nasty had happened and he knew he would have to call it a day.

He managed to get down the hill but it wasn't much fun getting his boot off and within a couple of hours the knee had swollen badly. He gave it the works with anti-inflammatory pills and an ice pack and next day went for a precautionary X-ray. Mike hated going to the clinic; it made him feel as though he was attending some sort of support group for middle-class wallies with self-harming issues. Although there was no serious damage he was told to rest the leg completely for a few days, after which he should do some walking and exercises. It was a bitter blow. Every day in Val was precious to him – but only if he could ski. A soul that has no skis feels pretty pointless in a place like this and the town centre of any ski resort is a depressing place in the middle of the day.

After five frustrating days, during which he'd been faithfully doing exercises to build up the knee and maintain his CV fitness, Mike put his recovery to the test, borrowed a pair of cross-country skis and set off on the langlauf course that encircled part of the town.

When he reached the trees at the north end of the circuit, just above the crossroads where it looped around a small frozen lake, he realised that he was in striking distance of Chalet Messigny. He'd heard people talk about the flashy new building that had replaced the ancient chalet, so when he saw something resembling a path through the trees heading roughly in the direction of the chalet, he turned off the circuit.

Chalet Messigny seemed to rise to greet the visitor emerging from the trees – a rectangle of concrete and rough-cut stone, with some wood-clad surfaces, apparently growing out of the rock on which it stood. It was an impressive sight. Quietly stylish, the ground floor was strangely windowless except for a long run of floor-to-ceiling glass one side – two-storeys high at one end – opening onto a large terrace of patterned wood decking. For all its elegance, it had the hint of a fortress about it.

There was a raucous din of dogs barking; they sounded large and quite cross. As Mike reached the terrace, a man emerged from a side door, shouting at the animals to be silent. He asked Mike in French how he could help. He seemed genial. Mike explained that he had heard a lot about the new building and was curious to see it. Now that he'd heard Mike's French, the man switched to English.

'You do realise this is private property?'

'I'm sorry – I was just passing and thought I'd take a look. It's as spectacular as people say.'

'Yes, it's quite something. I'd invite you in to have a look round, but we're in a bit of a flap at the moment getting the place ready.'

As he spoke Mike's attention was caught by the way the slender glazing bars of the chalet's wide rectangular windows seemed to be supporting the massive stone wall of the upper storey. It was a nice trick played on the eye using concealed steels cantilevered out from the core of the building. Mike suddenly became aware that his interrogator was staring at him.

'Quite understand. I'm sorry to have intruded.'

'No problem. Maybe another time. Are you here for the week?' Something in the man's tone suggested that this wasn't social intercourse, it was information-gathering.

'No, I've got three weeks.'

'Long holiday.'

'Not all holiday, I'm afraid. I'm really just here to do some work and get some skiing at the same time.' Mike didn't mention the Project because the Team were still keeping that under wraps.

'I'm Guy, you are . . .?'

'I'm Mike Warne.'

'Good, you know your way back.' His tone sounded cheery enough but this was clearly a statement and not a question.

The langlauf course took Mike past another set of new arrivals in Val. A bunch of environmental protesters had set up camp between the edge of the trees and the river. The Syndicat who ran the ski area planned to clear the trees and put in a drag lift. They had promised to plant two trees for every one that was taken down, but the protesters who were mostly Brits were having none of it and were going on as if the trees were prisoners they were rescuing from death row. The encampment, which had started with a couple of old camper vans, was getting bigger by the week. Mike counted nine vehicles as he trudged by. These people, known disparagingly by the locals as '*les druides*', made Mike uneasy but he had to admire their commitment. They had arrived in the summer when camping was no hardship and everyone thought they would disappear when winter came, but to the surprise of all they'd stuck it out. Mike dreaded to think what the living conditions were like.

The other excitement in town Mike had heard about was the presence of a gang of ski thieves. Given that Val's idea of a crime wave was a pushy Muscovite jumping the queue for the Belvedere cable car, it wasn't surprising that it was causing more than a flutter of alarm. The poor old gendarmerie was getting a lot of stick for failing to catch the culprits.

7

The purpose of a piste map is to mark the resort's ski runs, grade them according to difficulty and show where the lifts and restaurants are. These illustrated maps look pretty much alike: the resort with its little buildings is always as tidy as Toy Town and nestles at the foot of mountains covered with sparkling white snow tinged with the blue of ice and sprinkled with dark rock and clumps of trees. On these utopian extravaganzas an unseen sun is always shining so that the whole panorama sparkles like a toothpaste advertisement.

The artists who do this work often have to tinker with the unhelpful Alpine topology to force it lie flat on a page but the simple geography of Val de Ligne needed little help. Val was essentially a V sitting on a straight line which was the main road running along the Ligne valley. The town centre was the point at which the tip of the V met that line – the point where the three roads converged. The main road passed through the town and after eight hundred metres became a cart track that eventually petered into a footpath as it climbed steeply into the mountains leading to the Swiss border.

The lines that formed the V were two small roads running along the two great valleys that comprised the main ski areas. One headed south along the Vallée Gar; the other ran east along one side of the Vallée Brienne.

Val's winter landscape was exceptional; it offered vistas that appeared to belong to another planet. The almost sheer rock face of the mountains behind the town formed a stern backdrop when viewed from the south and east. On the other side was the smooth bowl of the glacier that lay beyond the resort and from which rose a formidable range of jagged peaks.

Much of Val's appeal for Mike lay in its sense of intimacy. He didn't want to be in a larger resort with its vast clusters of build-them-high-and-sell-them-cheap apartment blocks. Val was low rise and low key. In spite of attracting some serious skiers and mountaineers and a wealthy clientele who made it interesting, it was not furiously fashionable and its regulars were comfortable with its subtle cachet. Travel journalists lured here by freebie trips from holiday companies tended to describe it as 'The best-kept secret in the Alps!' This infuriated Monsieur Beluzon, Val's Chef de Publicité at the Bureau de Tourisme; he worked like a dog to get more visitors, but it was a struggle. This was probably because Val, at 1,600 metres, was the last town in the valley and not easy to reach.

There was just one road into the resort; the only other way in was by skiing, hiking or mountain-biking across country from the nearest resort, the sprawling Pentes du Paradis fourteen kilometres away, or over the mountains from Switzerland, which was seventeen. Apart from Oleg, who arrived by helicopter because he was seriously rich, or the poor sods who had to leave by one because they were seriously injured, everybody and everything had to come and go by that single road. And that was *everything*: spare parts for the lift machinery, cashmere sweaters for Maison Nicole, lake fish for Cézanne, where the top *prix fixe* could cost as much as the five-day ski pass, medical supplies for the infirmary; lingerie for Ola!; cutesy dolls for Orphée gift shop and a tonnage of double-zero flour for all the pizza places. To meet the town's needs, fleets of vehicles ground up and round the steep hairpin bends – tankers laden with fuel, armoured trucks carrying away the swag, vans bearing visiting rock bands, refrigerated trucks bound for the supermarkets and of course an armada of coaches laden with skiers ebbing and flowing in a weekly tide. As well as enough wine and beer to fill a lake, an ocean of spring water from all over Europe was lugged up here while the crystal-clear mountain waters of the Ligne, for some reason spurned, hurried by in the opposite direction, down a stony stream bed heading for the River Gellend and the Mediterranean Sea.

Val, then, was the last stop before miles of glacier ice and mountains, and very much on its own.

8

'Poor old Hedley Coram,' thought Owen. 'We thought you'd be part of us for ever.' The steady shrinking of the once great estate, which served as a training school for civil servants, had paralleled the diminution of Empire. Now they were selling it off. Who would have thought it? No more Hedley Coram. He, Glyn Owen, was to be one of the last performers on its stage.

> 'There is, however, a downside which I should mention. I'm not talking about the deaths and despair suffered by hundreds of thousands. That is a given. I'm talking about something more insidious and more destructive: the effect of the trade in the corruption of whole polities.'

Glyn Owen, academic and civil servant, technically still an employee of the Security Service, looked out at his audience. There were about thirty of them in all. Were they with him? Was he really engaging them? Of course, on a sunny day like this they'd rather be outside playing. He often thought of his audiences as schoolchildren. Well it was time for this lot to grow up. They'd had a chance to read the health warning he'd spelled out on the screen earlier.

The following events are true but some of them have not yet occurred.

By staying in their seats they'd ticked the box, so let them have it.

'Well, imagine, you've just got off your commuter train after a hard day at the Department when you are approached in the badly lit car park by a man you've never seen before and by the look of him you never want to see again. He tells you what he wants you to do and that if you don't do exactly as asked his people will tear your eyes out. As he talks, a couple of gents nearby make sure you notice that they are also on your case. Your new best friend advises you that if you report this conversation to your superiors or the police, his people, who are everywhere, will find out. He then outlines some of the interesting surgical interventions that can be made available to your wife and children. After he's given you a short list of verbal instructions, to make you feel better about yourself, he gives you an envelope containing a couple of grand in used notes.'

Owen had given this speech before so he wasn't using his mental bandwidth to capacity and as he spoke he was aware that two distinct patterns of thought were in play – three if you counted thinking about the other two. He wondered how he did it.

'The dynamics of the drugs trade are powerful enough to destroy a nation's respectability. What we are now seeing is a resurgence of state-tolerated if not state-sanctioned murder and theft in countries which had largely forsaken them.'

They were meant to be among the brightest and the best? Well, maybe – after the City had its pick. The younger ones looked a callow bunch, but you could never be sure. Did they have what it takes? Would they be any good when they were grown-ups, when they joined the silent war? Not that they were front line troops but would *they* be able to deal with *Them*?

That was how he thought of them: *Them*. 'Them' with a capital letter as in He for God (but God, for whom Owen himself had once been a part-time servant, was very much at the other end of the spectrum from *Them*).

Them was how in his mind he represented this fear that was always with him. It was an odd game they were playing. He was after *Them* and *They* were after him. *They* didn't know who he was and he didn't know who *They* were. He did know one thing though: *They* were getting closer. And that was why he was thinking more and more about Ludo.

9

Running through the heart of Val de Ligne was a massive fissure invisible to the naked eye. Its origins went back more than half a century to the years of the one known as the Ferryman, the one who in a long secret war took sanctuary in the surrounding mountains and led his warriors to an ill-fated battle on the Plateau. The Ferryman's presence tore loyalties asunder and compelled all to decide on which side of the divide they would stand. This fault line was so wide and deep that despite decades of education, marriage, migration, peace and prosperity it remained impossible for some of the divided people ever to reach across it and embrace each other again.

Mike, like other visitors who returned year after year, was all too aware of the scar that traced the division and the loathing that simmered in this little place. As his awareness of that division grew, he learned things that made him wonder if the war against the Axis had merely refreshed some chronic feuding whose origins lay in something elemental.

Here hatreds had a half-life of several hundred years.

10

This version would be different, Glyn Owen had decided. Sow the seeds in the minds of a new generation. Today would be as good as it gets, the culmination of his career. Not that his audience would realise that. Well, not for some time at least.

'Brunelleschi's dome, the aqueducts of Rome – the Italians have always had an innate feeling for structure and design, and the country's Mafias understand the need for form to follow function if they are to be as enduring as the edifices of the Eternal City. The Mafias' art is to suborn the state, not to destroy it; they must not saw off the branch upon which they sit.

'Like any business, high-end crime requires order and a stable economy. Organised crime functions at its best in an organised state. Of course civil anarchy presents its special opportunities but by and large it is unhelpful. Where there is general disorder everyone is to be prepared to use violence so the criminal loses his USP in the marketplace.

'We must commend the Mafias for their long-termism, which has allowed them to succeed where legitimate Western states and businesses fail. Why so? Politicians and businessmen depend on voters and shareholders; the Mafias rely on the family.

'Here is a structure which is truly robust, building blocks held together by the mortar of kinship, greed and terror. So while the lifespan of an Italian government seldom exceeds that of an Umbrian arts festival, the Mafias have been going for nigh on 200 years. Gino Mascarpone and Luigi Pancetta can deploy dynastic distillations of experience. Unlike their governments, their Families have a future. And because they can think long that they can think big.'

Owen looked out at the rows of faces. Was there anyone out there who understood what he was on about? He wondered if they would even notice if he started discoursing on the art of pruning fruit trees.

11

> Ski cuts snow, snow covers rock, rock cracks skull.
>
> *21st-century skiing proverb/Anon.*

Far, far beyond the poles that mark the edge of a ski resort, poles that say 'cross this line at your own risk', lie the mountains of the empty quarter where no ordinary skier can go. From a distance the bright white countenance of this terrain seems to smile invitingly, as innocent as icing sugar, but go closer, where you see rocks exposed like rotten teeth, and that smile looks like more of a snarl. Here the slopes are steep and treacherous and even the harmless-looking glaciers conceal crevasses ready to swallow and entomb intruders.

This is the territory of a tribe of madmen who go where common sense will not. They are known as extreme skiers or free riders and they practise skiing in its most dangerous form. They ski the impossible places by the cliff's edge, the 'you fall, you die' places.

This gilded breed possesses a fearlessness that is hard to explain. If they do have any fear, they cannot show it because overt fear and grace refuse to share the same pair of skis. And grace is key because, for these people, death on the mountain, as in the bullring, must be confronted in style. Perhaps this fearlessness is due to some irreparable damage – possibly sustained at birth – to the cautionary cortex of their brain that suppresses fear and this makes it harder for them to find excitement unless it is administered in massive doses. They are forever searching these mountains for untried stretches of terrain which will test their skill and courage to the utmost, terrain ribbed with narrow vertiginous couloirs, perilous ledges, giant snow-lipped cliffs and awesome slopes – challenges which offer a decent chance of death or at the very least serious injury.

The extreme risks taken by these men and women might suggest they constitute some sort of suicide cult, because free riders are almost by definition survivors of numerous attempts on their own lives, and while every now and then one manages to succeed, the others will not give up on their apparent attempts to access death. Some lesser mortals churlishly suggest that these daredevils are merely seeking to escape the realities of life, but any free rider able to express himself would insist that they are actually addressing them.

One of the greatest gifts life can bestow is the chance to earn a living from the work one loves, so the abiding preoccupation of the free rider is not just how to get down the mountain but how to be paid for doing it. To that end they have learnt how to harvest their adrenaline so they can eke out an existence on the margins of commerce: they video the rituals of their cult.

12

Warlords seek to take over the offices of state;
ganglords seek only to suborn them.

Prof. Glyn Owen, The Politics of Crime

Owen became aware he was sweating slightly. That was the problem with fear. Fear wasn't just a mental thing; it stimulated physiological processes that attacked the whole body. He must control himself. He didn't want them to think he was nervous of them; he wasn't. He could do this sort of lecture in his sleep. Sometimes he damn nearly did. In any case he'd given this talk elsewhere only three months earlier. And now that Hedley Coram invited him to fill in for someone at short notice he had resuscitated the Gangster State, which, as he was discovering day by day, was now even more pertinent than ever.

> 'Now, let us be clear: a thriving drugs industry is not the only means by which a nation arrives at this parlous condition, but it helps.
>
> 'We may feel sorry for those nations which have fallen into a condition of state-sanctioned criminality, but in truth the majority have never left it. The default option in this world of ours is Governance by Gangster.'

Who knew where the careers of these people in front of him would lead? His own path had been a chequered one, but it had been different in his time. Of course old people always say that. He'd intended to go into the Church because he wanted to be a preacher like his father. He still wanted to be a preacher. *That's what I am doing now: preaching.*

Owen thought back to his first long-ago war. The forest was quiet but for the sound of the fingers of wind ruffling the leaves – enough noise to cover his painful progress as he crawled along the sunken path dragging his wounded leg. There were troops everywhere combing the undergrowth in their search for him. He had to get back to Norah who was guarding the precious radio.

That was the first of his wars; the others had been very different.

So who to tell? That was the question that still nagged him. It nagged him even though he knew the answer: it would have to be Ludo.

13

As soon as Mike had finished work for the day he had a shower, checked his emails, called Anne, his wife, who didn't seem to be missing him much, and then headed to Sandy's, where he was due at a meeting of the Team at seven o'clock. The Team were big stars in the free riding business and videos of their daredevil stunts played in ski shops and resorts everywhere. Mike had been roped in to help with their most ambitious production to date.

He wasn't surprised that no one had arrived yet. Although they moved quickly enough coming down the hill, when you put them on level ground without any kind of physical emergency the Team were quite slow off the mark.

While he was waiting, Mike joined Sandy, the owner of Bar X, who was gossiping by the bar with a couple of regulars. Sandy was a baby boomer who had taken over the premises in the Sixties when it was a failing enterprise in the hands of some no-hopers who had named it Club Van Blonk. The only thing it had going for it then was its fantastic location at the junction of the town's three main thoroughfares. Sandy bought it with the help of Julianne, a rich Parisienne whom he married after a two-year affair. Although there had been another marriage since then, Sandy and Bar X had remained doggedly faithful to each other and looked after each other pretty well.

The son of an army officer and an early female tennis star, Sandy was by his own admission academically dim but found that life was made even more difficult by his dyslexia. He maintained he chose the name Bar X because it was the one word he could be reasonably confident of spelling correctly. Although the rest of the world called it Bar X, regulars like Mike called it 'Sandy's'.

Sandy was one of those laid-back old rockers who seemed untroubled by detail, but in fact he was as beady as hell and could spot a till fiddle from the other side of the room while his back was turned, as more than one foolish barman had found to his cost. He was a craggy old charmer whom everyone liked and respected.

He enjoyed his unofficial function in Val as a credit rating agency, dating bureau, news agency and database, all offering synergies with his core competence, which was decent and modestly priced food and drink served with unobtrusive efficiency by extremely attractive women. When anyone asked Sandy where he got his girls from he would tell them with a satisfied grin, 'The Newmarket sales.' The place was packed most evenings.

Everyone felt that Sandy deserved his success because he never just sat on his laurels and raked in the cash. Instead he kept investing. He developed the cellar into a private dining area, opened up the ground floor into an even bigger bar and bought the apartment above to turn it into a large gallery with more tables overlooking the main bar.

The place was floored and walled in seasoned pine planks, as was the ceiling. The effect was to create a mellow wooden womb, but because all the surfaces looked like floorboards, the inebriated sometimes became disorientated, with some quite spectacular results. The walls were decorated with bits of ancient skiing paraphernalia and Alpine and historic photographs of Val; the long wall that ran at right-angles to the bar was covered with ephemera daubed with jaunty messages and signatures from enthusiastic patrons paying tribute to Sandy, Bar X and some of the girls who over the years had served under Sandy behind the bar and in his bed. There were three giant plasma screens around the main room, one of which was clearly visible from the street outside to lure passing trade. These played a mixture of rock and extreme skiing videos.

The first topic of Mike and Sandy's conversation that evening was the new head of the gendarmerie who Sandy said was 'a bit of an unknown quantity'. Sandy much preferred known quantities because it was important for him to understand and get on with everyone. The last chief cop had left under something of a cloud, having fallen foul of the divisions in the town.

Sandy had also told Mike that a company that had taken Chalet Messigny for a week had stood down the regular staff because they were bringing in their own people. They talked about the Green protesters' camp, where the leader was causing a bit of a media stir. The mairie was worried about the effect they'd have on business in Val, but there'd been no sign of any downturn so far.

Sandy had news that a company of Chasseurs Alpins from the Chambéry battalion were to be deployed on a training exercise in the valley and that there had been a sighting of Oleg with a new Natasha.

Oleg the Oligarch was one of Val's treasures. The Bar X regulars thought he had chosen their resort because there weren't many other Russians around and here he could be an exotic big shot instead of being pond life over in somewhere like Courcheval. They saw Oleg as a bit of a cut-price version of his species. Some wags referred to him as the 'affordable oligarch' but most people thought of him as Oleg the Oligarch. Bar X regulars called him Oleg even though they knew his name was Vassily.

Oleg was not a man to inspire the awe that he felt was due to him. He would arrive in his helicopter with a bunch of bulky-shouldered goons in leather jackets who must have spent more time shaving their heads than their chins; they strutted around town like cage-fighters on their way to work. They surrounded and towered above little Oleg but none of them was half as high as the long-legged doll who was on their boss's arm. It was not always the same one but whichever one it was she was known by the Bar X regulars as Natasha. The Natashas usually favoured fantastical outfits of white jackets in fringed buckskin, peppered with glitter and trimmed with fur, which made folks wonder if they had escaped from the cast of a Las Vegas ice spectacular. Sandy, seeing one the Natashas at the top of Falaise, her long limbs unfolding as she emerged from the Pascal bubble, said it was like watching a giraffe being hatched from an egg.

14

The snow is always greener on the other side of the fence.

Kornie Løvland

Predictably, Tyler Rafferty was the first to arrive. Short and stocky with a broad-jawed athlete's face and a rasp of a voice, he got the usual warm welcome from Sandy because the Team were good for business and attracted the best-looking girls in town. He ordered a coke; like many athletes who had to train hard, he usually avoided alcohol and so had little resistance to it. Anyway, why would he need alcohol when he could get out of his mind on adrenaline and endorphins by skiing in situations which took him to the edge of his life?

For an athlete, Tyler was quite businesslike. He carried a slim leather document case because he had *documents*. He felt this set him apart from the others and defined him as the organising brains of the Team. He was the one who with the help of his girlfriend, the long-suffering Kirsten, kept the show on the road, making the accommodation, travel and training arrangements as well as, crucially, dealing with their chief and sole sponsor, Tyler's father, a litigator at a prominent New York law firm.

Jean-Luc arrived shortly after, with Kornie. Dark and good-looking, Jean-Luc Arnaud was your basic Type One French playboy and wore the regulation uniform: deep tan and perfect very white teeth. The son of a wealthy Lyon machine-tools manufacturer, he was the contented possessor of a charmed life. Kornie maintained that Jean-Luc's idea of a hard day's work was three minutes checking his investment portfolio and a disaster was when he was confronted by a pistachio shell that wouldn't open. Kornie Løvland, a teetotal vegan prone to Ashtanga yoga, meditation and burning incense, was the technician of the team. With his blue eyes and serene countenance he looked like – if it weren't for the ski outfit – a Victorian portrait of Jesus Christ. His long straight blond hair was parted in the middle and he had a way of drawing it back from his face with his index fingers like doll's house curtains that deeply irritated Tyler. Kornie's English was a salad of so many European pronunciations and syntaxes that sometimes it was hard to understand what he was on about but after a second or so you got there. His iPod was loaded with East Maine folk and Tyler maintained that at the start of every day of his life he thanked God that Kornie didn't sing or play the guitar. His eyes looked almost closed, as if they were acting as some kind of filter to allow in only those bits of life that were acceptable. Kornie, who in Sandy's words liked to 'graze in nubile pastures', was not in a relationship at that moment: he was in several.

The fourth member of the Team was Blake Bale, a Rocky Mountain skier from Telluride where his father was coach to some serious competitors. A little older than the others, Blake, withdrawn and preoccupied, was the only one of the group who was not concerned with projecting an image of contented cool. His demeanour suggested there was something more important in his life other than skiing. And there was. He was in the final stages of an acrimonious bust-up with his long-time girlfriend.

With their voracious interest in 'vertical slopes and horizontal women' as Sandy put it, there was a bit of the three musketeers about the four of them. They saw themselves like that too; they were certainly quite cocky, but Mike thought that was fair enough because they were talented and brave. Although they enjoyed socialising with their friends and rivals and the women who were always drawn into their force field, they exuded a sense of detachment that suggested they'd really rather climb into their spacecraft and fly back up to their own private snow-covered planet devoid of any other form of life.

Apart from Tyler's cowhide document case, which was a poorly fed beast at the best of times, the combined talents of the Team did not offer much in the way of commercial instinct. While this hadn't hampered them in accomplishing their fantastic feats, it had prevented them from making decent money. That's why they were banking on the Project, which they were meeting with Mike to discuss. He wasn't any kind of specialist but he was a good organiser and had offered to help – an offer he would come to deeply regret.

15

The object of the Team's new challenge lay in the range of mountains beside the road running to the southwest of Val de Ligne and dominated by Mont Galave. The faces were too steep for snow to cling to, however, on the northern windward side, the two spurs that broke out of the surface of the mountain like buttresses did catch some snow. Everyone reckoned they were unski-able – until, that is, the Team had started looking around the area the previous season. They spotted a fresh rock fall close to the chimney about a third of the way from the top of one of the couloirs which had created enough of a platform to extend the downhill drop by another two hundred metres or so. If they could ski it, they could get some pretty spectacular video footage – maybe enough to restore the ailing fortunes of the Team.

In truth the last season had not gone well for the four guys: their greatest rivals, the Daler Brothers, were beating them to the best locations and getting some great footage, while the Team's most promising video distribution deal had come apart at the seams. Then there was that serious black cloud day when their star, Thibault Reloux, was nearly killed.

They had decided on a couloir drop on Utah's Ruxton Ridge as their opening foray of the year. Reloux was to make the first attempt. It went badly wrong from the start. He completely misjudged the turn he needed to make when he came out of the first chimney and fell and spun down the 45-degree slope like a detached aeroplane propeller. When he finally came to rest he was in an unholy mess, with breaks to one femur, two vertebrae, four ribs and a shoulder cuff. This plus severe concussion and some nerve damage to his spine.

It had been a nightmare just getting to him, digging him out of the snow and easing him onto the gurney so they could lower him down to a point where the heli could get in close enough in to take him off the mountain. Reloux underwent a series of operations and was still in hospital more than a year later. They said it was unlikely that he would ever ski on anything but a nursery slope again. The accident had a disastrous effect on sponsorship – no one had admitted how much of a star he was – and the Team were facing a lean time.

Such success as the Team enjoyed had been made possible by Tyler Rafferty Senior's success in the New York court rooms. He had remained a loyal sponsor but this crucial source of revenue was now threatened by the arrival in his life of one seething piece of stereotypical high-maintenance Hispanic hot blood, Nina Marrero. Tyler resented this new influence on his father and for her part Nina questioned the wisdom of funding the Team so generously.

Anyway, with Nina chomping her way through Rafferty Senior's disposable income he was forced to inform his son that he now had 'Minus zilch to keep you boys playing in the snow.'

So when one day during this nadir in their fortunes Tyler got a call from a voice that said, 'Hi, my name is Saul Blomberg and I'd like to make a movie with you guys,' he all but sank to his knees in a prayer of grovelling thanks.

16

This call from Saul was manna from heaven. 'Oh, that's great,' Tyler managed to stammer. Tell me some more – like, why?'

'You guys have got it. I think you can go places. You need a lot of guidance, a lot of direction. That's what I bring.'

After a brief exchange of emails Tyler summoned the other three members of the Team to meet Saul in Vail where the great man explained his terms. And so after some lopsided financial negotiations the Team sold themselves into creative servitude under Saul Blomberg.

The format of your standard ski movie was simple enough: usually around forty minutes long with good clear camerawork and bags of stunts. There were a lot of smart people directing these little films but Saul, who himself had been a serious skier in his youth, was in a class of his own; he was not just a movie-maker, he was an entertainer and an artist.

The Team's one anxiety about their new master was that by reputation Saul was a nightmare to work with. They'd heard how skiers would be risking their limbs performing a stunt only to hear the director's voice over the radio saying thank you and that was real nice but I'm not happy with the cloud match and can we have another go at it in an hour or so when the light might be better? Saul seemed oblivious to the pressures on the athletes in his care who faced several options for imminent destruction as they stood poised to jump from the edge of a ledge.

But Saul, for whom life was an extended theatrical performance, often inflated his anger to exert his authority. He saw histrionics as an essential management tool. Anyhow, the fact was that the Team had taken in this tyrant to be their ruler because his talent was to show off their talent.

17

Yes, Ludo would be good.

He was an inspired researcher and that's what was needed for this investigation. Not a man of action exactly, he'd need help with that end of things if required, but he did have someone useful to turn to. Was he being fair to the man?

Owen remembered their first meeting. In spite of Ludo's intellect and commitment he'd slightly disliked his clever new student. He wasn't entirely sure why. Was it because of his quietly-spoken mannered shyness? Or was it the contentment on his narrow, sallow, privately educated face? As it happened a mutual respect superseded all this when Ludo handed in an essay entitled 'The War of the Jester'. It was a detailed analysis of the eccentric non-violent tactics used in the Seventies by the Uruguayan-spawned *Picadura de Pulgas* to discredit the authority of the military rulers and co-ordinate popular action to bring about their overthrow. Ludo had gone on to assess the implications of the adoption of these tactics in other territories by the new generation of digitally-powered insurgent movements. It promised to be a rich field and Owen and his student agreed that Non-Violent Insurgency should be the subject of Ludo's PhD. From that a friendship grew.

> 'Corruption brings a strange kind of darkness over the nation which obscures reality. Every matter, every transaction seems to have a hidden purpose. The daylight of transparent dealings fades to a twilight in which facts become unclear. In this half-light bad things happen.'
>
> 'Criminal forces edge ever closer to the seats of power, for corruption corrupts not only those who want a piece of it, but those employed to fight it. Before long crime has acquired a collar and tie and may stroll around in polite society.'

Owen regretted that Ludo had still not finished *Non-Violent Insurgency* because he could have made a name for himself. Nowadays whenever Owen asked him how *NVI* was coming along, Ludo would complain about the impediments strewn in his path.

'You can't believe how hard it is to get anything done. Basically I'm running a four-bedroom employment-opportunities centre for any cleaner, gardener, plumber and electrician within a fifteen-mile radius of Winslow.'

Owen couldn't quite make out whether he was making an excuse for not finishing a seriously worthwhile piece of academic research or subtly boasting about his enhanced status in life.

'And that's not the end of it. When I first knew you at university all I had was a bike. Now as well as the cars I've got a pony with a set of injury-prone legs whose sole purpose seems to be to keep our slightly too handsome vet in the kind of lifestyle he expects. What is it about women and vets, Glyn? He's never out of the house.'

'And how's the wonderful world of big oil?' asked Owen.

'Well, it's okay, I suppose. They see me as a conscientious worker who is a good communicator and functions well as a team player. I'm discreet. And I make a useful contribution to meetings in spite of seeming to be distracted.'

'You seem very sure of yourself?'

Ludo laughed.

'Well, that's how they described me in the last Getting to Know Yourself – one of those "360 degrees" exercises where your colleagues fill in some damn silly survey with harmless platitudes about you in the hope you'll do the same for them when their turn comes. It's something the HR people at A&G organise to justify their ridiculous existence.'

'I'm glad I've been spared the 360 degrees treatment.'

'Do you know, I sometimes wonder what would happen if I, Ludo James, as CEO of the James Family plc, was to run the same survey at home. I'd make damn sure the pony and the dog took part – they'd be the only ones who'd put in a decent word for me. Certainly Liz and children would be rather less charitable than my colleagues. Just imagine it: "Ludo would be well advised to finish his work at the office rather than spend hours working at home." "He needs to upgrade the casual sector of his wardrobe." "His performance on the dance floor disappoints."'

'And he sometimes fails to complete important assignments?' Owen added as an oblique reference to *Non-Violent Insurgency*. Ludo ignored him.

'They'd probably neglect to mention my generosity; as far as the girls are concerned I'm no more than a glorified ATM; they just have to press the right buttons and I cough up.'

> 'The smallest of wounds in the bark allows disease to enter. All that is needed are a few corrupted politicians here, some judges there. In the face of the evil, servants of the state are soon reduced to a grotesque abasement which would rival Versailles' cringing courtiers of Quatorze.'

'You ought to get it finished. You can't let all that research just rot.'

'I know, I know. But sometimes, Glyn, I become quite weary of providing. In fact at times I actually feel panicked by the responsibility. Is that how you felt when your boy was growing up?'

'Nope.' The Owen household had always been a rather more austere establishment. 'Recently I've been fantasising about jacking it all in and getting a perverse pleasure from the shock on the faces of my family when I tell them.'

'Nice idea,' said Owen. 'But you'd never do it; you're too soft.'

'I know, I know. I was just about to leave the office the other day when I got a suspiciously chatty text from Caroline, our youngest: "Dad, could u look in at DigiStore on your way home and pick up a laptop for us?" It was the "pick up" that got to me; as if she was talking about a pint of milk or something.'

But Owen could tell that Ludo's cheerful despair was tinged with a small sense of pride in managing to protect this creature from the realities of the outside world for so long.

Was it fair for Owen to involve a family man like Ludo in this?

I have no choice.

18

Tyler, who had become quite anxious about their new director, asked Mike to come with him to meet Saul at the airport. They spotted a tall figure pushing his trolleyload of luggage and skis as he emerged from Arrivals. Saul was your genuine antique hippy with a wiry frizzled grey-black ponytail, a firm paunch drooping over the waist of his jeans. He kept courtesies to a minimum and started asking questions before they'd even got to the car. Who was looking after the bookkeeping? Had anyone sorted out the comms? What had been done about transport?

Saul's interrogation of Tyler was brusque, in a showy kind of way which seemed designed to diminish all their efforts. Tyler and the Team were quite rattled by Saul's I-am-a-Hollywood-big-shot act; they would never understand that their director was dogged by insecurity. But he wasn't going to tell them that most Hollywood directors like him would happily swap their perilous commercial existence in Tinseltown for the comparative certainties of the life enjoyed by a sub-Saharan subsistence farmer.

Movie scenes don't necessarily get shot in the order they appear for logistical or other reasons. For instance, any sex scenes are, counter-intuitively, filmed early on because actors find them awkward to do when they have got to know each other well. In the case of *Conquest of the Couloir Noir* the shooting schedule pretty much reflected the storyline, beginning with action shots intercut with talking-head quotes taken from interviews with the Team, a poignant long shot of four tiny dots making their way across an expanse of glacier to the foot of a steep mountain, a hard climb up in crampons carrying skis on their packs, followed by a euphoric zigzag down through steep powder, Saul all the while manipulating the geography to suit the visual cadence of his narrative. Next they shot the Team skiing down contrasting terrains before converging at exactly the same moment for the final approach to the Couloir.

The reason for shooting the crucial Couloir action last was less to do with chronology than the unspoken assumption that if any accident was going to happen it would happen here. And even if it was as catastrophic as the episode that did for poor Thibault, they would already have enough other footage in the can to edit into some sort of saleable product though they might not be able to call it *Conquest of the Couloir Noir*.

The fragments of footage from each of several cameras would be stitched together by Billy Welzer, the American editor who arrived two days after Saul. He was a skinny long-haired blondish kid with spectacle lenses so thick his eyeballs seemed to be floating around in the space in front of his face. He didn't say a lot – working with Saul he didn't have a chance – but Mike, who found it instructive to watch Billy at work, volunteered to help him in any way he could.

Movie makers are neurotic about backing up their precious footage, so each day as soon as shooting had finished the cameras would be taken to Billy's rental apartment on the north side of town where Mike would help him remove the memory cards and copy the footage from each to a pair of hard drives. Mike who had mastered Billy's filing system would also help him index the sequences.

19

The eye has a tendency to see what it has already seen. Over the years, Owen had spent a considerable time studying how criminal gangs in Central and Eastern Europe manipulated the police and justice system for their own ends. He'd encountered a particular frequently recurring scenario: cop recruits criminal informer; informer corrupts cop and ends up employing him. Often the arrangement would turn sour, resulting in an unhappy ending for the corrupted official such as, maybe, loss of life. Owen was therefore always interested in cases in which any UK security officials came to serious grief – like the judge who had first caught Owen's attention. His body had been found entangled in the rigging, floating beside his upturned dinghy a mile and a half off the Kent coast near Ramsgate. The coroner recorded accidental death by drowning. It had been an uncontroversial verdict, but one aspect – not important in itself – that had struck Owen was how the investigation had been marred by sloppy evidence-gathering, administrative delays, the disappearance of documents and so on. But in spite of an examination of the judge's serious cases over a decent period, Owen could find no evidence of him being compromised by any criminal connection.

> "'There is something rotten in the state,' according to Marcellus, the guard at Hamlet's Elsinore. But this afternoon we are not discussing "something rotten in the state" but the state itself being rotten – when the canker of corruption has spread beneath the stone and stucco of the law courts and the ministries. Consider those states when every official, major and minor, demands a bribe, where you can't get start a business, pass a college exam or get a passport or a job, without paying off someone.'

There were two other cases he'd looked at in this context – a policeman and a prison officer who had died within a few months of each other. The former, a detective sergeant, had apparently jumped from a railway bridge into the path of a high-speed train; the latter had died of an overdose in his flat.

The police officer's apparent suicide surprised everyone. Transcripts of interviews with friends and colleagues suggested it was right out of character; nothing in his behaviour in the period before his death had hinted at such a possibility but in the absence of any other evidence, a verdict of suicide was given.

The death of the prison officer had a curious aspect. One witness had reported seeing a man delivering a large cardboard carton to the warder's block of flats on the evening of his death. When Owen had asked his research assistants to dump all the details of the case into the International Police Data Match Program, it had thrown up a matching phrase in the testimony from a murder case on the other side of the world in a suburb of Auckland, New Zealand. The occupant of a house in the suburbs, an immigrant who had just arrived in the country, was discovered bound with cord in the middle of his living-room floor with his face appallingly mutilated. The sickest aspect of the crime scene was a sheet of paper placed next to the body purporting to be a suicide note. They never even found a suspect to question, let alone charge. What raised a flicker of interest in Owen's mind was a witness statement by a neighbour who had seen a uniformed courier delivering a very large cardboard carton to the house on the day of the murder. The courier had never been traced.

> 'The stage on which its statesmen and its clerics strut is so riddled with rot one wonders that it doesn't collapse, but in truth it's the fungus which holds it up. A black economy is still an economy; never underestimate corruption's tensile strength. Meanwhile justice lies buried in an unmarked grave.'

While Owen had initially considered that the three UK victims might possibly be the victims of corrupt criminal relationship turned sour, he now knew they were something quite different.

So what linked them?

20

The seven-seater Scarabée flew through the lightening sky, the camera hoovering the floor of the valley and the sides of the distant mountains before climbing up to the back edge of the summit. As soon as the pilot had eased his machine down onto the tiny plateau above the Couloir, Mike was first out so he could film the Team disembarking and unloading their skis from the fuselage rack.

Last was Caspar, the dispatch man who was to video the take-off and the first few metres of the drop; after they had plummeted out of his view the skiers' head-cams would take over. To do this he needed to hang over the rock and see straight down without actually pitching over the edge himself. Mike's last job was to double-check Caspar's harness. That done, he wished the guys luck and climbed back into the heli.

The pilot took the aircraft up in a big loop to allow the Team to be videoed as they huddled together sheltering from the downdraft. As the machine curled around the rapidly shrinking figures, Mike could now get a clear view of what they would be coming down; it was a menacing sight. He had somehow assumed that everything would happen nearer dawn – that the guys would sneak up on this drowsy white giant while it was still half asleep and they'd slide down the Couloir before it could wake up and take retaliatory action. Instead, he was now staring at an unsmiling monster that, in broad daylight, looked very much awake.

Saul kept talking on the radio to his skiers, giving them seemingly useless information about the final checks on the ground. They knew he just wanted to distract them from the massive drop that lay a few feet in front of their toes and had come to appreciate this other, sympathetic side to Saul's character.

With everything nearly ready Saul came on the radio.

'I guess we'll be okay to go in a couple of minutes, guys. Okay for me to send the bird up?'

'Any time,' said Tyler.

Saul signalled to the heli 40 metres away. The pilot gave the thumbs-up and the bird – all two tons of it, an intricate gathering of a multitude of different kinds of alloy, commanded by a chip-brained engine gulping a litre of fuel every 30 seconds – began to shake with increasing fury until it broke free of its invisible bonds. A helicopter take-off always reminded Mike of his baby son's first unsteady steps. The machine rose, tottered unsteadily just above the ground and, in a sudden display of determination, dipped its nose and surged forward. Then it tilted to starboard and began a curling climb towards the mountain flaunting a newly discovered grace.

21

> As I approach she looks as if to defy me; I stroke her
> face and explore her with my whole body. I caress the
> contours of her white form as have her many lovers
> but she gives herself to me as to no other man before.
>
> *Bertrand de Moulliac, the philosopher-skier,*
> *in* A Lover of Mountains, *translated by Hugo Styles*

For everyone down on the ground, the roar of the engine seemed like the roll on a circus snare drum, a crescendo then a fade into near silence for the climax. Saul pressed the button to open the short wave radio channel. 'Ready to go, Camera One?' He checked each of the cameramen, and then looked up at the aircraft, which was hovering in position opposite the Team on the summit. 'Ready to go, Woody?'

Now Saul addressed the Team through Tyler who had Caspar's radio. 'Okay, guys, we're all ready for you. Let's see you do it, let's see you give this lady everything you've got!' Then he slid out of his coach-in-the-locker-room harangue back into a cool calm This-is-Mission-Control-Houston voice: 'Thank you, gentlemen; Jean-Luc, whenever you're ready.'

As Mike watched through his binoculars it seemed like an age passed and nothing happened. He was beginning to wonder if the guys had changed their minds – and who would blame them?

And then, there was Jean-Luc falling through the air.

This was always going to be the scariest part of the morning: the first one down. No one had ever done what he was doing. If they had got their recce wrong, it would be Jean-Luc who paid the price. There were a couple of moments when it looked as though he was going to have to do just that, but then they looked as though they were on the edge of disaster most of the time.

Everything they had been working for over the past three weeks was resting on the skill and courage of this lunatic up there among those rocks nearly bare of snow. At times his path grew so narrow that Jean Luc seemed to be balancing like a high-wire walker on a thin white ribbon. Then his path widened out into a steep open field dotted with ledges of rocky outcrops which caused the mountain to disappear from beneath Jean Luc's feet and leave him airborne for two or three very long seconds before he plunged back into snow so steep and deep that he repeatedly disappeared from view.

For those watching from a distance there was a strange soft grace in this shape sliding, bouncing and falling down the mountain. But when Mike glanced across at a monitor screen showing the close shot, he was confronted with the ringside reality of a brutal fight: Jean Luc, battling to stay upright while the mountain used all its power to try to knock him over. The lonely figure was a strange fusion of carbon-fibre coated wood fixed to epoxy resin and polyether, clamped around a bone-chassis wrapped with sinew and muscle, plaited with nerves and capillary pipe-work all fired by an elemental furnace located somewhere inside his skull.

When he finally re-emerged and came back down to earth, he pointed his skis at the final camera and came hurtling towards it. At the last possible moment, with a sideways flick of his heels, he angled his skis steeply so that he came to a crunching halt a few feet from Saul, barely smiling at the waiting earthmen, who found it hard to believe that the mortal standing in front of them was the same ethereal creature they'd just seen falling through the air and snow between the long sharp ribs of that big bad mountain.

Pausing just long enough to catch his breath and receive

congratulatory slaps on the back from the crew – more violent than they realised because they were partly relieving their own nervous tension – Jean-Luc got on the radio to Tyler and Kornie and briefed them about a couple of unexpected hazards they needed to watch out for.

Kornie went next. At Jean-Luc's suggestion he dropped more to the left and got a better landing. He did some typically Kornie stuff in the deep snow – doing just two turns in the steepest bit where Jean-Luc had strung five together and skimming over the rocks in the narrowest parts. But because Kornie was Kornie, swathed in confidence, he got too cocky. And that's what did for him. When he came to the ridge that marked the edge of their route, he landed awkwardly at the wrong angle, momentarily lost control and his speed drove him not just up to the edge but over the edge. On the far side were snowless rocks that threatened serious injury or worse. For a few nerve-wracking seconds, Kornie skeetered along this skinny spine before he managed to slip back onto his needle-narrow course. He had got out of trouble as fast as he'd got into it and completed the run without further incident. When he reached the ground crew he too had advice for Blake, who was now alone with Tyler and Caspar at the top of the hill.

There was a long pause while they waited for word that Blake was ready to go. Saul flipped his radio switch. 'You okay there? We're ready for the next one.' There was no answer for about thirty seconds, which, in the circumstances, was an age, and then Caspar's voice came on sounding odd – slightly forced. 'We have an equipment failure.'

'Okay,' said Saul. 'How long you going to need to fix it?'

'I don't think we can fix this one, Saul,' said Caspar. 'Tyler is coming down next.'

'What's that all about?' muttered Saul. Jean-Luc and Kornie exchanged looks and shrugged. They could imagine Blake edging back from the edge of the summit and Tyler shuffling forward until his skis pointed over the abyss.

'Dropping in ten!' called Tyler.

They all stared at what looked like a piece of dark rock that had become dislodged and was tumbling down the mountain. Eventually it turned into a person skiing at speed. Even though this was the third time they'd seen it, those watching found themselves sucking in their breath as if that would somehow help Tyler get through that tiny gap in the rocks. Then when he got to one of the lower drops he threw in one of those stiff-legged back somersaults that were his speciality, landing with such a tendon-tearing crunch that some of the watchers wondered if the force was so great it hadn't knocked his eyes out of their sockets. And now as he hurtled downwards, accelerating all the time, they felt as though they needed to reach out to steady themselves so they too didn't go plummeting down the mountain and share some terrible fate that might be lying in wait for this overconfident snow dancer. Instead Tyler sped towards the last camera and came to a halt a few feet from the lens in a calm and controlled ending to a stylish evasion of the mountain's perils which said, 'Sod you, Calamity, catch me if you can.'

They'd done it.

22

'Okay, listen up, everyone,' said Saul. 'This job isn't done yet. We need some quality head-cam footage of the ski into town please. We've been through this, so you all know what to do. The lead camera team are going to head down here and go through the lower town. You'll drop the gear off and then come on up for the lunch at Chez Michel. Tyler, Jean-Luc and Kornie are going to stay high and head for those trees by the big chalet and come down into town that way. The rest of us will cut in between.'

He paused. 'Have we got that?'

There was a lot of nodding but no one said anything.

'I think so, Saul,' Mike answered. He didn't want Saul to feel he was on his own. Mike was like that – always keen to help things run smoothly. It had been Mike's suggestion that someone went by Chalet Messigny, not just because it made for a picturesque scene but because it would annoy the snooty creep who'd sent him packing.

'Good. Bill will do the camera checks? And Kirsten, do you want to call Michel's and tell them we're on our way?'

As he was talking, Saul had kept looking up at the sky and now, as Tyler said, 'Let's do it,' Saul held out his hand, palm down, and said, 'Wait a moment. I think we have a visitor.'

Sure enough, the sun was slowly making its way through the clouds.

'Aw c'mon, Saul!' groaned Tyler.

'No, wait. This is important.'

'No, that was important,' he said, pointing back over his shoulder in the direction of the Couloir Noir. 'This isn't.'

'It's all important, Tyler,' said Saul patiently. 'Just give it a couple of minutes, that's all.'

So they waited with an edge of grumpiness on their euphoria, watching as the sun, unhurried, ambled out from behind the cloud.

'Iss movink like old men crossing de road,' growled Kornie.

Finally Saul was satisfied.

'Okay, let's go!'

Liberated by their sense of a mission accomplished and their spirits lifted by the newly sunlit landscape, off they shot like bats out of hell.

23

The Team and some of the crew were already at the restaurant when Mike arrived. They were in the back section, which had been reserved for Saul's party, and everyone was chattering ebulliently over drinks. Lunch had been laid up on a long table by the window.

At a neighbouring table Billy Welzer was backing up to a pair of hard drives the memory cards with the mornings footage from each of the cameras that the Team and the crews had used that morning.

Saul summoned everyone to gather round. 'Let's have all your phones off now, guys. And let's leave it that way until the end of lunch. This is all about just us. Okay? Thank you.' After a pause he stared at the floor for a moment, put his fingertips together, stared round at his audience and gave them his What-you-have-all-done-here-today-is-something-very-special' speech before he led the way to the table. There they devoured Michel's special *tartiflette* – cream and molten *Reblochon* poured over waxy potatoes, still fizzing on its surface from being grilled to varying shades of evil brown. It was accompanied by a crisp sharp salad of chicory and walnuts and followed by a dessert of fat black cherries swimming in schnapps. Everyone agreed Saul had done them proud.

During the meal the Team sat among the crew, but now after they had collected their coffees everyone had drifted back to the tables and regrouped themselves by caste – Team, cameramen, assistants.

Mike heard a voice behind him.

'Mike, we need to talk.' It was Tyler, who took him over to Kornie and Jean-Luc. They were sitting some distance from the rest of the party.

As Mike sat down he realised someone was missing.

'Where's Blake?'

'He left,' said Tyler.

'Why?'

'He is needing some space,' said Kornie. 'He's not happy with what happened.'

'What did happen exactly?'

Tyler answered quickly before Kornie could. 'It's complicated. But we need to tell you about what happened on the run into town.' He pulled his chair closer to the table. 'Kornie, tell Mike what you saw.'

'I think we causing some troubles,' said Kornie.

'That makes a change.'

'No, Mike, seriously,' said Tyler. 'I think we went in a place we shouldn't have been and we saw something.'

Instinctively Mike glanced towards the tables in the main part of the restaurant but all he could see was a quiet elderly couple planning their afternoon's skiing over a piste map and a loud English family who were making enough noise to drown out any conversation at the Team's table.

'We split up just like Saul said we should. Jean-Luc was taking the highest route; I was in the middle and Kornie downhill from me. I'd guess that most of the time we were about seventy-five to a hundred metres apart. About three kilometres out of town we come to that woodland above the langlauf course. Jean-Luc's line took him above the trees; Kornie was also on clear open ground. My route took me straight through the wood.

'Obviously this place is never skied and the going was patchy. The trees in this part are quite recently planted so there is not a lot of ground cover and the snow gets through. Suddenly – say maybe ten metres below me – I see a guy dressed in white from head to foot – white suit, white headgear, something white over his boots. He has white goggles pushed up on his head. And as he turns and looks up at me I can see his face and it's covered in this white cream or something. Then I'm noticing a long, long barrel thing, which I think is a gun because it's wrapped up in some sort of white stuff, but I'm now guessing is a camera on a tripod. The guy looked kind of unhappy to see me.'

'Well, he would be, wouldn't he?' observed Jean-Luc.

'Then I was past him. This all happens in seconds, you understand, I don't slow down. It was all too fast and I'm ducking through the trees. I knew I wasn't meant to see him; I just wanted to get out of there.'

'So what was he filming – or photographing?' Mike asked, his pulse quickened as he realised what the answer would be.

'At that point I was just above a big chalet. I could hardly see it. It must have been that. But Kornie got a real close look.'

'For sure I went right by it,' said Kornie. 'It's fancy place. Top luxury type. As I'm coming near there is a couple of guys in dark jackets. When they see me they come running, waving arms, but they haven't skis and I pass them. I was at the big house quite quick. There were all people out on the terrace taking coffee. They were real surprised to see me. Some more guys in black ski gear shout at me to stop. Everyone real angry. Dogs barking and trying to chase me, so I ski on quick.'

'So you think the man in white was filming these people, why?' Mike asked.

'Maybe the police,' said Jean-Luc. 'Undercover cops. Who else would be videoing like that?'

'I understand that, but it wasn't your fault that you saw him . . .' Then an idea occurred.

'Maybe a paparazzo,' he suggested. 'Those people will do anything.'

'Now that's a thought.' Tyler was grateful to have a more harmless suggestion. 'This is just what they do to get their pictures.'

'Have to be someone famous, seriously famous,' said Jean-Luc.

'Okay, so what sort of people were they – the people on the terrace?' Tyler asked.

'I don't know. But rich, I'd say,' said Kornie, then, after an uncertain pause, 'but not skiers, I think.'

'Why's that?'

'I don't know. Anyway, you can see what I saw, what Tyler saw; it will all be on our head-cams.'

Mike went over to Billy to ask if he would show them some of Tyler and Kornie's head-cam footage and made some space for the laptop among the debris of dirty plates. Billy loaded Tyler's material first.

It started with his camera glancing back at Jean-Luc and Kornie as they set off. The open terrain slipped by either side until Tyler reached the wood, where the video quality deteriorated drastically as he jinked round trees and ducked low branches.

'This is the bit but you need to look very carefully,' said Tyler. 'It's only a moment.'

The four of them huddled closer to the screen as the head-cam bounced around, crashing through the low snow-covered branches.

'There! Look,' said Tyler in an excited half-whisper, his finger stabbing involuntarily at the screen. 'Can you see him?'

'Well possibly ... but not really,' said Mike, who could see nothing more than a faint blur of a moving shape caught by the camera as it hurtled past on its wobbly course. Almost instantly it was gone.

'Billy, can we have that again, please,' he asked.

The picture quality was lousy but on the second viewing there was no doubt about it. First they saw the path ahead jumping from side to side and then, a few metres down the slope in the trees beside the track what at first looked like a snow-covered boulder rose up and unfolded into a human figure clad entirely in white from top to toe. Tyler said he thought the man was very small and seemed to be carrying some sort of cylinder swathed in white cloth, but when Billy played it again for them frame by frame they all agreed it looked more like a powerful telescopic camera lens.

Billy clicked on the file with Kornie's footage. Chalet Messigny looked pretty beguiling sitting down there on the edge of the trees on a sea of sparkling white. It grew a little bigger on the screen every time Kornie turned out of the trees until there it was, its tinted windows glinting in the sunlight, the stylish angles of its timbered outline sharp against the sky with fifteen or so people on the decking enjoying the sunshine. Kornie was right, Mike thought, they did look rich and one knew instinctively they weren't skiers. And the fact was that anyone who was standing around drinking coffee on the first decent day Val had had in days couldn't possibly be a skier.

It was a striking bit of footage because some of the chalet's occupants had drifted away from the terrace and were strolling across the snow in small groups. Then, like the world's fastest gatecrasher, Kornie shot right through the middle of the party like a speeding arrow, capturing the scene all around him. The net effect was to hose down the whole party with his lens as they instinctively turned to look at him.

They asked Billy to replay it a couple of times, then to freeze-frame the groups. Many of the faces in the images jolting across the screen would have been pretty much recognisable to anyone who knew them, even allowing for the dark glasses that the sunshine and snow glare forced most, but not all, to wear. Sunglasses may hinder recognition but they do not prevent it.

'I got it!' announced Kornie. 'De guy in de woods is nothing connect to the chalet people. He is wildlife photographer!'

'You could be right, Kornie,' said Tyler patiently, "but I have this funny feeling you aren't.' Just like Kornie to seize on the most pleasing and innocent possibility, he thought.

'Well, I don't think he was a paparazzo,' said Jean-Luc. 'I can't see anyone famous here.'

'We wouldn't know, would we?' said Tyler.

'I can't think,' Mike said. 'What does Saul say?'

There was an exchange of uneasy glances.

Tyler answered. 'We haven't told him. And I don't think we should. You know how he doesn't like complications.'

'For sure I think we don't tell him,' said Kornie. He was surprisingly nervous of Saul. Their relationship was not good and it didn't get any better following an incident three days earlier. A curious bystander asked what equipment was in their huge pile of aluminium cases. Unaware that Saul was in earshot, Kornie pointed to the smallest case and said it was for the camera and 'all der udders are for der director's ego'.

'We weren't meant to see that man in the trees,' said Tyler, 'and I kind of feel that the fewer people who know the better.'

The party was starting to break up. Saul and Billy were keen to get away and work on the footage. Before they left Saul invited everyone to Bar X at 7.30 where he'd be doing a bit of promotional work for the Project but he wouldn't say what. Mike took Billy aside. 'Billy, it's maybe best for everyone's sake if Saul doesn't see that stuff with the guy in the woods. Can you just take out that white suit footage and keep it somewhere safe?'

'No problem,' said Billy.

Outside the restaurant Mike turned on his phone and found a text from Sandy: WHERE U? PEOPLE LOOK 4 U ALL OVER TOWN. He wondered who that might be. Normally they'd have been easy to find, but because Saul had wanted the lunch to be a private affair for just the guys and the crew without a crowd of well-wishers tagging along he'd chosen Michel's instead of one of their usual haunts.

Mike felt slightly depressed. Now that the conquest of the Couloir was in the can, his work was done; he wouldn't be needed any more. There was one sure cure for this mild depression so he hooked up with some of the crew for a couple of hours of hard skiing.

24

Owen realised he had ventured beyond the boundaries of academe and was now deep in a very complicated clandestine investigation. What had started as playful academic speculation but had now turned into something very different. The hypo had become detached from his hypothesis.

The more he learned about his prey, the more he understood the dangers of hunting it. He was a minnow chasing sharks. What would he do when he caught up with them? Worse, what would they do if *They* caught up with *him*?

A growing fear haunted his waking hours. The intelligence he had accumulated was so toxic if *They* ever found out he had it they would destroy him just as they had destroyed others. Every line of his enquiry was a risk. He now knew that his enemies were able to watch their own backs by suborning the technical services of the state they were meant to be serving. Owen had to take a lot of care: laptops leave bloody great footprints for surveillance to see. Electronic eavesdroppers suck phone conversations out of the ether and pass these trillions of words to intelligently programmed cyber gangs of robots working round the clock in a doughnut in Gloucestershire. It would have been safer for Owen to carve his findings on a wall in the middle of Whitehall than trust any digital record, so best to keep all his key research in hard-copy form in a single file and mark it . . . 'Swanborne'.

'A state in such a rotten state as I have described might be said to be "on the brink of collapse". But collapse is quite difficult to achieve, although some states have had a decent crack at it. Rather they just totter on with all reduced to a few flyblown warlords fighting over the wreck of a radio station in a city abandoned by all but the sand.

'The trappings of order remain intact. A carapace of ceremony to covers the corruption with pantomime salutes and bows and the swearing of solemn oaths. The clerical robes are the whitest of white, justice the blackest of black. The breastplates of the royal guards still glitter in the sun; the rumps of the palace cavalry still gleam, and those that cheer this cavalcade are no wiser than the horses.'

Owen knew people in all almost every police force and academic institution operating in this field as well as having contacts in the Village, as the government intelligence community informally refers to itself, and he'd talked to a lot of them. He was worried that he might have been a little careless. Every conversation leaves its vapour trail. But how else could he get to the truth?

Aware that the task was more than he alone could handle, Owen sought someone to help him – someone who could take over if anything should happen to him.

The obvious candidate was Ludo; in fact, there wasn't anyone else. He'd been his star pupil and had become a good friend, but more to the point he was up to the task. He'd get to the truth. So why was he delaying? Owen knew why and hated to admit it to himself. As the career of his protégé advanced he had experienced a glimmer of professional jealousy and now he found himself questioning Ludo's involvement. *Why should I leave him with all the glory?* But glory might not be only thing Ludo would get if he was caught.

25

Before Mike set out for the evening he called his wife Anne. The girls were fine but Dahlia had cut her paw on something and Anne had had to take her to the vet. She wasn't overly impressed by the Team's achievement but made an effort to sound pleased.

The bars in Val de Ligne start to warm up about an hour and a half after the lifts close, which is how long it takes for people to ski back, have some tea and shower before going out for an early drink. By the time Mike got to Sandy's it was just after eight; news of the Team's conquest had spread and the place was heaving. When Tyler arrived twenty minutes later with Kirsten and Kornie he was without his document case, which signalled he was in ready-to-rumble mode.

'So,' Tyler said to Kornie, rubbing his hands together in gleeful anticipation of the evening ahead, 'what did the Saudi adulteress say to the Iranian pole-dancer?'

'Let's get stoned,' replied Kornie dutifully.

'Well, you'd better buy the drinks then!'

Tyler always enjoyed making Kornie buy him alcohol and

started to push the back of his shoulders towards the bar as if he was a trolley. Jean-Luc and Blake joined them soon after. People kept coming up to them and offering congratulations, which was quite tough for Blake; he was in no mood to party but was trying to put a brave face on it. He drifted off quite soon to distance himself from the Team's success.

Saul didn't make his entrance until half past eight. He came over to the Team, took a memory stick from his jacket pocket and held it up at shoulder height like a plainclothes cop showing his badge. 'So guys, this is it. It may only be a quick rough-cut but it's sensational. We'll have a sneak preview LA-style. Mike, maybe you'd ask *le patron* if he'd be so good as to play our movie for us.'

Mike went off to find Sandy. As the others watched, the giant plasma screen below the balcony railing went blank then after thirty seconds or so kicked into life again.

Given that they had only had a few hours Saul and Billy had done an impressive job. It wasn't much more than two minutes, but Saul's magic was clearly visible. The narrative jumped from camera to camera and quite a narrative it was, with Kornie's near disaster, the impact of their landings, the cat-like recoveries and changes of angle, bodies hurtling within a whisker of menacing rocks. It ended with head-cam footage of the run back to town in the sunshine, past the tiny cluster of ancient houses by the stream, past the party people at the Chalet Messigny and through the outskirts of the town to the lift area. They had used the last sequence to pad out the clip because Saul didn't want to give away too much of the main action footage.

As the crowd in the bar saw what was playing on the screens, the volume of the conversation dropped. Everyone stopped talking to watch. At the end of the footage prompted an eruption of cheering and table-thumping before the movie, which was on repeat, started to play again. Soon everyone was going over to congratulate the guys while Saul stood there beaming proprietarily. And so the evening progressed, with the movie going round on its loop, the audible excitement of the newcomers seeing it for the first time, more congratulations, more beer and wine, more beaming goodwill.

Mike first became aware of a problem when Sandy came up to him and said, 'Chap making enquiries about your movie. Not happy.' Over the years Mike had developed a deep respect for Sandy's radar.

'Where?'

'To your left. Black jacket. Expensive.'

As Mike edged his way through the throng, he could hear a polite English voice.

'I gather you are responsible for this video on the screen?'

The speaker, who had his back to Mike, was addressing Tyler and Kornie.

'Who's asking?' said Kornie.

'Who's asking "who's asking"?' said Tyler, who was now well oiled and ready for the fray.

'My name is Guy Dubois and I represent the current occupants of Chalet Messigny.'

Mike immediately recognised him as the man who had ordered him off the Messigny premises. The recognition was not mutual but then Mike had been wrapped up in ski gear at the time. So what was he, Mike wondered, this smoothie with his vain semi-bouffant hair, his gold ring and cold charm? He guessed corporate lawyer.

'What your friend did is quite serious, but we can settle it quickly,' said Dubois. 'We need to take this video off the screens very quickly.'

'*We* do, do we? Go and ask the barmen. They run the video,' said the Tyler. He hadn't actually drunk much, but enough to edge him into a truculent phase.

'I've already asked them; they said it was there at your request and I'd need to talk to you.'

'Well? We're talking.'

Unruffled by Tyler's tiresomeness, Dubois smiled and shrugged. Mike didn't want the evening to turn sour, so rather than let Tyler provoke him further he decided to intervene.

'Tell us exactly what your problem is?'

Mike knew exactly what his problem was. If his guests were the kind of people who attracted secret surveillance they certainly wouldn't welcome an involuntary cameo appearance in a movie that relayed their faces in high definition on giant screens for all to see.

Tyler, resenting Mike's involvement, tried to regain the new arrival's attention. 'I'm Tyler Rafferty; I'm in that movie.' Dubois ignored him and addressed Mike.

'As I say, I represent the residents of the Chalet Messigny on the southwest of town where someone intruded earlier today. I am sure no harm was intended, but it was trespass and it was aggravated by unauthorised filming which infringed the privacy of the chalet's guests. Just look.' He nodded in the direction of one of the screens. And indeed, there they were again, the smart set taking their coffee on the terrace whizzing by the camera lens. 'I am sure that with your help we can get this cleared up without any expensive proceedings.'

This had an inflammatory effect on Tyler.

'Proceedings? Are we talking legal proceedings here? Listen, Mister Big Shot,' he snarled. Mike could guess what was coming next and sure enough it did. 'My father's a senior partner in a big New York law firm; if I get him onto this we'll sue your ass off.'

Mike realised this was going nowhere, so in a quiet aside he asked Dubois, 'Why don't you and I go and talk about this somewhere a little more peaceful?' They moved away to a spot near a window.

Dubois stared intently at Mike for a moment before he spoke.

'Am I right in thinking that we've already met – when you came to the Chalet the other day?'

'Yes, that's right. I hope you've forgiven the intrusion.'

'You seem to be part of another one, a rather more serious one. Was this your idea?'

'No, nothing to do with me.' Mike lied. 'I've just been helping out a bit on the movie.'

'So can you speak for everyone here?'

'No, no one speaks for anyone – but right now I'm probably your best chance.' Mike was uneasily aware that he was taking on a responsibility that wasn't his to take.

'We need – you need – to get that video taken off the machine right now.'

'Hang on a mo, tell me exactly what your objection is and I'll see what can be done.'

'I've told you. Number one: some of the material on this video is the consequence of trespass. Number two: it is also clear invasion of privacy. It has to be edited. This presumably isn't the only copy? And is there any more of this material in existence which relates to our interests?'

'I don't know what you interests are.'

'Is there any more footage taken at the Chalet?'

'Don't think so. It's just one camera on a skier's head passing at speed by a house in an Alpine ski resort. It only lasts a few seconds. What's the big problem?'

Mike was curious to hear his answer.

'I work for an international management consultancy which represents the interests of a major corporation.'

'Which corporation is that?'

'For the moment it must remain nameless; you'll understand why.'

'Of course,' Mike said heavily.

As he talked Dubois's eyes flickered around the room and over Mike's shoulder. He was sure Dubois was communicating with someone he couldn't see. A couple of times he gave a slight negative shake of the head which he built into the gestures of his conversation. It was done in quite an accomplished way.

'This is a good company, Michael. They employ a lot of people around the globe and they're doing a great job. They pay their taxes, they look after their workforce and they clean up their mess. One of their main trading partners is facing a hostile takeover. The bid comes from an unorthodox and, if I may put it like this, highly unsavoury quarter.'

This was class bullshit and Mike was enjoying it.

'The senior management organised a meeting to prevent this undesirable outcome – to save the corporation from dubious ownership and to save jobs.'

Mike groaned inwardly. Oh yes? And reduce its carbon footprint? Why can't people tell the truth and just say it's about making more money? Nothing wrong with that. Folks have got to eat.

'But of course,' said Mike.

'Obviously we had to arrange everything in the utmost confidentiality.'

'Confidentiality?' said Mike. 'Confidentiality is just secrecy in a suit and tie.'

'The meeting was between members and shareholders of the company and some of the more understanding members of the other party. The arrangements for the gathering were highly complex; everything has had to be done without the markets or the media finding out. We took a lot of trouble to guarantee total privacy. Everything was going well until that long-haired hooligan comes crashing right through the middle of the event with his video camera.' Dubois paused for a moment; the expression on his face seemed to plead for sympathy. 'So this is the nature of my problem.'

'I see.' Mike thought for a moment. 'You know what? If I were you, I'd fire your security people.'

Dubois stared at the floor then looked Mike in the eye.

'*We are* the security people.'

Mike had to admit that, for a moment, he actually *warmed* to Guy Dubois. He liked the way he admitted to a professional failure.

God knows, everyone cocks it up at one time or another. Mike was all too aware of the mistakes he'd made in his time – that's why he sometimes thanked his lucky stars that he wasn't a brain surgeon. Dubois was talking again.

'I've spent the whole afternoon trying to trace the source of the intrusion and then I was passing by here a few minutes ago and I discover this. You will appreciate my position.'

Mike understood how tough this must have been for him, a serious operator having to play a bit humble, a bit helpless. Interesting act; Mike admired his performance. As Dubois spoke he kept thinking of that man in white hiding in the trees above Messigny and he thought to himself, 'If only you knew, Mr Dubois – that hippy with the hair wasn't the only one to intrude on your privacy today.'

'Each time that video footage of the terrace goes up on these screens, everything my people are trying to do is placed in severe jeopardy, you understand this? That's why I'm asking you to stop playing it immediately and then we need to talk about removing the material obtained through trespass.'

Mike started to feel things were getting out of hand. Anyone who provoked such determined surveillance could be quite dangerous. And this wasn't really his problem; it was Saul's.

'I tell you what,' Mike said. 'Give me a moment and I'll go and have a word with the director.'

Mike found the great man holding court to a circle of admirers and managed to take him aside, but as soon as he was told about Dubois's demands Saul bridled.

'No way!' He seemed to inflate with indignation. 'I love that scene. Apart from anything else, it's a great location. It's got a Sixties vermouth commercial shtick. It's glam, it's stylish. No, the terrace scene stays.' Mike wondered how a talented person like Saul could be such a pompous arse; he tried to remonstrate and then wondered why he had bothered.

'You don't understand, Mike. That terrace scene,' Saul persisted, 'points up the rest of the action. You have our brave heroes falling down the mountain and then you see these nice rich folks taking their coffee on the terrace in the sunshine. Okay, yes, you can have them take it off the player now. It's done its job, but the terrace scene stays in the movie.'

When he added the loopy alcohol-induced pronouncement, 'Without the party scene, this movie is nothing,' Mike felt his right hand curling into a fist.

'One day you must remind me to quote you on that to Tyler and the guys,' he told Saul wearily, seeing as he spoke an alarmingly clear image forming in his mind of Tyler decking the pompous prick.

Saul was clearly beyond reasoning; no way was he going to convince him of their tricky predicament. Mike had a bunch of people on his hands whose metabolisms were being confronted with more alcohol in a few hours than in the entire previous twelve months. But booze was not the only problem here. They'd all been taking something that could play more havoc with the brain than a bucket of raw ethanol: they were off their faces on success.

Mike went to find Dubois and tell him the bad news.

'I'm sorry, but that's not acceptable, Michael. Mr Blomberg is being unwise.'

Dubois now gave Mike a speech about the perils of infringing privacy under French jurisdiction and the legal costs that their little film company could incur – costs which could equal its production budget. Wipe them out. Wouldn't that be a waste? Then he began to unfold an enticing scenario with talk of his clients' two media companies.

'We could maybe offer distribution, publicity, marketing. All this is possible, you know.'

'It's a really kind thought but the Team have got all that sorted out,' said Mike. 'They aren't quite as dumb as you think.'

'Please, I wouldn't suggest …'

'I know. Let me get them to consider your generous offer.'

Mike pitied Dubois. God knows, he thought, we all have to do stuff for the corporation that we find distasteful. And this Dubois had a tricky hand to play: it was a more complicated version of the classic Please-Mister-can-we-have-our-ball-back scenario. Dubois was playing Mr Nice Guy, but if that didn't work, Mike feared for what he might try next. That made him worry for the safety of the Couloir Noir video, which had cost so much money and effort; more than that, Tyler, Kornie and Jean-Luc had risked life and limb for it. Mike was getting worried that Dubois's desire to delete those few seconds on the terrace might not end there. If there was any kind of problem he and his unsavoury associates would happily wipe the lot. The Couloir material had to be put out of Dubois's reach. Yes, of course it was Saul's responsibility to do that but he would only inflame the situation; he wouldn't understand that he was up against a seriously unsavoury opposition who could turn very nasty. Mike was the only one who was sober enough to save the footage from possible destruction. First he needed Dubois to believe that he could count on him.

'Monsieur Dubois, would you like to come with me?' Mike led him over to the bar and caught the eye of the nearest barman who was Auckland Keith and gestured to the video player. He pushed his open palm towards the equipment as if to signal 'help yourself'. Mike reached over and removed the memory stick.

'Keith, would you do us a big favour and pop this in the microwave at 100 degrees C?'

'Seems a bit harsh, mate,' said Keith. 'I didn't think it was that bad.' He placed the stick on a foil plate with a little flourish, slipped it into the oven, turned the temperature dial and flicked the 'on' switch. The silver casing began to bubble as its innards underwent a massive chemical trauma. Not a nano-byte of data could survive that. Mike turned to Dubois.

'I think that takes care of that, don't you?'

'Yes, thank you,' he said. 'I appreciate this.'

Mike nodded and turned to leave; he considered the business done and felt he could now rejoin the party. No such luck.

'Now we need to deal with any other copies of this footage.'

Dubois was no fool.

'I guess there might be some but I don't know where,' Mike lied.

'You have to let me have those so we can edit them. I'm only talking about a few seconds of footage. It's not a lot to ask. If we deal with this sensibly, we can keep everything civilised. None of us want this to turn unpleasant.'

Dubois was moving from charm to menace. Mike instinctively plumped for the I-must-play-along-and-appear-to-be-rattled option.

'No, absolutely, of course.'

'So Michael, where is this other footage?'

'Our editor would have it but he's not here. We need him because he's the only one that knows how everything is filed.' Mike wanted to show he was keen to help. 'He usually hangs out with his fellow tekkies but I'm not sure where they'll be. But let me try and find him.'

That wasn't actually Mike's plan but he needed some time. He took out his phone.

'I'm going up to the balcony to make some calls. I might be able to hear myself talk up there.'

'Of course.'

Mike's real reason for going up to the balcony was to find out what he was dealing with. He was convinced Dubois wasn't alone and indeed two men, probably mid-thirties, had caught his attention when he turned to scour the room. They were hardly talking, just casually looking around while everyone else was engaged in animated conversation. They weren't really drinking either; their half-full glasses of beer would be at room temperature now. The pair of them looked as though they could handle themselves, which is to say they looked as though they could handle other people. One a bit stocky, the other a bit wiry, they might have been middleweights by avoirdupois but they looked more like heavies by trade.

Mike climbed the balcony staircase and went over to the rail. He texted Billy the Editor – no one ever phoned Billy because he didn't really do the spoken word unless he was in front of a screen. Billy was a genius at his work but when it came to communicating with the rest of humankind he was definitely Special Needs. 'The operating manual for talking to Billy,' Saul had said, 'advises avoid facing him or looking him in the eye because this will faze him. Better to sit beside him facing a screen and think piano duet, then he's fine.' Mike had found it to be quite a common Geek thing. Anyway, text it had to be and Mike tapped out: VITAL U STAY AWAY FROM YR APRTMNT TIL U HEAR FROM ME MIKE.

Now Mike pretended to be talking on the phone while he surveyed the room below. The tables up on the balcony were occupied by diners unconnected with the party below. There was a clear open space by the balustrade. Someone else was using the comparative quiet of the balcony to make a phone call. Mike could hear him; his voice was raised in anger.

'This is the first bloody holiday I've taken in more than a year for Christ's sake, and I can't even trust you to do the basics . . . Okay, then you'd better get him to call me this time tomorrow, okay? And tell him it would helpful if he had the fucking figures.'

There would be calls like this being made all over the Alps at that very moment. 'I know the feeling, mate,' thought Mike, 'been there myself. I go on holiday for a few days and everything in my department goes pear-shaped.'

Mike scanned the mass of people below and saw that the two heavies were talking to Blake. What was that all about? He hurried back downstairs to talk to the rest of the Team, who, apart from Blake, were with Saul and a group of friends. But he'd have to be quick because he didn't want to leave Dubois on his own for long and he didn't want the Team to start getting Saul over-excited. He was beginning to feel like that old Chinese ferryboat man who has to get a tiger, a goat and a cabbage across the river without leaving the goat to eat the cabbage and the tiger to eat the goat and so on. Mike reckoned that he was the only one who had the faintest idea what they were dealing with. He could smell trouble. Dubois had power and Mike could imagine what kind of person you had to be to have someone freeze in the snow so they could secretly video you and your pals.

When Mike got back to Dubois he found him being harangued by Tyler. Encouraged by the man's apparent interest – which even from three metres away Mike could detect was fake – Tyler was leaning over Dubois and stabbing uncertainly at his lapel, the man's patient expression being destruct-tested by Tyler's index finger. Mike gave a silent groan; the cabbage was eating the tiger.

'Our editor is not answering his phone, Mr Dubois,' said Mike, interrupting Tyler's monologue, 'but I've talked to a mate of his. He'll get Billy to ring me ASAP.' Dubois nodded casually, searching Mike's face for signs of deceit.

'I'll come with you when you go.'

'Sure,' Mike said. But that wasn't going to be possible. He had something else in mind but he'd have to hurry, and before that he needed to take some precautions. Caspar, the camera assistant, was the safest available pair of hands. He found him talking to some girls by the door.

'I'll explain later but I have to go now,' Mike told him. 'Can you make sure the lads don't talk to any strangers who are asking questions? If anyone wants to know that I have left or where I've gone; just tell them you don't know. And make sure no one on the crew tells any stranger where we edit our footage. If anyone asks, say the editor works on it down in Le Bas.'

Mike was about to leave when he took a last look round. As he did so, on the other side of the room he caught Guy Dubois watching him with an expression that seemed to say: 'So, Monsieur Nosey, going somewhere?' Mike raised his now empty beer bottle in an acknowledging toast to Dubois and signalling, 'No way, mate;

I'm here till this place closes,' and adjusted his route with studied casualness. Mike didn't see Dubois signal to his heavies but as soon as he was out of sight he looped back towards the bar and edged his way through the crowd to the counter. He gestured urgently to Keith, who interrupted an order to come over.

'Keith, please, I need to get out of here quick.'

'Sure, no problems.' He waved Mike through and he slipped behind the counter and through the swing door into the kitchen. As he crossed that threshold Mike had a vague sense that he might have taken a course of action from which there would be no way back.

26

The kitchens were like a smelting shed: hotter and noisier than hell. Chefs and their staff, faces glistening in the heat, shouting, weaving between their furnaces. Mike eased past three pork chops hissing on a hotplate and headed towards the back door beyond the big steel sinks where a couple of ski bums were paying for their habit by working as *plongeurs*. Then out into the still, ice-chilled night.

Mike headed for Billy's apartment, texting as he went, asking Billy to call him urgently. Mike couldn't be sure if his departure had been unobserved so he walked fifty metres beyond the first junction and ducked behind a corner, from where he could look back. His anxiety was justified. There, about 150 metres away, coming up the road at a brisk pace, was a figure scrutinising the ground and peering down the side roads at the junction.

Mike hurried down the road at right angles to his pursuer and after another 100 metres ducked into cover and looked back. He had a clear view of the crossroads. Sure enough, within a short time a figure appeared and stood stock still right in the middle of the junction, looking down the three roads in turn, tilting his head as he listened for footsteps. Mike was no longer nervous: he was scared.

His pursuer took the road straight ahead while Mike carried on as quietly as he could for a further fifty metres before breaking into a run. He paced himself because he still had a half a kilometre to go. Running along an ice-rutted street in snow boots isn't easy at the best of times and a few beers and a dodgy knee didn't make it any easier. Several times he checked behind him but the road seemed deserted.

Rue Clarines was silent and Mike made his way to number 127 at the far end. He rang the buzzer to Apartment 9 without expecting a reply. He tapped in the combination on the entryphone and walked up to the top floor. He had his own key to the apartment and let himself in. He passed the doors to Billy's room and the spare room, which was used to store camera and lighting equipment, sound gear, bright rescue-orange anoraks and bits of plastic sheeting, and made his way to the living room at the end of the corridor. Billy had left the lights on, but closed down the terminals. Mike sat down at the desk with the editing computer and turned it on.

While he was waiting for the system to boot up he opened the safe in the cabinet, took out the pair of hard drives and began to search for that day's footage. The files were all marked 'Couloir Noir, Day 11' with the sub-files marked 'Team', 'Crew' and 'Afters'. As he was opening up the files his cell phone purred. It was a text from Tyler. Saul says transfer all footage to stick. Vital include terrace + white suit footage. Don't use email or send any footage email Explain later. Gluck. Good for Saul, he wasn't as drunk as Mike thought. It was smart to think about avoiding an incriminating email trail. One thing puzzled him though: Saul didn't know about the man in white, so Tyler must have told him – or maybe Tyler had just added it to the instruction on his own initiative, so in that case, good for Tyler too. Mike texted a reply: Had already started. He wanted Tyler to know he'd taken the initiative. Something else puzzled though. How on earth did Tyler know he was at the Billy Welzer's apartment? But this was no time to ask.

Mike put in a brand new forty-gigabyte stick and started copying across batches of footage from each of the cameras. He was making good progress when he got another text from Tyler. MESSIGNY FOLKS HEADING 4U. U HAVE 10 MINS MAX TO WRAP + GET OUT.

The Messigny folks? *Grief!* How had they discovered the whereabouts of Billy's place? As instructed he had deleted the white suit footage after copying it over to the memory stick and had transferred almost all of the main files; he'd nearly finished.

As Mike was closing down another text came in. It simply said: GET OUT NOW. Moments later the entryphone buzzer sounded. He froze. A friend of Billy's? Wishful thinking; all his friends would be with him now down at the geekfest. No, this must be 'the Messigny folks'.

Mike scrabbled in the desk drawer among the debris of discs, manuals, paper clips and yoghurt-covered-raisin packets, found a lanyard for the memory stick and put it round his neck. Now another text: BREAKING IN DOOR.

That wasn't good. Once they'd got into the hallway downstairs they'd have cut off his escape route through the back door via the boot room. He really didn't want these people to find him: they'd be very cross about his deceit in sending them in the wrong direction.

Mike looked round frantically. The sparsely furnished apartment didn't offer much in the way of hiding places. He could sit in one of a couple of cupboards – how obvious can you get – and wait for the intruders to find him. He could get onto the veranda and jump two storeys into the snow below, but as he'd never seen the place without snow he didn't know what kind of nasty rock might lie just below the surface. Anyway, Mike admitted to himself, he didn't do stunts like that; it wasn't his thing – especially with an injured knee. It would have to be the front door and he'd have to get out after they had got in.

The living room had to look inviting so he left the lights on and the door half open before going into the store room.

'You hide out in the open,' one of Mike's army friends had once told him. 'They don't see you there.' He slipped onto the bed and got under the debris of coats, anoraks, tarpaulins, bags and miscellaneous cases of film gear and waited.

As he lay there Mike felt a bit stupid. Why was he doing this? His initial attempts at being helpful had now got completely out of hand. He felt resentful about Saul's behaviour towards him back at Bar X earlier that evening; his attitude had changed now that Mike's work was done and he was surplus to requirements. So why bother? He'd done his bit for the *Conquest of the Couloir Noir*; his loyalty was well past its use-by date.

There was a sharp crack as the intruders broke the lock on the apartment door and they were in. They hardly talked but Mike guessed there were two of them and they were coming along the corridor towards him. When they reached his door he tensed; the light went on and he heard one of them come over to look inside the wardrobe right beside the bed. The man was so close Mike could have touched him.

As soon as they had gone into the living room Mike searched for 'Welzer' on his mobile to get the apartment's landline number. When he heard the intruders searching drawers and shelves by the edit suite, he slid off the bed, waited by the door and pressed the RING key on his mobile. Soon as he heard the phone ringing in the living room he had crossed the corridor and made for the front door of the apartment; he was counting on the noise of the phone ringing to cover the sound of his exit. In fact the apartment door with its broken lock was half open anyway. He crept out and hurried down the stairs.

Once outside Mike ran like hell. To avoid being seen from the edit suite window, he had to head uphill further out of Val before circling back towards the centre of town. He had no idea where he was going; he just wanted to get as far away from these Messigny people as possible.

At the first roundabout he turned down the narrow street that led to the centre of town. He needed to catch his breath. There were three bars here, which offered some cover. He chose the Auvergne and joined a group of smokers gathered under a heat umbrella. Mike's phone had been ringing on vibrate several times in the last twenty minutes so he checked his messages. The first was from his wife. THANKS SO MUCH FOR CALLING. R U HAVING A NICE TIME? That wasn't good. By that time of night Mike had almost always called her. Now she was going to have to wait even longer, which would make matters worse. And what could he tell her? The truth would sound scary – if it didn't sound laughable – and he didn't want to alarm her. That conversation would have to wait; first he needed to text Tyler that the footage was safe and he'd let him have it tomorrow.

The next was a message from Saul's assistant about tomorrow's arrangements; then came another from Tyler: DON'T GO HOME. BAD FOLKS HUNTING 4U. TAKE NO CALLS. WE GOT BIG PROBLEM.

What am I meant to do now? He felt he was a stranger in foreign territory trying to follow some unfamiliar set of rules. In a search for reassurance he touched the stick on the lanyard round his neck.

Urgent problem: somewhere to sleep. He thought of pitching up at a hotel; he would say he'd been locked out of his apartment to explain his lack of baggage, but who was going to have a vacancy at the height of the season?

Suddenly Mike felt very tired. It had been one hell of a day, starting with a five o'clock alarm call. There had been the shoot and the lunch and the shindig at Bar X and then this last ridiculous escapade. He needed to stop for a few minutes and sit down, somewhere private, somewhere safe. What about the Cutlers? They weren't too far away; he'd try his luck with them. Paul and Sophie were old friends. He was a biologist doing research on the snow flea; she painted landscapes which were sold in various outlets around town. They spent the winters in Val and the summers on their houseboat on the Thames. Mike called to ask if he could drop in briefly. Paul answered.

'Sure, but come quickly because we are stuck in some really bad television and we need you to get us out of it.'

Chalet Mazot, the Cutlers' home, was a tiny little single-storey structure sitting on a shelf halfway up a steep rock-faced slope and reached by a double zigzag of stairs which started by the side of the garage down on the road. Mike was pretty knackered by the time he'd got to the top and rung the bell. Sophie, all warm brown eyes under a tangle of auburn hair, welcomed him in.

The chalet was just a studio with a kitchen and bathroom off to one side of one decent-sized room with a double bed at one end and a dining table at the other. No room for a guest. Paul turned off the television and offered Mike a drink.

Mike entertained them with an account of his morning at the Couloir Noir and, having recovered his strength, left after about forty-five minutes, using the back door. This opened onto a path that went up and over the tree-covered ridge to join the road leading down into town.

The list of people Mike could count on for hospitality at this short notice wasn't a long one. He considered a number of possibilities before remembering Ken Simmonds. Ken wasn't really a friend – more of an old acquaintance, but Mike reckoned he was his best chance, so he called him.

27

Ken was one of the eccentrics of Val. A mountaineer who worked part-time as a power linesman for electricity companies back in the UK, he was the tightest bastard Mike had ever met. Ken prided himself on being a man of few words and there he was not wrong. He liked to play the Professional Northerner: I'm-a-straight-talking-no-nonsense-sort-of-chap-as-honest-as-the-day-is-long, but that was bollocks for he was as devious a bastard as you'd find in any City snake pit. He insisted on being self-sufficient but he had to be because no one who knew him would buy him a drink; he had never stood his round in his life. And that was the way Ken wanted it. So no one in their right mind would do what Mike was about to do and throw themselves on Ken's hospitality; it would be like jumping onto a cold wet rock.

When Mike phoned and explained his predicament Ken agreed to take him in without a single question apart from 'When do I expect you?' Mike told him about fifteen minutes.

Mike kept his eyes peeled on the way but there were few people around on the streets. En route, he checked his phone. There was a text from Kirsten: Do u know where Tyler is? He guessed she suspected that he might be with Saul's attractive assistant, of whom she'd become irrationally but deeply jealous in the last couple of weeks.

'Long fifteen minutes.'

This was what passed for an ebullient welcome from Kenneth Simmonds, son of Leeds. He kept his words to a minimum and this must have used up a month's worth of his ration. Mike had long known not to bother to fill the silences that Simmonds created. He was a stocky figure with an alert, defensive expression on the front of his heavy-jawed weather-beaten face. Mike followed him into a cheerless living room furnished with a sofa, a cupboard, a table and some chairs, two or three of which were broken and lying in one corner.

The only pictures in the place were on an almost empty book-shelf: some people-less photographs of K2, Mont Sangalette and Sierra Hualpa in a triptych frame as if they were pictures of his loved ones. In a way they were, although one of them had tried to kill him. Three years back he'd been in a group that got to the summit of Sangalette when the weather changed for the worse and the descent got messy. Two of the party fell to their deaths. Ken and the other climber only survived by jamming themselves in a crevasse and hanging there until the following morning when the storm was over.

To show an iota of kindness Ken regarded as a mark of rank effeminacy and he ran his minimalist life with maximum dourness, glowering at an increasingly deteriorating world. He was a loner – watching, cautious, avoiding any human contact. Some people, curious about his solitariness, attempted to befriend him, maybe buy him a meal, but it was an unrewarding experience – he regarded them and their offerings with deep suspicion, took the food or drink hurriedly and disappeared with no sign of gratitude like a feral cat. People soon gave up on him. Sandy at Bar X had this theory that Ken's constant tetchiness was because he'd been cursed with a name like Simmonds instead of something properly Northern like Postlethwaite or Grimshaw.

The only company Simmonds sustained for any length of time was that of his fellow climbers, but some wag suggested that was only because they were tied to him with a rope. Those who thought they knew him suspected that there was a decent guy flickering beneath the curmudgeon; certainly the bouncy Véronique, a redhead of uncertain years from the Auvergne who worked at Le Coq, the *pisteurs'* bar, and with whom Ken had had an on-off relationship for some time, maintained to all that he was a good man.

Anyhow, from Mike's standpoint Ken was the soul of discretion and he had no long-term nosey neighbours in his apartment block, just short-term visitors. He'd never find a more secure berth than this.

'You'll be here.' Ken pointed at the sofa and handed Mike a thin rug. 'I were turning in anyway. I'll be done with bathroom shortly. There's tea in cupboard.' That last bit was Ken-speak for 'You can have a brew but touch one crumb of food and I'll bloody kill you.' As he sat on the sofa wrapped in the rug and huddled over a mug of black tea – Ken didn't do milk – staring glumly at his socks on the radiator, Mike felt he was paying a high price for this discreet accommodation.

He texted Tyler to arrange somewhere safe and out of town to meet the next morning so he could hand over the footage. Let's

MEET NOW SAY WHERE came the reply. Mike wasn't going to move an inch so he replied Now NOT GOOD. 10.30AM LA DURASSE. It was a small restaurant and bar at the edge of the ski area halfway down Les Cascades. He was looking forward to the meeting already because he'd be glad to be shot of that memory stick. It might only have weighed a few grams round his neck but it felt like half a ton on his mind. He was just about to ring Anne when his cell phone came to life; Anne's name flagged up an incoming call. Mike cursed that she had beaten him to the draw.

'So what's happened? Where have you been?'

'Darling, I am sorry. Something's going on here. It's quite complicated. I can't really explain now.'

'Oh, really?' Mike could hear the edge in her voice. He often wondered how she achieved this special effect.

'You have to understand, I'll explain—'

'Where are you?'

'I'm at Ken Simmonds' place, he's—'

'Who's Ken Simmonds?'

'He's a climber, you won't have met him. He's put me up because I can't go to the apartment.'

'You what?'

'I can't—'

'Why not?'

'I . . . I can't really explain.'

'I'm sure you can't.'

'Let me tell you about everything later.'

'That'll be interesting; I look forward to it.'

'Darling, it will all make sense.' Even as he said it he knew that wasn't true. Why should it make sense to her when it didn't make sense to him?

'Well, all I can say is I hope you're having a nice time!'

The phone went dead and Mike sat there staring at the desolate walls of Chez Simmonds, imagining Anne conjuring up an angry fantasy of him and a mistress in an Alpine love nest. The one source of solace in his rapidly changing life had now vanished. As he was considering the fact that his despair was complete, his phone buzzed again. It was an historic phone call: Billy Welzer talking *live*.

The poor chap was distraught. He had been with his friends at the Electric Leopard when three men came in and demanded he take them to the apartment. He was forced to open the safe where the paired hard drives were kept. They told him he would have everything back in due course. He hadn't dared to tell Saul what had happened and desperately wanted Mike's advice.

Mike was glad to reassure him with a brief account of what he'd done and that he now had a copy of everything. Billy was nearly sobbing with gratitude. When he'd calmed down Mike told Billy that he'd arranged to give the footage to Tyler the following day. They agreed not to say anything to Saul, who would never even know it had gone.

Mike finished his tea, turned out the overhead light, stumbled back to the sofa and wrapped himself in the rug and several layers of self-pity. He fell asleep wondering what on earth he was up against.

28

Owen was spending a lot of time these days thinking the unthinkable. Even now while he was talking at Hedley Coram. He worried that if They got him, Ludo would have all the glory. Well he wouldn't. When the full truth came out the people in this audience would remember that they heard it here first. *My peers will applaud my prescience.*

> 'There are three primary models for the gangster state: one in which gangsters act at will in spite of all the state's efforts; one in which the state colludes with gangsters; and one in which the state is run by gangsters – when the state is itself a gangster.

'Just as you have sovereign debt, so you can have sovereign crime, which has a history as long as it is dishonourable. We are spoilt for choice when it comes to contemporary examples: Zimbabwe, China, Russia and so on. The sign on the desk of the President of the Gangster State says, "The bucks stop here – and I can't get enough of them."

'We understand the military industrial complex, so we must understand the military-criminal complex, for the Gangster State is a collaboration of the criminal and the police and/or military.

'Consider the Russian model, where sovereign state gangsterism suffuses commerce. The Quasi-Tsar grants chosen supporters control of state enterprises as a medieval monarch granted land to buy the loyalty of his barons. Commerce features blackmail and threats of violence – if not violence itself – to get rid of CEOs who are not on side, and install place-men to secure control of a corporation.

'Mexico is an example of the first model – a state full of Gangsters. Swathes of territory have fallen into the hands of the drug lords; more than 30,000 people were killed in the first few years of conflict as the state tried to fight the gangsters and the gangsters fought each other. Such a war, waged by a weak central power against ganglords who are beyond its control, faithfully reproduces the England of warring barons in the reign of King John . . .'

Clunk. The laptop died and the screen went blank. The power had failed. There were some muffled exclamations from the audience.

Don't be flustered, stay good-humoured, keep them with you.

'The Colonel's jammed and the Gatling's dead,' announced Owen cheerily. Polite laughter. Well at least some had got the archaic reference. Somewhere people still knew about this stuff? The Director rose from her seat; she looked slightly sinister illuminated only by the glow from the screens of their mobiles that people had turned to provide some light.

'I do apologise, everyone. It's not the first time this has happened. This old place is on its last legs. We'll move to one of the upstairs rooms.'

29

Mike slept deeply until around 6 a.m. when he was awoken by a series of scufflings and grunts culminating in an almighty crash and the sound of splintering wood.

'Boogger!' Mike sat up and saw Ken flat on his back on the floor, entangled in the shattered remains of a dining chair. 'Boogger!' and he slapped the floor angrily with the palm of his hand. That must have hurt too. It was only when Mike noticed Ken's footwear that he understood what had happened. Ken was doing his morning training routine of weights, press-ups and hanging by his fingers from the architrave of his bedroom door for a dozen sets of three minutes. It culminated in doing several circuits of the living room without touching the floor, which on this occasion ended when he lost his grip on one of the main ceiling beams by the fireplace.

Mike studied the wreckage of the chair, guessing it would soon be joining its injured colleagues in the corner of the room.

'You won't be having any more of your famous dinner parties for a bit then?' Mike immediately regretted his slightly spiteful remark but he'd had quite an uncomfortable night. Ken ignored it and proceeded to massage his sore hip.

'It'll not be getting any easier.'

Time to get out; Ken was getting garrulous.

It was a filthy day with the sky firmly grey and the wind jumping about all over the place, snatching at piste maps and making the marker flags dance. The visibility was poor down in the town; up at the top it would be terrible. All to the good, thought Mike. Less chance of being seen by Dubois and his people.

He texted Tyler to confirm their meeting at La Durasse; the reply was almost immediate: BRING ALL FOOTAGE. After breakfast, which consisted of two mugs of milk-less tea in Ken's wordless company, Mike broached a tricky subject. 'I want to ask you a couple of big favours. I have to be on the hill by mid-morning, but I can't risk going home for a ski suit or getting my skis and boots from François's place. Can you lend me a suit and pick up my skis for me?'

Ken didn't look up. A silence followed.

'Aye.'

More silence.

'When do you need them?'

'Within the hour?'

'Right.'

That was the thing about Ken: his curiosity was as minimal as his conversation.

Mike made a mental note to buy him a small packet of teabags. Some might think that a mean thank-you but Mike knew that receiving disturbed Ken almost as much as giving. It was incurring debt. While he waited for his host to return with his skis Mike phoned Anne, but she was refusing to answer so he sent her an email saying he'd explain everything when he had the chance. He got no reply before he left.

30

Even though he'd pulled his hat and goggles low on his brow and his neck-warmer was pulled up to his nose, Mike felt very vulnerable on the short walk through town. He also found that Val de Ligne had somehow changed; it had lost its innocence; what had been familiar and friendly now looked different and threatening. Last night had changed everything. Val would never be the same again.

It was when he turned down the walkway leading to the main ski lift area that he had the distinct sensation of being followed. So he did what he'd seen people do in the movies and stopped at Orphée's gift shop, pretending to look at the window display while he tried to see in the reflections who was in the open space behind him. There was no one there and he felt a bit foolish. He saw Madame Orphée looking at him from inside the shop. She knew him quite well because his wife spent a fortune buying junk from her whenever she came to Val. Normally she would have waved but not this time: she didn't recognise him, which was good.

Because of the lousy weather there was only a small group of people in the queue for the chairlift so Mike didn't have long to wait. At the top was a choice of a lazy red or a cut through the trees down a narrow black with some moguls. He decided on the latter: it was quicker and it would shake him up – give his preoccupied brain something else to think about. He was just about to set off when a text came in. It was from Tyler: U GOT ALL FOOTAGE SAFE?

Mike replied: YES ROUND MY NECK. ON WAY, and pushed off down the slope.

He enjoyed the run. For the first time since the events at Bar X the previous night, he stopped thinking about the video footage. That was what was so great about skiing: it was all-absorbing. If you were thumping down through a mogul field at speed there was no room for anything else in your brain.

Mike stopped to take a breather about fifty metres above the point where the run forked. Normally there was a great view from here but today a curtain of mist lay across it. It was also getting colder. The wind had increased, the sky was developing a sulphurous tone and the gimmicky little thermometer stitched onto the left sleeve of his jacket read minus two degrees C. When he reached the foot of the two-man Morillon chair there were only a few hardy souls forming a short queue, so he was soon sitting on a chair being carried up the mountainside.

The Morillon chair was, as the Val tourist literature liked to remind everyone, at almost three and a half kilometres the second longest chairlift in the Alps.

'I think we are in for a long cold ride.' Mike suddenly became aware of his fellow passenger talking, his voice raised to compete with the wind. He was British.

'Yes.'

'It's odd, isn't it, all of us in rows like this? I always feel it's like someone's run off with the aeroplane and left us sitting in the sky.'

That's all I need, Mike thought, a talker. Usually the camaraderie of the slopes would have made him respond sociably, but today he wanted to be left in peace to think about his imminent meeting with Tyler.

'Yes, it's a bit like that I suppose,' he said, un-encouragingly. Not un-encouraging enough.

'They say it's the longest lift in the resort.'

This was going to be seriously tedious.

'Indeed.'

'But not the longest in the Alps. The honours for that record go to the Dopler chair in the Ötztal, which is 3.9 kilometres.'

Mike said nothing. The idea of being stuck on the longest lift in the resort with the Alpine equivalent of an over-talkative trainspotter wasn't what he needed.

'Anyhow, enough of that; I wanted to talk to you about that video footage you got at Chalet Messigny.'

Incredulous, Mike swivelled round sharply.

'What?'

The stranger didn't look at him but just stared ahead.

'What did you say?' Mike asked.

He hadn't really registered the man before; now he stared at him. There wasn't much of him to see: a stocky figure probably of middling height in a dark grey middle-of-the-range ski suit with a largish black knapsack on his back. He was no more identifiable than Mike was. He'd kept his goggles down over his eyes so that with a black woollen hat pulled low over his brow and a neck-warmer covering the bottom half of his face, the only part of him Mike could see was a very small patch of cheek just below the goggle line. It was white Caucasian, which was confirmed by his voice – quite sharp and clear, his accent middle-class. No geography in there but a hint of armed forces '*Okay chaps*' about it. Mike didn't quite know how, but from the man's skis and gloves he formed an impression of a middling skier.

'I'm aware of what you did last night at Bar X. Destroying the memory stick; doing the editing business in the apartment. And getting away. A bit cheeky, eh? You did well. Really well. I was frankly impressed. It's a pity though.'

'What's a pity?'

'That you don't understand what you're dealing with. But then there's no reason why you should.'

'No I don't know who I'm dealing with: who the hell are *you*?'

'Tell him it would help if he had the fucking figures.'

For a moment the non sequitur left Mike puzzled; then it clicked.

'You were the one on the balcony of Bar X last night. You're the poor sod who can't go away on holiday?'

The stranger nodded.

'So this is about the people on the terrace at the Chalet, isn't it?'

'Correct.'

'How long have you been following me?'

'It's not important.'

'Are you police?'

'Sort of. Sort of not.'

'What's that meant to mean?'

'Let's just say that I represent a Non-Governmental Organisation.'

'Doing what?'

'Our focus is on the area of fiscal irregularity.'

'Working for whom?'

'Working for you actually, chum, if you're a taxpayer, that is.' Businesslike tone; urgent in a controlled sort of way.

'I'm no wiser,' said Mike.

'We work on contract for an EU department to assist member states in recovering tax revenues. We have had the Chalet Messigny under surveillance because some of those who were present are suspected of, among other things, massive tax evasion.'

'What taxes? UK taxes? VAT?' Mike was shouting over the noise of the wind.

'Among others. They are very significant players. These are going to be very big cases when they come to court in their various jurisdictions. This one is about billions, Mr Warne.'

He knew Mike's name but Mike couldn't even see his face. Mike felt at a serious disadvantage.

'So that's why there was a man wrapped up in white hiding in the woods above the house? He was your man, yes?'

'Yes. Presumably everyone in your movie crew knows about this?'

'Actually, no. Just four of us.' Mike didn't know why he told him that.

'You're in a bit of trouble. You need my help . . .'

'Trouble? What kind of trouble?'

'. . . and I need yours.'

They sat in silence again as they travelled through the air.

At the time it had hardly registered but now Mike remembered there had been a small kerfuffle just behind him in the lift queue. His fellow passenger must have been the cause of it as he jostled for position to get on the same chair as Mike. How had he found him? How long had he been following him?

'You need to listen very carefully. We haven't got a lot of time. I'm going to have to ask you to give me that video footage.'

'You're crazy. Why do you want it?'

'I just need to check it, make some edits. Just a few seconds of footage that has no bearing on your project. I can assure you that you will have it back. This is a promise.'

Mike said nothing.

'So please give it to me. Now.'

'I don't have it. Do you seriously think I carry that stuff around with me?'

'Yes, I do.'

'I haven't got it.'

'I know you have.'

Mike said nothing.

'So please hand it over,' insisted the stranger.

'And if I can't?'

The man took off his right glove to reveal a close-fitting black glove beneath and slipped his hand inside his jacket to produce a small bright chrome syringe with a very long needle. His index finger was curled around the trigger.

'Jesus Christ!' exclaimed Mike. 'That's the kind of thing they use on horses.'

'Two possible scenarios, Mike. You hand it over and all's fine. You don't hand it over: you'll be unconscious by the time we get to the top. They stop the chair and we pull you off and put you in the pisteurs' hut. I tell them I'm your friend and you've had another one of your attacks. You have "a condition". It will so happen that someone who's in the chair behind us turns out to be a doctor. He'll have the stick off you while checking you over and we'll disappear as soon as they've taken you off in the blood wagon.'

'I left it down in town.'

'Not true.'

He pushed his upturned palm towards Mike. 'Give me the stick now please.'

'Alright, alright.' Mike's idea was to play for time, so he reached for his knapsack.

'Oh Mike, for fuck's sake don't mess me about. It's round your neck.' With that he reached across and deftly whipped off Mike's hat. Mike was shocked by the speed of his action; he was even more shocked that the stranger knew where he'd put the memory stick and by the peculiarly threatening way he'd used Mike's Christian name.

The wind howled round them like some menacing backing chorus.

'Now don't drop it because I'm really good with this,' the man said, raising the syringe slightly.

'Are those things standard issue in the Inland Revenue these days?' Mike thought that made him sound quite cool.

'Probably,' said the stranger.

Mike took off his right glove for the handover, the wind icy on his knuckles.

'The juice in your toy water pistol will be frozen solid in this temperature.'

'Not this juice. Do you want to give it a try?'

'If I drop this you'll be stuffed. It'll be like trying to find a contact lens at the bottom of a bottle bank.'

'Just give it to me, chum.'

Mike opened the top of his collar so he could pull the lanyard over his head.

'I'm really looking forward to telling my friends that I haven't got their footage. What am I going say to them?'

'Just tell them the truth. I'm sorry about this. But you can tell them you were promised you'll get it back when we've finished with it.' He pushed the stick into a breast pocket, patted the Velcro seal of the flap and put on his glove.

'How will you find me?

'We found you this morning.'

More uneasy silence. It was cold and they were just about to be carried beyond the shelter of the mountain, when the east wind would hit them full on. As he was talking the stranger took off his glove again and tapped something into his cell phone.

'Now you'll have to forgive me because I'm going to have to get going any minute now.' He unzipped the back part of his knapsack and took something out. He fiddled with it for a moment down by his left hip on the far side of the chair out of Mike's sight. 'It is very important that you and your friends don't mention the man in the woods to anyone. Not a soul. If you do, I'll know about it and I can assure you that you'll never see that footage again. Understood?'

'Seems clear.'

'I wish you luck. Please do as I have told you.' As he put his knapsack back on his shoulders the lift stopped moving and they were left bouncing gently in the air.

'Okay? Now can we . . .?' the stranger said, making as if to raise the safety rail. Mike couldn't make out what was happening but obediently moved his arms out of the way and slid his skis off the footrest. As the stranger swung up the rail he turned to Mike and said, 'Mike, you need to take care, okay?'

With that he edged out of his seat, dropping his whole weight onto what Mike could now see was a thin rope looped around the armrest of the seat. His movement made the chair bounce erratically. Mike looked down to see him descending smoothly, his karabiner clipped on the double rope – not an easy thing to do while wearing skis and carrying ski poles. When he reached the snow he pulled the rope loose so it landed at his feet. Coiling the line quickly and neatly, he pushed it into his knapsack before skiing back down the slope – his action not stylish but workmanlike – and disappearing into the fog.

Mike pulled the safety bar back down and sat there angrily contemplating what had happened. How did the stranger know where Mike kept the stick? He thought about the text to Tyler reassuring him the footage was safe: YES ROUND MY NECK – but Tyler wouldn't have told anyone.

The jolt of the lift moving again nudged Mike's mind from the recent past to the near future. What was he going to tell the Team? Billy had told him that he'd been forced to hand over both the hard drives; which meant that Mike had had the only remaining copy of the footage and now he'd lost it. After risking so much to make the video the Team had – thanks to him – nothing to show for it. The promise that the stick would be returned didn't really help.

When he got off the chairlift he took the red run that would take him to the restaurant rendezvous. His predicament was now affecting him physically: he ached and felt slightly sick; his skiing was sluggish and unfocused. He felt a cold pressure on his chest and had to stop and rest beside the piste. There weren't too many people around. Mike tried to work out how he'd break the news to Tyler.

One way and another he was feeling pretty lousy.

31

Tyler was sitting at a corner table when Mike arrived at the restaurant.

Mike told him the news before he'd even sat down.

'Someone has just taken the stick.'

Tyler didn't say anything.

'On the Morillon chair. There was this guy. He had a syringe.'

Tyler didn't react; he must have thought Mike was winding him up.

'I'm being serious, Tyler, I don't have it!' Mike tore open his ski jacket collar and bared his neck to emphasise the point. 'He took our movie, for God's sake.'

'It isn't your movie.' It was an unkind remark. Mike hadn't meant to sound possessive, but he felt he had contributed quite a lot. But the odd thing was that Tyler seemed quite unsurprised by anything in Mike's detailed account of what had just happened to him on the chairlift.

He just stared at the table.

'Tyler, believe me.'

For a moment they both watched the arrival of a family of four, faces flushed with cold as they removed their hats and gloves. Mike's predicament made him envy them. They were arguing noisily about what they'd all have; the father was trying to impose budgetary restraints.

'Mike, I believe you. We've got ourselves into the middle of something weird. I also had some unusual stuff happen to me last night. After you went off to talk to that man from the Chalet, a complete stranger came up to me and said if I really wanted to know about the Messigny people's interest in the Couloir footage he had a colleague outside who could tell me. I'd had a couple drinks by then and I was curious, so I went along with him.

'When I get outside there's a black SUV with the back door open and a guy sitting inside beckoning me in. Suddenly I'm nervous but when I try to get away I'm pushed into the vehicle and it moves off. I'm between two guys. One of them warns me not to try anything and gets out this great big syringe – yes, chrome, with a helluva long needle. The other one put plastic ties on my wrists and a soft cloth bag over my head – like the bags your new ski boots come in – and pushes my head down out of sight. I'm freaking out. He says he needs my cell phone; I'm about to tell him where it is but he already knows which pocket and just takes it. They turn up the radio – I guess to stop me hearing anything that would give away our location – and they start asking me about you. "Who is Warne? What does he do? Whose boss is he?" They weren't thuggish or anything, they were quite courteous actually, but they were sort of insistent.

'We drive for maybe ten minutes and end up in a garage under an apartment block. When my blindfold is taken off I see the two guys are in balaclavas. They take me up to a room. They're polite. Apparently I have made some enemies and I need protection. I say I can't afford protection and they laugh and say they don't want any money. They say our movie is at risk for reasons I wouldn't understand. They'll keep it safe, but they need my co-operation. It may sound crazy but I sort of believed them.

'All the time the other guy is looking at my phone; he says he's sorry but he needs to check some calls and texts. Then one of their phones rings and the guy who answers it listens for a while then he says, "Warne has just turned into Rue Clarines." He wants to know why you're there. I tell him that's where all the footage is kept and you've probably gone to take care of it and he starts texting on my phone.'

Mike realised that this must have been the text that told him to copy the footage onto a stick and not to email it.

'Then we wait for a bit and they ask me about the movie. They want to know who did what, who had hired the helicopter, stuff like that. They ask about Billy, what sort of guy he is and so on. Every now and then one of them takes a call.

'Then when more calls come in things get very tense. They ask me where you could be. Visiting friends? Who were your friends? Did you have a woman? If you didn't go home where would you go? Then there's an incoming text and one of them goes off.'

It became clear to Mike how he had been manipulated all along by these people using Tyler's phone but that it all went wrong when they lost him. Without realising it he had shaken them off at the Cutlers' chalet, where they saw him go in the front but didn't know he'd left by the back.

Tyler's captors had let him dictate a text to Kirsten, his girlfriend, which they sent for him but of course would not let him tell her where he was. They used him to help respond to Mike's texts, along with other emails and voicemails that were coming in on his phone – mostly messages of congratulation on the Couloir. Kirsten had tried to ring back but they wouldn't let Tyler take the call; they were sorry about all the precautions but they were necessary for his sake as well as theirs. They put him in a basement room for the night. In the morning they gave him some breakfast and dropped him back at his apartment – that was just a couple of hours ago.

'They told me not to talk about the time I'd spent with them and they said I'd find you at this restaurant. So here we are. I'm sure they're watching us now.'

Mike looked round the room. It was too early for the main

lunchtime crowd so the restaurant was quiet. As well as the English family, there were only a group of Italian students, a wealthy-looking middle-aged man with his own *Ecole de France* ski instructor and two girls who judging by the sound of them came from Newcastle and were showing some nonchalant interest in the Italian party.

'So,' said Tyler, 'that's why I believe what you've told me.'

They sat in silence for a bit before Tyler spoke again.

'I really don't want to tell Saul anything about all this until we have to. He'll just make matters worse.'

'Okay,' said Mike, 'but tell me, how would you describe the people that kidnapped you?"

'I don't know. They were kind of . . . average.'

'Well, that narrows it down,' said Mike. 'Anyway, they were obviously connected with the guy who took the stick from me. For some reason this footage is more important than we ever thought. They don't give a damn about four guys falling down a mountain; it's clear that what they want is the stuff that Kornie got outside the Chalet – and your footage from the woods. I was warned that none of us should say anything about that man in the white suit. If we did we could say goodbye to the stick for ever.'

'That's what they told me too.'

'There's something else,' said Tyler. 'Our friend from last night, Monsieur Dubois, has been in touch. He invited me to join him at Cézanne for lunch today.'

This must be a serious charm offensive. Cézanne was the priciest mountain restaurant in the resort. Oleg the Oligarch and his entourage spent a lot of money in there.

'Dubois was asking about you, Mike – he wants you to join us.'

'How did he know how to reach you?'

'Don't know.'

'What did you say?'

'I said yes and I'd ask you if I saw you.'

'Why do you think he wants to see us?'

Tyler shrugged.

'My guess: he wants to see if we are what we say we are.'

Mike's first reaction was to not go. It would be embarrassing. The last time he'd seen Dubois, Mike had told him he'd find Billy; instead he'd done a runner.

'Come on, Mike, let's do it,' said Tyler.

Mike agreed – they had to do what was necessary to keep in with these Messigny people to secure the return of the Couloir Noir footage.

'But remember,' said Mike, 'whatever we do we say nothing about the man in white.'

32

Mike and Tyler got to the restaurant first and saw Dubois as he arrived, removing his hat and patting and stroking his hair as if he was soothing an agitated cat. When he saw them his face lit up in a convincing display of pleasure.

'Gentlemen, excellent! Tyler, very good to see you. Mike, so glad you could join us. I hope you're having a good day?'

'Yes, indeed,' Mike lied. Tyler, uncouth and direct, told the truth.

'Not without our video we aren't.'

Dubois bridled for a moment at the lapse of courtesy but he let it be.

'As soon as we've removed the short section of sensitive material obtained as a result of your trespass everything will be returned.'

'When will that be?'

'Our people are working on it now, so later today. But meanwhile, shall we have something to eat?'

After a quick glance at the menu Dubois said he was going to having lobster bisque and Chateaubriand. These were among the priciest dishes on offer so he was signalling to his guests to order anything they wanted.

'Is this on your expense account?'

Mike found that Tyler's directness could be quite jarring at times. Dubois just smiled as if to say 'Does it really matter either way?' and didn't blink when Tyler ordered steak tartare followed by *côte de boeuf*. There followed some inconsequential chit-chat about the weather and the conditions on Mont Lazare, which Dubois said he had just skied.

'So, Mr Warne, how do you come to be associated with Mr Rafferty? Are you in the movie business?'

'No, engineering.'

'So you are working on the film?'

'A bit.'

'He's been helping us out,' offered Tyler.

And so it went on in its own tedious, faltering way. On the face of it Dubois was an attentive and generous host, but his faultless charm that made Mike uneasy. While he and Tyler chomped their way through the best part of a cow, Dubois shifted his questions between the generalities of the ski video business to the details of the Couloir Noir production, but Mike suspected this were merely to conceal his real interest, which was the timing of Kornie's run past the Chalet. How was it he came to be going past at that particular time? Tyler and Mike could only tell him the truth. Then came the question from Dubois that Mike really didn't want.

'You disappeared last night, Mike. We tried to find you. What happened?' No accusation of deception, just a chance for Mike to explain.

'I heard you'd managed to get hold of Billy before I did; after that I reckoned you didn't need me.'

'So you went home?'

Mike stonewalled with a shrug.

'What is the nature of your work as an engineer?'

'Structural.'

'An interesting area, Mike.'

'That's Mike all over, really interesting.' Mike didn't think Tyler was being entirely complimentary here.

When the meal ended and Dubois decided he'd got as much as he was going to get from them he called for the bill.

'Please be assured that your video will be returned,' said Dubois as they parted.

33

The Fear. The Fear justified. Owen knew the game was over when he saw a solitary drinker on the other side of the saloon bar staring hard. The man didn't realise that Owen was watching successive reflections of *him* in three of the large repro Edwardian etched mirrors that hung on every wall of the Castleford. Owen knew the angles. He followed the man's head as if he was reverse-engineering a snooker shot that was ricocheting from cushion to cushion. Yes, the man *was* looking at him and there'd be others outside. Once he had left the sanctuary of the pub they'd snatch him at the first opportunity and when they'd got him they'd want to find out what he was doing and who was paying him. How they'd approach this task hardly bore thinking about but in recent weeks he'd thought of little else. If he told them the truth – that he was working on his own account – it would only make matters worse because they would never believe him.

Owen had had his disappearance all worked out. He just needed to get to a certain village in the Cévennes in central France, where they'd never find him. He had already abandoned his Marylebone flat and moved into a B&B on the other side of the Edgware Road, so God alone knew what had made him return to his old haunt, the Castleford Arms. Actually he knew exactly what: a craving for familiar company, a brief moment of fellowship before he disappeared for a very long time. And it was two nights after the last of the Seven Nations so there'd be a lot of excitement and a large crowd to disappear in. A good time to say goodbye.

But he'd got it wrong. He had been too cocky and now they'd got him. So he had to do just one thing before they caught up with him: the handover. Rhys would be the best man for the task. He was one of the more taciturn members of the circle. Owen took him aside, gave him a few phrases to memorise and very precise instructions on how to contact Ludo.

Owen saw the van as soon as he came out of the bar. Time for a couple of quick phone calls. The first was to his Department's Mayday line; the second was to the Emergency Services reporting that several men of foreign appearance, one possibly armed, had chased a terrified black teenage girl and forced her into a white transit van – he gave its registration number. Short of including a member of the Royal Family this was the best combination of elements designed to push Owen's call to the top of the Emergency Services priority list.

Owen's pursuers now made their move. Two men ran up behind him and forced him into their van, which had drawn up alongside them; they drove to Kings Cross where they parked outside a noisy nightclub. The vehicle had been kitted out like some sick parody of a mobile operating theatre with a sort of table in the middle for the Bulgar to do his business.

Pliers are the workhorse of the proactive interrogator when there is no running water or mains electricity to hand and the Bulgar got to work immediately as prescribed by the doctrine of 'fresh and fast' which the rubber-apron men hold so dear. The surgeon's report and the post mortem that succeeded it suggested that as well as pliers, a culinary blow torch and some kind of a needle-fine stylus had been used, as well as a substantial dose of hypersodium thiopental. In fact the extent of the damage was limited because the Bulgar and his master had needed him alive so he could tell them crucial information such as who he was working for and how much he'd found out. As Owen himself had to explain in countless lectures, 'The *bien pensant* are fond of saying that torture doesn't work. That's nonsense, of course. Mere self-deception. It keeps their world pure. Those who are actually in the business know better but they also try to perpetuate the idea as a way asserting that they would never stoop so low. But you could fill a city with the people who in the course of history had been tortured into betrayal. No, it's not that torture doesn't work, it's just that it doesn't *always* work.'

The hideous ordeal that Owen was now undergoing forced him to confront the veracity of his words. Academic theory had come face to face with practical reality.

It was certainly not the Bulgar's intention to kill him. He wanted to extract the names of those Owen was working for and send a signal loud and clear that anyone else who presumed to oppose them would be caught and would be in for a sorry time. So the second part of the work was cosmetic in nature. Owen's subsequent death was an entirely unintended consequence; his tormentors could not have guessed that his metabolism would have such an adverse reaction to the hypersodium thiopental.

As conference calls went it was quite unusual. No way was the Bulgar's boss going to risk being on site, so he'd got the snatch team to set up a webcam and sound link so he could conduct the interrogation from the safety of a remote location. He went straight in with the most important question.

'We need to know who you're working for.'

Owen stalled. He concocted names and detailed descriptions but none were known to his interrogator. He started to talk about a big player in Georgia who was paying top money for information on rival operations but he, Owen, had no direct dealings. He then fabricated a time-consuming account of a Swedish intermediary based in Finland who was associated with . . . and so it went on. To further prolong the proceedings he took a long pause between each of his answers to make space to construct his next set of untruths. Each pause provoked a vicious new assault from the Bulgar. Owen's bogus revelations worked at first but soon the wealth of extraneous detail made his interrogator realise that the patient on the operating table was just playing for time.

In these situations the Bulgar's antennae were usually reliable. He dearly loved his work but if the figure writhing around on the table was deliberately delaying he would be doing it for good reason: he must believe help was on its way. When he heard the voice of his boss on the line saying, 'He's taking the piss,' his suspicions were confirmed. He had to be quick. He ordered the driver and his assistant to get out immediately. Leaving the wretched Owen clamped to the table, the three of them ran from the van to their nearby car.

Only minutes later an alerted police patrol located the abandoned van. When they broke into it shouting, 'Where's the girl? Where's the girl?' all they found was an appallingly disfigured man strapped to a stretcher. It was only when they heard him whispering 'Section S38' that they realised what they'd got on their hands. A few minutes later, amid screeches of tyres, the first of a series of unmarked cars arrived delivering various mystery men – men who had come to the rescue of one of their own.

Owen managed to tell them that there were three assailants who'd left minutes earlier. He was rushed to hospital where he underwent several hours of critical surgery. Now, as he lay delirious in the ICU, swathed in bandages covering his burnt flesh, festooned with tubes and catheters, he was forced to accept that he had fallen victim to the very phenomenon that his researches had identified. His fate was appalling proof of his thesis. Worse: he had been caught by the Fox without even finding out who he was. And worst of all: he was facing the terrible truth that he hadn't properly completed his arrangements to secure a successor to continue his work. Owen would take his findings with him to the incinerator. *I will die in vain.*

True, he had arranged for his key research to be delivered to Ludo but this was mere data shorn of its thesis. He had planned to give him a full verbal briefing on his theory of Extreme Impunity.

He also hoped that the passage he had added to his Gangster State text might have excited the curiosity of someone in the Hedley Coram audience, but that was a pretty slim chance.

So the surprise appearance of his niece Angela at his bedside gave him some hope. Under any other circumstances he would never have involved her but now he had no option. If he didn't take this chance he'd slip out of Wessex Ward into the great hereafter leaving unfinished his finest contribution to the civilised world. He would have to rely on Angela to cope. She was a sharp lawyer with a good memory and a clear head; her training would prevail. His problem now was to find a way of communicating that his niece would understand, but which Special Agent Big Ears sitting in the corner would not. He had to put Angela in touch with Ludo, who in turn would contact others. In this way he might create a fragile filament just strong enough to carry the light of his precious information and illuminate the terrible truth.

34

At around 4.15 p.m., just as Mike was heading for home, Billy Welzer called – again talking live – in a state of some excitement. A courier had just arrived at his apartment with two packages. One contained the two hard drives, the other was a half case of champagne with a handwritten note that read, 'Thank you for your co-operation. Guy'. Billy had checked all the footage carefully. Everything was there except for the terrace scene.

In replaying these events in his mind later Mike would often find himself trying to hit the pause button, to call a halt to it all then and there – for that brief moment when everything was just fine.

35

The next morning was cold with poor visibility but now that all the nonsense was over Mike was desperate to get some skiing. He'd been working on his knee whenever he could and now he wanted to really test it. He made an early start and headed for the Plaisance chairlift, where a group of children and their instructor were waiting for it to open. As the attendant cleared the snow from the take-off area, the empty chairs started to move; the sound system blared into life and the damp air was filled with the sound of Verdi's *Hebrew Slaves' Chorus*.

Mike was staring upwards, vacantly watching the procession of chairs emerge from the white gloom, when he was startled to see one of them was occupied. As it got nearer he could make out a snow-caked figure, no skis or poles, face covered by goggles and a muffler, sitting quite motionless as it glided serenely to earth through the gently swirling flakes and the luxuriant swaying sounds of Verdi. The moment Mike realised this passenger was showing no sign of preparing to get off the chair he called out to warn the pisteur, who had his back turned and was unaware of the new arrival. It was almost too late.

'Whaaghh! *Alors!*' The pisteur flung aside his shovel and leapt for the lift control switch, hitting the red stop button just as the passenger reached the lift's lowest point. His workmate had rushed out of the hut and the two of them started ministering to their unexpected visitor. By now Mike, like the instructor, knew this wasn't going to have a happy ending so he helped in the difficult task of shepherding the swivel-necked children away from the scene which now transfixed them.

When Mike got back to the lift the attendants were fiddling with the frozen ropes holding the body upright in its chair. They brusquely rejected his offer to help. One phoned the gendarmerie. Mike guessed they must have been told not to touch the corpse because they stopped their work and waited. A police car drew up nearby on the edge of the car park and two gendarmes got out and hurried across to the chairlift; they examined but did not touch the frozen figure and then marked off the area with black and yellow hazard tape.

While they were still doing this M. Beluzon, Val's Chef de Publicité, bustled onto the scene. He was in an excitable state, remonstrating with the officers and trying to untie the tape. Mike looked on as a snow ambulance with caterpillar tracks drew up and two medics emerged. They freed the body and lifted it onto a stretcher; unfortunately the corpse had been frozen solid in the sitting position so there was a minute of black slapstick as they made repeated attempts to drape a blanket over this troublesome chair-like shape all the while being chivvied by a Beluzon anxious to obliterate any sign of the unpleasantness before the morning queues began to form.

It was clear that this lift would be going nowhere for some time so Mike skied over to the other group of lifts, which took him up to Pelle. He had a great morning's skiing; his knee performed well and, although the corpse on the chairlift had been a bit of a downer, the slopes of Val reassured him that they could still work their old magic.

36

Towards the end of the afternoon Mike, who'd being queuing for the Pascal four-man bubble, stepped aboard as it came alongside the platform. The clumsy middle-aged novice behind him was having trouble with his ski poles, which got wedged horizontally across the doorway. He took so long to untangle himself and get aboard that the doors closed before the next two people in the queue could get in. Mike's sole fellow passenger was in a bright red and yellow suit and silver mirror sunglasses – he looked like a sort of comic-book garden gnome and Mike marked him down as another dumb punter whose skiing gear was at odds with his skiing ability. As this clown fought to gain control of his errant sticks and settle himself on his seat, he leaned forward to address Mike.

'Sorry about all that, Mike, but I thought we ought to have another one of our little chats.'

Mike stared at him. It took him a moment to recognise him as the man who'd forced him to hand over his memory stick at needlepoint the day before.

'I didn't recognise you.'

'One does one's best.'

'So what now?'

The man didn't say anything for a bit, but seemed to be looking for the answer in the skiers on the slope below them. Eventually he spoke.

'I have to tell you that you are in serious trouble.'

Mike didn't say anything. Let him make the running. His travelling companion took off a glove and produced a cell phone from his jacket pocket. He tapped at the keyboard and passed it to Mike.

'Please take a moment of your time to look at this short movie.'

Mike peered at the screen.

'Recognise anything?'

It wasn't exactly the Saul Blomberg school of film-making; the camera panned jerkily around a room. It took Mike a moment to realise he was looking at his own apartment – it was in a state of disarray. The place had been ransacked; cupboard contents had been tipped on the floor.

'What's this about?' Mike asked.

'Come on, you know who. You know why. They were looking for something.'

'Like what?'

'Something on that video footage?'

'Yes, but we've been through all that. We let them take out what they wanted.'

'Apparently not.'

'I don't know what else there could be.'

'I don't know either. But something has changed their view of you.'

Mike felt sick.

'These people now believe that the intrusion at Messigny wasn't a chance incident, but that you orchestrated it.'

'They didn't think that yesterday – Dubois was fine. He bought me an expensive lunch.'

'I know. But today they've changed their mind. They are hunting for you. And it's not because they want to invite you to lunch again. If they get hold of you it'll be a far less pleasant experience. We have to get you out of town. You need to be where they aren't. You've seen some of their handiwork today already.'

'Do you mean that poor sod on the chairlift?'

'Yes.'

'You knew about that?'

'Yes, we'd been following him for some time.'

'Blimey, was he late with his VAT?'

'Not quite.'

Mike was trying to understand his situation.

'Hang on a mo, if these people are as dangerous as you say, I won't ever be safe again?'

'No, they'll eventually realise you are not the threat they thought you were. But at the moment they are convinced you are their enemy. Your situation may be temporary but nevertheless extremely dangerous. Believe me.'

'Well, why can't I just tell them that it has been a terrible misunderstanding? Face them up – explain the facts?'

'Not a good plan, chum.'

'Why not?'

'They wouldn't believe you. Not after what you've done. Or what they think you've done. They'd want to put your story to the test.'

'Well, fine. So what sort of test?'

'You really don't want to know, Mike, I promise you.'

Mike still didn't understand what the man was talking about, but his words were deeply unsettling.

'You need to be clear about this. You've got a big decision to make here. Either you believe me and let me get you to a safe place where you'll be kept under our protection or you toddle off and take your chances. You'll be a free man for as long as you live, which could be several hours.'

Mike reckoned he had no choice and gave a resigned shrug.

'Alright then.'

The man tugged his knapsack round to his front and partially unzipped it so Mike could see a tightly packed bundle of clothing inside.

'Jacket, trousers, hat and a neck-warmer – all very different colours from what you're wearing now. You'll be unrecognisable. When we get to the top I want you to ski down to somewhere like Plantes Rouges. Duck into the trees and get these on – they'll fit over what you're wearing. Wait for the rush hour before you go back into town. Safety in numbers and all that. Not that there'll be so many today with this weather. You'll see a black SUV on the far side of the car park with a red pennant on the radio aerial. We'll be there waiting for you.'

Mike unzipped his jacket and pushed the package inside.

'Mike, are you using the same mobile as before?'

'Yes.' Mike recited his number.

'Okay, now I'm texting you a number for emergencies. You must on no account make or take any calls.'

'Okay.'

'When you get down to town go straight to the rendezvous. Do not go anywhere near your apartment. Have you got that?'

Mike nodded glumly.

'Good luck. See you later.'

37

Ludo turned down the radio and sat staring ahead, his hands resting on his desk as if to steady himself. He had not even heard the details but was shocked to hear the short news bulletin reporting Glyn Owen's death.

Owen dead? Owen, the guiding influence of his career since he'd been Ludo's tutor at Oxford. They had been very close but hadn't seen much of each other in recent years, so Owen's influence was unseen but no less important for that. Ludo would have liked to see more of his mentor but, apart from the occasional conference and email contact, their work and geography kept them apart.

Part of Owen's work was in the public domain but some of it emphatically was not. For much of his career he had acted as an intelligence analyst for the Home Office and Ministry of Defence.

Ludo's own career had started on a similar path. He started as a lecturer in Modern History while in the spasmodic employ of the Security Services, where his speciality – developed on the advice of Owen – was the area of national security known under the umbrella term of Unorthodox Threat Field.

Now Ludo was in a very different world. Big Oil. He'd had no choice. Serving your country was all very well – if you had a private income. But, as he had explained to his wife, Liz, to pay school fees on his salary would have meant making sacrifices – 'like giving up food'. His section chief at the Service was very understanding and arranged for him to talk to 'a helpful chap' at A&G Oil, where he soon found himself with a new life. He was now one of eleven executives in the Central Services Department at A&G, which handled a variety of special projects and troubleshooting tasks, all reporting direct to the Chief Executive's office.

As soon as Ludo signed up with A&G he was asked to meet his new boss, Reggie Peplow, to be briefed about his responsibilities. He had turned up at the office for his mid-afternoon appointment only to be told by Peplow's PA that Peplow was out but he'd find him in 'the recovery position'.

'Good Lord, poor chap,' said Ludo, alarmed. 'What happened?'

The Recovery Position turned out to be a raffish basement drinking dive in a quiet street a couple of blocks from the office. Lined with red banquettes and chipped gilt mirrors it had only one occupant, a portly figure, red-faced and rumpled, who sat on a stool at the bar communing with a bottle of red.

'*Reggie Peplow?*' ventured Ludo, acutely aware this was a bit of a Dr-Livingstone-I-presume moment.

'Ludo! Come into my office, dear boy,' said Reggie, pointing to the neighbouring bar stool, 'and welcome to the Recovery Position, which you should know is a Site of Special Scientific Interest. Another glass for Mr James, Jolanta, if you please. You are going to be seeing a lot more of him.'

After some small talk Reggie gave Ludo the first of many lessons in the meaning of life and more specifically their role in Central Services, which was 'to paint oil whiter than white'.

Although it had now cleared Ludo's salary off its books and transferred it to A&G Oil, the reality was that the Secret Intelligence Service, aka MI6, still held Ludo firmly in its grasp. Ludo unofficially served as a liaison figure for the Service, which periodically used the oil company as cover for various intelligence functions. His other task was to complete his much delayed research thesis, *Non-Violent Insurgency*, now partly funded by the Service and partly by the Research Unit at the Ministry of Defence. His failure to make proper progress with it had become a source of almost daily guilt.

It must have been more than a year since Ludo and Owen had been in touch. Ludo scrolled through their email exchanges. There was a thank-you note for a book Ludo had sent him on his birthday. Cheerful and optimistic, Owen wrote that he was enjoying country life and getting plenty of work but he had discovered 'some serious irregularities in the accounts department'. That last bit sounded interesting but Owen had not elaborated. Typical of him: he loved to suggest mystery.

The second contact was much more recent. Ludo stared at the postcard on his pin-board, a sepia photograph of workers in a Welsh slate quarry. It arrived about twelve weeks after the email. Second-class, West Country postmark and unsigned, it read: 'Have discovered the Swanborne Riot which explains much . . . Will tell all when we meet, but leave me to contact you. Working hard on big stuff. Am summonsed to perform at Hedley Coram! V short notice so will reprise Policy Studio lecture!'

This was all very Owen-ish – teasing clues, the just-wait-until-I-tell-you-about-this-one tone, promise of mystery to be unveiled. He could make a failure to pay a parking fine sound like a plot to overthrow the state.

The Hedley Coram note was Owen's last. And now that news bulletin which began: 'An academic with Ministry of Defence connections has died from his injuries following a brutal attack in North London.'

38

'I need to join you for a couple of minutes.'

Ludo was sitting at his usual table in the café by his flat soon after he heard the news of Glyn Owen's death. He was being addressed by a man he half recognised who was pulling up a chair at his table.

'I'm Rhys. We've met before . . . when Owen brought you round to the Castleford.' Ludo remembered that he was one of Owen's drinking mates.

'Of course,' said Ludo.

'I'll be quick. Four days ago I was with Owen and the usual crowd in the pub when he suddenly seemed preoccupied; he took me aside and told me how to find you and gave me a "vital" message for you. He made me repeat it twice. The message was: "I may be about to leave the premises. Seek help from the son of a friend of the family and guidance from the child of the Blessed Virgin Mary. Collect the cases from the Cockatrice Den. Do not contact me."'

That was it. Ludo asked Rhys to repeat the words while he wrote them down. Ludo offered him a coffee which Rhys declined, explaining he had to get to work. After he'd gone Ludo stared at his notes. The phrase 'leave the premises' said it all. It was one of Owen's many typically chirpy euphemisms for approaching death. So Owen knew he was in serious danger and had decided to pass some information to Ludo – information presumably that had put Owen's life in jeopardy. That instruction to get help could only refer to one person, the one completely trustworthy person who was in a position to give it.

39

Ludo was uneasy about the prospect of having to contact 'the son of a friend of the family'. When Owen had used the phrase in his message to Rhys there was only one person he could have been referring to and that was Clay.

Clay had been a strange presence in Ludo's life; quite an absent sort of presence really. They met only once a year at the Remembrance Service in a small village outside Hereford, and when they did, the quietly understated academic and the combative and cautiously indiscreet former infantry captain and SIS officer were not natural companions. They came together only because of what they both saw as a solemn duty to the memory of their fathers and the traumatic event which linked them.

Clay exuded a let's-get-on-with-it sense of urgency but usually arrived slightly late. Short and stocky, he had a squarish jaw and cheerfully pugnacious face, topped with a haircut that seemed to have involved a strimmer. Now out of the Service he had joined the ranks of the 'brass plates'.

Security consultancy was regarded as a graveyard for spooks, but it was also known as the 'gravy yard' because its work could be handsomely rewarded. There was an army of firms out there gathering intelligence for commercial clients – work once undertaken by management consultants but that now constituted a sector of its own. Because it required pretty much the same the range of skills as military and political intelligence – the ability to acquire and analyse information from miscellaneous public or confidential sources – former spooks were valued recruits.

There were those who said that in truth much of the work was the sort of thing a competent temp could pull off Google as soon as she'd finished meeting her obligations on social media and before she got down to her nails. But clients felt a lot happier if this 'intelligence' was offered up on expensively bound weapons-grade cartridge paper by a cabal of gentlemen hinting at spooky connections from a few thousand square feet of deep-pile carpet behind a brass-plated entrance in Mayfair, rather than a cut-and-paste job emailed by Dawn from TipTopTemps.

During one of their annual encounters, Clay had explained in that sharp and breezy military kind of way he had, the workings of his firm.

'So let's say the CEO of Consolidated Wheezes plc wants to invest in some joint venture in the badlands – say a vodka-canning plant in Kalashnistan – he commissions some research from a "brass plate" like us. We'll begin our report with the fact that this exciting young republic consists of varying terrain occupied by a population of thirty-seven people and a goat and conclude with the assertion that "Although its business environment presents a number of challenges due to the vagaries of the legislative process and the volatile relationships within the president's family who control the levers of commerce, transport, gambling, politics, military, judiciary and secret police – i.e. they're all fucking crooks

– the state is rich in commercial opportunities. We take the view that clear and substantial rewards await those who seek exciting possibilities while having due regard for the associated security risks." That last bit is to cover our arses so when your Head of Operations disappears within a couple of hours of arriving at the airport and is found four days later hanging from a water pipe in a derelict factory with his balls torn off, we can tell 'em, "Don't say we didn't warn you, chum."'

Ludo found he was often irritated by the way Clay revelled in this I'm-a-right-callous-bastard act.

'But to be serious we actually provide a damn good service and you'd have to be a bit daft to go into one of these territories without hiring us first. We can introduce you to everyone who matters in the country and tell you who to bung to get your construction permit, where to buy protection and how much to pay, sexual foibles of the people who matter, financial status of the leading companies, leverage that might be applied in the City of London if things get tricky. We know which centuries-old family blood feud is on the front burner at the moment and exactly who wants to kill who. We can tell you where to find a safe source of Fair Trade hookers for your visiting investors, and if we don't know something we'll know someone who knows.'

Well, that's how Clay had described it, and it made him the right kind of man to help Ludo uncover the truth behind Glyn Owen's death. True, Ludo did not know Clay well; they did not see much of each other, although their work had a lot in common. But then that was understandable given the delicacy of their family connection, which made for a certain awkwardness between them. But it would also meet the need for the kind of unhesitating mutual loyalty that now came into play.

Loyalty aside, Clay was in a good position to help. As a gently prospering freelance consultant, he had the freedom to take on or reject any assignment, so when Ludo contacted him citing the 'friend of the family' message from Owen delivered to him by Rhys in the café, without hesitating Clay said he would do whatever he could to help.

40

In recruiting Clay for the task, Ludo had carried out one of Owen's three instructions. The second was to 'seek guidance from the child of the Blessed Virgin Mary'. Owen had told him how this was one of the nicknames he used to tease his sister, Norah. 'Not to be confused with the other Mary,' Owen had said, 'whose son gave up on his carpentry business and came to a sticky end dabbling in radical religion.' It went back to their nursery-school days when they had appeared in the Nativity play together. Owen was part of the crib menagerie and was fidgeting around in the background wearing a huge baggy brown sweater and a home-made cardboard ox's mask while Norah, two years older, had the starring role of Virgin Mary.

So Ludo needed to talk to Norah's daughter, Angela, not only because Owen had instructed him to seek her guidance but also because she had been Owen's only visitor in hospital and the last person to see him alive. He rang her office in the Temple and they arranged to meet after work at a bar just over Blackfriars Bridge.

It was a place that served wine in a passable pastiche of seventeenth-century alehouse: timber beams, oak barrels and sawdust on the floorboards to suggest that if you were to hang around for another ten minutes you'd probably bump into Samuel Pepys. A warren of candlelit nooks and crannies, it was a favoured location for office workers' gossip, conspiracy and romance.

Ludo arrived first and chose a corner table near a crowd of noisy girls celebrating a birthday, who would insulate them from any eavesdroppers.

'Hello, you must be Angela. I'm Ludo James,'

She had arrived punctually and when Ludo had returned to the table with his beer and her cranberry juice she stared at him rather disconcertingly and said, 'So you're Zebedee's boy, are you?' Ludo could see a faint resemblance to Owen in the set of her eyes beneath a broad forehead and dark hair.

For Owen the name James on its own was unsatisfactory. If he was James, he had to be James the son of Zebedee. Owen enjoyed using words like Zebedee.

'I need your help because I'm trying to find out what happened to your uncle.'

For a moment or two she looked at Ludo and then said softly, 'I wondered when someone would get in touch. And I'm very glad you have because I wasn't sure what to do.'

'In what sense?'

But Angela didn't seem to want to get down to the point quite yet.

'So tell me how you and Owen came to know each other.'

Ludo gave her the background and reminisced about his trips with Owen to Resistance sites in France and Holland. She asked him if he was the one who'd been with Owen in France when he ditched the car. Ludo said that he was and still had a dodgy shoulder to show for it. It had been an incident-prone trip culminating in Owen driving the car deep into a ditch outside Vercors, where they were stuck until a farmer came by with a horse-drawn cart and pulled them out. Angela remembered a postcard from Owen reporting that the expedition had been rescued by 'a pair of passing Percherons', which became something of a family catchphrase. She laughed at the memory and, now more relaxed, asked how she could help.

'Does the Cockatrice Den mean anything to you?'

Angela looked startled.

'Yes. Yes it does. Glyn used the phrase. I'll explain how in a minute but I also remember my mother mentioning it.'

'I don't suppose you know what or where it was exactly?'

'No, you'd have to ask my mother.'

'Can you do that for me?'

'Not really. We don't get on. Haven't had a sensible conversation for twenty years. She's pretty impossible.'

'In what way impossible?'

'Well, she's got religion.'

'Oh I see.'

'Actually it's more that she's got religions. She is forever discovering new ones – signing up, trying them out, moving on. Owen used to say she was "spiritually incontinent" and that her problem was that she had peaked too early. He said that if you've given birth to Baby Jesus before you're six years old, from then on it's going to be downhill all the way.'

Ludo laughed. 'He was probably right.'

'Norah's been working her way through some of those boutique religions. The current squeeze is the Zen Tantric Evangelical Church,' said Angela. 'She's been on that one for two or three months.'

'So where does that happen?'

'Thamel, Kathmandu. Typical Norah.'

Ludo knew the type: the ones who were forever in search of some remote corner to live in, an endless quest for the warm embrace of a Utopian community. He could understand what they were after, the trouble was when they got there, they'd find a retired bank manager from Chorleywood and an uncolourful collection of mid-life crises stumbling around in saffron robes.

'Can I reach her on the phone?'

'Well, I haven't been able to.'

Ludo could imagine the set-up. Elderly divorcee with a bit of money. The shaven-headed spivs in sandals and SUVs who run the place wouldn't want to let her go. They'd keep her passport and mobile. Maybe that was why she didn't come back for the funeral. Or maybe, he guessed, she was so wrapped up in herself that she just could not be bothered.

'I want you to tell me everything you can remember about Glyn's final hours,' said Ludo.

41

'The first thing I knew was when a police officer came to my house sometime after 10.30,' said Angela. 'He told me that Glyn had been critically injured in a mugging. That he was barely conscious but had repeatedly asked to see me.'

'I found him in a private room in the intensive care unit with a plainclothes police officer. When I said I wanted to be alone with the patient the officer said it wasn't possible. I was annoyed. He was sitting on one side of the room but of course he could hear everything.

'My uncle was only semi-conscious but he clearly recognised me; he even managed to reach for my hand. Once he'd got it he clung to me for dear life. When I spoke to him he answered, mumbling very softly in a hoarse whisper. I had a lot of difficulty understanding what he was saying. Sounded like strange, sort of religious ramblings, phrases which he repeated several times. He was desperately trying to tell me something. Because he kept repeating the words I was eventually able to understand what they were.

'Before I left the hospital, I sat down in the reception area and texted myself everything he said. It wasn't much,' she said, reaching into her bag, 'and this is it.'

Ludo unfolded a single sheet of paper.

'This isn't the only copy, right?'

'No, of course not.'

'Good.'

There were just four lines. At first glance it looked a bit like poetry.

> *The truth lies in the Cockatrice Den*
> *Trust the son of Zebedee*
> *In Balmoral I spoke the truth*
> *The riot is with us now*

It seemed to Ludo as though Owen had in his dying hours reverted to the language of his childhood chapel; these were the rantings of a barmy brimstone preacher. At the same time he had to admit the 'Zebedee' and 'Cockatrice Den' made some sort of sense. Owen had called him Zebedee and sister Norah had confirmed the existence of the Cockatrice Den.

Angela sensed Ludo's doubts.

'You're quite wrong if you think he'd gone mad. I know this was part of a clear plan he had in his mind.'

'What makes you think that?'

'Just before I left, Glyn pulled my hand even closer to him, then eased his grasp slightly and tapped my fingers four times. Then he paused and did it again, he so weak I could hardly feel it. It took me a few moments to understand what he was doing and then I got it. He was giving me a secret signal. And whatever he was trying to tell me, he didn't want the plainclothes officer to know. This was code. But what code? Short pauses and long pauses. Dots and dashes? Morse code! He was doing Morse code on my hand. Brilliant! He was messaging me in Morse code right under the nose of his minder!

'That was a rubbish idea, of course. For a start, nobody knows Morse code these days. I certainly didn't know Morse code; I was pretty sure Glyn didn't know Morse code; and more important I knew that he knew that I didn't know Morse code. But his hand was still tapping on the sheet: tum-tum-tum-tum pause tum-tum-tum-tum. Then eventually it stopped.'

As she spoke, she tapped the table with her fingers and looked at Ludo expectantly.

'V for Victory?' he ventured.

'Exactly! He was conjuring up the past. Trying to link me with Mum's memories.'

Ludo could imagine it: Norah and Owen hiding in the woods of their childhood home. He, brave hero of the French Resistance, taking his sister into this fantastical construct of his ten-year-old imagination: they were gallant guerrilla fighters crouching in their forest hideaway while swarms of German storm troopers tried to hunt them down.

And that was their call sign. Tum-tum-tum-taaaaah. Those few seconds of lone timpani, ominous and hopeful: the opening bars of Beethoven's fifth. For those who heard it in 1940s France its effect was spellbinding. Not a message, not a sentence, not a word, just one letter – the combination for V as in Victory. So, actually, it *was* Morse code after all, used in a way that became lodged in the minds of millions – a tattoo which was to become the call sign of the French Resistance, presaging instructions from London to the Maquis, the Free French resisting in towns, hills and forests all over France.

'So, if he was trying to say something, what was it?'

'I don't know, but I do know that every one of those words meant something.'

Ludo sat there absorbing her story in silence.

'I must have spent less than ten minutes at his bedside when a nurse came in and asked me to leave; she said the patient needed to rest.'

The memory of being asked to leave seemed to upset Angela more than anything; Ludo watched her eyes well with tears.

'I told him I would come back and see him again the following morning but he had already drifted out of consciousness. I kissed him goodbye on the one part of his face that wasn't covered by bandages.

'That was the last time I saw him. I was woken by a phone call from the hospital at around 2.50 a.m. It was the ward nurse: Glyn was dead.'

Angela looked at her watch.

'Listen, I need to get back to my chambers and to put the finishing touches to another marriage.'

Ludo smiled, reassured that the caustic Owen gene ran through her side of the family too.

'You've been very helpful. I'm grateful for your time. I'm not sure who you can bill it to. Maybe put it down to "client development" and recoup it from some of your other clients' bills?

Angela smiled. 'You shouldn't know about these things.'

She stood up and shook Ludo's hand. 'You will let me know what you find out, won't you?'

42

The police and the public have been content to delegate the control of anti-social behaviour to the peers of those committing it.

The Journal of Social Order Report on Unregulated Enforcement and Informal Judicial Initiatives in Public Sector Housing Developments (Vol. III Case studies 1945–59)

Central London had long lain beyond the reach of Middle England, so Clay lived south of the river in Wandsworth in a stylishly ugly late-Victorian terraced house. In the hallway: obligatory shrine to pastoral roots consisting of large log basket sprouting golf clubs, cricket bat, walking sticks on which perched rural headgear all proclaiming, 'Though we may dwell on the edge of this dank urban park, our hearts lie far away in an England of weald and wold where the lark is forever ascending'.

Sitting room: inherited Victorian dark-wood furniture in uneasy symbiotic relationship with selection of white laminate and chipboard items of Scandinavian parentage. Underfoot: selection of un-valuable kelims on stripped pine flooring topped with selection of toys (suitable for four to six-year-olds). In dog basket: Henty, Labrador, adequate for fallen bird retrieval duties and appearances at low-beamed hostelry when shooting with chums in Gloucestershire. Armchair occupant: black cat with white splodges called Hashtag who 'is a bit of a character'. Above fireplace: Victorian curve-top wood-frame mirror known in the brown furniture trade as a 'Clapham altarpiece' garnished with wedding and 'drinks and nibbles' invitations from neighbours who would have been aghast if they ever discovered exactly what Clay got up to in office hours. In fireplace: some cleverly fashioned asbestos shapes giving convincing performance of a real log fire. In front of fire, standing: Clay in jeans and T-shirt bearing the bold legend PARKING FINE SURVIVOR in discussion with Ludo, on the sofa, curled over a notepad on the floor between his feet. Key personnel absent from tableau: wife and children. Mr and Mrs Clay had decided on a trial separation. Now, two years later, the jury was still out. 'The Boss' had moved back to Yorkshire to be near her parents while Clay had stayed in the London home and had the children for sporadic visits when he was in the UK, which wasn't too often.

'Clay, you realise we just can't do all this ourselves.' said Ludo. 'We've both got jobs to hold down.'

'I know,' said Clay. We'll need some help.

'But where from?' asked Ludo.

'I've got a few ideas. And what are we going to call this thing?'

'Thermidor,' said Ludo. 'We'll call it Thermidor.'

'Sounds good to me, but why Thermidor?'

'It was the month in the French Revolutionary calendar which brought to an end the Reign of Terror.'

'Excellent!' said Clay. He was always impressed by Ludo's knowledge and intellect, which was why Ludo didn't mention that the events following the death of Maximilien Robespierre was a convenient rationalisation. His actual inspiration had been an enticing photograph in a weekend magazine illustrating a lobster recipe.

43

The paranoid artery located in the soft tissue
separating imagination from truth may in certain
conditions become inflamed.

Prof. Glyn Owen, Information Dissemination in
Counter-Terrorism Contexts

'What did he *do* to provoke such treatment?' asked Clay.

'Owen wasn't a "*doer*"' said Ludo, 'he was an academic. But, to begin at the beginning, he was Welsh nonconformist. Father ran a small building company in North Wales. Devout Methodist, an official at the chapel and a lay preacher.'

Ludo outlined Owen's career as Owen himself had described it to him. He related how as a young man Owen had followed his father's example and become a lay preacher. He had studied comparative religions at Cardiff with half an eye on the ministry but became drawn to secular, notably military history. From that he developed an interest in counter-insurgency, with an emphasis on criminality as an element in nationalist struggles – and that became the subject of his PhD at Oxford. It attracted the attention of the Village and he was recruited into the research department of the Pol-Mil branch of MI5.

It had been a desperate time – Northern Ireland and so on; the Service trying to find new ideas and approaches to the perennial problem of terrorism. Owen was a moderate success but he wasn't at ease with the culture and the politicking and after six years returned to academe. He took up a post as Professor of Modern History at York College, Oxford, which was where Ludo had met him. York, new and aggressively classless, was reputedly 'spookier than St Antony's'; while there Owen continued to do research for his former masters in the Security Services.

Since he'd left the Village, the Catania Agreement had heralded a new focus on organised crime, which coincided with the Northern Ireland Good Friday agreement. There was no shortage of funding for Owen's work and he was awarded a series of nicely paid research contracts. 'I am getting a piece of the peace dividend,' he was telling friends.

Owen had been asked to examine aspects of the drugs trade and he published *White Powder, Black Money*, a structural analysis of the trade in the countries of the European Union. Meanwhile he was still pursuing his lifelong interest in insurgency and terrorism; he produced several papers that were respectfully received.

After leaving Oxford Owen had moved to a flat in Bloomsbury close to the libraries at Kings College and at the School of Oriental and African Studies and within easy striking distance of Whitehall. He had had numerous acquaintances at the Castleford Arms round the corner from his home.

'I went to the Castleford myself a few times with Owen,' said Ludo. 'He seemed to be well liked but little known. Most of his crowd were under some vague impression that his work was to tutor high-ranking civil servants in various aspects of history and administration. But basically he came across as your typical Professional Welshman with a hunger for conspiratorial gossip and the worship of his gods, whether at the Bloomsbury Central Methodist Chapel or Cardiff Arms Park.'

'Married? Family?'

'Yes, his first wife, Katherine, a social sciences lecturer, died of pancreatic cancer only four years after they were married. They had one son, David, in his late twenties, who was working for an overseas aid organisation but with whom Owen seemed to have little contact. Owen was one of two children. His sister, Norah, two years older, was a civil servant who married a colleague in her department; they had one child, a daughter called Angela. Norah, now divorced, was in Nepal at the time of Owen's death and still is. She's at some kind of a monastery; it's very hard to reach her.

'As well as the Bloomsbury flat Owen had a cottage on the edge of Danford, a small village a few miles outside Dorchester. He spent a lot of time down there after his wife's death, when he was in a relationship with a languages teacher. She was about ten years younger; that ended when she returned to her native Australia about a year ago.

'And that,' said Ludo, 'is about all I know. I don't think he was ever involved in the Village at the sharp end; as I say, he was just an academic with some interesting theories, a researcher.'

'So nothing one can think of to provoke what they did to him?'

'No. My guess is that he discovered something.'

44

Days of subtle inquisition, socialising with colleagues and acquaintances, cautiously promoting the subject of Owen's demise. Focused enquiry masquerading as casual conversation. The Village was abuzz with speculation about Owen's death and if people didn't have their own theory – the Russians, the Chinese, the Iranians, and, of course, the Azerbaijanis – they were happy to hear another one, or talk about it. They processed a lorry-load of silt without finding a single speck of gold.

They talked to their colleagues, colleagues of colleagues. They talked to the Police, Special Branch, and the various niche outfits, the military, police and civil service training colleges, people in 5 and people in 6 – every available source in the rambling apparatus that had been erected to ensure the security of the realm. They also talked to those who laboured on the outskirts of the Village: the Brass Plates – other intelligence consultants like Clay. And it was one of these, a contact of Ludo's called Freddie Jackson, who was key in pointing Clay and Ludo in the right direction.

Jackson was a partner in an operation called ComIntC21 – 'Commercial Intelligence for Century 21'. He had been out of the

Village a year and a half but he was knowledgeable and a talker and happy to help because he had known and respected Owen when they had briefly worked together in the Service; he was also someone Thermidor could trust. It was he who told them about Hedley Coram.

'The last thing I heard about Owen,' Jackson told Ludo, 'was from a young chap in the Service in his department who had been scheduled to go on a two-day course at Hedley Coram.'

Ludo knew all about these courses. They gave them fun titles like *Perception versus Perspective in the New Security Landscape* or *Cyber Dimensions in Developing World Emergency Contexts*. All sorts of speakers were called in to fill the bill. Hedley Coram had been until recently a Civil Service college outpost in Hertfordshire and had since fallen victim to departmental cost-cutting. So: big house, big grounds, rows of people, long tables, a bottle of water for you and a socket for your laptop and you sit there all day listening to know-alls banging on about this and that, presenting their PowerPoint displays. It was a thriving subset of the entertainment industry, except entertaining it wasn't. Ludo would often wonder why they bothered. Anything worth saying could be said in a short email; but no, everyone had to travel in and sit there while they strung it out for forty minutes. Of course it happened in the private sector too, where they liked a motivational speaker – maybe an explorer who'd found a viable career explaining to a bunch of small-town suits why his epic tale of surviving a plane crash in the Amazon jungle would assist your Baldock-based Sales Team achieve exponential first-quarter growth.

'Well,' said Jackson, 'come the day when my man was due to go to Hedley Coram he was halfway down the motorway when there was an all-hands-on-deck alarm and he was called back to the office to deal with a passing panic on the part of the nervous cove on the duty officer's desk. It was the day that some local lawyer went bonkers in one of the Gulf States – I think it was UAR when they had one of their rock concerts – you know, stoning to death some wretched woman for something or other. Young radical lawyer got into a bit of a state about it and started taking pot shots at the royal princes. Didn't get anyone.'

'Don't know how he could miss,' interjected Clay. 'Royal Princes? There are *hordes* of the buggers and it's only a little place.'

'. . . but he did remember hearing from someone else who went that Owen had made controversial assertions and caused a bit of a stir.'

'. . . easy as shooting fish in a barrel.'

'Clay, please,' but Clay wasn't letting go yet.

'. . . these chaps get too used to firing into the air . . .'

'Indeed,' said Jackson as he pressed on doggedly. 'According to my man who was in touch with someone else who got to the course, Owen was apparently the one speaker who was really interesting – his talk was called something like *A Response to Organised Crime*.'

Ludo frowned. He thought that sounded a bit limp for Owen.

45

It was early evening and Ludo had just got back from the West Country where he had been scouring the village of Swanborne. He was recounting his findings to Clay. They had been joined by a young man, the son of an old friend of Ludo who had also known Owen and could be trusted. Recently graduated, he wanted to get some work experience and Ludo hired him. Clay insisted he should be given a code name – so he became Colza, which was the twenty-seventh day of Thermidor. Also with them was Candy, a friend of Colza's. In her late-twenties, she liked her freedom and to preserve it worked freelance, doing miscellaneous chores for a group of charities. Ludo didn't really see her as a Candy, more of a Fiona or a Pippa. Not bad-looking, she was a sturdy blonde Home Counties pure-bred with thighs designed to subdue mogul fields and crush unbroken horses, along with a pair of lungs that could carry a quarter of a mile and stop a runaway whippet dead in its tracks.

Thermidor didn't have much to go on for their investigation: Owen's communications to Ludo constituted about half of it. The second of these mentioned 'the Swanborne Riot' and Owen had used the word 'riot' on his deathbed so they thought it must be significant and concentrated on finding out what it meant. Apart from a lot of people called Swanborne, there were a few places as well, but no name or place that they could connect to a riot.

The best bet was a Swanborne in Dorset near Owen's cottage. There was nothing in any of the books to suggest it was the sort of place that could ever have rustled up a riot. As Ludo pointed out, the most subversive element in the place, if you didn't count the Women's Institute, was a largish stone building dedicated to an internationally renowned animal rights activist – the Parish Church of St Francis of Assisi.

As he drove west Ludo rehearsed in his mind the gist of a cover story. 'I'm doing this history of the West Country for the Shireland Press, this dingbat little publishing company that you've never heard of before and never will again 'cos it doesn't exist but this card has a telephone number that will get answered. Yes, we do have a website but unfortunately we've had some ongoing issues so it's not actually fully functional at the moment.' And so on.

'Well, not a great success,' Ludo told Clay and Colza that evening when he'd got back. 'I went to see all the right people – the church warden, the vicar, the two big farmers, the publican – and some of the wrong ones: the guy who did motorbike repairs and dealt in scrap metal among other substances, the trustafarian in a disintegrating Georgian farmhouse waiting for a tsunami of money to hit him while getting gently out of his skull on dope in between forays into some project in the visual arts . . .'

'Visual arts!' snarled Clay.

'You've never been much of a one for your arts, have you, Clay?' taunted Ludo for Colza's benefit, but Colza had already gathered that.

'It seemed like any other village in England with all the traditional offerings: Yoga and Pilates classes, web design lessons, courses in Life Skills, a spray-painted bus shelter and a pub serving typical English pub fayre, which is to say, Thai food dinners from Monday to Thursday. Today was chicken curry with coconut and lemongrass.

'The vicar was one of those trendy types, all cheerless enthusiasm. I made out that I was interested in all that parish pump stuff, his wife's valuable role in his work and so on. She was a qualified tai-chi teacher, knew a bit about websites and was setting up a "community presence" on the net, which he said was much needed in a rural area like this. She had had some success with a similar enterprise in their previous parish on the outskirts of Burnley, but it was proving a bit of an uphill struggle in Swanborne. The one attempt at a community magazine thirty years earlier hadn't been a great success. It had been started by a retired civil servant, "a bit of a maverick" who was "not very positive" about church affairs. Carling, he was called. Anyway, he wasn't popular in the village and the thing only survived for a few issues before disappearing.'

How 'not very positive'? Ludo had asked. 'I didn't really want to know, it was just that in my experience the negative is usually more promising. "Oh, some quite disobliging stuff about the Church actually," says the vicar. "I must admit I was glad to see the back of *The Riot.*" "The *what*?" I said. "*The Swanborne Riot*," he said, "that's what it was called."

'"Now why was it called that, then?" I asked. "Oh, I don't know. I suppose that's what Carling thought he was trying to do, cause a riot." "Is this Mr Carling still here?" "Oh yes," says the vicar with a glint of malign pleasure. "You'll find him near the fence in the southwest corner. Unpolished granite, gable top. It just says, 'Richard Carling, Servant'. I forget the dates."

'I asked where I could get a copy of this magazine, at which point Our Lord's representative on earth for Swanborne, Danford and Highditch got a bit antsy and said he hoped it wasn't going to be an negative history of the county and went to a little archive of local stuff in his bookshelves and produced the sole surviving copy of *The Riot*.

'"I can't let you have this," he said, "but you're welcome to read it here." It didn't take me long. There were just a few short items about darts fixtures and IT support, some nature notes, a recipe and a few small ads. The heart of it was a column called "Thursday Country" and signed "Swanborne Fox".

'This Fox read like a crotchety old-fashioned civil servant who'd been let off the leash. It was vituperative stuff, mostly complaining about the lack of support for the publication, which had undertaken the vital task of monitoring the actions of the allegedly great and good of the Parish. There was a line about Swanborne having its reputation to preserve "as a source of rebellion and unorthodoxy following the example set by a maverick resident of the area one hundred and fifty years earlier, an incident from which this publication takes his name".

'I asked the vicar what this "incident" was about but he didn't know. I thanked him and set off knocking on doors around the village but of the few people who were at home nobody had a clue.

'Before I left I drove over to Danford so I could have a look at Owen's country retreat. It was one of two late-Victorian semi-detached brick cottages on the edge of the village. There was a van parked on the road by the gate; the front door was open. Owen's half was visibly more neglected than the house next door, where a young pregnant woman was working in the garden. I didn't like the look of the van so I didn't hang around.'

'And you can't find any other reference to a Swanborne Riot?' asked Colza.

'No, not a thing. My guess it's the usual story – starving farm labourers protesting about the price of bread or something.'

Colza shook his head and frowned.

'I don't think so. This is all about hunting.'

'Why do you say that?'

'Some of the words. "Thursday Country" – and "riot", come to think of it.'

'Maybe some kind of hunt saboteurs' stuff? You'd know about that!'

Ludo was referring to Colza's student days, when he had been a militant hunt saboteur. He and Clay liked to wind him up about his past and Colza knew what was coming next.

'A hunt saboteur! You Bolshevik hooligan,' said Clay. 'Remind us what it was daddy used to do?' Clay went into a parody of a sergeant major. 'Yew 'orrible ungrateful little class traitor, yew!' then switched to a caricature upper-class drawl: 'Tell me, what did dear papa have to say about that?'

'I think we've been through that one, Clay,' said Colza coolly.

'Papa was only a bloody colonel in the Foot Guards! A colonel! In the Royal blinkin' Household!'

Ludo enjoyed the irony that Colza's qualities of subversion and cunning as a hunt saboteur had so impressed one of the undercover cops who'd infiltrated the group that he passed his name on to his superiors and Colza was eventually recruited into Her Majesty's homeland Security Service.

'My point is,' Colza persisted, 'I don't think it's anything like that at all. A riot means something different to hunting people.'

'So what are you saying?'

'I'll probably be able to tell you if I can get down there myself.'

46

There is no English term for *coup d'etat.*

Prof. Glyn Owen

Grand houses are as insatiable in their demands as any woman. They can be veritable gold-diggers, relentless in their quest for rich men to keep them in the style to which they are accustomed. The Hall at Hedley Coram was no less demanding than the rest of them. Built in 1827 by a local landowner, it had bled dry several patriarchs before kicking them out and captivating another. The old place was still engaged in a quest for a wealthy incumbent in the 1950s when halfway through the decade it seduced the richest of them all: the State.

Hedley Coram had been chosen for a miscellany of Civil Service uses including the training of the upper echelons off the Foreign and Colonial Office. But as Britain managed its orderly decline with the shedding of overseas responsibilities, the Hall increasingly came to be lent out by what some of the Foreign Officers privately referred to as 'other ranks', aka the civil servants of the ministries of Transport, and Agriculture and Energy. Once the preserve of discussions concerning *Tribal Politics in Waziristan* it was now *Holistic Approaches to Infrastructure Plan Implementation in the East Midlands Conurbation.*

Come a new era of consolidations and Hedley Coram was put on the market. The Security Issues Course at which Owen spoke was one of the last engagements it would host. The first buyers were a leisure group with plans for a 'luxury spa hotel' but they had gone bust in the interim. Hedley Coram was now back on the market.

When Ludo called the agents handling the sale and asked to view the property, he was put through to someone called Giles.

'What did you have in mind?'

'A conference centre,' replied Ludo. He could almost hear the little blighter smirking down the phone.

It was a large building, not beautiful but handsome, thought Ludo as his taxi emerged from the trees. The effect of its tall windows sweeping rhythmically down to the ground was marred by gloomy steel fire escapes and an air of abandonment. The once great estate had been reduced to its gardens but most of its flowerbeds and borders had been grassed over; everything had been reduced to a sort of fairway that was getting rougher by the day.

Giles was waiting for Ludo on the steps.

'Is it really a conference venue you've got in mind?'

'Yes.'

'You don't look like the conference type,' said Giles, scanning Ludo's elderly full-length check tweed overcoat.

'Teachers have conferences like everybody else.'

Giles seemed happy with that.

They walked through a grand hall into one of the main reception rooms, with Giles doing his spiel in a glib, off-hand kind of way. The poor old place already smelled of damp plaster; no wonder it was having trouble seducing a new master. The tiresome Giles droned on '. . . a very rare opportunity . . . clear growth indicators in the conference market . . . we're fielding a serious number of enquiries.'

Ludo imagined Owen giving his lecture. Perhaps this was the room. There would have been the rows of tables facing the speaker's rostrum at one end by the window with Owen spinning his prophetic vision of some impending threat to the nation, a Welsh chapel Jeremiah preaching against new evils in a Victorian plutocrat's drawing room.

It was only on their way out that Ludo saw it. For a moment he stopped in his tracks. On the outside of the door was a small black wooden plaque with a single word painted in dull gold: 'Byzantium'. He hurried along the corridor checking each door. The next one was 'Mesopotamia', the one beyond was 'Anatolia'. He swung round and headed back towards the staircase ignoring Giles who was startled by the sight of the distrait Ludo, long coat flapping as he hurried up the stairs.

Ludo, heart pounding, reached the top and looked down the long main corridor now chopped up at intervals by ugly regulation fire partitioning.

The plaque on the first door was 'Windsor'; the next one along was 'Sandringham'.

'Balmoral' was just across the corridor.

47

As soon as he had seen Jackson, Ludo tracked down the secretariat that administered Hedley Coram and asked for a copy of Owen's talk. As he suspected, Jackson had got it wrong: the title was actually *Triumph of the Gangster State*. The Hedley Coram people said Owen had left them a hard copy of his lecture rather than a digital version but they were pretty disorganised what with having to cope with the aftermath of the move, staff off sick, someone on leave etc and couldn't actually find it. However Owen had told Ludo in his note that the lecture he was delivering at Hedley Coram was the same as the one he'd given to the Policy Studio so he approached them.

The Policy Studio was one of the middle-ranking players in the think-tank business. It was a world Ludo was more than familiar with, this community of ideological policy wonks, each convinced that he had the perfect plan for the governance of men. Odd folk – men and women, all sorts of intellectual shapes and sizes, their shoulder bags full of legislative tweaks and blueprints for the dawn of a new world, tugging at sleeves, hustling for funding, battling against Westminster's fierce centrifugal forces to get to the centre where lay the power to drive their dreams.

Ludo wanted a low-key approach so he called in without an appointment. The Director was there and more than happy to help, particularly now their party was in the chill of opposition. That's politics for you: one minute you're the bright new kid on the block with offices in Westminster and the Government's ear in your pocket; then a sudden election changes everything, no one cares what you think and you're a dying duck in a couple of rooms at the wrong end of Chancery Lane, hanging on to the whim of an ambitious hedge fund manager with deep pockets and long-distance plans for political influence.

The Director emerged after a few minutes and passed him a folder. Ludo glanced at a few passages.

'Yes, this looks like it.'

'I can't understand why but there doesn't seem to be a digital version; so let us run off a copy for you.'

As Ludo watched an office junior photocopy the pages he wondered idly if this keen youngster would get anywhere in the great game. Certainly a lot of successful political careers had begun in hatcheries like this; maybe this one would be running the country in twenty years' time. Anyway, she should certainly go a long way with legs like that.

48

The only creatures with clean hands in the City
of London are the workers who tend to the toilets
and the carp that swim in the atria ponds.

Prof. Glyn Owen

Ludo walked down to the Temple gardens and found an empty bench where he could read Owen's words in peace. He flipped through the pages. 'Oh yes,' he smiled to himself as he flipped through the pages, 'this was Glyn Owen alright.'

'For the most accomplished realisation of the Gangster State we have no choice but to look to Italy and its Mafias who have managed to combine two models of the Gangster State, in that it is a state full of gangsters and is to a great extent run by them.

'And is their corruption so surprising, given this is a land where they offer bribes of cash and candles presumably on the basis of a conviction that even He can be bought?'

Oh yes, vintage Owen, the Welsh nonconformist lobbing a rock at the Romans. And there was Owen the melodramatist:

'There comes a slow dawn of realisation that a mild illness has turned into a terrible contagion and now a new climate of malevolence prevails. As the plague rats enter the city the angels start filing their flight plans.'

And Owen the alarmist:

'And what if the judiciary were to be corrupted? What if juries could be 'got at'? What if the criminal lawyers became criminal? How very fine that borderline between presenting a client's explanation and fabricating an explanation. It must be tempting to transgress it – the rewards can be so great – so maybe this almost undetectable offence is committed routinely?

Is it possible that our criminal barristers have found a way of committing the perfect crime?'

Owen was never keen on lawyers. 'I'm all for the rule of law,' he would say, 'but not if it means the rule is by lawyers'.

'Cast your eyes up to the Old Bailey's dome where gold-gowned Justice makes her rooftop protest and imagine how her judgement might be swayed when someone chucks a bloody great lump of Charlie on her scales. Might that persuade her to exchange her sword for a razor blade to hold aloft instead and signal that she too is poised to take her cut? She would only be following in the example of our venerated financial services community?'

Bankers too! Owen always used to talk about the City as the 'criminal overworld'.

'Now, a question for you. Fingers on buzzers. Ready? Which is the more guilty – the man who commits a bank robbery or the bank which launders the proceeds? Each and every day, even as we smirk at the nigh comic corruption of the allegedly emerging nations, the Square Mile opens its sluices to a torrent of asylum-seeking criminal money from those very kleptocracies. The City is basically a bloody great panic room for nervous bank notes, most of which are on the run.

'In terms of turnover, we are probably the most corrupt nation in the world. In spite of being the world's largest receiver of stolen treasure, our financial community has managed to confer upon itself an aura of stylish respectability. One wonders if this is the real and least understood achievement of the tailors of Savile Row.

'The City also launders an ocean of home-grown criminal money, which, once washed and dried, confers the trappings of respectability. After trading some charitable donations for a peerage, the lawbreaker becomes a lawmaker – the vermin wear ermine! They who were once running mules now stable racehorses. Their children go to the schools for the elite where they become the friends of future business leaders, politicians and judges.

And so the rot spreads.'

And here he was in one of his favourite roles, the Biblical harbinger of doom:

'Beware the days when good men are cowards and bad men are brave.'

This is the stuff. *Oh Glyn, I miss you, old friend.*

Ludo carried on flicking through the pages until he got to final quarter. 'I told them in Balmoral,' Owen had whispered to Angela, so Ludo must look for something that Owen said at the end of the lecture after they had moved upstairs. Among the florid phrasing he found one passage, stark and unadorned, concerned with foreign crime.

'The scale of their profits has provided criminals with access to the sort of human and technical assets which were once the preserve of the State. In consequence, in the unending war on crime, the advantage has swung so far in the criminal's favour that, in some territories, it has culminated in the most toxic iteration of the Gangster State which is when Extreme Criminal Impunity prevails.

'This is the phenomenon in which high harm criminal forces have grown so powerful that they proactively engage the agencies deployed against them. By a combination of violence, bribery, intimidation, the elimination of courageous individuals in authority and the penetration of the State's criminal intelligence organisations they render the law-keepers too frightened to act against them.'

Nothing exceptional there, thought Ludo, that's what happens in a lot of places – not something to get excited about. So what had Owen said that he thought was so important?

49

Ludo rang Angela to get the address of the cottage in Monmouthshire where Owen and Norah had spent most of their childhood. He wanted to have a look around, just in case. It was near Tredunnock, about four miles outside Caerleon. Ludo found the spot by following the Usk road, which made its way through open countryside dotted with copses and clumps of woodland and the occasional small farmhouse. The Owen house was easy to find because it still had a small pond in front just as Angela had described it, except that whereas it had once been on the edge of woodland it was now surrounded on three sides by a dozen tightly packed L-shaped semis ranked in orderly curves. Peering beyond the neighbouring hedge into the back garden, Ludo could see it was now nothing more than a big bare lawn. There were limits to what could be done sitting at one's desk and doing an online aerial search like this, but it showed him everything he needed to know; there'd be nothing left of the Cockatrice Den so no need to drive down there. He told Clay and Colza that they'd have to get an audience with the Blessed Virgin Mary herself. Ludo tried to persuade Angela to go out and visit her mother but she didn't like the idea at all, so Thermidor dispatched Candy with an effusive letter of introduction from Angela explaining she was preparing an appreciation of Owen for his university alumni journal and would appreciate any co-operation Norah could give her.

Within a fortnight, over mint tea in some dysentery-inducing café on a muddy street in Thamel, Kathmandu, Candy was patiently listening to Norah's bright-eyed account of the joys of the Cognitive Judaeo-Tantric Church before coaxing her back to her childhood days with Owen, and asking, among many other things, about the Cockatrice Den.

'Oh, that?' said Norah. 'That *is* going back a bit. That's when we were in the French Resistance.'

'You what? How come?'

Norah laughed.

'Well, not really, of course. As a child Glyn was in awe of a man in the village who'd served with SOE. He'd tell my brother tales of heroic agents parachuting into France and I was forever being dragged into Glyn's French Resistance fantasies. He said we had to have a hiding place for our radio, ammunition and food supplies. The Cockatrice Den was Owen's name for the remains of an old chicken house by the trees at the end of the garden where we would hide everything safe from the Gestapo.'

'Why Cockatrice Den?' Clay asked Ludo after they had read the report of the conversation.

'Oh that,' said Ludo. 'That was typical Glyn Owen: it was biblical and portentous; he'd obviously developed his taste for melodrama at any early age. Also, he would have liked the sound of it, the click and the hiss of it – a bit more exciting than, say, the Chicken Shed.'

'So what do we do now?' said Clay.

'The new housing development at the Monmouthshire cottage would have obliterated any trace of the 'Cockatrice Den' and we aren't going to find much in the way of accommodation for chickens where he lived in Marylebone. That leaves Danford, his last country lair. We need to get down there.'

'Great, can we take the bikes?'

Three days later, accompanied by Colza, Ludo on a borrowed motorbike and Clay were bombing down the motorway to the West Country. A couple of miles from their destination they stopped to put on the false registration plates in case there was any hidden CCTV gear rigged up by Owen's enemies and made a couple of passing runs by the cottage. It was apparently deserted. They knew the neighbours weren't in because Candy was treating them to dinner in Luigi's Grill in Dorchester on the pretext of being a freelance journalist writing about their former neighbour.

Colza waited in some trees where he could watch the road while Clay and Ludo went round the back of the cottage. There, sure enough, at the end of the scruffy garden was an empty chicken hutch.

They'd brought a torch lantern, trowel, jemmy and a couple of collapsible spades, and had a good poke around but found nothing – until Ludo noticed that the little wooden ramp up to the entrance was quite a solid affair with a double thickness of timber. Odd, considering it didn't need to support the weight of more than a couple of chickens. They jemmied the layers apart and there it was: a black polythene package containing a brown envelope.

They tidied up carefully and pelted back to town, breaking off at a service station for coffee, doughnuts and, at Clay's request, 'a quick peep at the goodies'.

50

'What's this little arrow thing he keeps using?' asked Clay.

'It's a crescendo sign,' said Ludo. 'Musical notation. Owen would often mark it on written text; he used to use it on my essays. That crescendo is his shorthand for "expand, needs more". The three fs – fortissimo – for "very loud", which he uses for something that is "extremely significant". In fact you could call this whole thing a score for a criminal symphony.'

The contents of the Cockatrice Den package consisted of a bundle of papers in a thin card folder on which was handwritten: Swanborne.

Twenty-seven pages freeze-framing Owen's investigative process; a chaotic assembly of numbers, words and phrases, sprinkled with underlinings, questions marks, linking arrows. Colza said it looked like the work of a particle physicist having a nervous breakdown.

Most of the pages were handwritten, in some places neatly, in others hurriedly scrawled; some pages were printouts of typed notes, photocopies, transcripts. No discernible structure, no chronological ordering, just raw notes, lists, charts and occasional pieces of text.

'I need to spend a bit of time with this on my own,' said Ludo, who proceeded to immerse himself for days on end, reading and re-reading the file. Most other avenues of enquiry came to a halt as he kept the others busy with a mass of requests for information to be sought or checked.

Some of the material was grouped under headings: investment banks, hedge funds and domestic and overseas charities; there were lists of service companies – motorcycle couriers, notes on leading criminal lawyers, police forces and HM Customs officers, judges and prison governors, civil servants in the Home Office and Inland Revenue. There were roughly sketched organisational charts, and logistical graphics featuring UK and European cities. Under the name Justus Lipsius were seven sets of initials.

As well as organisational charts of UK and overseas companies, there were incomprehensible diagrams and a welter of detailed but disjointed notes on a string of events ranging from large and small commercial transactions, robberies, assaults, criminal damage, sudden resignations from major companies, violent or suspicious deaths, and chronological lists of incidents, events and procedures mostly concerning the Police or the Security Services. There were several of these with little indexes of people and place names like Vox and the Park in the margin.

Vox was an abbreviation commonly used in the Village for Vauxhall Cross, the headquarters of the Secret Intelligence Service, MI6, on the river opposite Westminster. Anyone who wondered why a nation would move its most secret institution into one of its capital's most flagrantly attention-seeking buildings might have been reassured to know that very little of any significance happened here. Apart from its library, archive and image analysis section housed on two basement floors, the place was little more than a sparsely occupied back office.

Ludo was always amused that when MI6 sought to influence a decision maker or secure co-operation from anyone it flattered them with an invitation to its riverside headquarters, where they were taken on 'a necessarily very limited tour' beginning with the Service's museum on the south side of the second floor. On their way they passed along the gallery that ringed the large double-height space of Cummins Hall. Nothing was said, but, in the belief they were observing the nation's elite spymasters at work, visitors were in fact staring down on a large clerical force processing invoices and expense claims from around the globe and, in the northwest corner, the transport department of MI5 administering the complicated demands for vehicles in the UK. Making them share office space was one of many – over-optimistic – attempts to enforce a degree of co-operation between the two squabbling institutions.

The pointy end of MI6 was actually the massive Department of Operations (DO), but in the Village more often referred to as 'the

Park', located intentionally close to Heathrow Airport fifteen miles due west on the edge of Osterley Park. The apparent function of the eighty-acre office campus was to house the Defence Procurement and Support Agency since its move from Bristol – along with a handful of sensitive MoD and security specialist units. Its covert function was to accommodate the misleadingly named Defence Logistics Division, which occupied a seven-storey building (three of them below ground level). It was from here that MI6's case and desk officers controlled and administered agents around the world. The Park made repeated appearances in Owen's Swanborne File and attracted the largest crescendo marks.

51

When he'd done all he could Ludo outlined his conclusions to Clay.

'Owen lists seventeen violent deaths in this document but focuses on three of them. His notes are peppered with question marks and arrows suggesting that they were in some way connected.

'What's interesting is that he seems less concerned with the murders than in the manner of their investigation. He's always highlighting the length of time taken to gather evidence and the inadequacy of witness interviews, careless procedural failures which caused delays in an investigation, evidence going missing, evidence neglected, leads not followed up.'

'So standard police procedure followed at all times then,' interjected Clay.

'And that's what our enquiries confirm: people who'd been close to the two UK police investigations, unprompted, remarked on the low priority they had been given considering their seriousness.

'Now while much of his work had concerned foreign territories, Owen also conducted a study on wholesale distribution patterns in the UK drugs trade – this had become part of the security services' remit because it was inextricably linked with organised crime.

'So Owen was more than familiar with the industry and police methods to tackle it – devices like the Met's Kirby List, a sort of league table listing high-end villains in order of importance to help prioritise the allocation of surveillance resources. Owen's notes suggest there were some decisions that were puzzling not so much because of who was on it, but who wasn't – who had been relegated or removed. This was probably what he was referring to when he sent me that postcard mentioning "some serious irregularities in the accounts department". The most notable example in Owen's eyes was a criminal family called the Parsons, which gets several mentions in the file.'

'My problem,' he said, 'is that I can't explain the words written prominently across the foot of the last page: "S Fox: alive + well". I think we need Colza to get down to the West Country.'

52

'Ludo, it's Angela here . . . Glyn's niece. I have been thinking about you and your friend. Your investigation – how is it going?'

'Slowly and expensively but we have made a bit of progress.'

'I think I can help. I've just got the details of Glyn's will. He was better off than I imagined and he's left me quite a decent sum. If you want it it's yours – to help with your costs.'

Ludo wondered if many bequests were used to investigate their donors' deaths.

53

Colza searched the bookshelves in his Hammersmith flat. It was still there, his *Bailey's*. This had once been his greatest treasure. *Bailey's Hunting Directory* listed all the hunts in the British Isles – gave a short history of each, the name of the master, the secretary and the hunt servants. It had been like having a complete plan of the enemy's forces.

That was the thing about fox-hunting stuff: it was all on paper. Colza liked that. Hunting people were Pre-Pixelites. They didn't bother to put their stuff up on the net. It wasn't that they were pre-Internet, it was just that they were *not*-Internet. Whoever it was had got it right when he pointed out that the 17,000-year-old database, the Lascaux Cave paintings, didn't include anything about sex but had tons of stuff about hunting, whereas with the Internet it was the other way round.

The cramped double-column type in Colza's *Bailey's* told him that there was a Swanborne Hunt until 1847 when it became the subject of the first of many amalgamations. Its country was part of what came to be known as, at the time of the hunting ban, the Old Pytchvale and Pike. Its last huntsman was called Jim Lightfoot; who Colza traced to a semi in Turlford, just outside Dorchester.

Lightfoot's wife answered the door. Colza explained he was compiling a book of hunting anecdotes – another publication from the tireless Shireland Press. Would Mr Lightfoot see him? She showed him into the little sitting room where the old huntsman was sitting in a large motorised reclining chair; he apologised for not getting up. Colza felt sorry for the man – he'd spent most of his life on horseback out in the countryside and now, crippled with arthritis, he was confined to a chair in this tiny room.

Lightfoot was now a good deal bigger than he was in the photographs on the walls and the sideboard, which showed him slim and red-coated on a big bay with two whippers-in, surrounded by hounds. There were others of him blowing the horn at the hunt ball, judging at a puppy show, walking the hounds and receiving a trophy on his premature retirement.

It's always the way, thought Colza. There were plenty of pictures of the panoply of it all, but nothing showing the crucial action when the hounds were almost on the fox. God knows, he and his fellow hunt sabs had tried hard enough but it was almost impossible. And even if they succeeded, no blurry photograph could ever satisfactorily show the collaboration of huntsman, hounds and the field. The elements were too scattered; the art too subtle.

When Colza got back to Clay's place late that night Clay and Ludo were anxiously waiting for him.

'How did it go?' asked Ludo.

Colza told of his meeting with Jim Lightfoot. Clay was amused by the idea.

'Must have been a grand day out for you, eh? Meeting the old enemy, eh? Just like those telly programmes where they used to put old Spitfire pilots together with Luftwaffe chaps and have them sit down and chat with each other and everyone's chums.'

'Maybe,' said Colza, 'except that Lightfoot didn't know that I was on the other side.'

Colza told them how he had begun by asking Lightfoot about his own career before moving on to the history of the Swanborne.

'So was there anything remarkable in the story of the hunt?'

'We had a few alarms and excursions, but nothing to write home about. No, not in my time there wasn't.'

In fact Lightfoot had looked at the history and the accounts and he didn't know of anything. 'No, nothing since the Riot but that happened nearly two hundred years ago!'

The Riot? Thank you! We have ignition.

'Tell me about the Riot then; that sounds interesting.'

'Fetch down my scrapbook from that shelf there, would you. It'll be in there.'

Lightfoot found what he wanted, a photocopy of part of a page from a local newspaper. The title and date had been handwritten: '*The South Dorset Chronicle*, February 11, 1824.'

When Colza had finished reading it, he asked Lightfoot permission to photograph it.

Before he read it aloud to Ludo and Clay he explained that the word 'Riot' in the headline was the hunting term to describe hounds chasing anything other than the fox – maybe some geese or whatever.

FOXHUNTING FIELD RIOT

Mr John Partley's hounds met at the Cock tavern on Saturday last. They were brought there by the huntsman Paul Stobbs and his first and second whips, Jim Packman and Albert Cronin. It was a good scenting day following an overnight frost and the sun making a late appearance.

Stobbs led his pack numbering seventeen couple along Green Lane and into Squire Ben Hartley's land running by the Baldon Stream. Crossing over into Ferret Wood they picked up the scent and a field of some seventy-four souls had a good run up toward Gibbs Hill where the scent went cold.

Mr Partley now called for Stobbs to draw Fielden's Copse one mile and a half to the South West. There a fox broke cover and headed East across Cawley Vale. Stobbs blew Gone Away and the field followed at a goodish pace.

There now followed a seven-mile run that took them North East by Pike's Ridge, through Gapps Wood before turning back in open country again. Some formidable obstacles in the form of high post and rails on the edge of Weaver's Acre accounted for not a few of the field.

The pack was gaining on their fleet-footed prey when occurred a remarkable turn of events.

Colza paused in his reading.

'What happened next wasn't strictly speaking a riot,' he said, 'but there was no term to describe it so they just reached out for the nearest one. It's what happens.'

As to what did occurred next, Colza said he'd never heard of anything like it but by the time he'd finished reading to the end, Ludo began to see what it might have meant to Owen.

54

The cold wind had dropped and a fog had descended. The slopes were spookily quiet but for occasional voices muffled by the fog and snow. Mike knew he ought to change into his spare suit as he'd been instructed but he was reluctant to delay his progress. 'Anyway, I'm safe here,' he thought, 'because they can't even see me.' But then he couldn't see them, not that he knew what they'd look like. He felt alone and frightened – frightened by the idea that his pursuers could emerge from the fog at any time. He skied on and was halfway down to town when his phone purred. Thinking it might be his mysterious new best friend he stopped immediately. It was a text from Blake: CAN WE MEET SOONEST? MAYBE PERIGORD? Mike replied: NO V DIFF. But Blake wasn't giving up. WHERE U NOW? Mike felt sorry for him. He'd been in a bad way since the shoot at the Couloir. Mike didn't want to make him feel rejected so he replied: AT VARGONNE HEADING 4 BASE. TALK LTR and hurried on his way.

Mike thought he ought to use the trees that run down beside Automne to change into his new gear. When he got to the point where the run forked, a pisteur was roping off the entrance to Blanche so he had no choice but to stay on Marmotte. When he had reached the foot of the run he found two skiers hunched over their piste maps arguing about the route. As Mike came level with one of them moved towards Mike waving his piste map.

'*Monsieur*, which run do we take to . . .'

Actually the man wasn't that interested in finding the route to anywhere. He just wanted to get close to Mike and keep him focused on his map while his mate came up on the other side. Now they were in a position to grasp his elbows and force him down on to his side in the snow. They didn't say a word.

Nor did Mike. One of his assailants had his hand clamped over his mouth.

Then Mike saw that help was at hand. Half a dozen skiers coming down the slope. They stopped a few yards away.

'Is he alright? Do you need help?'

Mike started to writhe in an attempt to escape but four powerful hands held him firm.

'No, he's going to be fine, we can cope, but thank you.'

Mike couldn't shout out because they'd stuffed a cloth in his mouth and pulled his neck-warmer back over it. He struggled furiously and tried to shout through his gag, but restraining hands put an end to the wriggling and two fingers pinching his nostrils reduced him to silence.

The group sped off, satisfied they'd done their duty. By the time the blood wagon drew up, Mike was unconscious.

55

When Mike came round he was staring at the ceiling of a large shed that smelled of engine oil. He tried to move but could feel that one of his legs was trapped between two solid blocks. Out of the corner of his eye he could see that the wall beside him was lined with neat racks of tools. He realised that he was lying on a workbench equipped with a couple of vices; his head was in one and his right boot in another. His arms were tied to his sides by a length of wide webbing around his chest and upper arms. There was a draught from an open door beyond his head. The whirring of great steel wheels and the rumble, clatter and clank of arriving and departing cabins told Mike he was in the maintenance area of a lift station.

'*Je pense qu'il est prêt pour toi maintenant,*' said a voice from behind his head. A figure in a dark blue ski suit, face masked by a balaclava, came into Mike's vision and proceeded to blindfold him.

'Okay, *maintenant.*'

He could hear two or maybe three sets of footsteps approaching, ski boots clumping across a concrete floor.

Then the questions started. They were spoken in English with an Eastern European accent.

'So, *monsieur*, are you having a good time?'

'Not really, to be honest.'

'I say, are you having a good time?' His tone was insistent.

'And I answered you. No, I'm no . . . I'd rather be skiing.'

'I am saying what does it mean, "Are you having a good time?" This it says here. On your mobile. He held up Mike's phone so he could see it. What is meaning?'

Oh, I get it, thought Mike. He was talking about a text on his phone from Anne.

'It's a message from my wife.'

'Where is she?'

'At home . . . England.'

'This wife likes you to have a good time?'

'It's difficult to explain.'

'Try explain. We have plenty time.'

But Mike was spared because another text had caught his interrogator's attention.

'Who is Dahlia? She your girlfriend?'

'Dahlia is my dog. My wife's dog.'

'Clever answer, Mr Warne. Is he friend or colleague?'

'It's a she. She's a bitch.'

'A bitch?'

'She's a Dalmatian.' As soon as he said it Mike regretted it. It might be offensive; maybe his interrogator was from another Balkan tribe who hated the Dalmatians for burning their villages and killing their firstborn or something. Mike was struggling; he hadn't envisaged Dahlia in a broad geopolitical context before.

'If she dog how she text kisses?'

'It's my daughter. She sent the message.' In an attempt to lighten the atmosphere Mike added, 'The dog doesn't use the phone. It is not permitted.' *It is not permitted?* – he groaned to himself. Now he's got *me* speaking English as a foreign language.

'So why message ending "Love Dahlia"?'

Mike didn't know where to start.

'This is strange story, Mr Warne.'

'It's a family thing,' he said limply, wondering how he could possibly convey the status of deity accorded domestic pets in the English household to a psychopath from some godforsaken land where animals were seen as nothing more than a source of food, shoes and underfloor heating.

'Here is message of interest. WELL DONE. SAUL SAYS TRANSFER ALL FOOTAGE TO STICK. VITAL INCLUDE TERRACE + WHITE SUIT. DON'T USE EMAIL OR SEND ANY FOOTAGE EMAIL. EXPLAIN LATER. GLUCK.

Why didn't I delete this stuff?

'What is all this meaning? What is White Suit? Who is Gluck?'

Start with the easy bit first in the hope that before his interrogator got to the trickier stuff the good guys will come flying through the door on a zip-wire and carry him off.

'Gluck is like "Good luck". But the white suit . . . I'm not sure what he was talking about.'

'You are fucking liar. For sure this is really bad for you.'

'I don't understand.'

'Mr Mike, you know what we are wanting. You must give to us.'

'Give you what?'

'We are needing the answers to some questions . . .'

'Who are you?'

'. . . right answers. Wrong answers will be very bad for you. Then we are needing to begin the procedures.'

Mike felt cold steel explore his fingers, possibly a pair of pincers.

'Skiing you like?' he asked.

Mike wanted to say 'No, I don't like skiing; I hate skiing; I came here for the fucking golf.' Actually he didn't *want* to say that at all. He *wanted to want* to say that. In the event he just nodded and croaked out a 'Yes'.

Now he felt his right trouser leg being pulled up towards the knee and a small ice-cold surface pressing against his shin as it was drawn up and down it in a hideous parody of some blindfold 'guess-the-object' party game. Mike guessed a hammer.

Half his gibbering brain was processing these immediate realities; the other half was churning the notion that in just twenty-four hours his life had changed beyond all recognition. How come he got to be lying trussed like a chicken on a bench at the mercy of some sick psycho who kept his DIY kit in a chill cabinet? One moment he was in a glorious Alpine resort and the next he was in a dank chamber reeking of engine oil at the gateway to hell. So these then were 'the bad guys' that his chairlift companion had been talking about. The people he needed to avoid at all costs, people whose methods he 'really didn't want to know about'.

'Why you visit Chalet Messigny?'

'Because I'd heard about the new place – I remember the old chalet that was there before – I have been coming here for many years.'

'You not ski for a morning just to see a house? Not true. This skiers don't do.'

'I was just doing the langlauf course. Messigny is close by – I couldn't ski properly because I was still recovering from an injury.'

'Injury?' Mike's inquisitor was interested. 'What is injury?'

'My right knee.'

'Where in knee?' Mike really wished he hadn't mentioned the knee.

'The medial.'

'Where is medial please?'

Mike shuddered as he felt the cold steel moving around his kneecap. It had a sharp edge. He now guessed a chisel.

'Skier's knee is Achilles heel, I think?' Balaklava man sounded pleased with this question.

Mike's panicky mind slid off its track to marvel at the way a Greek warrior who probably never even existed could die beneath the walls of Troy and pop up in conversation in an Alpine workshop twenty centuries later. There's fame for you. Mike wondered how his brain could make time for such a fatuous diversion. It was displacement activity of course. His coping mechanism wasn't coping.

'Maybe we doing some more surgery for you? No charge.'

'I'd rather not, if possible.' *If possible?* Mike admitted to himself that by this stage he wanted only to ingratiate himself.

'So this is depending on you. Tell me, Mr Mike, why your friends making video at the Chalet Messigny?'

'It was just part of a video of a skiing stunt. Skiing the Couloir Noir. Very dangerous.'

'Not clever stunt to ski past Chalet Messigny. Dangerous, I don't think? I think more like easy green!'

'The Chalet is on a route between the Couloir and the town.'

'The Chalet is private property, Mr Mike.'

'I am sorry but it is not clear. It is not marked.' Now he tried some more ingratiation. 'No harm was intended.'

'But harm done.' After a pause Mike felt hands adjust his leg. 'Why you tell lies where Mr Video Man was?'

'I wanted to save the footage. I thought some people wanted to steal it.'

'What people?'

'I don't know. Maybe you can tell me?'

'You not know what people? You not know why?'

'Yes, that's right.'

'Not true. You not thinking this thing. Why someone steal this?'

'I wasn't sure, but there were people who were definitely trying to get it.'

'So big question, question number one for you, Mr Mike: who is your friend in white suit?'

'He is not my friend. I don't know who he is.'

'Good fairy-tale for fairies, Mr Mike, but bad for you. You tell who you work for. You tell who white suit work for. If no, time for some procedures. This is to be hurting now. Very bad hurting. You maybe make some screams.' He raised his voice. 'Gérard, please start engine.' Now he addressed Mike again. 'Vacations people are not liking screams.'

The massive horsepower of a piste-basher's engine outside

the building roared into action, battering what was left of Mike's resolve, adding new layers to his terror.

'Who told you to visit Chateau Messigny?

'Nobody told me to go there. For God's sake, if I knew I'd tell you.'

Okay, thought Mike. This wasn't exactly the proudest moment of his life. But he would defy anyone who was scared, cold and trussed like this, with chilled sharpened steel moving round their kneecap, to do anything different. No, nothing painful yet, just thickening terror fed by an imagination flickering with foul imagery of the consequences of hammer on shinbone, of chisel edging into the kneecap like the teeth of a miniature alligator with time on its claws. And people say engineers are not imaginative types? *If pushed we can all have our moments.*

Mike kept reassuring himself that he'd be alright because he could just tell the truth. He didn't have to lie and give Mr Psycho a chance to catch him out.

'Big question for you now, Mr Mike Two Suits.'

Oh, now this was bad. Of course they'd found the other suit in his knapsack.

'Why two suits? Eh? Is big puzzle?'

'I was given it as a disguise, to help me hide.'

'Who gives you this? Why you want to hide?'

'A man on a chairlift. Someone I don't know. He said I was in danger. He said I must get away. He told me to change clothes so I wouldn't be recognised.'

'But we find you.'

There was nothing to say but Mike said something anyway.

'What can I say?'

'What he looks like?'

'I couldn't see. I tried to see but his face was covered. He was about my height.'

'So we come to meat course, Mr Mike. We know you lying to us. You fix intrusion. You copy video – we have your orders from Mr

Tyler. You working with him. You have a bad story about giving up the memory stick. You have two suits so you escape us. Question is, who make you to do all this? We ask you once. You give bad answer we begin the procedures. Last chance. Is clear?'

'For God's sake.' These, Mike would remember, were his final whimpering words on the subject when over the din he heard some approaching footsteps followed by a muffled conversation.

'It is now coming need for us to move to new location before we begin the procedures,' said his interrogator. 'We going now.'

Mike felt the vice opening and his leg being lifted out. A pair of ski goggles with opaque lenses was pulled over his eyes. They were in a hurry.

'I don't think I can walk. How am I going to get anywhere?'

'Same way you are coming here.'

This conversation ended when a gag was fixed over Mike's mouth and he felt himself being lifted, moved onto a stretcher. His was a head-to-toe terror, sandpaper searing the soft tissue of his brain.

Mike's fear was as big as the sky, whose void he could feel but could not see as they carried him out of the oily smell of the lift station into the cold fresh air. When they put him down, he understood exactly what was happening. He was in a blood wagon. Brilliant. A blanket concealed the bindings around his legs and arms and his neck-warmer was pulled up over his gag. They were going to take him down the slope in full view of everyone as if he was just another poor bastard who'd caught an edge.

56

When the eyes close down the ears work harder. Mike searched for sounds as a blind man must, sifting the air with his ears. He could hear skis hissing, snowboards rasping, the shifting sound of the wind as they slid in and out of sheltered terrain and even the near silent scuff of ski-suit polyester. As they lost height Mike could detect the snow getting slushier under the blood wagon's runners. Now came the clanking of the chairlifts as they jumped over the stanchions then the wheels-on-hawser whirr of what must have been the Marchette cable car and below it the tinny spring-loaded chink of the riderless pomas. From all around him he heard voices dampened by the thick air but none remarked on their passing: the blood wagon is a card that can be dealt to anyone at any time; its appearance is a bit of a downer and therefore best ignored.

Now the shrieks of children told Mike that they were close to the nursery slopes, then the din of music from bars and restaurants said they had reached the car park and there they came to rest. Mike felt himself being lifted out of the wagon, carried a few steps and dumped in the back of a car. Doors slammed and they moved off almost at once. *Did anyone see what happened to me?* Maybe some people sitting in a black SUV with a red pennant on its aerial witnessed all this and would follow? *Well, it is a hope to cling to.*

The distinctive thump of the Palais Ceroc told him they were on the east side of town, so they could well be heading for Chalet Messigny. He was right. The surface changed from road to stony track. They must be in the trees.

It was only a matter of minutes later that he heard one of his captors curse and the car came to a halt. Mike wondered why; they couldn't have been even halfway along the road to the Chalet. There was some muttering from the driver and his passenger before they opened the doors and bedlam broke out.

First a roar of perhaps a dozen people, then the shouts and oaths and scuffling sounds of a struggle. The rear door opened, the blanket covering Mike was snatched away and he was dragged out feet first. Hands pulled up his goggles revealing his rescuers: two figures from among a ragged mob, faces masked by balaclavas. They cut his bindings and between them dragged him upright a little way down the track to a waiting flatbed trailer hitched to a snowmobile. When he looked back he could see a tree trunk lying across the track in front of the car. As Mike took in the scene and regained his mental bearings it dawned on him that his rescuers were the environmental protestors, *les druides*.

After a short ride he was transferred to a waiting SUV where he found himself back on the floor again and covered in another blanket.

'What about my skis?'

'Casualty of war, I'm afraid, sir.'

Sir? What was that about?

ACT TWO

1

'Why are you quibbling about every last penny like this?' asked Abricot.

Ludo was arguing with him about the size of the expenses he was incurring in his surveillance of Parsons, one of the recurring names in the Swanborne File. Abricot was insisting, 'You could be making some decent money to pay for all this work.'

Ludo was both irritated and impressed by Abricot. He was the son of one of Clay's army friends who was trying to get into the Special Forces. Meanwhile he needed a job that would allow him the time to train for the notorious Black Mountain Cakewalk, the bitterly ironic and geographically inaccurate nickname for the ultimate test: 24 hours, nearly 50 miles across the hills carrying a 55-pound backpack. He found some part-time work at an outdoor adventure school, one of those places usually run by former soldiers which convinced companies that their senior executives would perform so much better if they were dunked in freezing water and run ragged for four days in the wilds of Wales. It was there that Clay found him and invited him to help Thermidor. He became a useful asset, doing much of the early surveillance work.

Abricot understood their problem. Thermidor were convinced they knew why Owen was killed but not who killed him; their efforts to find that out were proving expensive.

'And how could we could make some money?' said Ludo.

'I've been tracking medium-sized drugs dealing operations implicated in the Swanborne File and I've followed the route of cash as it moves around. I've been thinking how vulnerable it is when it's in transit, so why don't we help ourselves – to cover costs?'

Ludo looked doubtful.

'Margins on recreational drugs are still pretty good,' Abricot persisted. 'It'd be a very handy income stream.'

'How would it work then?'

'We identify a medium-size dealer in an area – he's got to be big enough to make it worthwhile, but not so big as to be too organised and dangerous. There are hundreds of people who'd qualify. We find the point in the cycle when your man has got all his cash from his sales and is about to make the pass – pay it over for his next consignment. There's this small window when all the cash and all the gear is in one place. That's when we move in. And the great thing is that the little darlings can't report the theft.'

'Well, yes, that's nice,' granted Ludo. 'But you make it sound too easy.'

'It is easy. Plan things properly and it's high yield for low risk.'

'Let me think about it.'

Later that afternoon Ludo called Abricot over to talk through his proposal with Clay.

'Interesting idea,' said Clay, 'but who'd do the heavy lifting?'

'I know some people,' said Abricot.

2

'At the moment we're gathering information that will lead us to those who did for Glyn Owen,' said Ludo. 'If we take up Abricot's idea we're going to need another type of intelligence to identify the targets that will fund our investigation.'

'The cops would be a good place to start,' suggested Clay. 'Good cops. Honest cops.'

Ludo feigned surprise.

'And where are we going to find *them*?'

'They say there's always one good apple in every barrel,' said Clay.

'Okay then.' Ludo suddenly understood the possibilities. 'So angry cops . . . frustrated by failure to get convictions?'

'Yes. We tell them we can help them if they help us.'

'Alright, so how do we find these paragons?'

'The usual. Have some people hang around the courts. Always a good recruiting ground – for both sides of the law.'

'So we'd be trawling for failed prosecutions,' said Ludo. 'Then we call a few of the most promising police officers. 'Hello, you don't know me, my name is Summers . . .'

'Summers – why Summers?' asked Clay.

'Thermidor . . . July and August. They'll probably be in the drugs squad – keen but frustrated. The ones that take it really badly when a prosecution collapses in a "not guilty" verdict after months of work; the ones who go home to their wives railing about the prosecution lawyers always being such crap.'

'You realise what we're talking about here. This is nothing short of a PJI!'

'Exactly!' The idea resonated for Ludo with his former work for the Service in the Unorthodox Threat Field, where he'd been identifying the principles and characteristics of activist movements, notably the Private Justice Initiatives.

'Our pitch is simple,' he continued. 'It's "Give me a little information and I can help you do your job and improve your career prospects."'

'We'd need to offer a bit more than that,' said Clay. 'That sort of cop would want the bad hat to get his just deserts. We arrange some bad luck for him. Maybe his house goes and catches fire and he bumps into a lamp-post or something.'

The faintest of alarm bells began to ring in Ludo's mind; now they were working together for the first time, he was getting to know Clay a little better.

'I don't know about that,' said Ludo, aware as he said it that he was sounding a bit prim. 'But then, maybe. As long it wasn't the only thing that we did. The essence of our pitch is that Our Good

Officer will receive some useful information – most likely a tip-off, details of a pass by another dealer. That'd give him an arrest and an increased chance of promotion.'

They considered these new possibilities in silence for a bit.

'Obviously,' said Clay, 'no one meets anyone. They don't know who Summers is – won't want to either. For them it all has to be deniable. The Good Officer is just happy to pass on information about suspects he hasn't got time or enough evidence to investigate. Then we go to work on them.'

Clay thought they shouldn't confine their approaches to serving officers in the police and Customs but that they should include recently retired officers who'd be less nervous about providing tip-offs. And Ludo, prompted by incidents cited by Owen in the Swanborne File, wanted Thermidor to seek help from those who had a motive for giving it: the victims – the families and friends of people lost to addiction, the factory owner who'd been forced into paying protection; the bank employee whose children had been threatened, people forced to sign over deeds to properties and businesses, the juror followed from the courtroom and intimidated, the council housing officer bullied into assigning accommodation.

'There's no protection for these people,' said Ludo, 'so when they get an offer from our man called Summers saying, "I can help you strike back", they'll want to co-operate with information – or in any other way they can.'

However, while Ludo could certainly see the possibilities he had some nagging doubts about the practicalities.

'All this is going to call for a massive intelligence-gathering effort.'

'I should say,' said Clay breezily. 'Massive, but we can buy it. We subcontract to the private sector.'

'So what does that mean?' said Ludo.

Actually he knew damn well what that meant. The private investigation industry was available to anyone who could afford it: around 12,000 agencies employing thousands of men and women, most of them highly skilled. They could get into bank accounts, cars, PCs, phones, boardrooms and bedrooms. And who was their biggest client? The Government, which used them to investigate tax fraudsters, benefit cheats, illegal immigrants, fare dodgers and people who hadn't bought a TV licence. They could offer anything: human and electronic surveillance, forensic accountancy, electronic data intervention, research and analysis. This mosaic of enterprises constituted a large and formidable private sector secret service.

'The trick,' said Ludo, relenting, 'will be to conceal our intentions. We can't tell these people what we are really trying to find out. We need to break up our target information into discrete parcels which we allocate to several different agencies. One does the bad boy's wife or the girlfriend, the other his business, another, his clubs and favourite bars and so on. Thermidor alone has all the information; it's only when we put it all together that any clear picture emerges.'

Some of Ludo's lingering doubts were allayed by the knowledge that they wouldn't be asking these people to do any more than most firms of management consultants working on a takeover used to do as a matter of routine. Some of Ludo's university friends had joined these well-paying outfits and found themselves counting staff in and out of office buildings, following vans to check a distribution network, counting cartons in the loading bays to make sure production numbers really matched claims. Nicking an internal phone directory was always a good start, but there were occasions when they'd even set up a sandwich delivery business or a shirt-laundering service to get inside a company's offices. Legislation had brought that to an end for management consultancies but the work had merely drifted over to the Private Investigation sector.

But Ludo could see that the Abricot-inspired model constituted a serious case of mission creep and said so.

'Better Mission Creep than Mission Droop or Mission-called-off-cos-we've-run-out-of-money,' was Clay's retort.

'Okay, so I say we give it a shot,' said Ludo. 'But first, two cardinal rules: although most of our intelligence-gathering will be outsourced, anything directly concerned with the investigation into Owen's death has to be handled by us, by Thermidor itself. And let's agree that the name Thermidor is never to be used outside the organisation. We are safer if we are not perceived as an entity. That would make people uneasy. We are just a bloke called Summers who seems nothing more than a very well-funded eccentric soloist, works on his own, a player who doesn't concern himself with legality or paperwork. He's just a voice on the phone who always delivers.'

And so the days of Thermidor began.

3

The Swanborne File generated a daunting number of leads for Thermidor to pursue, so Ludo thought it best to focus, just as Owen had, on those three *fortissimo* deaths. His notes suggested that their investigations were stalled and sidetracked by systematic obstruction masquerading as incompetence, so investigate the investigations, find out if Owen was right. And if he was, who was responsible? And so, hours of enquiry: probing conversations, searching, tracing people, archive-trawling. The process guzzles time and money. The scope is vast. How far back should you go? You've got to stop somewhere. A statute of limitations? Say three years then? Arbitrary but reasonable, but that still leaves a lot to look at. A judge, for instance, can sentence a lot of people in that time.

'Well, let's leave him till later,' said Ludo, 'and get cracking on the other two.'

It was a good call. Meanwhile better get a move on and recruit some investigators to do the digging and some muscle to carry out Abricot's funds acquisition strategy.

The search for suitable investigators was not easy. Sharp brains are not uncommon, but finding the principled ones with a slightly overdeveloped sense of justice proved rather more difficult. They needed some people who had the time to commit and who could be trusted. Friends or friends of friends, like the poor human rights lawyer hiding for his life in the middle of a trailer park by the seaside out of season. He was a lawyer whom the law could not help, a man on the run. He'd entered the murky world of the paradipping – acting as an unofficial diplomat to negotiate between government and rebels when the leaders of neither side can be seen to be talking to the enemy. While acting as a back channel in some fraught dealings in a treacherous Gulf kingdom, word got out and rebel hawks put a large enough price on his head to make it worthwhile for the bounty hunters to pursue him to the UK. A mutual friend had put him in touch with Ludo who hired him. 'Blessed are the Peacemakers,' Clay had declared with Biblical portentousness at the end of their meeting in the blacked-out trailer home. 'From henceforth you will be Salicor.' And so he joined the days of Thermidor.

Even as Salicor was shuttling between the offices of a Gulf prince's import-export business and sipping mint tea in a courtyard residence in the Bab el Oued quarter of Algiers, a crisp young man whom they would come to name Carthame was working as a casual barman in a chain of East Midlands pubs while he was actually acting as a private investigator for a brewery to catch managers who had been fiddling the takings. His inspired general surveillance expertise impressed Thermidor when they hired him to do a very tricky job on a little drugs gang. He was among a handful of others like him who accepted Clay's invitation to join the ranks of Thermidor.

'We're fine on the phone and keyboard,' said Clay, 'but apart from Colza and Abricot we're seriously lacking in kinetic skills.'

It was Candy who'd told them about a friend, a troubled former member of the Special Forces who'd caused catastrophic collateral damage in the course of an anti-terrorist operation. To get him out of the way for a while he had been sent on attachment as an adviser to the police, but his advice proved lethal for a temporarily deranged but entirely harmless and much respected Asian businessman who was drilled through the head by a sniper in a grossly mismanaged siege. The one-time elite soldier had now been reduced to working on the doors of a Chelsea nightclub when Clay contacted him at Candy's suggestion. He accepted the name of Brebis if only to stop Clay calling him Captain Blue-On-Blue.

Abricot and Brebis between them brought half a dozen into the Thermidor fold. Ludo discerned that they appeared to come from the same sort of template: clinically anxious, wilfully subversive, steady in action, flighty in life and all of them misfits searching for somewhere to fit.

At first, the action they sought was slow to come, but as intelligence dribbled in and the targets were identified, they began to purloin the takings of hard-working dealers up and down the country. Although much of their effort bore no relation to discovering who killed Owen, they provided the wherewithal to prosecute the investigation. Their role prompted Ludo to name them Messidor.

'Why Messidor?' asked Clay.

'It's the month before Thermidor; it means "harvest".'

Thanks to the effectiveness of the intelligence gathering and the deft operational skills of Messidor the finances of Thermidor were soon more than adequate to fund its investigation but for all its successes it was a vulnerable entity. As a criminal organisation engaged in large-scale law-breaking they all faced the risk of imprisonment if they were caught by the police. Something more catastrophic awaited them if they were caught by those they were hunting. The fate of poor Glyn Owen was an ever-present spectre. Better not make the same mistake as he had. But, as Ludo often pointed out, 'Unfortunately, we don't know what that mistake was.'

4

The recruitment of a former senior police officer as an investigator proved invaluable in untangling the police work that had been done, or rather not done, on the three cases Owen had highlighted in the Swanborne File. The career of Chief Superintendent Stella Taplock had recently ended with a loud bang and a non-disclosure agreement after she'd been found guilty of the most heinous crime a police officer can commit: blowing the whistle on a corrupt colleague. Ludo had the inspired idea of inviting her to join Thermidor.

'You will be joining a criminal organisation,' he told her, 'but then you've only just left one and at least your new employers are honest.'

Stella had agreed that they should start with the case of the unfortunate Detective Sergeant Cope, the officer from the Regional Drugs Squad who'd caught the fast train at the railway bridge outside Leicester. Early enquiries painted a picture of an effective and unpleasant police officer whose zealous commitment had sent a lot of people down; so there was no shortage of candidates who'd have liked to see him go. They drew up a list of the six likeliest culprits and investigated each of them. One suspect who had been completely overlooked by the Police investigation at the time was an unconvicted crim called Don Parsons, whose territory was part of Cope's patch and who, more significantly, was named by Owen in the Swanborne File. Parsons had a clean record and a handful of legit businesses – automotive spare parts, office cleaning, IT support – but enquiries suggested he was almost certainly using them to launder the profits of drug dealing. Within a very short time of starting her enquiry into the investigation of Cope's death, Stella managed to unearth crucial evidence which had somehow got discarded: photographic evidence showing a series of faint grooves on the masonry of the railway bridge. No great expertise was required to work out that they had been created by the Detective Sergeant's fingernails.

Thermidor's early enquiries into Preece, the one who'd come to a sticky end in New Zealand, revealed that he was a police informer who'd been relocated from his home in Staines, Middlesex as part of a witness protection programme after his UK cover had been blown. Stella had a number of trusted former colleagues still in the Force whom she could count on for some cautious help. Using these along with some private investigators and a variety of questionable methods, they reconstructed the Police investigation into Preece's death, which turned out to be entirely inadequate: their main suspects were small fry who'd have had trouble scraping together the fare to the airport let alone New Zealand while it was clear that this crime could only have been done by a serious player with a serious grudge.

So, start the investigation again and proceed from the 'possibles' to the 'maybes' and then the 'probables'. Put some boots on the ground in and around Staines and, after a lot of trawling, interviewing, coaxing, sifting and checking, they came up with a list of names who might have been beneficiaries of the demise of police informer Preece.

'How do we find any connection between the names on two lists of suspects that we suspect but cannot see?' said Ludo. He was addressing the question to the twenty-three-year-old hacker Colza had found them and whom Clay described grandly as Head of IT.

'You need OmegaScan or something like it. A program which trawls the net for matching data. The Inland Revenue love it because it can chomp its way through a mass of data bases and flag up any connections which aren't overt. So the transaction taxes for a property in Spain are maybe linked to an undeclared bank account in the Caymans – and so on.

'Nice, but the Revenue aren't going to let us play with their toy?'

'This is true but there's someone I use at a market research company which has got the program. I'm sure he'll give us access if you make it worth his while.'

Thermidor's offer was accepted and all the data they had on the two lists of suspects was fed into OmegaScan's maw. It dutifully responded by flagging up a promising connection between two of the names on their two separate lists of suspects. It revealed that Parsons, the main suspect for the police officer's murder, used a firm of accountants in Birmingham; it was one of those 'they're-fly-but-not-crim' outfits who'd do you a set of accounts that was 'so clean you could eat your dinner off them.' This firm also had premises in an office block named Albion Buildings in Cord Street, in the City of London. What OmegaScan revealed was that Albion Buildings was the main office of the firm of solicitors used by another unconvicted player, a Hounslow businessman called Harry Drake whose name also appeared on the list of people suspected of involvement in the murder of the informant Preece.

The promising possibilities of the Albion Buildings prompted Thermidor to focus their full attention on Drake and Parsons. They turned out to have been partners in crime from their early schooldays at Grain Vale near Hounslow, where they used to steal the other kids' lunch money or sell them drugs from the pushers at the gates. During their time the school won some notoriety following the murder of one of its pupils – not that there had ever been any suggestion that either Drake or Parsons were involved in the murder. When they left school, they surprised their friends by going their own separate ways.

'So Colza, how do we get inside Albion Buildings?' asked Ludo.

'Office cleaners?' said Colza.

'Correct.'

'I'll have a crack at it myself, if that's okay.'

Ludo was beginning to appreciate Colza as a bit of an operator. Beneath an honest demeanour was a practised deceiver who was able to give himself a makeover convincing enough to get some shifts with Albion Buildings' cleaning contractors. He found that the offices were nothing swanky but everything tidy and well run. Eight floors occupied by seventeen different businesses. Bit of retail on the ground floor – key cutting, minicab office, motorcycle couriers; half the space on the first floor given over to meeting rooms for the use of all the tenants.

When Colza reappeared with the photographs he'd managed to snatch along with the floor plans, Ludo could see it immediately. *The meeting rooms are the asset.* Two firms each book rooms in the same corridor for overlapping times. Anyone can move from one room to the other without being seen. Drake and Parsons, who were based in different parts of the country, had a secure place to meet each other without anyone knowing.

'It's quite clear what's happening here,' pronounced Clay. 'The business of accountancy is facilitating criminal activity.'

Ludo smirked.

'Well that's a first!'

5

'So where are we,' said Clay, and what happens next?'

'Well,' said Ludo, 'we know that Owen said something he thought was significant and that he said it upstairs in Balmoral after the power failure. We need to talk to some of the people who were there and find out what it was.'

'But that's a helluva job,' said Colza. 'No one is going to want to talk.'

He was right. They managed to have some sort of contact with seventeen of the thirty-four attendees. They were a mix of civil servants from Defence, Home and Foreign Offices and the Treasury, plus fast streamers from the Police and Army colleges. There was also a sprinkling of representatives of Critical Non-Governmental Security Organisations – trusted blue-chip private security firms and cyber specialists with large government contracts which were increasingly being included in events like this.

Ludo and Clay divided the list between them and contacted the lot. As far as they could gather from the ensuing casual conversations generated by 'accidental' encounters, none of them had been much interested or impressed by Prof. Glyn Owen or his talk. This was largely down to, the various specialisations they represented. These were not front line troops; more tail than teeth and high harm crime was not in their field of vision. They detected no great significance in anything Owen had said; it was just good scaremongering stuff. Most had assumed that Owen was there merely to provide a bit of drama and excitement on the last day and that the content was prone to exaggeration. The only real surprise was the way Owen had left hurriedly without waiting to take any questions.

It was one of the names allocated to Clay that turned out to be the most promising. Her name was Rebecca Rawlings and she was serving in C43, one of the sections with the thankless task of liaising with the UK's European allies.

The due diligence on Miss Rawlings showed her to be the daughter of a Scottish doctor and an English nurse. Promising material or what, thought Clay. She was clearly one of Her Britannic Majesty's Own Regiment of Crack Civil Servants That You Can Absolutely Count On, aka The Impeccables. She had split from her boyfriend some eighteen months earlier and was one more intelligent, attractive women in her early thirties in the capital who was having trouble finding a worthwhile man. She went to the cinema and the opera with various single friends of both sexes, saw her parents in Hampshire for occasional weekends, sailed with friends in Ventnor, skied a couple of times a year. The most predictable part of her routine was her early-morning walk with her dog in Kensington Gardens. Colza managed to get some clear if unflattering photographs of an auburn-haired figure in a waxed raincoat with slender ankles disappearing into a pair of incongruously large white trainers.

On the basis that two of them would be less sinister, Clay contacted his old mate Julian and arranged to pick up Desmond early one weekday morning. Julian always described Desmond as his lodger, which would prompt an outbreak of ribbing from Clay.

'Oh come on, Julian, why don't you just admit it: you're in a civil partnership!'

Desmond made the introductions as planned. His tough guy looks brought more than a tinge of Essex to the Royal Park but somehow he never failed to charm women. As a chance encounter it was completely convincing. Rebecca was a lot better-looking than Colza's photographs suggested and pleasant to talk to in a distant kind of way. Clay and Desmond showed some interest in her dog, Clay doing all the small talk. How old was she? Very beautiful. A rescue dog, was she? That's interesting. It was all quite affable until Clay played his hand, although he tried to do it as gently as he could.

'I'm a neighbour of yours in the Village and I wanted to ask your help.'

A pause as she adjusted to her new situation.

'Which village is that?' Aloof, convincing.

'It doesn't really have a name, but you could call it Hedley Coram if you wanted to.'

No response but a definite thickening of the air between them.

'I wanted to ask you about Glyn Owen.'

'Look, I don't know who you are, but I have to get to work now so if you'll excuse me . . .'

'Please understand, my intentions are entirely honourable.'

'Indeed?'

'You were at Hedley Coram when Glyn Owen spoke. He was the last speaker at the seminar.'

Although she gave no obvious sign, Clay sensed she was rattled and pressed on.

'I used to work in Acre House. A friend of mine was taught by Owen and knew him well. I'm trying to help him find out what happened to him.'

Rebecca looked blank.

'You know he was killed, don't you?' asked Clay.

'This is completely irregular and you should know that . . . but yes, of course I heard. Really horrible street attack. He was just a harmless lecturer. One of those wrong-place-at-the-wrong-time events.'

'No, they got him in exactly the right place at just the right time.'

'I wouldn't know.'

'I've found out that he was maybe not so harmless after all.'

'He was certainly a *colourful* lecturer, more of an entertainer than an academic. I'd say entertaining, provocative but not informative.'

'What about his thesis that the UK could become a Gangster State?'

'Well it created a bit of a buzz but everyone could see it was just melodrama.'

This is the moment! Clay knew he had to risk it – he had to put his trust in her. He took the plunge.

'Please can I ask you not to mention our meeting to anyone.'

'It's hardly a meeting. No sign of anyone doing the minutes.'

She was a cool one, was Miss Rawlings, but Clay wasn't giving up.

'What about ECI . . . Extreme Criminal Impunity?'

No answer.

'Surely you remember?'

'I don't remember much about that . . . Jacaranda, come here!' she said, suddenly becoming absorbed in concern for her dog.

'You must remember,' Clay persisted.

'Yes, vaguely . . . Jacaranda!'

Clay persisted.

'So what did you think?'

'I think he liked to scare people to get some more speaking engagements.'

'Don't you believe it could be true?'

But Rebecca was now shouting, 'Jacaranda, come here this instant!' Then she swung round to face Clay. 'Would you please control your fucking dog?'

Clay was shocked by her sudden outburst of bad language but she had a point. Desmond was starting to give Jacaranda a lot of hassle. He certainly couldn't fault her on grounds of technical accuracy. Quite a struggle ensued before he could get the priapic bull terrier back on his lead and haul him off.

Desmond's antics had rather broken Clay's fragile line of questioning and Rebecca was clearly relieved by the distraction. Inwardly Clay was cursing Desmond. The luvvies had got it right when they said never work with children or animals.

That was as far as Clay dared go for the moment. They parted awkwardly. Clay offered her a phone number and asked her for hers.

'You seem to know how to find me,' was all she said.

The encounter in the park didn't carry things forward and they all focused on getting back to sifting through the list of partners in all of the firms in Albion Buildings. But for Clay this Rebecca Rawlings line of enquiry was by no means dead. She was different from the others: he sensed that she had actually listened to Owen's lecture while the others had merely heard it. She had dismissed Owen but had actually taken his talk seriously. He was sure she knew something – under her cool she was jumpy. Clay felt a sense of frustration. It was like trying pull out a pigeon that's got stuck in the chimney but the wretched thing doesn't understand you're trying to help it.

6

The call. The big call, the this-will-change-your-life call. Georgi Tsanko had been working at the warehouse on the outskirts of Sofia for about eighteen months when his boss Nico was contacted by someone in the office of Lefko Kalomiris, the owner. The big man's personal security people were looking for a replacement for a couple of weeks. Nico had recommended Tsanko and, given that it meant both extra money and a change from the warehouse routine, Tsanko was more than happy to apply.

Pale-skinned, cropped black hair, Tsanko, in spite of his war-wounded foot which gave him a limp, had that athlete's presence which even in repose suggested a powerful engine idling. His demeanour was, given his line of work, surprisingly pleasant and open. Indeed he took pleasure in the moment when his victims discovered the difference between the Tsanko they saw and the Tsanko they got. He was perfect for the task in hand because he was effective as well as presentable. The young man with the quietly cheerful countenance, easy charm and converging eyebrows had undergone a gruelling audition at one of the more earnest mixed-martial-arts gyms in the city and had impressed.

Even though he was the most junior on the security team Tsanko's main duties were to accompany Mrs Kalomiris shopping or visiting friends and now, for the first time in his life, Tsanko got to see how a rich man lived. He couldn't wait to tell Nico and the others at the warehouse about life in the Kalomiris villa, of gold-plated cutlery, chandeliers and gilded mirrors; the luxuriant garden and the sexy little maid's heels clicking on the white marble floors. There were expeditions to luxury shops, restaurants, and the soothing cleanliness and order of a smart residential neighbourhood; it was a world away from the grim warehouse in an industrial area and the cramped ninth-floor apartment by the motorway he shared with three others, who took it in turns to curse the plumbing and stamp on the cockroaches.

The night shift was best. That's when he would go with Kalomiris to meet with friends or business associates in the restaurants and clubs around Vitosha Boulevard. Tsanko was one of five minders in the retinue and would wait on the pavement watching the passing cavalcade of chauffeurs, doormen, minders, fixers and fetchers – and, when she came out for a cigarette and a chat, the lovely Agneska, one of the cloakroom girls at Babkava. Tsanko loved being close to the rich and their beautiful women, being part of the self-important kerbside arrangements of their retainers.

'When Tsanko came back to us at the warehouse two weeks later, he was a changed man,' his boss Nico would later recall. 'He was restless, ambitious. He wasn't interested in making extra money from evening shifts at the warehouse any more; now he'd do anything to avoid them. He wanted to spend all his time on the Boulevard.' Tsanko had discovered a world of possibilities.

Tsanko acquitted himself well during his fortnight with Kalomiris and was soon asked to do some more shifts. It wasn't long before Tsanko became part of the Vitosha fraternity and was greeting the chauffeurs and the security men like old friends, harvesting information, passing on gossip. One of the regulars, an elderly limo driver and all-round wise bird called Stephanos, became a sort of mentor.

When Tsanko wasn't engaged in taking urgent-looking phone calls or hurrying off suddenly to attend some unspoken duty – or appear as though he was – he was always ready to help find a taxi, dispatch a beggar or moderate in disputes. He was soon included in that core of regulars who were offered sweetmeats and pastries sent out from the kitchens by the wiser restaurant owners.

So this pleasant and helpful young man with the war hero's limp became a familiar figure among the pavement folk. Tsanko learned from Stephanos that first he must be noticed, then valued and then sought-after. He developed his own heart-winning response when given a tip: 'May God bless you, my brother will thank you for this,' the brother-less Tsanko would say with a dignified incline of his head. 'It will help him to pay for his medical studies.'

Requests from the Kalomiris office were not confined to personal protection. Sometimes Tsanko was required to make up the numbers of a small goon squad who'd go round town in a couple of SUVs collecting money, presenting gently menacing reminders to slow payers or administering a beating to more serious offenders. He also found that the skill set he had acquired to obtain the location of Kurdish rebel arms caches in the Taurus Mountains had its uses here in Sofia, where it was routine to identify a well-placed employee in a rival business and extract commercially sensitive information along with, if necessary, his toenails.

Tsanko was happy in his work.

7

For some months Tsanko's boss Kalomiris had been negotiating to buy a marble quarry, but just as he thought he was closing the deal the property was sold to a businessman called Roy Faulds. Kalomiris went tonto. This was not the first time their paths had crossed. Kalomiris was so mad that he decided that Faulds would have to go.

Such a high-profile murder carried all sorts of risks. It required the kind of careful planning he wouldn't normally have bothered with if it was just about dispatching some piece of pond life. Kalomiris reckoned that the young Bulgar would serve his purpose and offered a tidy sum (roughly half the price of a mid-range SUV) to do the deed; Tsanko accepted.

Two nights before Tsanko was due to do the business he went down to Vitosha Boulevard to hang out with his mates. He met his mentor Stephanos and steered the subject around to the business of contract work. The old man had a fund of stories – tales of fine workmanship, near misses, total cock-ups and finally, one notable own-goal. This last concerned a casino owner and general bad hat called Vazov who, needing to dispose of an enemy, hired a young newly arrived country boy called Todor to do the deed. Todor duly carried out his contract but two cops at a nearby traffic incident heard the gunshots and hurried to the scene. Seeing a furtive figure running from a villa, they challenged him and when he failed to stop they shot poor Todor dead.

It was a complete set-up of course. A fat wad of cash along with items of jewellery were 'found' on Todor's corpse so he was assumed to be a thief rather than an assassin – the policemen received commendations from the Mayor; as well, of course, as being paid off by Vazov in used notes from his blackjack tables.

Now this tale rang alarm bells in Tsanko's head and one bloody great bell was clanging louder than any other; it was making Tsanko sweat. The deal Kalomiris's people had offered was to give him half the money in used notes immediately before he did the job, with the balance on completion. Poor old Tsanko, who had thought he was about to make some real money, was now convinced that Faulds's death would be rapidly followed by his own. He'd go the way of Todor and be gunned down by a bunch of cops on the take.

Tsanko hadn't got a lot of time to wriggle out of his predicament. Going to the police was not an option: they'd sell him to Kalomiris as meat on the hoof. But Tsanko also knew that there was no way he could back out now and carry on his warehouse work as though nothing had happened. His days in Sofia were over. This was not a city – or a country – that people could get lost in. He needed protection, a ticket out of town and a new home in a faraway place. Calculating that his most valuable asset was the detail of his contract to kill Faulds he figured that his intended victim would pay the most for it. Tsanko rang a senior security man at Faulds's office and told him he had information of utmost importance for the boss which he could only deliver in person. When he got to

Faulds's office he was searched and ushered into the presence of Faulds, who dismissed his bodyguard.

'Sir, I have crucial information for you,' began Tsanko, 'but I want a cash payment, safe passage out of the country and six months' accommodation plus work anywhere in Western Europe. This, sir, is a modest demand of someone who has access to cargo ships and aircraft.'

Faulds was impressed by Tsanko's desperate but cheeky pitch; however, it wasn't his style to offer anyone an easy ride.

'Why,' he asked Tsanko, 'should I do anything for you when I know what you are going to tell me? You are going to tell me about a plot to kill me, right?' Poor Tsanko said nothing and just tried not to look ill as he contemplated the smouldering wreckage of his rescue plan. But after conducting an intensive interrogation, Faulds, with a show of magnanimity, accepted Tsanko's terms.

'You'd never have got me anyway,' Faulds told his would-be assassin as he ushered him to the door.

'You want to bet on that?' said Tsanko.

Faulds liked this killer's impertinent cool and he thought he knew just the right home for him. He gave orders for a car to take Tsanko to a house owned by one of his office managers, where he could lie low until a temporary UK visa came through. He needed to keep the Bulgar safe from the clutches of Kalomiris's people, who'd soon be scouring the town for him.

8

What a shambles; there were *tens of thousands* of them. Rebecca scrolled through the A list. In the Department this was known as 'dredging'; the more cynical, who believed most of these horses had already bolted, called it Operation Stable Door.

Mid-level recruits to MI5 began by completing six attachments, three obligatory: immigration, narcotics, terrorism; three optional from a list that included research, cyber operations, trafficking, finance, tax and political extremism. Some monthe before she went to Hedley Coram Rebecca was doing her four-month stint at L32 of the Immigration Section based at Pitt House in Stockwell, where they did all the Long-Term Immigrant Remedial Checks (LTIRC) in the UK. It was part of a belated effort to get a grip on the chaotic situation brought about by the Home Office's awe-inspiring failure to manage its immigration control processes and to identify latent threats to security and public order.

Rebecca's group had to meet a quota of checks while also carrying out any current investigations that might be passed to them. She had just opened up the LTIRC pool and pulled down three files when she was diverted by a request to help on another inquiry. If she'd followed procedure she should have returned the files to the pool for the next available person to process; instead she held them in her working queue until she finished the new inquiry. When she had some time she called up the files she had held over and gave them a cursory read. Three of them looked interesting so she hung on to them and passed the others to the 'Completed' folder. A couple of hours later her boss came by.

Mary Grigor was normally a cold old fish but today she was chatty and solicitous.

'You've done well since you've been with us,' she said. She was built like a small truck and a lot of ambitions had been flattened by this small-time tyrant.

'You've got a good eye and I'd like you to do a special check for me. Leave your current work and pick up the file that I'm just about to have sent to you.'

Rebecca was understandably flattered but for reasons she couldn't explain to herself she felt that the three files she was working on were worth another look. Everyone who did this job had that feeling at one time or another. Something could arouse your curiosity and you didn't want to let go. It was partly because everyone was scared about being the one who let a bad one through.

So instead of closing the files and sending them back to oblivion, as soon as Mary Grigor had gone she copied them over and slipped them into an admin folder in her queue.

It was three weeks before Rebecca returned to her former duties and one evening just before she left the office she pulled the three files out of hibernation. No more than fifteen minutes passed before she had a visit from Pit-bull Mary.

'What are you working on, Rebecca?'

'A few files I haven't quite cleared in my mind yet.'

'Rebecca, the pressure is really on and we're falling behind on our targets. We have important cases waiting for checks. You've had the names; you need to get to these soonest. But the reason I'm here is that I need some feedback on the Systems Value Assessment. What can you tell me?'

Odd, thought Rebecca. Everyone said Systems Value Assessment was a classic case of the DDAs – Departmental Displacement Activity – and not to be taken seriously. Rebecca gave her some guarded thoughts on the subject and Mary Grigor seemed to go away happy.

Every screen in the unit could be monitored at any time from Grigor's desk. The fact that there'd been two interventions while she was looking at this group of files made Rebecca uneasy. She wasn't going to let go.

When she did get to read them without interruption, only one of the three remained of any interest to her; it belonged to a thirty-six-year-old Bulgarian national called Georgi Tsanko.

9

What have we got here, then? Wednesday evening at Hedley Coram, two days before Glyn Owen was due to speak. Terry McCall stood in the doorway fiddling with his lapel badge which labelled him 'Foreign Office, Trade dept' but might just as well have read 'Pushy little bugger from the End User Certificate Monitoring Desk, Arms Control'. There was a blatant impertinence about the way he was scrutinising what had turned up for 'Welcome Drinks in the Grand Ballroom 6.00 to 8.30'. Some of them looked like real crashers; he could see a couple of groups that would need serious avoidance. He fiddled with his badge not because he was nervous – he certainly wasn't the socially nervous type – but because he was impatient to extract some professional gain from the event. It didn't look too promising, but it wouldn't, would it? It was a gathering of the professionally discreet. *Hello! What was that?*

A momentary sight of well-groomed auburn hair before the intervening heads closed over it. Then they parted again, revealing a strong face, long straight nose, pale skin, tucked-in chin making for a hint of haughtiness. Gone again. *Must get some more of that.* Terry edged through the crowd. She was saying nothing, feigning interest. Poor thing was with a couple of Grade A crashers. Good.

Terry didn't hesitate but eased his way into the group, his eyes swiping her name badge as he took his place beside her.

'Rebecca, hi! I'm Terry McCall – didn't I see you at the Royal Yacht Club Ball?'

She turned to contemplate the new arrival. A little on the short side, but okay. Certainly a bit pleased with itself. Cocky.

Terry watched her appraise him. *Yes, definitely a bit haughty. I like it.*

'Yes, it was quite a do, wasn't it?' She hadn't missed a beat.

Terry had judged it right: the imminent threat of socialite chit-chat was enough to send the other two scattering in search of more serious-minded company.

Quite striking, is our Rebecca, thought Terry. Tennis, he said to himself. Tennis and bed.

'I'm sorry, I seemed to have frightened off your companions.'

This little chap had quite a nerve.

'Yes, wasn't that a surprise. Do you always have that effect on people?'

'Only certain kinds of people,' he said. 'You're still here.'

He was pleased that she had no reply beyond the who-the-hell-do-you-think-you-are-Mr-Smart-Arse look that she gave him. *Press on. Don't give her time to recover.*

'What did you think of the Yacht Club Ball then?" he said.

'I'm surprised you recognised me, considering I was just there as a waitress trying to earn a few quid.'

And from this mutual improvisation one thing led to another.

10

Among the other attendees who were having a hurried talk in the hall after Owen's talk at Hedley Coram before saying their goodbyes there was very little discussion about the Triumph of the Gangster State. A couple of people cautiously admitted that they found his assertions plausible but the others ranged from the non-committal to the dismissive. According to a young woman from the Foreign Office, Prof. Glyn Owen was what happened when people spent too long working in a job like that, while the man from the Customs Service called Owen 'a Welsh windbag brim-full of piffle'. A snarky graduate police officer complained, 'I don't need to be told by some deadbeat polytechnic lecturer that "Corruption brings a strange kind of darkness over the nation".'

While everyone set off in their various directions, Terry and Rebecca slipped off for dinner at a pub in a nearby village. They'd hung out together since meeting on the first evening and now they enjoyed themselves with gossipy speculation about various characters among the lecturers and their fellow attendees.

By the time the steak Béarnaise arrived ('serves two, minimum of 20 minutes') with its 'trio of seasonal vegetables', Terry had steered the conversation to Rebecca's own career and personal situation. She changed the subject back to the Hedley Coram lecturers.

'Well, the Welsh guy didn't get much support on the old comment thread, did he?'

'True,' said Terry. 'I think they all found him a bit too showy.'

'What did *you* think?' she asked.

'I wouldn't dismiss what he was saying. Everything is possible in love and war.'

Rebecca didn't respond to his attempt to lever love into this unpromising territory.

'One of his ideas seemed quite plausible,' she said.

'And which one was that?'

'His suggestion that there could be criminal as opposed to political infiltration of the intelligence services.'

Terry was disappointed. He'd had her down as less gullible than that.

'Tell me more,' he said.

And so after they had had some fun at the expense of the Dessert Selection – she ordered the Concerto of English Cheeses and he went for the Peach and Pistachio Extravaganza from the collection of laminated photographic portraits on the Ice Cream and Sorbet Menu – Rebecca told Terry about Tsanko the Bulgar.

11

Terry had listened without interruption as Rebecca told him about the file and her unease about the interventions. She was relieved that he appeared to accept that her suspicions as reasonable and she was grateful and excited when he suggested that they might try and find out a little more. As they drove back to London they contemplated the possible consequences of the evening, the most immediate of which was that they ended up in bed together. They later admitted to each other that in their heart of hearts neither of them was entirely sure if their ensuing affair was fuelled by the pursuit of the conspiracy or if it was the other way round.

'Yes, I can see why you were curious,' Terry told Rebecca after he'd read the copies of the files. 'One somehow wants to know a bit more about this Bulgarian Turk who didn't want to stay at home with his folks and mind the goats.'

The facts in the possession of the UK Home Office concerning Georgi Tsanko were that he was working as a security guard in the City of London at the offices of the Grus Corporation. He'd been employed there for just over four years. He had arrived in the UK five years before to work as a security guard at a warehouse owned by a trading company in South Manchester. Born in a village in the Stara Mountains, Tsanko was in his teens when his family, like many other Bulgarians, moved to Turkey in search of work. He did his military service in the Turkish Army, where he saw action against the Kurdish rebels, was wounded and invalided out. He returned to Bulgaria with his mother and father and was employed as a guard at a warehouse in the Burgas industrial zone.

Terry had to avoid making any formal request for information about Georgi Tsanko through the system for fear of alerting the wrong kind of attention, but he knew the Deputy at Sofia Station well enough to ask for a favour. The response revealed that the Bulgar was referenced in a file on a British businessman called Faulds.

The warehouse company which employed Tsanko was owned by a businessman called Kalomiris who was described as 'a Class A criminal, unconvicted and known to be involved in smuggling and currency fraud', and who therefore enjoyed a large measure of police immunity which was par for the course in this patch. The note on the file concerning various employees recorded that Tsanko had served as a warehouse security man for Kalomiris but had been used to do occasional personal security work for the boss himself.

Tsanko had walked out of his job suddenly without warning nine and a half years ago and travelled to the UK on a temporary visa that had been arranged for him in London. Kalomiris had been shot dead in Sofia along with his two bodyguards while walking in Zapaden Park six months later. Tsanko's sudden departure inevitably made him a suspect until it was established he was in the UK at the time of the assassination. This was aside from the fact he had no discernible motive while, as the Sofia Station Deputy put it, 'Kalomiris was so loathed that you could have filled a stadium with people who'd have been happy to kill him.' Among those at the head of the queue would have been a Brit called Roy Faulds, who operated a trading company from an office in Sofia and with whom Kalomiris had had a long and intense business rivalry.

Rebecca and Terry were now both convinced that Tsanko's file was being monitored to protect the Bulgar; the fact that there had been three interventions during Rebecca's possession of the file was beyond coincidence. It was evidence, if only a fragile strand of it, that there might be corrupt operators inside the Service as Owen had suggested at Hedley Coram. Their suspicions inflamed, Rebecca and Terry intensified their enquiries.

'I think we need to go to Sofia,' Terry suddenly announced.

'What is purpose of your veesit to our country, Mr Engleesh?' asked Rebecca in an attempt at an immigration officer impersonation. 'Beez knees or pleasure?'

'Business, of course. But mostly sex. Wild sex in a seedy Bulgarian hotel with sateen curtains, grubby shag-pile carpet and nylon leopard-skin bedspread.'

'And I was planning on lovely white linen in the Cotswolds.'

Sofia was looking magnificent in a faded sort of way. The trees along the Vaptsarov were just breaking into bud. The grand but now grubby Hapsburg buildings lined the boulevards like aristocrats in their faded finery. Released from half a century's imprisonment by the Soviets, even in their shabby state they looked way too overdressed for the time and place. The hotel Terry had booked obligingly lived up to his caustic imagination.

On the pretext of gathering references for a recruitment company, they arranged to see Nico, Tsanko's former boss at the warehouse. With Kalomiris dead and buried he was happy to talk when Terry offered 'a small fee to cover expenses'.

'Georgi was useful boy,' said Nico, who spoke just enough English for Rebecca and Terry to piece together an account of Tsanko's time at the warehouse. It seemed that he'd just come out of the Turkish army when he started here. He had been with the Hakkaris – the Mountain Commandos and was decorated twice. In the end he got wounded in the foot which left him with a limp and the Army let him go. When his family returned to Bulgaria from Turkey because they'd inherited some land from a relative, Tsanko decided to join them. With his military training, security was an obvious choice of employment and he eventually turned up at the warehouse. As well as security the boss had apparently used him for other jobs like 'cleaning the house', at which point the old boy drew his fingers across the knuckles of a fist by way of explanation. 'He useful to boss. Good man. I hope he okay. Say Nico say "Hello".

'There's something there,' said Rebecca after they'd left Nico. 'Why would he leave his job in such a hurry?'

Before they could find out, something happened which changed everything.

12

After their encounter in Kensington Gardens, Clay was convinced Ms Rebecca Rawlings had something to offer and Thermidor put her under close surveillance. They learned she was having an affair with a Foreign Office employee called Terry McCall, which was interesting because he'd been on the course with her at Hedley Coram. It became even more interesting to observe them meeting one evening in St James's Park within sight of but not visible from Collingwood House. They talked for some minutes before Rebecca set off purposefully towards Pimlico. After 200 metres or so, Terry followed; and then he overtook her. After conferring over their radio link the Thermidor watchers worked it out. Rebecca and Terry were trailing someone.

The task of identifying someone who is being followed by someone you are following is the one of the trickier challenges in the art of surveillance. 'Doing the Conga', they call it in the trade.

'Really?' said Ludo when they told him. 'So who was it they were following?'

'Someone called Mary Grigor; she's a supervisor at Pitt House. She's known as Pitbull Mary. Rebecca used to work under her before her current placement.'

A couple of weeks later their watchers rang Clay.

'We've just gathered that Rebecca and her man think Mary Grigor is going to meet someone on Sunday afternoon at the History of Britain Museum. They want to know who she is meeting. So I guess we do too?'

The History of Britain Museum hadn't been open long and was attracting huge crowds; it was already the top attraction for every divorced father with custody of his child for the day. When Clay said he'd go along for the ride, Ludo suggested they should take Rufus Elmwood, who'd be an asset in an operation like this. Rufus was keen on the idea.

Clay hadn't been to the Museum before. The landscaping was half finished and they were still building some of the satellite halls, but the bulk of it was completed, a quarter-of-a-mile-long structure running along the old railway line on the edge of West Kensington. Clay and Rufus were there in good time, waiting with their tickets in the big glass-walled entrance hall beside one of the circular kiosks. Ludo was lurking in the bookshop at a decent distance but with a good view of the main entrance doors.

As they arrived almost all the visitors paused for a moment to stare up in wonder at the high atrium roof. Hanging from steel beams among a mass of colourful heraldic banners were scale replicas of historical figures and objects, among them a biplane, a knight in armour, a galleon and a space-walking astronaut, all bouncing gently on spring-loaded hawsers like slow-motion bungee jumpers.

Rebecca and Terry didn't look up when they arrived but hurried straight across to the dispensing machines to collect their pre-paid tickets before moving into the cover of a cluster of steel pillars. Rebecca was wearing dark glasses and a woollen hat pulled low over her forehead hiding her auburn hair.

Ms Mary Grigor looked pretty much like the snatched pictures that Clay had been given. Cropped grey hair, pugnacious features, dark-framed spectacles. Not quite as wide as she was tall but getting on for it. She bought her ticket and went straight to the rail platform. Rebecca and Terry followed her at an interval; Ludo was not far behind, followed by Clay and Rufus.

A replica of Stephenson's Rocket with five small carriages was waiting at the platform.

Ludo's voice came through on Clay's earpiece.

'Grigor is on the second coach. Rawlings coach four.'

Clay and Rufus stepped into the fifth coach.

The train gave a gentle lurch and rumbled out of the station. Somewhere between the sixteenth and seventeenth century there was a strange hissing sound and it came to a halt. There was a long pause and then it slowly reversed back into the sixteenth century. The railway's teething troubles had been widely reported and the crowd waited good-naturedly. Everyone was disembarked.

Eventually the next train, drawn by a replica of the *Mallard*, drew up and there was minute or two of confusion as some of the passengers tried to alight onto an already crowded platform. Clay was wondering if they had seen the last of Mary Grigor for the day when he got a text from Ludo: WITH GRIGOR COACH ONE. The platform was now badly crowded with some struggling to get into the sixteenth century as other tried to leave and station staff began to marshal the crowd. As helpless as swimmers caught in a rip tide, Clay and Rufus were swept along the platform and into the third carriage, where they came nose to nose with Rebecca and Terry.

Clay didn't know whether to laugh or weep. So much for

tradecraft or 'operational skills' as they now called it. This was the Spooksville equivalent of a motorway shunt.

Rebecca spoke first.

'What a coincidence,' she said in a steely tone of arch insincerity. 'I know . . . isn't it?'

Rebecca stared at Clay's chin. 'You seem to have grown a beard since we last met.'

It was an ace. There was no way he could even get to the ball although he tried.

'I almost didn't recognise you what with the hat and the tinted glasses.'

Excruciating embarrassment or what? Then there was a bit of 'how-are-you-ing?' and 'fancy seeing you here' and so on. To add to the embarrassment they were acutely aware that only a few people in the carriage were talking.

'This is Terry, a friend of mine. Terry, this is . . . ?'

'Clay. And this is Rufus.'

'Hello, Rufus!' A different, more effusive tone for him from Rebecca, who having now regained the upper hand after their meeting in the park wanted to take advantage of her superior position.

'So how's your friend Desmond?' she asked.

'Oh he's fine', said Clay. 'On good form actually, good form.'

'Is he? Oh that's nice! Still rogering everything in sight?'

The packed carriage at this point was silent except for the whispering of a group of teenage girls sharing some terrible private joke.

'Oh my God, did you *hear* that!' said a wide-eyed giggly girl, the largest and the loudest of the bunch, cupped hand over mouth. 'I can't believe she just *said* that!' An outburst of hysterical giggling all round.

Clay scrabbled for some words that would establish Desmond's canine credentials.

Rebecca saw his game and was determined to retain his human potential.

'You should have brought him. He's just the type to enjoy a bit of history.'

Clay decided he'd go along with this but then he heard himself saying,

'Yes, he was really keen to come.' It left Rebecca with an open goal and she didn't fluff it.

'Yes, he was last time we met.' That was all that was needed to send the girls into further paroxysms of histrionically-enhanced teenage mirth.

'Why don't we all have a bit of a chat over a coffee?' Clay suggested just before they got to the eighteenth century. Rebecca was really un-keen on the idea but Terry was all for it. He looked at the map in his museum guide.

'There seems to be a place just behind the Highland Clearances.'

'So do you come here often then?' asked Clay mirthlessly as they sat and waited for Ludo to arrive and while Terry bought the coffees. Rebecca didn't reply but just smiled at Rufus, who seemed sullenly mesmerised by her.

'How old are you, Rufus?'

'Six.'

'My, six! So what do you think of this place then?'

Rufus stared around at the massive project that had been born before he was and swallowed millions of pounds of investors' money along with acres of prime real estate and the time and talent of an army of designers and craftsmen.

'Alright, I s'pose.'

Ludo now appeared and sheepishly admitted to Clay he'd lost Mary Grigor. Clay introduced him to Rebecca and Terry who had reappeared with the coffees. 'Okay,' said Ludo, 'we might as well admit we are all doing the same job. We better just hook up and get on with it.'

Rebecca didn't seem to be listening; she was fishing her wallet out of her bag and asking Rufus if he wanted to get himself an ice cream. Then she turned to Ludo and said:

'I'll need to discuss this with my associates.'

'Only two scoops, Rufus,' said Clay, 'and don't tell your mother or she'll kill me.'

'Listen, Ms Rawlings,' said Ludo, 'you haven't got any associates. Your "associates" is sitting on the chair beside you.' Terry smiled brusquely, conceding the point.

'This,' said Rebecca, giving Ludo and Clay a gorgeous big, defiant smile, 'is true.'

That almost wrapped it up. They'd all got each other bang to rights and agreed to meet again within forty-eight hours in a properly secure location. Everyone shook hands on it, which was as close as they would ever get to pricking their thumbs and taking an oath of loyalty in blood. Suddenly Terry was on his feet.

'Are we all done now? This bagpipe music is getting on my tits.'

13

The consequence of the collaboration between the two groups was very soon to produce a startling result. Now that they had access to Rebecca and Terry's research on Tsanko, there was a mass of material to be drawn into the Thermidor data bank. Digital does long and it does deep but it doesn't do wide, so Stella organised what every large police enquiry has to have whether it's for real or on the telly – a large hard-copy display. It filled three large pin-boards along the wall of one of Clay's children's bedrooms which already featured an exhibition of primary school artwork.

A mass of mug shots – Faulds, Drake and Parsons among a crowd of bit part players – were dotted among grainy snatched pictures of figures in the street, at cafe tables, diagrams and maps, including one of the City. On this Colza had ringed with a red felt-tip marker Albion Buildings in Cord Street which linked Drake and Parsons. There were company logos and illustrative material of all the key locations: the railway bridge where Detective

Sergeant Cope died, a chart of the section of Kent coast where Judge Sparrow was drowned, a photograph of the upturned dinghy, distribution points and key locations of the Drake and Parsons operations. There were newspaper cuttings, strips of printout of material pulled off the web.

Sometimes they would move the stuff around, maybe putting the judge's boat next to the Midlands warehouse, the railway bridge next to a photo of Albion Buildings and so on, all the time looking for new connections. One evening they made one.

Ludo had been 'shuffling the pack' and found himself staring at two thumbnail maps. One showed the detail of Saffron House in Antwerp Place where Tsanko's employer, the Grus Corporation, had its offices; the other showed Albion Buildings in Cord Street. *It couldn't be?* He hurried over to a computer, pulled up the satellite view and zoomed in on Saffron House. *It was.* The Grus offices in Antwerp Place backed on to a row of buildings in Cord Street and Saffron House was immediately behind Albion Buildings.

From the street, the fronts of the buildings formed a continuous façade lining the pavement but at the back they were all very different. It was a Dickensian jumble of rooftops, light wells and alleyways. Saffron House shared access to a fire escape with two neighbouring buildings that led to a walkway leading from one rear flat roof to another, down a flight of iron stairs along a narrow passage. Terry spent a morning inspecting the planning maps held by the London City Corporation planning department and found his answer. It was quite a common solution to the demands of the fire regulations. The emergency escape from the back of Saffron House in Antwerp Place, was over the roof of the rear extension, across the adjoining extension, down a stairway then through the kitchen and dining area of a wine bar and out into Cord Street.

The most promising vantage point seemed to be the loft of the neighbouring building, which had windows in the mansard; they'd give a view of most of the fire escape steps and the walkway over to the other building. Colza used the office cleaners routine again to do a recce which established that the top floor was used only for storage. They snuck in a two-man surveillance team who spent four days in a pile of discarded office furniture before they got lucky, but when they did they struck gold.

As dusk turned to dark at the end of their third day, one of the watchers saw the door at the top of the fire escape open. He roused his dozing mate and they trained the camera and the night vision goggles on the three security men in baseball caps making their way down the ladder and across the roofs, testing the walkway railings as they went. They looked like any unhurried routine security patrol. Now a security guard from the building next to the restaurant appeared on the fire escape and greeted the group of three. They stopped, lit cigarettes, chatted for a bit and then returned to their respective buildings. One hour and fifty minutes later the same routine occurred.

It was only when they got the video back, enhanced the picture and scrutinised it properly that they could see what had happened. One of the group of three security men, a taller man with longish black hair, had changed places with the man from the building opposite. And when they came to enhance the image and look at him more carefully they were presented with an intriguing puzzle: why would health and safety issues like a fire escape be the responsibility of Frank Crane CBE, Chairman of the mighty Grus Corporation, registered offices: Saffron House. And if he did feel compelled to get involved in such minutiae, why would this silver-haired gent deem it necessary to wear a black wig?

Inspecting a fire escape while wearing a wig might not yet have become a criminal offence, but they knew they'd snared some serious vermin. Crane had spent more than two hours in Albion Buildings, which Thermidor had established was the nerve centre of a substantial criminal organisation, and he'd taken a lot of trouble to avoid being seen there. It was perfectly clear that the Albion operation was being clandestinely controlled by Crane.

Who'd have thought it? This pillar of society, this respected ruler of a prosperous commercial empire, champion of charities, was at the heart of the whole filthy caboodle. The modest, the charming, the respectable Mr Frank Crane was up to his axles in the world's nastiest businesses, a sponsor of misery, punctured veins and broken lives, of addled wretches beaten, broken and pimped to within an inch of their lives and almost certainly, on occasion, beyond.

Crane's people thought they had laundered the Bulgar, but Rebecca and Terry (or the Hedley Corams as Clay was inclined to call them) had together uncovered his past. And, thanks to Thermidor's cack-handed performance at the History of Britain Museum, the two separate investigations were merged and Georgi Tsanko was able, albeit unwittingly, to make his greatest and perhaps only contribution to the world of the righteous by establishing the connection between Albion Buildings and Saffron House.

When he heard the news Ludo offered the nearest thing he knew to a prayer of thanks. Owen had done it by a whisker; he had indeed spoken the truth in Balmoral, just as he had told Angela on his deathbed. And Angela had told Ludo. Ludo had told Clay. Clay had delivered Rebecca. Rebecca had alighted upon Tsanko. Between them they had managed to make the connections which would in the end let them find the Fox.

The words that Owen spoke as he approached his death were to be the most important of his life.

Thermidor's focus now shifted to Frank Crane. They assembled any open source information on him that they could get. Then same as usual: feed everything into the digital files and get all of it onto the wall: names of Crane's companies, photos of his family, friends and associates, favourite haunts, Crane's London house. Crane's missus, Crane's son and daughter, Crane's missus's family. Pics of Crane at charity events, the cover of Anglo's annual report; gossip column item about Crane in the Caribbean; drone shots of his place in the country. Random dots of information. Every bit of data that might bring something to the party.

14

Thirteen million of them passed through this place each year, coming in, going out, an unending modular tide of giant steel ribbed boxes ranged in ranks, maybe forty, maybe fifty-six foot long but still imperially measured, piled in stacks ten high. All day clanging and banging, booming like thunder, trundled by shuttle lift trucks to construct the tower blocks of a vast ever-shifting grid-plan city.

The crane lines and container parks of the great port of Busan were massed in batteries which sprawled along the estuary of the Nakdong River on the southeast coast of South Korea. It was the fifth busiest port in the world and the Korea Customs Service employed more than 300 customs officials here. By special arrangement there were also a company of US customs agents at the port. Among its many functions, Busan played a key role in the trade in North Korea's illicit exports, notably in counterfeit currency and drugs. These injected desperately needed foreign currency into this basket-case economy to secure vital materials including components for its vast but ageing military arsenal and, even more important, for the purchase of luxury goods to retain the loyalty of the Looney Tunes leadership's crony elite.

Given that North Korea was a mentally unstable nuclear power with the potential to sell on weapons of mass destruction to other rogue states, the Western powers kept a close watch on what passed through Korea's ports. The UK Intelligence Service recruited local customs officers as undercover agents in the port of Busan to report on suspicious consignments being moved to and from the North. Among them, when the new millennium was still in single figures, was a keen young officer called Han Jin-Ho. When one of his supervisors excited the suspicions of the Intelligence Service,

Han had arranged to switch some of his shifts so he could be part of the suspect's team on Quay Number 17 searching containers from a PMV (Priority Monitoring Vessel), the term for a highly suspect vessel from North Korea.

A glorious spring day. Han and his team were at Park 11B, about to tackle a dozen containers that had been taken from their stacks and brought to ground level for inspection. The supervisor pointed to one; the doors were swung back and the unloading began. When they were halfway into the container, the supervisor selected batches of cartons laid out in rows on the quayside; he picked two, seemingly at random, and instructed his men to open them. *How did he know which to choose?* Each contained rows of white china plates stacked between sheets of polystyrene. The innocent packages were resealed. Han had been watching as the man worked, secretly memorising numbers when he could get sight of the manifests. *This is a game; this is not for real.* He searched for any signs on the cartons as he helped stack them back in place but could see none. *There must be something.*

It was clear to Han what was happening. The supervisor was picking on the containers that did contain contraband but was selecting innocent cartons. When he got home at the end of his shift, Han noted down all the numbers he had memorised from the manifests, encoded the data – names of shipping companies, agents, dates, cargo and so on – and zipped it to his controller at the Park.

And that did for him. Not that it caused his death, but it did put an end to his life.

15

Criminal organisations can maintain levels of secrecy
which are never attainable in advanced democracies.

Prof. Glyn Owen, Crime in the Kingdom

The one thing that everybody knew about Frank Crane was that nobody seemed to know anything. How did he make his money? Crane didn't look like a crook. His suits were quietly expensive and with his distinguished groomed silver hair, shrewd steel rims, thin lips, cool eyes one might even mistake him for the respected chairman of a well-run hospital trust. It was a cause of mild unease among those who knew him, the way he seemed to have systematically erased almost all the details of his early life from public and private record. If a tenacious reporter managed to track down anyone who would have known the Great Man in his earlier days he'd be greeted by a refusal to talk about him. And that was true of anyone – not just relatives, friends and ex-neighbours but former associates and, assuming that they had managed to find where he was educated, school contemporaries and teachers. Some who were particularly tenacious were bought off with jobs or contracts with one of his many companies.

How did Crane achieve this veil of secrecy? He or an associate would have had to contact each and every acquaintance to ask, bribe or threaten them to say nothing. Whatever he did, it worked: the *omertà* was complete. Quite creepy, people thought, but they set aside their reservations in the face of the man's surefooted charm, his wealth and his charitable contributions.

Crane was always going to be a criminal; it wasn't a vocation for him, just a clear understanding of where his talents lay. Criminality was in his nature, if not in his genes – his parents were fastidiously honest. But that was part of the problem. The twelve-year-old Crane had watched with disbelief as his father abandoned a long struggle to keep alive his failing electrical repair shop until his bank foreclosed on him and he was forced into a poorly paid job maintaining equipment in a nearby food processing factory. In Crane's eyes the road paved with honesty and hard work looked unenticing.

In his late teens he had friends with crim connections but he didn't like what he saw. He certainly had no desire to be one of them. He didn't want to be the kind of gangster who wanted everyone to know he was a gangster; the type who craves respect, struts around in noisy suits generating more menace than revenue. He reckoned that some of these clowns would have been better off working for the council emptying bins. For a brief period he hung out with a crim set in their bling-lined homes, their tacky drinking clubs; he witnessed their showy charity, sat with the other lads ringside at unregistered bloody bare-knuckle prize fights. He'd joined them when they went mob-handed, burning up the motorway in an SUV full of greyhounds. They'd bounce over the moonlit stubble of the South Suffolk arable prairie until the headlights trapped a running hare, then they'd chuck the dogs out and the chase was on. Afterwards it was back to the seedy unglamour of the Lucky Dice Casino for a bloody great nosh before heading off for Josie's, where girls who were not hairdressers offered them the joys of the Barber's Chair. This Crane did not want. He wanted to get away from his native scrubland of kennel sheds and stables and guilty-looking breezeblock buildings with doors festooned with padlocked chains, dotted among clumps of nettles and grass chewed to the quick by piebald Gypsy horses. And by 'out' he didn't mean a deluxe ranch-style dwelling on the southern coast of Spain.

No, Frank Crane wanted an upgrade. He wanted to sit in a completely different part of the aeroplane, to move in decent society, to be among the rich, the famous, the respectable and the effective. He knew this was possible, you just bought a ticket, he just needed to get hold of the money for the ticket.

What made Crane exceptional was that he got so wise so very early. He realised the importance of a clean slate. True, what he did while still at school hardly constituted a clean slate, but only two people knew about that and they certainly weren't going to tell anyone about it. He opted to learn the art of legitimate business because once he had crossed the line into criminality any mistakes he made would be much more expensive. He'd seen that happen to people he knew, who'd got into trouble in the deep end before they had learned to swim. They ended up starting life in gaol.

Crane began work at eighteen as a trainee motor mechanic in a garage specialising in delivery van fleets. In his spare time he salvaged some of the vehicles his firm had written off, repaired them and hired them out for cash until he was ready to formalise the business. Within seven years of leaving school he'd established a substantial commercial transport fleet. But precisely how he parlayed a fleet of vans in Essex into a major international property company, an interest in a bank and a slew of trading companies remained a mystery.

With the enterprising reason of any youth who finds himself contemplating the criminal horizon, early on Crane came to the inevitable conclusion that a stall in the pharma's market had got to be the way forward. So when he judged the time to be right he got in touch with Drake and Parsons, his two closest school friends (actually, they were his accomplices but no one knew anything about their sin) and moved into the Great Trade; he kept his transport business at arm's length except as a means of laundering his profits. Unremarkable and presentable, Frank Crane didn't look like someone who might unleash extreme violence but then he didn't: he preferred to subcontract. Since the early van hire days, he always had access to some discreet muscle for his enforcement work and he made sure that he was never around when there was an 'event' on.

Takings from the street dealing were distributed among by a platoon of foot soldiers recruited from all over the UK who used it to buy services and products from the Parsons and Drake chains of businesses.

As the operation began to absorb substantial sums of drugs cash, it became prudent to limit the amount laundered in the UK, so most of it was moved abroad. Cash consignments were smuggled in selected cargo vessels bound for Spain, one of the Caribbean islands or West Africa. It was collected by a local agent who would charter a yacht for a fortnight, during which it was moored by a quiet beach; the boat party would come ashore for a picnic, bringing the cash in picnic hampers and beach bags. Another party appeared by road, also to swim and picnic. While the two groups socialised the bags would get switched. The local agent used the cash to buy some run-down real estate with some potential, which was then developed and extended using more cash, before being sold at a profit. The now accountable funds were spent on another property in a better area. The process, of course, called for substantial quantities of palm oil for local politicians and government officials.

The chain of transactions continued until it reached into the blue chip legitimate property in prime locations. The drugs money had become what the fraternity called 'white goods' and it was now just down to competent estate management. In this way the stash of dirty cash that had bought a breezeblock barn on a patch of donkey-dung in a Caribbean kleptocracy had over time morphed into a luxury apartment block on the edge of a Swiss lake.

By his mid-fifties Crane had made an impressive fortune. His ambitions for status had been achieved. The house in Knightsbridge was preceded by one in Maida Vale and before that, Barnes. Why choose places so far from his roots? *Because* they were far from his roots; they were places people like him didn't go. His carefully calibrated social life embraced fellow businessmen and the great and the apparently good, whom he had befriended with generous hospitality and some tactical charity work fronted by his prepossessing wife Adele, a sturdy Italianate beauty, daughter of a respectable owner-manager of a small office supplies company.

Crane cut an impressive figure in the City; some big cheques to the major political parties gave him access to politicians. An invitation from Crane, whether for dinner in Knightsbridge or a week in the Mediterranean on *Azure Cloud*, his 190-foot Kerplartz yacht, could deliver a high-rolling financier, politician or opera star to dance attendance.

As with most successful people, charm was his first line of approach, and Crane was a very charming man; but when he got riled he was seriously scary. Crane's great achievement was to create a successful symbiosis of criminal and legitimate activity with illegitimate capital gains funding legitimate acquisitions. The key point was to keep the two very separate, and the man who achieved all this for Crane was a fiscal alchemist called Maurice Betts.

Maurice Betts was one of Crane's most valuable assets. He was Crane's money man who acted as his financial adviser, his chief accountant and his Yes-I'm-sure-we-can-do-something-here person. Betts didn't seem like an interesting man. Indeed he was decidedly colourless, but once into his digital ledgers he morphed into a conceptual artist of startling originality whose works were much admired by some of the finest minds in the Inland Revenue and the accountancy profession.

When the street takings came in it was Betts who took them to the laundry. Betts loved his work; he derived pleasure from solving the problems that Crane set upon him. He'd known Crane and worked with him since their schooldays. Betts had his own office in the Knightsbridge house and he and Crane lunched together once or twice a week when Crane was working at home. Apart from his finance-related duties Betts acted as something of a confidant on the non-kinetic side of things, such as the soundness of Adele's latest charity of choice, the progress of son Max's education, and the dietary requirements of Debbie, Crane's neurotic King Charles Spaniel.

Betts was spared the messy details of Crane's progress because he didn't want to know. As with Adele, his was a wilful moral myopia. He didn't like to see any blood on his spreadsheets.

16

If Betts was the man who knew where the zeros were buried, Cropper and Dubois knew where the bodies were; this was largely because they helped to put them there.

Cropper Dubois purported to be a public relations firm; in fact it was a suave and discreet security consultancy fronted by a PR operation for the benefit of those kinds of clients who felt it indelicate to be seen hiring security. These included industrialists, financiers, nervous media figures, politicians retired from high office and an assortment of the privately wealthy. It was all low profile – no riffraff, no attention-seeking clowns from sport or entertainment and no tone-lowering robber-rich Russians. They operated from a period brick and stucco building in a quiet street in Mayfair close to Park Lane. The two directors spent ninety per cent of their time working for Crane, looking after every aspect of his covert interests and overseeing the security arrangements.

People who get as rich as Frank Crane can only be seen as nice if they have people to be nasty for them, someone as nasty as Kevin Cropper, a tall well-built shaven-headed toughie with the deep jaw of a raptor and skin as taut and blue-pale as a budget-price chicken. He had been forced to resign from the Metropolitan Police in his late forties when he was a chief inspector overseeing a DTIU (Drugs Trade Investigation Unit) running a network of informers. It was said that he had left 'under a bit of a cloud'; in fact he had left under a lots of them. A talented and energetic detective, he'd nonetheless long been distrusted by his colleagues, who believed he'd got in too thick with the thieves and was on the take.

Cropper's inspired act was to play at playing the bent cop while actually being a bent cop. 'Yes, I keep bad company, that's my job and of course I'm going to make out I'm a bent cop: no respectable villain wants to be seen talking to a straight one.' Cropper's superiors didn't know what to believe and he remained in office until eventually the growing pressure of his colleagues' suspicion made the situation impossible. Nothing was proven and the Met's 'you-resign-and-we'll-bring-no-charges' deal, now worn threadbare with over-use, was brought out yet again. Cropper departed, telling all who enquired, 'The Force has been everything to me and the day I left it was the saddest day of my life. I have been the victim of a most terrible misunderstanding but I bear no grudge.'

Cropper had already decided on a career in the more lucrative world of private security and spent his first year out of the Force with an outfit that specialised in protecting commercial secrets. Once he'd learned the essentials of running a private business, he handed in his notice and went off to set up on his own account, taking the firm's three most profitable clients with him.

Private enterprise suited Cropper. He preferred working for himself because, in truth, that's what he had been doing all his life. He built an impressive client list by recruiting talented and honest executives from decent backgrounds. One of these was a former Security Services officer called Guy Dubois.

Dubois was a smooth and effective operator, but cursed with a flaw which Cropper was quick to identify. His father had been a regular soldier turned gentleman farmer who had proved to be better at the gentleman bit than the farming. He found himself unable to keep his son at a public school with a merciless bursar who demanded fees that grew faster than the pupils, and one day the sixteen-year-old Guy suffered the humiliation of being collected by his father without the chance of saying goodbye to his friends. Cast out from his world of cosy privilege he was sent to a mediocre comprehensive where he was forced to make some serious adjustments in order to survive.

The whole experience fired in Dubois a fervent ambition to fight his way back into gentility; he got a short service commission in the Army, which secured him a place at Clare College, Cambridge, after which he went into the Foreign Office, who liked his combination of charm, cunning and savvy separateness. For each of the three institutions struggling to avoid accusations of elitism Dubois was gold dust – a palpable gent but one with a state education that ticked the inclusivity box.

To secure the lost social territory he had re-conquered, Dubois, church-goer and charity treasurer, sent his own two boys to public school, which his wife's family finances made possible. That source of finance dried up when his father-in-law made a foolish investment in an alleged friend's no-hoper company. This was calamitous for poor Dubois, who had to cope with the demands of a wife smarting under the unhelpful combination of very little money and lots of rich friends. Dubois dreaded inflicting on his sons the humiliation he himself had endured, so he started hunting for better-paid jobs in the burgeoning commercial intelligence sector.

Kevin Cropper, with whom Dubois had had some dealings in the past, was not the sort of person Dubois would have normally approached for employment. Dubois's frank explanation of his situation appealed to Cropper, who offered him a job; he knew that Dubois's needs would keep him loyal, at least for the duration of his boys' education. Moreover, Dubois, public schoolboy, Army and Foreign Office smoothie, would lend a bit of the class that Cropper could never offer. Dubois would be the acceptable face of Cropper, good cop to his bad cop. And so it proved. Cropper the bastard who knocked the cigarette out of your mouth; Dubois the nice one who put it back in.

It was not long before the magnet of money began to play havoc with Dubois's moral compass and he proved he would stoop to any unsavoury task that was asked of him. After testing him on his more prosaic clients, Cropper introduced him to the Chairman of the Grus Corporation, his star client, Frank Crane, who gave his approval. Dubois became immersed in Crane's complicated corporate interests and privy to some of his darkest secrets. Now he need not worry about the school fees but he was uncomfortably aware of his daily betrayal of the very values he was paying the school to imbue in his sons. Cropper revelled in his moral plight. When the two of them were plotting a particularly sordid aspect of some unspeakable scheme, the ex-cop would taunt him.

'Oh Guy, if only the headmaster of St Giles's could see you now. And d''you know, I've half a mind to tell him the truth about you.'

Cropper and Dubois carried out key functions in the Crane organisation, which included organising the chairman's personal security, and left the running of the PR accounts to half a dozen executives who were quite unaware of their double life.

The other member of Crane's inner circle was his son, Max, who worked for a small merchant bank and was ostensibly clean as a whistle. Crane planned for Max to do what he had done: learn how to work within the rules before starting to break them.

17

Warlords seek to take over the offices of state; ganglords seek only to suborn them.

Prof. Glyn Owen, Swanborne File

Crane had long held a deep respect for the more committed foreign exponents of crime. They seemed to have a vision that extended beyond the manor – in his eyes a crim couldn't be labelled 'international' by dint of owning a three-bedroom villa on the Costa Brava. Crane was an admirer of the various versions of the Italian mafias, but it was the children of the East who drew his greatest approbation for their willingness to go to charnel-house extremes. True, Albion had its own serious nasties, but nothing in the Eastern European league. Like Polish plumbers or Italian lovers, they just seemed to be better at the job. He detected in them a level of commitment that was altogether lacking on the home front, not just among the CEOs but also among the knuckle-and-bullet foot soldiers. Crane needed to go international and put out feelers; he wanted to find the best of the worst.

18

We must consider job satisfaction. Many a low
caste crim would make more money if he got a job
in a shoe shop but he wouldn't be so happy.
Prof. Glyn Owen, 'Nine Criminal Myths' – lecture to
Canberra Police & Security College

It was almost inevitable that at some stage Crane would be enlisting the help of Pegram Schwarzkopf, a collection of venal semi-criminal financial con artists who called themselves a bank. One of the partners introduced Crane to Carlo Podesti at a charity gala dinner in Monaco when they were both guests on his table. Podesti, an Anglo-Italian, was not the first Family man whom Crane had encountered but he was particularly impressed by this Italian's quietly stylish respectability which was the tone that Crane himself worked so hard to strike. He and Crane got on well and discussed, at first in elliptical terms, the nature of their work, after which a modest business collaboration began.

Podesti shared Crane's convictions about criminal performance in the West, which he saw as cosy, settled and lacking innovation. The mafias were suffering from a form of cultural inbreeding – a consequence, Podesti suggested only half-jokingly, of seeing too many portrayals of themselves in the movies and on TV. Like Crane, Podesti admired the business style of the Balkan crime bosses, who were making serious incursions into Italian enterprise. They seemed more earnest and less inhibited – always happy to go that bit further. Podesti's response to these Eastern intruders was to join them. Accordingly, after some careful trial transactions he had forged some trade agreements with a handful of operators. In the belief that the UK could be a valuable partner Podesti asked Crane if he too might be interested. Indeed, Crane was, but on the strict understanding that there could be no overt or traceable link between himself and the others, and so over the following months Podesti arranged for Crane to meet his new partners – or 'the Board' as they referred to them – in a series of clandestine encounters in airport car parks, yachts at sea and, in the case of a Romanian bandit called Shandor Pallengro, behind the bullet-proof glass of the high-security suite in a West London hospital while the old rogue was recovering from heart surgery. Pallengro liked to describe himself as *Mamioro* – a spirit that brings terrible illness; this was sort of true, in that he was one of the largest narcotics dealers in the Balkans.

Another of the main players was Zoltan Pivic, a Serb who trafficked diamonds in West Africa, where he operated a private security firm – in fact a small but brutal, largely white mercenary army whose UK contingent fondly referred to him as Blood Diamond Geezer. It was Pivic who financed Bad News Bapoto's Army of God's Light in his bid to rule over the three tribes of the West African Democratic Republic who had been fighting each other like rats in a sack ever since they were encircled and trapped together by a colonial mapmaker's pen. God's Light was a grotesquely vicious bunch of brutes which included child soldiers zonked out of their skulls on hallucinogenic drugs, limb-lopping and mass rape. By the time they'd left town the TV news reports would have to warn 'some viewers may find some of the following scenes distressing'.

One of the Board's nastiest members in a closely contested field, Pivic was co-opted at Pallengro's suggestion. As a child in 1941 he had escaped death at the hands of the fascist troops of the Croatian Ustashe who sought to eliminate the Serbs. The Catholic Ustashe so hated Orthodox Serbs that they began a holocaust of their own equal in horror to the Nazi version if not in scale – with only one million Serbs they lacked the raw materials. Nevertheless, in a frenzy of killing the Ustashe did manage to get through one third of them in such places as the concentration camp in the marshes at Stara Gradiška, where they sent Pivic's mother to die along with 12,000 females, many of them murdered by the Ustashe using knives, hammers, machetes and saws. The epicentre of this horror was in the cellar of a building known as the Gagro Hotel. His two sisters were taken to a special camp for children at Sisak where they were among some six thousand who perished. Pivic spent the war surviving in tunnels in the forest running errands for the resistance.

The Serbs never forgot about the Gagro Hotel and the other horrors inflicted upon them. When Yugoslavia imploded and it all kicked off again in the Nineties, Pivic did not shirk his bloody duties and was in the forefront of directing the slaughter. This sort of high calibre hatred held an immense appeal for Crane, who believed it informed Pivic's work. Indeed when they first met, Pivic told him, 'Only two of my family are still alive and we will be together until the day I die.' When Crane dutifully asked, so who were they? Pivic told him, 'A brother called Hatred and a cousin named Revenge'.

In crime as in so much else, the Eastern Europeans were happy to do the dirty, the difficult and the dangerous. Trafficking, prostitution, protection and enforcement were a natural fit for Pallengro and Pivic, for whom violence was a first rather than last resort. For most of the Board it was the opposite. The business of rigging a financial market, running a chain of casinos, conducting illegal arms deals and money laundering, counterfeiting and harvesting the rich opportunities presented by the worlds of finance, art, fashion and entertainment sectors demanded a subtler, less visceral approach.

So, there they were, an elite loosely-harnessed assemblage of mutually supporting talents with interlocking interests, a multiplicity of human and physical resources, global in reach, engaged in a magnificent mosaic of high-end criminal endeavour: pushers, hookers, hustlers and thugs plying their trade down in the streets; diligent denizens of the internet fraud centres and the legal and accountancy firms laboured in the offices above while in their penthouse boardrooms the bosses schemed – each of these myriad of citizens in their own way playing an active role in the community.

As the alliance grew and prospered, the work of some of its cohorts – though not, of course, Crane himself – came to the attention of the British authorities, who began to take action. Midlands drugs distribution began to suffer serious interference; the tentacles of Albion Buildings were getting trodden on. It was a meeting with an Israeli Board member, a former Mossad man called Avi Gelfand, who was pivotal in Crane's next phase.

When Crane expressed surprise at Gelfand's Mossad pedigree, Podesti pointed out that intelligence-gathering and crime both call for the same skill set.

'That's why,' Podesti explained, 'sooner or later they're all at it. CIA staffers became accomplished drug smugglers; the Zetas, one of Mexico's most voracious drugs gangs, came from the Special Forces and former members of the Russian KGB stole the entire country. Gelfand's Mossad duties included monitoring organised crime and he succumbed to the infection.'

It was Gelfand who would define for Crane the signature tactic of the Board.

19

'You know what your problem is?' Avi Gelfand said to Crane. 'I'm going to tell you.'

And he did.

Meetings with anyone from the Board had to be clandestine, so Gelfand and Crane shared an hour and a half of quality time behind the tinted windows of one of Crane's limos driving round the purlieus of Maidenhead apparently looking at houses with For Sale signs before stopping for lunch at an almost empty riverside pub. They sat at an outdoor table; their security sat by himself at another table out of earshot; the chauffeur had stayed with the car.

Crane had mentioned some problems he was having with some big police and customs busts. Gelfand's response was characteristically prescriptive. 'You're taking too much crap from the authorities. They aren't showing you respect. You need to teach them about that.' Gelfand's noisy Middle Eastern vehemence made the softly spoken Crane cringe. Avi was going on as if they were alone in the middle of the Negev, not in the garden of a genteel gastro-pub in Penlow on the Berkshire Thames.

'You have to tell them: "Why are you wasting time on hard-working business people like us when there are people out there committing parking offences? You tell them there are plenty of enterprises they can go after, but yours is not one of them.' It was then that Gelfand articulated the simple principle that would henceforth guide Crane's approach. 'If they come after you,' he told Crane, 'you go after them.'

'But Gelfi, this is England.'

Gelfand stared at Crane as if seeing him in a new light and not liking what he saw, then shrugged and stood up.

'Let's go.'

It was a humiliating moment for Crane. Gelfand clearly thought he wasn't up to it. From then on he determined that 'This is England' would never again constitute an obstacle to his plans.

20

One of the consequences of Crane's riverside tryst with Avi Gelfand was a new acquisition for the Saffron House security contingent.

In the course of one of Crane's occasional conversations with Roy Faulds, his Sofia-based crony, recruitment had been a recurring theme.

'Give me a foreigner every time, Roy,' said Crane. 'They've got more go to them and they've got no local baggage to trip them up.'

Crane had been particularly struck by an 'Eye of History' television programme about the Janissaries. It had explained how the Turkish Sultans had taken the strongest and brightest youths from their Christian families in the subjugated Balkan territories and trained them as soldiers for their own palace guard. The idea was that the sultans could count on the complete loyalty of these foreigners because they had no other source of employment or protection to turn to. Crane, who was quick to see the application of the idea to his own fiefdom, reckoned that this advantage outweighed the downside that strangers were an unknown quantity and less easy to read.

Although Roy Faulds wasn't overly interested in the socio-military structures of the eighteenth-century Ottoman Empire, he did pick up on Crane's general point, so when the young Tsanko appeared in his office offering his skin-saving deal in exchange for a new life abroad, Faulds immediately called Crane.

'Frank, I dunno if I'm doing you a favour or calling one in.'

'Try me, Roy. Try me.'

'Well, I think I've found a Janitor for you, Frank.'

It was a moment or two before Crane picked up on Roy's reference.

'Tell me more.'

'I need to find a nice home for this party. A very useful pair of hands.'

'Useful for what, Roy?'

'All sorts, but very good for the heavy lifting.'

Crane could detect from his tone that Faulds really needed to oblige this party.

'Send him over, Roy. Talk to Cropper.'

21

When everything was ready, Tsanko was put on a flight to Heathrow where he was met by a driver and taken to a modest flat in a mansion block in Maida Vale. There he received a call from a man speaking in Russian who gave him instructions on how to access a modest weekly cash allowance. He was told he had a place on an intensive English language course at a language school in the West End of London just off Oxford Street that has been fully paid for. He needed to take this very seriously because after six weeks all their conversations would be conducted in English, and his money would be cut or increased depending on his progress.

After two weeks, his minder, whom he still had not met, phoned to explain the plans that had now been made for him. In his third week he would be given the name of an employment agency that would offer him a security job in West London; it would be menial because of his lack of English, but as his English improved, so would his employment and salary. Meanwhile he must do nothing to compromise his reputation or the respectability of any organisation he worked for.

Tsanko did what was asked of him; he worked hard to learn the language, kept his nose clean, forged contacts and friendships in the respectable sector of the Bulgarian expat community, and prospered. After six months his English was satisfactory. His basic salary wasn't generous but he was soon earning extra money in cash when his boss began to ask him to carry out occasional assignments. For these Tsanko had to travel to various parts of the country but mostly to Middlesex and East Anglia, where his tasks included personal security, couriering cash and miscellaneous strong-arm work. Some of the assignments were in Europe. He was always clearly briefed by his masters and the operations were well researched and organised. Tsanko was confident that he was working with professionals and he felt that the confidence was mutual.

After some nine months, Tsanko was told to visit another employment agency, where he was seen by an ex-serviceman. The agency specialised in supplying security-related personnel for a variety of industries and organisations and sent Tsanko to an interview with a firm of public relations consultants in smart Mayfair offices a block from Park Lane. There he was interviewed for an hour and a quarter by two men sitting at one end of the long polished boardroom table. One was a charmless shaven-headed bully, the other a smooth diplomat type. They turned out to be the firm's chairman and CEO. This was a long time for two expensive suits to spend in the company of a doorman, so Tsanko realised he was being considered for a serious job. They pressed him closely about his past in the Hakkari Mountain Commando Brigade, in Sofia and in the UK; they asked him about his childhood and his family's move to Turkey. Throughout, Tsanko realised that they knew much more about him than they were letting on. They said they'd be in touch in due course and they parted on good terms.

Two days later Tsanko was called back. This time he was kept waiting for an hour and a half before being shown into a tiny office with scarcely enough room for the desk and three chairs. The same two interviewers were there but this time the atmosphere was very different. His interrogators were curt and unsmiling as they took him back over everything, but deliberately scrambling the chronology – his job in West London, his army service, his arrival in London, his childhood, his duties at the Kalomiris warehouse. Throughout Tsanko displayed a courtesy and charm learned from his Vitosha Boulevard days, where he had developed the good waiter's ability to pamper the dignity of others by firmly retaining his own. Although the tone of their questions became increasingly aggressive his composure did not crack until the interview culminated with the unpleasant one asking, 'Why did you lie to us?'

'How I lie to you?' said Tsanko.

'You lied about the work you have been doing.'

'What work?'

'Mr Tsanko, we ask the questions.'

'What you want me say?'

'Why didn't you tell us what you do for these people?'

'If I tell you their business, you want I tell everyone your business?'

It was the right answer. Cropper and Dubois, who'd been briefed by Faulds, knew exactly what he did for these people, of course, and Tsanko knew they knew.

The suicide of Detective Sergeant Cope from a railway bridge just outside Leicester was administered by Cropper Dubois and committed by Georgi Tsanko. The good policeman had been digging where he shouldn't and a lucrative part of the Drake operation was being jeopardised. Crane needed to know how far the officer's investigation had got (rather too far, judging by the information they extracted from a merciless interrogation of Cope, after which his death became essential).

Judge Sparrow's watery demise soon followed soon. To the outside world both murders looked like accidents but colleagues of the deceased understood that they were a stark warning. The passing of Preece, the police informer on a witness protection programme within hours of arriving at his 'safe house' in New Zealand, was a more extravagant notification for the benefit of potential informers or undercover agents. It was Crane's own way of saying, 'You cannot hide from me.' Not that anyone knew who 'me' was.

22

One of Frank Crane's most valuable associates was a high-rolling businessman called Cho Min who combined legitimate commerce with a thriving illicit trade with North Korea. This was almost entirely due to his excellent contacts among the crooked clique that surrounded the lunatic who ruled in Pyongyang. Cho Min found Western Europe offered him the best opportunities to buy goods and sell illegal drugs. He was equally impressed by the educational possibilities and seeing an advertisement in a glossy diplomatic magazine, he sent the boy Nam to a public school named Viva College.

It was the creation of a cynically high-minded group of investors who had bought a neglected baronial Hertfordshire pile in which they conjured the ambience of a country house hotel. Adding a mix of traditional trappings and educational modernity they created a lucrative public-school-lite offering for a growing new foreign clientele – people like Cho Min.

After a lonely and uncertain start at the school young Nam fell in with a sly and clever clique which included a cool operator called Max. Frank Crane had been highly tempted by the idea of one of the brand-leading public schools but then decided that in an ever-globalising world somewhere like Viva College would provide his son with a broader set of contacts.

Max and Nam became firm friends and would spend part of their holidays together with one or other of their parents. Crane senior liked the sound of Nam's father as described by Max so he invited him and his wife to come over from Seoul and stay with them in London. They accepted and had hardly left the airport before the two fathers were up to their elbows in sin.

Given the prevailing international market prices and its government-sponsored advantage, synthetically produced drugs from North Korea were, for the foreseeable future, going to offer better margins for any UK dealer – better, for instance, than the crystal meth and methamphetamine manufactured by China. They agreed that Cho Min would broker a trade with his contacts in the North on behalf of Crane, who would be the conduit to the European market through a number of subsidiaries.

Those subsidiaries were operated by Parsons and Drake.

23

Cho Min secured the necessary line of supply and Crane's people finessed the arrangements for freighting to the UK and distribution. The operation was complicated and not without risk, but by paying the right people in the right places the supply line was secure and profitable – until one evening when Cropper requested an urgent meeting with his boss. Crane was just about to go out on Puccini patrol with Mrs Crane at Covent Garden so they met during the interval in the street outside the Royal Opera House.

'We've got a problem,' said Cropper. 'The Cho Min show has gone haywire. Some customs officer in the Busan docks has found out what's going on. We don't know how bad it is but Min says we need to put a lid on it . . . set an example. You happy for me to send someone?'

'You better had.'

24

Han was working on the late shift at the docks when he heard them coming. The cadence of those footsteps wasn't right. *They are coming for me.* And they were. They grabbed him, bound him and threw him into a Jeep that delivered him to a forty-footer at the base of a stack in the northeast sector of the container park. A round-eye was waiting for him. Han saw that he was wearing rubber gloves. *I will be okay. I activated my panic button before they got me.* He prepared to face the immediate future in the certainty that his controllers at a faraway place called Osterley Park were watching over him every minute of every hour of every day. Now they had been alerted they would get him out of trouble.

Wrong.

25

Real name: Molly Lee Reed. Older daughter of a Korean mother and American father, he the manager of a US-owned chemical engineering plant.

Mo went to a good university in Seoul and studied English, Russian and Commercial Practice. Her professor told her parents, 'Mo is a natural linguist but frivolous; lacking in ambition.' Her parents disapproved of Mo's approach to her early career, which meandered between croupier and PA to a rock band. There were a number of boyfriends but none that lasted; she enjoyed partying with her friends in the Western expat community, but always made time to look after her elderly aunt, deaf and bedridden, who lived with the family. Mo was also close to her younger sister, who was outgoing and materially ambitious but had a kind of naivety that worried Mo and made her feel protective. To her parents' relief, Mo eventually found a decent job in the marketing department of a bank which valued her English, and to Mo's relief her sister found a good husband with a secure job as a customs officer in the port of Busan. His name was Han.

Han's terrible fate had driven every action in Mo's life ever since. When she first heard what had happened she found her whole being convulsed with rage; but when she visited him in hospital and saw what they had done to him, she made a promise to her grief-wracked sister, that she would find the culprits and Han would be avenged.

Mo's odyssey began one weekend when she was at her sister's apartment in the Seoul suburb of Yangcheon. One of Han's Customs Service colleagues, a man called Lee, came to offer his sympathy, and in the course of their conversation he revealed that, shortly before his kidnap, Han had confided his suspicions after he'd witnessed his supervisor's handling of the inspection at Quay 17. Given what had happened to Han, Lee was now too scared to go to the authorities. Lee also told Mo that he'd heard two reports of a European who'd been seen at Quay 17 on the day that Han was assaulted and who, according to one of the main gate security staff, had produced a British passport as identity.

Mo enlisted two people to help her pursue this lead. One had been a university friend of her brother-in-law called David Kang. He was the son of a British mother and Korean father. Kang, a sales executive for a travel company, was newly divorced and had some time to offer. The other was Mo's childhood friend Shin, now a moderately successful freelance sports photographer whose working time was flexible enough to allow him to help.

A fortnight after his last visit, Mo's informant from the Customs Service reappeared with some new information. The name of the European who'd been seen at Quay 17 was recorded as Geordie Sangster. Lee also passed Mo a list of companies whose goods featured in the suspect consignment. With this slender evidence Mo, Kang and Shin began researching the ownership of the companies on Lee's list. Given the presence of the Brit at Quay 17, they started with the one UK-bound consignment. It belonged to MPL Trading Ltd, whose directors and top management were all Korean.

On most days the senior executives of MPL Trading liked to eat in a noisy noodle bar by the dock gates. There'd usually be four or five of them talking either about sport or business. Mo followed, listened and watched as only she could. For a long time she got nothing of value, but one day when they were discussing business prospects over lunch one of them mentioned the possibility of another toy consignment; the fuss had died down since the last one; Wui Chon had done a good job. One of them rocked sideways and back upright in his seat a few times; the others laughed; they switched to baseball and the woes of the Doosan Bears.

Wui Chon translated as 'a man with a limp'; Mo wanted to know more. Through her Customs Service contact, Lee, she established from the security staff on the gate that the visitor named Sanger did indeed have a limp; he *was* Wui Chon. Mo hoped to learn more from the MPL executives about the man, but as the name never came up. *So how about I try to prompt them?*

One lunchtime Mo arranged for Shin to be seated near the MPL table. When she heard a lull in the conversation she nodded to Shin. He got up and made his way to the gents' past the MPL group, limping ostentatiously as instructed. One of the honchos nodded at the retreating figure. 'There goes Wui Chon.' There was a short silence, then one of them said, 'Now he was good at his job. SP company people could use a few more like him.' The remark provoked some ribald laughter. Hardly conclusive evidence, but to Mo it seemed like more than a worthwhile lead.

It was fiddly but not that difficult. The MPL consignment had been handled by a UK company called Sappel Freight Forwarding PLC. Mo, Kang and Shin all set to work on tracing the ownership of the firm. It turned out to belong to another Felixstowe-based freight company, which in turn was owned by a trading operation called Coldingsby Holdings registered in the UK. Mo realised that the only way she could get close to Coldingsby was to give up her bank job and go the UK herself. Kang and Shin said they wouldn't let her go on her own.

Three weeks later, armed with a tourist visa, Mo flew to London and checked into the Tudor House Hotel in Barons Court. Kang and Shin, arriving three days later, rented rooms in a chaotic but friendly lodging house in Hounslow run by a retired baggage handler where a shifting cast of taxi drivers, airline catering staff and cabin crew came and left at all hours of the day and night.

26

For six weeks they did little other than reconnoitre the territory, watch and develop their plan. Meanwhile as the trio staked out their prey, Mo intensified the coaching of her collaborators in her special skill. A tricky skill, a rare skill, a skill she had made them work at morning, noon and night almost as soon as their collaboration began. Although they trained intently, Shin did not find it easy and would only ever be barely adequate, but Kang had some talent for it and quickly reached a competent level. As for the plan they were developing, they had to make sure that Coldingsby's people, not Mo, would appear to be responsible for what would happen next. It was they who must see her vulnerability and appreciate her possibilities; the approach must come from them.

Tommy Pollard was, as always at this time of night on a Tuesday, sitting in the car outside the Golden Bar Casino waiting for his boss. The street was empty so it was inevitable that he noticed a slim young woman in a dark grey mac who slipped across his wing mirror as she came out of the casino, walked briskly past him and turned a corner fifty yards down the street. He didn't give her a second thought until a few minutes later when two men hurried out of the club, looked up and down the street, then split up and ran down the street on either side. Just as they had disappeared round the corner at the end, the woman reappeared at the opposite end and headed towards the casino on the other side of the road. What was odd was that she was holding her shoes in her hand.

Tommy Pollard sussed it immediately: she didn't want her footsteps to be heard. Suddenly she ducked down behind a car. Pollard now saw one of her pursuers, who'd given up his search and was hurrying back to help his mate. As soon as he was round the corner and out of sight, the young woman reappeared from behind the car. He saw her bend down, presumably putting on her shoes. Now she had crossed back over the road and was walking hurriedly in his direction, Pollard could see she was Oriental and plainly frightened. He leapt out of the car and held open the back door.

'Quick, love. Get in. They're sure to be back.'

The woman hesitated, suspicious.

'Come on, hurry up!'

She seemed frozen to the spot.

At that point Pollard saw that her two pursuers, one much shorter than the other, had reappeared at the junction and were staring down the other road with their backs to him.

'Look, they're back – get in, you daft bitch.' Her eyes widened in terror and she turned to look. Still she made no move, but when Pollard firmly but gently shoved her into the car she didn't resist. Pollard went to the boot and took out a long dark raincoat.

'Get down on the floor and keep this over you.' He got back into the driver's seat. They were both silent while they adjusted to their new circumstances.

Pollard spoke first.

'So, love, what's all that about?'

The girl didn't reply.

'Well then, was it love or money?'

Still no reply.

'There was two of them, so I guess it's money, eh? You be quiet now 'cos your pals are coming back this way.'

After an interval in which her two pursuers passed them as they went back into the Golden Bar, Pollard tried again.

'So what's the story?'

'Yes, it was money. I have to say thank you.'

'Glad to be of assistance. Whose money would that be?'

'It was theirs but not really. Now it's mine.'

'That makes sense. Good on you.'

'They weren't meant to have found it was missing quite so quickly. I have to get away from here.'

'You stay put, love. Mr Harry'll understand.'

'Mr Harry?'

'You'll see.'

Pollard was waiting on the steps when Mr Harry came out of the casino.

'There's a bit of hopscotch in the back of the auto, Harry. It's in a spot of bother.'

'What you on about, Polly?'

'I thought it might come in handy. I dunno . . . you know what I mean?' He opened the rear door and his boss peered in.

'Yes, indeed. I see. Hello, love. Mind if I join you? I'm Harry Drake, registered owner of this vehicle.'

As Drake's silver saloon took them inside the outer walls of Frank Crane's defences as surely as the Trojan horse, Drake coaxed Mo's story from her: personal assistant in a big corporation in Korea . . . misunderstanding over 'borrowing' money from the promotions budget . . . had to leave Korea . . . came to the UK after friend of a friend had promised employment which didn't happen . . . yes, she'd got a UK passport; no, it didn't come from the Passport Office . . . looking for work as a croupier, meanwhile doing some temping by day . . . had done a lot of translation work translating for a dodgy Chinese guy trying to win orders from Seoul . . . he vanished owing her money but she'd hunted him down . . . had got her own back robbing him as he was processing cash at the Golden Bar.

'So, Mo, what did you get?'

Mo patted her large black leather handbag.

'Let's have a look then.'

Mo held open the bag for Drake to see the bundles of fifty-pound notes.

'What's that then? I'm guessing . . . four or five K?'

'Six and a half.'

Drake grunted. 'They always say I'm a pessimist.' But now he looked faintly puzzled. 'So what went wrong that you ended up in here?'

'I was meant to have longer to get away before he discovered the bag was missing. But I can pay you for what you and . . .' she nodded towards Tommy Pollard at the wheel, '. . . have done for me?'

'Yes, you can pay me, certainly can, young lady, but don't need any; to be honest with you I got more than I can handle! Got it coming out my bloody ears, I have. No, you hang on to it. You'll pay me another way.'

Here we go, thought Mo.

'No, don't mean . . .'

What Drake meant was: *You might be just what I need . . . no local baggage . . . probably sharp around the office . . . croupier, so good with figures . . . you're an illegal so you'd depend on me. And, it has to be said, a nice bit of popsie.*

What Drake said was: 'You can't go back to your job 'cos they'll find you there, so why don't you come and work for me?' He produced a card from his wallet.

'Be there, nine o'clock, day after tomorrow and we'll see what you can do. You need to tuck your chin in until then, lie low, yes? I know a place.' He raised his voice.

'Polly, we'll drop this young lady off at the Nevada Suites.' And turning back to Mo, told her, 'Little place, maybe dozen rooms; got Jacuzzi and everything.'

Mo nodded.

'You'll be alright. They won't find you there. Barry owns it; friend of mine; I'll have him look after you. Looks like you can afford to pay the bill.'

27

During Mo's early days in Drake's office – a suite of four rooms over a parade of shops on an estate on the outskirts of Staines – she made her mark as an employee who combined fastidious bookkeeping with a pragmatic understanding of what account-ing was really about. Drake was quick to appreciate the asset. Mo's private task was to see if the company had any connection to a container full of she-didn't-know-what at the port of Busan. Mo sent a stream of information from the documents she'd memorised and the gossip she'd overheard back to Shin and Kang, using the system they had so carefully rehearsed.

The weekly cadence of the office routine consisted of a steady pressure throughout the week, culminating in a highly tense period late on Wednesday afternoons as Drake demanded a mass of spreadsheet printouts for what Mo gathered was an important meeting somewhere in Central London. As the time approached Drake would grow increasingly twitchy and nervous; for all his I-am-the-boss front, he was a subordinate taking orders from someone. So one Wednesday afternoon Shin and Kang tailed Drake from his office to a building in the City of London – Albion Buildings in Cord Street. Checks on the companies that used it produced nothing of significance beyond the fact that Drake's accountant was there.

Mo watched Drake tense as he took the call, body language loud and clear. *He is talking to his superior.*

'Tell Cathy to come with me and bring the CB working files,' he said to Mo when he had finished the call. 'And give Polly a shout and tell him to get the car round here pronto.'

'Cathy's had to go home, Mr Drake, she's poorly.'

'Christ. Of all days. . .'

'What's the problem?' asked Mo. 'She got me to do the last of the checks on the CB stuff – maybe I can do something to help?'

'You know enough to talk through the current positions?'

'Sure I do.'

'Well you get those files and come along with me.'

28

Tommy Pollard drove Drake and Mo to a hotel near Windsor used almost exclusively by East Asians. It was done out in a Dallas-born fantasy of an English country house: sporting prints hanging from silk ribbons, elaborately coiffed curtains. The receptionist, who was expecting them, directed them to a small sitting room with French windows leading out to the garden. Drake flipped nervously through the spreadsheets while they waited.

Cropper, tall, unsmiling, shaven-headed, entered the room. For Mo he was a viscerally threatening presence.

'Who's this?' was all he said, no greeting.

'This is Mo who's joined us,' said Drake. 'Cathy's regrettably indisposed.' He didn't bother to introduce Cropper to Mo.

'Okay, we'll get the basics out of the way first. Himself will want to talk about some of these things on Wednesday so let's see what you've got.'

Drake and Cropper didn't quite get on. Drake and Crane went back a long way and he saw Cropper as an intruder who got between him and his boss.

After a ten-minute inspection of the paperwork and some questions, the tall man appeared grudgingly satisfied and rose and moved towards the French windows.

'We need to talk about other stuff . . .' He glanced at Mo. 'Let's take a stroll.'

While she waited Mo considered her next step. This man was Drake's superior. He had referred to the Wednesday meeting with 'himself', suggesting someone superior to them both. This man could be her conduit to Drake's boss and it might be a long time before such a chance came her way again. *Play the big card as soon as you get the chance.*

Some twenty-five minutes passed before she saw the two of them coming back down the stone path towards her. That was lucky because sideways was almost impossible. Their business discussion was over and they were both laughing. Although she couldn't hear, Mo knew why they were laughing and it was something she could work with. She held open the glass door for them as they came in. Then she spoke.

'I'm not offended at your comments about my appearance – in fact I appreciate them – but you should know I don't eat dog.'

The two men stared at her aghast. Mo met Cropper's eyes. For a moment he was no longer in control of the situation.

'Actually very few middle-class Koreans eat dog these days.'

Cropper smiled apologetically.

'How did you know . . .?'

Mo said nothing. Cropper and Drake exchanged edgy glances.

'You must have read my lips,' Cropper said, trying to make light of the situation.

Mo still said nothing, just returned his stare.

Then he got it.

'You *did* read my lips.'

Knowing that interesting possibilities would have already been flooding into Cropper's crooked mind, she merely nodded before turning to go. She hadn't even moved a step before he called out.

'Wait a minute.'

29

'*What is it with these people?*'

Crane was unhappy. His new friends were causing him a shedload of grief. They just didn't get it. How they conducted their own business was up to them, but any operations carried out for the Board had to be clandestine and deniable. They'd all agreed that, but some of them had broken their word several times. Crane knew that if he didn't read the riot act, sooner or later they'd compromise him. He confided his fears to Drake one evening after making the rooftop crossing to Albion Buildings.

'Yes, Harry, they've done me proud. Done good stuff. And we've had some nice economies of scale. Some of them are okay – like Luciano and Avi. But some of the others, like that Pallengro, they're insane. I had a couple of meetings with him before we got into bed and he seemed to get it. I said we couldn't have him doing any stuff he did in the UK. Then what happens when he needs to give a good tonking to some little hero from Bucha-bloody-rest who's been half-inching funds and come running to London town to get out of sight? What does the fucking gyppo do? Takes the little bugger's arms off – which is only his bleeding signature tune!'

'Oh deary, deary me,' said Drake, who was always amused by the way that Crane, the respectable boardroom Big Beast, lapsed into his old self-satirising crim-speak when talking to other faces from the fraternity. 'That's well out of order,' added Drake, mirroring Crane's indignation while also picking up on Crane's style of dialogue which so often seemed to have come from off of the telly.

'This is it, Harry,' said Crane. 'Do you know what? They're fucking uncouth, these people are. Fucking animals.'

'But Frank, that's why you wanted them,' said Drake. This mild criticism of his fearsome boss would come over as sturdy independence and made him a valued advisor. It was the impertinence born of loyalty presenting a subtle form of sycophancy at which Drake excelled.

Crane was now wondering why he had ever thought that people like this could be suitable business partners. The more he thought about it, the more he realised that he had been seduced by the idea of being a world-class player.

At the same time Crane contradictorily found himself increasingly uncertain about domestically reared employees. He'd only recently had to let a girl go who'd been on his staff for over two years. He'd suddenly felt queasy about her. He couldn't explain why but he'd had to go with it: when someone agitated his antennae he was never at ease. And God knows those antennae had served him well over the years. And she hadn't been the first.

For Crane, getting rid of someone when they were on the inside was a delicate business. There was no question of firing them. Even if they weren't 'in the know' about the full truth of his business affairs because they could never see the full picture, they knew quite a lot, so they had to be detached *gently*. The fact that there was an unwritten non-disclosure agreement in play had to be made very clear to them. As for the shedding process: they'd be moved to the outer circle, maybe assigned to Cropper Dubois, where they could be eased gently away from Crane's affairs to one of their genuinely respectable clients.

So what was it about an indigenous employee that made him uneasy? They understood too much. They had their own points of reference, their own understanding of things – too much baggage. That's what had made Georgi Tsanko such a good proposition. Clean slate, uncomplicated, he was dependable because he depended. These were the sort of people Crane needed. He only wished all the Board members could have been a bit more like Tsanko. That was one of the reasons why Crane wanted to do something about the poor sod's foot. Roy Bloody Faulds had never said anything about damaged goods. *I should have got discount.* If there was one thing a goodbye man didn't need was a visible trademark. The limp would have to go.

'Georgi, my boy, I'm sending you to hospital; you're going to have an operation.'

30

What an amazing asset, thought Cropper, what a wicked little app. Surely a game-changer in negotiations and so on. And far too valuable to be wasted on Drake out in the wilds of Hounslow; he'd bring her into Cropper Dubois to see what she could do.

A few days later Mo was employed as a general assistant at the offices in Charles Street, Mayfair for a trial fortnight while they ran some background checks. For Mo this was the most formidable part of the ordeal. She knew what kind of people she was working for and that, particularly in the early days, they'd almost certainly have her under surveillance. Guessing that Cropper Dubois would monitor her mobile phone, she'd kept it spotless. As soon as she had arrived in the UK she had begun a routine of calling her mother every morning so that a record of the routine was established. This measure, along with intensive daily rehearsals with Kang and Shin, made Mo confident of her communications. She was also reasonably satisfied with the arrangements she had made to prevent anyone from discovering that she was related to the wretched Han now languishing in his military hospital. She had simply become someone else.

Using a forged passport, she had assumed the identity of a high school contemporary who, after a bitter quarrel with her unloving and now divorced parents, disappeared to Europe, severing all her local connections. Her father had since died and her impoverished mother quickly agreed to Mo's proposal. In exchange for a monthly payment she agreed, if asked, to identify Mo as her daughter and have some pictures of Mo taken at various ages ready to display in her apartment. As for Mo herself, she would say that 'Mo' was merely her nickname.

Mo was quick to pick up the essentials of her new employment: the tasks and routines, the culture of the organisation, the hierarchies and the politics of the relationships. This was partly down to her experience, but her special skill gave her a distinct advantage.

Dubois, much less scary than the charmless Cropper, frequently took her along to client meetings and social functions as well as some of the bars and restaurants used by business associates and rivals to see what could be gleaned. The answer was quite a lot.

To her colleagues she seemed quite uncurious about everything that went on: she just did her work and went home, and the day came when Cropper Dubois pronounced the new recruit clean as a whistle and offered her up to Crane for his household staff at 27 Brompton Crescent.

Mo became one of four personal assistants who provided round-the-clock cover for the great man. They shared a quiet admiration and fear of Crane and a moderate tolerance of each other. Crane usually rose at six and whichever of his four assistants was on the early shift would arrive at seven (unless they had worked late the night before and slept in a flat in the staff quarters on the top floor). On most days Crane would be at his office by nine, but sometimes he would work at home, in which case Maurice Betts, Crane's money man, would arrive at around 9.30 and later lunch with Crane. Adele Crane, having spent the morning in her first-floor office dealing with household affairs, social engagements or her charities, would usually go out for a rich-girls' lunch at a chic restaurant.

At first Mo's duties were mundane – organising meetings and social functions, taking Crane's dog, Debbie, for a walk around the block, booking theatre tickets, making travel arrangements and helping Mrs Crane to compile lists of potential guests for charity functions. Sometimes she would accompany Crane to Saffron House with Cropper Dubois and one of the accountants. Mo had one routine of her own that she quietly insisted on and everyone tolerated – even Crane. She would call her mother most days at around 10 a.m. – 6 p.m. in Seoul – and they'd have an anxious-mother-and-caring-daughter chat. Mo would tell her what she was doing, how work was going, what movie she had seen and so on. Then she would ask about her mother's news – what was her neighbour up to now? Had she heard from the landlord about the tiles by the front gutter?

Although by this stage of her life Mo had learned that charm was often the weapon of choice for nasty people – until it failed – she was annoyed with herself for finding Crane pleasant and attractive. He even seemed genuinely concerned for her welfare, but maybe that was because he valued the extra set of antennae she provided him. At the same time Mo was unsettled by her boss's watchfulness and the latent menace that seemed to lurk beneath the surface of his charm.

Crane for his part succumbed to the sort of mildly racist

stereotyping of a stereotypical Chelmsford lad who'd had a high time of it in Pattaya and formed an Estuarine-shaped assumption that this Asian doll was another quietly ruthless mercenary who'd pitched up in the UK with an eye for the main chance. Well, he'd give her that chance. She got on well with the other girls, her special skill offered a level of intelligence-gathering that could give him a vital advantage over his business rivals, she had no local baggage. She was an asset to his permanent staff, a model Janissary.

The hours of training soon began to reap rewards. Mo passed Shin and Kang a wealth of detail on Crane's activities, associates, friends, corporate structure, addresses, deals, timings, trading figures, bank accounts, all of which the two men compiled into a growing dossier. At first much of the material seemed no more than innocent organisational detail, but as Mo became familiar with the many facets of Crane's commercial empire she learned to understand its workings, its half-truths and lies, its distortions of facts, the figures of speech needed to reconcile the sometimes conflicting needs of regulators, Revenue officials and the transformation of grubby banknotes harvested on desperate streets into profits with an impeccable pedigree. In all these dealings she sought to find any correlation between apparently legitimate commerce and the bare-knuckle end of things which was run from the offices of Cropper Dubois. Most of all, she was searching for the existence somewhere within Crane's empire of a man with a limp.

31

An urgent request from Spider for a face-to-face was the only reason in the world that would have permitted Cropper to postpone a meeting with Crane. And Crane understood; Cropper set off for Hounslow.

Spider was waiting for him and immediately gave Cropper the news.

'He's a High Access freelance called Glyn Owen and he's been very busy, made a few connections. Thought he'd covered his tracks and he nearly had.'

'You done well,' said Cropper, but he needed to know much more – most importantly, who was Owen working for? They'd have to extract those answers from him quickly, so who better for the task than Georgi Tsanko? Of course, Cropper could never have guessed that Owen was a sole trader who wasn't working for anyone.

Cropper and Dubois made the necessary arrangements to snatch Owen at his cottage in the country where there were less likely to be any interruptions, but just before they did, Owen left and went to London. It had to be Plan B.

Cropper briefed Tsanko accordingly.

32

It wasn't easy for Mo. Every second of every waking day she was fearful of making a slip, that some investigation by Cropper's people might reveal her link to Han, that her story might betray some inconsistency.

It all happened soon after Thermidor had started following Crane, gathering information on his contacts, his routine and his people. The operation called for the highest calibre of surveillance. The CEO's chauffeur was, of course, much more than a chauffeur; his car was always accompanied by one, sometimes two unobtrusive security guys on motorbikes who kept their distance. Mrs Crane had a minder with her wherever she went. There were at least two staff inside the house at every hour of the day and night; sometimes there'd be a couple of people in a parked car or van in the road keeping watch over the house and over Crane when he emerged to walk Debbie before he went to bed. Any contractors who came to work in the road – tree surgeons, or utility engineers – always had their credentials checked. On top of all this was a pair of gloomy Romanians with dark waterproofs and large dogs who patrolled the road at random intervals through the day and night; as in many other expensive neighbourhoods, the residents had clubbed together to hire their own security.

In these circumstances surveillance wasn't easy, but by using remotely controlled cameras in parked cars or trees they gradually assembled a picture of the house, its people and their routines. Lights came on in the big office soon after 7.00 a.m.; Crane's driver would arrive at 8.45am and have a cigarette with the cleaner under the porch of the side door. Any deliveries would be taken in by the Filipino housekeeper. The arrival of Maurice Betts's at 9.30 was roughly when one of Crane's office staff, an Oriental Asian girl in her twenties, probably a PA or something, would appear at the window of the main office talking on her mobile; there were occasional visitors, usually chauffeur-driven. The Asian girl would often come out for a cigarette with an Eastern European crop-haired toughie who they assumed was security. Certain members of staff took it in turns to walk a small King Charles spaniel around the neighbouring blocks but it was almost always Crane himself who took the dog out last thing at night.

After surveying the scene for some time Colza found his attention focusing on the Asian girl at the window – and not just because she was cute. She would appear at the window several times throughout the day, but for her first appearance of the morning there was something oddly emphatic in her delivery that differed from the other calls.

It was a long time before he understood what she was doing. But when he did it was a key moment for Thermidor – the moment they realised that they weren't the only ones who had Crane in their sights.

*

Not easy to find, but Colza reckoned he'd found it. Beautifully concealed in a tree branch using bark and lichen, a camera with a high magnification lens. He went to tell Ludo and Clay.

'Okay, this is how I think it works. The girl is usually at the window talking on the phone at roughly 10 a.m. But that phone call is just a cover. She seems to be talking to someone on the phone but she's actually communicating with someone *outside* the house.'

'How is she doing that?' asked Clay.

Colza paused before delivering his triumphant conclusion.

'Someone is reading her lips.'

'I don't understand,' said Ludo. 'So what would anyone inside the room hear?'

'She is making a genuine phone call and having a proper conversation but when the other person is talking and she is meant to be listening she is actually silently mouthing the information to her confederate outside.'

'Not bad, Colza,' said Ludo. 'Not bad at all.'

'Two ears and the tail,' said Clay.

Thermidor knew nothing about Mo, let alone who she might be working for, but on the 'my-enemy's-enemy-is-my-friend' principle they agreed to risk confronting her.

33

It was lunch-time on a weekday and Mo was queuing in the Knightsbridge sandwich bar, looking forward to her break in the sunshine. She felt a light nudge in the small of her back that made her turn round. There were two of them; the shorter one nearer her was holding a large notepad across his chest.

'I'm sorry,' he said and as he adjusted the pad he revealed four handwritten lines in thick very clear felt-tip capitals. It was easy for Mo to read but impossible for anyone else. As she saw the words her world crumpled. She was overcome with a leaden despair.

WE KNOW YOUR GAME. WE CAN HELP. YOU'LL BE SAFE. FOLLOW US. Mo had no choice.

34

Mo paid for her food and drink and followed the two men to a secluded bench in the small public garden.

'Please sit,' one of them ordered without looking at her. 'Look ahead. You are by yourself. We are separate and are apparently having our own conversation. Please eat your food and please listen.'

And so she did. Anyone looking at the bench would have seen two men engrossed in conversation, heads close together, ignoring a solitary girl eating her sushi.

'My name is Ludo and this is Clay. Firstly, you don't need to be scared. You must keep looking ahead. We know what you are doing. We also have a substantial interest in Mr Frank Crane but we need to know your purpose. You must keep eating your sushi. You need to tell us why you are doing this. Who are you really working for – taking this terrible risk?'

Mo said nothing.

'We are pretty certain that you want what we want.' It was still the taller man doing the talking. 'So why are you doing this?'

Mo knew there was no point in delaying; these two had her life in their hands. 'For what Crane did to my family.' And, dabbing her lips with a paper napkin to hide the fact that she was talking, she briefly told them about Customs Officer Han.

'What's your plan?'

'I'm not quite sure yet.'

'We can help.'

'Why are *you* doing this?' she asked.

The taller man, who was called Ludo and had his back to her, answered.

'For the same reason as you. To destroy them.'

Mo closed the lid on the barely eaten sushi. 'I need to get back. What happens now?'

'We will now leave. You stay here and finish your lunch. We know you are collaborating with others. Tell one of your friends to be here tomorrow afternoon at 15.05. We can make arrangements for us all to talk properly and then we can tell you how Han was betrayed. Meanwhile, good luck and keep safe.'

At a second, lengthier meeting following the sandwich shop encounter the Korean trio and Thermidor began a massive exchange of information concerning Crane, Cropper & Dubois. By far the most important piece of evidence to come from Mo and her two associates was Mo's story of Cropper's rendezvous with the man on a bike which had taken place more than twelve months before.

35

The West's security agencies have more to fear
from penetration by serious criminal interests than
the agents of foreign governments.

Prof. Glyn Owen

Mo had been in Crane's office taking notes of a discussion he was having with Cropper when there was a buzz from Cropper's cell phone. She recognised the emergency ringtone.

After listening for a moment he interrupted his caller.

'Wait a moment.' He turned to Crane. 'Spider,' he said, nodding in Mo's direction. 'She needs to go.'

When Crane called her back into the office twenty minutes later, Cropper was on his mobile asking for his diary for the next day to be cleared between eleven and three. That night Mo risked an emergency contact with Shin and Kang to tell them they must follow Cropper the next day.

With Shin and his violin case in the passenger seat of their hire car, Kang tailed Cropper's SUV on to the M4 until it turned off at Junction 2; from there he followed it to Gunnersbury Park where it stopped in the shadow of some trees. Cropper got out and walked over to a cluster of picnic tables which were unoccupied apart from a young man in serious cycling gear with a pedigree racing bike lying on the grass beside him. Shin got as close as he dared and, from the cover of some shrubs, took his video camera and telephoto lens from the violin case. When the two men left, Shin and Kang followed the cyclist, who headed west, but only a bike can trail a bike and in the car Kang couldn't follow unnoticed so he soon lost him.

Mo didn't appreciate the crucial significance of the location, but for Clay and Ludo, familiar with Glyn Owen's Swanborne File and its references to the Park, one possibility was too tempting. Gunnersbury was close to Osterley Park, the operational head-quarters of MI6 which housed its intelligence hub, the Combined Operational Security Data Centre (COSDC), containing details of officers and agents at home and abroad. The timing of Cropper's rendezvous in the park with the cyclist was also significant: six days before the kidnapping of Glyn Owen.

Thermidor's first task was to find out if the cyclist was still working at the Park now, almost a year later. Colza took Shin and a Thermidor surveillance team out to Osterley, where they staked out the two roads leading to the entrance and for three successive days photographed every cyclist coming in and going out. A pollution mask, wrap-around goggles and skid lid didn't leave much of a person to identify, but only one of them matched the video of the man with a bike seen in Gunnersbury Park with Cropper. As he zipped past, Shin gave the signal to Thermidor's two cyclists waiting nearby and they followed him to his home.

Their target turned out to be Ricky Phibbs, a twenty-six-year-old Cambridge physics graduate and one of the platoon of brilliant young brains who developed, managed and serviced round the clock the phalanxes of encrypting software which protected MI6's most crucial data from cyber attack. Ricky did not go to many social occasions, but when people asked him what he did, he would say he worked 'in Defence Procurement on comparative production cost analysis'. They didn't press him any further because although they suspected it was a bit top secret it also sounded pretty boring.

Phibbs's official job title within the Service was Encryption Supervision Officer, but given that he was searching out and selling some of the OSDC's most sensitive information, a more accurate title would be Traitor, Grade One. The fact was that Phibbs, like most of his colleagues in the building, would have earned more money as a primary school head teacher and the temptation to augment one's salary was powerful. Thermidor discovered that the root of his treachery lay in a gambling habit which took the form of some serious plays in the precious metals markets. It had made him hopelessly beholden to Frank Crane – not that Ricky knew it was Crane because he dealt only with an intermediary.

At lunchtime on the day of his appointment with Mr Cranford, Phibbs logged off from the terminal in his glass cubicle in the most secure part of C3 and told his colleagues that he was going out on his routine training run. He took the lift up to the ground floor and a few minutes later emerged from the locker room in his RoHo cycling kit with the BB helmet; after passing through three sets of security doors he made his way to the car park. There he unlocked his beloved Hoffman 270, which weighed almost as much as a teaspoon, headed for the main perimeter gates and rode out into the ordinary world. Within fifteen minutes of leaving his terminal Phibbs was speeding along the back roads to Gunnersbury Park, where he found Mr Cranford waiting.

Phibbs had been fed with a list of sensitive search terms with instructions to report when they were accessed and who by. During his duty rota he'd clandestinely spun a web of meta trip-tag clusters across the main database. This had been a high-risk, time-consuming task because he had had to set up a plausible pretext (e.g. unscheduled maintenance) to switch off the cyber-security patrol programs or 'brushes' which check for debris and intrusions. In essence, Phibbs, the Spider, was rigging temporary nets across various paths in the form of pieces of pulsed code which morphed into undetectable configurations at the approach of any cyber-security patrol. And it worked. Eventually something got caught in one of his traps. From this, Spider established that at a number of the sensitive files were being accessed by someone with Level Four Clearance which meant they were outside the Park.

A firewall prevented Phibbs from finding out who it was but Cropper Dubois owned people in all the right places, among them a divorcee called Marian Close who worked on the other side of the firewall at GCHQ, Cheltenham. Recently impoverished and embittered by the evaporation of her investments at the hands of a crooked personal financial adviser, she fell prey to an offer from Cropper Dubois. When she received the co-ordinates from Phibbs via Cropper, it was the work of moments for her to come up with the name.

It was a high-graded consultant intelligence researcher called Glyn Owen.

36

They lay there locked together flickering on the edge of wakefulness, sometimes slipping into sleep. Maybe an hour had passed like this when he felt Mo's body tighten. She drew his head towards hers and kissed him. Not gently, but in a desperate way which alarmed him. He knew that she was trying to evade the fearful thoughts that were chasing her. They made love again, escaping in each other.

'I will protect you. You will come to no harm.'

'Only I can protect myself.'

There was a long silence before Clay spoke.

'Remember, I'm never far from you – me, my people, your guys, we're all close, ready to bring you out.' They both heard the soft sound of the car.

'You have to go now,' he said. 'When shall I see you again?'

'I can't say,' she said. 'It's getting so risky.' In silence they contemplated the terrible looming void.

'You will keep your vow to your family,' Clay said. 'That is my vow to you.'

When he heard about it Ludo was furious. It was a fury fuelled by fear. This Clay and Mo business was the last thing Thermidor needed. This crazy infringement of basic security procedures put them all at hazard. Ludo became depressed; this uncalled-for development could be their undoing – and a couple of times it damn nearly was. But Thermidor depended on Mo's information. Thermidor had no choice but to do as best it could.

'We can take you away at any time – now.'

'No, I need longer to do what I came to do,' she said. 'I will stay until they've had their meeting.'

That was when they began to plot.

37

One fine day – actually it was pelting down, but Ludo would always remember it as a fine day – an envelope had finally arrived containing the transcript of Owen's Gangster State lecture from the now nearly defunct Hedley Coram secretariat. Ludo took it to his desk and hurriedly turned to the final section, searching for text that Owen would have delivered after they had all moved upstairs to the Balmoral room. He found a section on Extreme Criminal Impunity that was not in the earlier version. A chilling list of examples of the phenomenon Owen had gathered from abroad culminated in a variation from the Policy Studio text.

Extreme Criminal Impunity need not be confined to banana republics or the lands of the Stans but could embrace the legitimately ordered countries of Northern Europe. And, yes, that could include the United Kingdom.

Could, for instance, that scenario I earlier described of a bureaucrat being threatened in a railway station car park befall of our civil servants in Wokingham or Pinner?

Our United Kingdom is surely qualified to make a bid for Gangster State status? Why shouldn't our police be thoroughly corrupted? They have been before – swathes of officers have been fired in a succession of metropolitan and regional purges. We know our Prison Service has been infiltrated by criminals who get jobs as warders so they can smuggle drugs. What if our Security Services were to be penetrated by criminal forces, just as they were by foreign intelligence agencies during the Cold War?

If I ask you what prevents these things from happening here, you will probably argue that it is *culturally* impossible for us to let our institutions succumb to criminal domination. It is not in our nature. That sort of thing happens elsewhere. But there is no 'elsewhere' any more. Borders are a figment. There used to be talk of 'the end of history'. Well, it was not history but geography that ended.

Britain's uniquely specialist contributions to criminality are pretty much limited to Six Counties Knee-capping and Financial Services (aka money laundering), but globalisation has opened our doors to a raft of new possibilities to enrich our own sparse criminal menu.

We have Arabians to whip domestic servants, Somalis who can offer female genital mutilation and Kurds to run protection rackets. Indian sub-continentals have brought us facially disfiguring acid attacks, Nigerians are masters of financial scams, Tanzanians trade in the body parts of murdered albinos, while there are Congolese and Ugandans who may pass the time with some ritual child sacrifice.

These exotic specialities have all found accommodation in the mild British climate of benign tolerance, post-colonial guilt and a sort of pro-active languor. There is no reason why Extreme Criminal Impunity cannot do the same.

Well, I can report to you that it has.

Ludo sensed his pulse quicken.

It is an unspoken truth that one of our larger police forces has been infiltrated at a high level by organised crime and lives in terror of the consequences. Colleagues in other forces regard it as institutionally criminal and co-operation is routinely refused by other forces because they do not trust many of its officers. A number of public servants in the fields of law enforcement, the judiciary have met suspicious deaths and national employees have almost certainly been suborned. The threats uttered to a public servant in a station car park actually did occur on UK soil – Chorleywood, in case you're interested.

It may be wrong to shout fire in a crowded theatre, but if anyone happens to notice smoke rising from the footlights, they are obliged to mention it to those whose duty is to deal with it.

That is what I have tried to do in addressing you today.

Thank you.

Ludo thought back to the night Colza returned from Swanborne with a newspaper report of a 'Foxhunting Field Riot' two centuries ago and read out the final paragraph.

> With all but thirty paces separating the fox from the hounds, those leading the field saw Mr Reynard draw to a halt and come back on his own course towards his pursuers. When their paths met he set about the dogs with great spirit before he was dispatched by weight of their superior numbers. Careless, at eight years, the veteran of the pack was found to have bites to his muzzle and several others had sustained injuries. Our inquiries have failed to discover a precedent for this remarkable occurrence.

Now he understood.

The long-dead fox had presented a moment of epiphany for Owen. The tale of the Swanborne Fox was a stark parable for Extreme Criminal Impunity, one of the defining conditions of the Gangster State in which high harm criminals hunted down any members of the police and security forces who threatened them. In the first version of his Gangster State lecture at the Policy Studio he had identified it as a phenomenon present in foreign states and warned of it as a potential threat to the UK. By the time Owen came to speak at Hedley Coram he had discovered that it was already entrenched. And that was his desperate message to Angela from the edge of his life. His very last words on earth were, 'The riot is with us now'.

38

'It has all come down to cultural differences. Crane likes to keep everything low profile; some other Board members do not. For Pallengro the Gypsy, for instance, it isn't enough to be making money by illegal means; he needs everyone to know it.'

Ludo was addressing a gathering of Thermidor operatives and was giving what Clay called, 'a tour of the horizon'.

'The law is for the small people. *He*, Pallengro, is above it and must be seen to be above it. His power lies in his reputation, which is measured by the volume of the sound of the skulls he cracks. Crane shuns publicity; his criminal partners revel in it. For Crane, violence is a last resort; for his associates it is the first.

'The problem,' said Ludo, 'is that Crane's entire operation depends on his alliance with these people remaining clandestine; if he was to be seen with any one of them his whole position would be compromised.

'Crane has been trying to warn the Board that they were putting their collaboration in jeopardy but to no avail. No amount of encrypted messages, trusted emissaries, secure lines, party phone calls or video conferencing made any difference. He realised he'd have to talk to them all face to face. He'd have to show that he wasn't just a decent club player but could hold his own at international level and that you didn't have to be born in a cave in the Caucasus to have the skillset and the bottle for the work. So Crane did what he had to do, even though it was the last thing he wanted: he called a meeting of the Board.'

Ludo explained that the idea of Val de Ligne as the venue came from Dubois, who had skied there a couple of times. In his Foreign Office days on the North African desk he'd read about the talks conducted between the French and the Algerian rebels in the Sixties. Secrecy had been vital to prevent either party's more hawkish followers finding out; ski gear was useful in disguising the Arab and other delegates.

Crane had approved the idea. The plan was for Dubois, who spoke good French, to go to Val with Mo to prepare for the event and oversee it. Cropper would stay in London.

39

As soon as Mo told them that the venue was to be a secluded chalet called Messigny in Val de Ligne, Clay and Colza flew out in advance to do a recce for what promised to be a both technically tricky and extremely hazardous operation.

'We've got a raft of evidence against Crane but,' as Ludo pointed out, 'if we can show Crane to be associating with some of the very worst international high harm criminals, we'll have brought him down.'

Ludo had strong views as to how Thermidor would release its evidence. No point in going to the authorities. With his criminal lawyers and his rotten contacts in high places they'd be lucky if he even got a speeding ticket. No. Only one way to do this: put all their evidence in the public domain, whip up a frenzy of international indignation, enough to create a firestorm of interest that would outflank Crane and the Board's placemen in all the jurisdictions and force the relevant authorities to act.

Excited by this prospect as he was, Ludo tried to contain his expectations. *The consequences may not be as dramatic as you'd like. Don't assume the world will be put to rights. You want bangs; you end up with whimpers.* It didn't stop him indulging in the prospect of an almighty media eruption that would unmask a worldwide rabble of politicians, officials and collaborators followed by a welter of arrests, sackings, surprise resignations, disappearances and, who knows, maybe some suicides. The exposure of Crane and the Board would be the climax of Thermidor's work. Owen would have been avenged.

40

Europe is always telling us that there has to be a
political not a military solution. This is not correct.

General Uğur Ozkan, Turkish regional army
commander in operations against the PKK in an
interview in Turkish Voice.

Even the humblest employees of an organisation can be valuable sources, which is why Mo made an effort to befriend everyone on Crane's staff at every level. Among the regular Knightsbridge security men, for instance, was a pleasant young Eastern European. Mo often found herself alone with him for long periods while they waited for Crane to emerge from meetings; they got to know each other quite well.

Swarthy, with cropped dark hair and a pleasant open face, he had little education or conversation and wasn't someone Mo would naturally befriend, but they were both foreigners in a strange land and they had the shared experience of working for Cropper Dubois. Moreover, the conscientious and twitchy Tsanko was a loner who sometimes got lonely and needed to talk.

When he learned that Mo was from Korea, Tsanko said he had been there once on business but only for a few days. Mo's pulse began to race: he might be the man to lead to her 'Wui Chon'. Careful not to press him too obviously, she talked a bit about her own past and offered small confidences to encourage him to tell her more about his. Bit by bit she pieced together the story of his childhood, military service in Turkey, his duties for Mr Kalomiris and the nightlife on Vitosha Boulevard, where everybody knew Georgi Tsanko.

'One day when I have made money I go a long way from here and have easy life.'

'Where will you go?' asked Mo.

'New Zealand. New Zealand is beautiful country.'

They were having a cigarette outside the entrance of a light engineering firm on an industrial estate on the outskirts of Leicester where Crane was attending a meeting.

'You've been to New Zealand or just seen it on TV?'

'Of course – on business. I will buy small farm. My family too can come.'

'You may never see your village again,' said Mo. 'It's a long way from your country.'

'This why New Zealand has no war. It is so far away it has only peace.'

'So have you been in a war, Tsanko?'

'Yes, in mountains in Turkey. In the East.'

'Was it a big war?'

'Any war seem big if you are in it.'

Tsanko told her of the Kurdish rebels' fight for independence in a long and dirty struggle against the Turks. He told her how the Kurdish PKK forces would ambush Turkish army patrols, take control of villages, committing atrocities before disappearing back into the mountains. The Turks would arrive and take reprisals and these reprisals would prompt reprisals and so it went on. Tsanko was in the worst of it and came to know well the smell of burning flesh. Crane's reappearance brought an end to Tsanko's gruesome memories and her boss's dictation kept Mo busy on the journey back to Knightsbridge. She welcomed the distraction.

For most of the time Tsanko was around the house with the others minding Crane, but occasionally he would be absent for days. He would offer no explanation to Mo, who knew better than to ask for one; however, Mo did find that although Tsanko was extremely discreet about his work for Crane he was always happy to talk about himself.

'They looked like they *smiled* at us. Was bad,' said Tsanko, his voice hoarse and somehow distant.

'Smiling is bad?' asked Mo.

Tsanko said nothing. Mo pressed him gently.

'Tell me about the smiling, Tsanko,' she said. And he did.

He told her about the morning in the second summer of his military service. The war was not going well for the Turkish army. Tsanko was with his unit on patrol in a notoriously dangerous valley when they received orders to go to the support of another company which had been ambushed three kilometres away.

By the time they got there it was too late; the patrol had surrendered. At the approach of Tsanko's unit, the rebels retreated but not before killing their prisoners and laying out the corpses in a row on the rocky hillside.

Tsanko's commanding officer wanted reprisals. He led his troops to the nearest Kurdish-occupied village – it was called Kasrik – and there a killing spree began. Egged on by their officers, the men behaved like butchers gone berserk. The obscenity culminated in the selection of a dozen prisoners who were taken to the open ground in the centre of village. There the commander gave the order.

Tsanko's tone, which had been flat and matter of fact, now changed; his throat grew hoarse and the words became forced.

'What was this order, Georgi?' asked the soothing Mo.

'He ordered us to make the prisoners smile.'

Mo reached over and put her palm on his warm damp brow.

'What happened next?'

Tsanko had seen bad things; this was the worst. In the following days his mind was flooded with visions of mutilated faces on the rocky hillside, of the massacre at Kasrik. It was three days before he snapped. No cathartic rage, no running amok: one night while on sentry duty he simply put down his automatic and walked away from the camp. After three or four hours he stopped, crawled into a rock crevice and slept.

When he awoke his mind was calm; he faced the dreadful

realisation of his crime. He had deserted his post in hostile territory. He knew what he had to do and set off to rejoin his comrades, but by that time a search party from his platoon had been sent out, and unfortunately for Tsanko they saw him first. He was given a bad beating and dragged back to camp. His prospects were not good.

Tsanko's punishment, one specifically devised for deserters, was carried out in the course of a Friday parade. The regiment was drawn up in three sides of a hollow square; the Sergeant of Colours brought out the wooden block and a junior orderly followed carrying a large white-painted rock taken from the circular kerb around the flagpole outside the guardhouse. There was a doctor in attendance.

Tsanko, hands bound behind his back, was marched forward flanked by two of the largest troopers in the unit. They took off the boot and sock from the prisoner's right foot, placed the foot on the wooden block and held his leg firm. The adjutant read out the charge; the Colonel nodded in assent and the rock came crashing down.

Following an inexpert bone-setting operation by a trainee surgeon, Tsanko spent a week in an army hospital.

'Then they send me to *disko*, eighteen months. Is very bad.'

'Disco?' said Mo, puzzled.

'Is prison for military. Bad people there. Then they send me out of army.'

'I am sorry to hear all this.'

'No, is alright now.'

Tsanko's next words came out of the darkness and seemed to strike Mo's whole body.

'Mr Crane he paid for operation to reset bones or I still be limping bad today.'

Waves of elation and hatred surged and swirled through Mo's head.

'What is wrong?' asked Tsanko, startled by her sudden movement.

'It is a horrible story,' Mo replied. *My search is over but I must keep control.* 'I'm sorry you suffered like this.'

'It is past,' said Tsanko, reaching out to touch her naked body.

'You must sleep,' she said tenderly. Then, in her desire to protect what she planned to destroy, she gently pulled up the bed sheet to cover his shoulders.

41

'That's not enough,' said Mo.

'It's how Ludo wants to settle his obligation to Owen.'

'What about me? What about Han and my promise to my sister!'

'Sssshhh.' Clay tried to soothe her, stroking the soft skin of her back.

'No, they'll have to be punished more severely than that. That plan has no hope. They'll never even get taken to court. Crane poisons everything he touches. You'd be relying on a system that Crane and people like him have corrupted. Believe me. I know him and how he works. I have been with him for two years now.'

'I'm not alone. This isn't my decision.'

'Then better not confide.'

'Let me think what we can do.'

'You must. I have risked everything. You owe it to me.'

'I know.'

42

Once they had removed his blindfold, Mike's two minders from the forest ambush helped him out of the SUV. They were in a dimly lit garage with room for half a dozen vehicles; so they were under a small apartment block. There was another SUV, a couple of motorbikes, and one of the breezeblock walls was almost covered by a neat log stack. In one corner were various piles of cardboard boxes, a couple of kids' mountains bikes and a purple space hopper.

A man, probably late twenties, in a ski jacket was waiting at the door to the internal staircase. He was wearing a Bluetooth earpiece and microphone.

'Hello, Mr Warne, I'm Colza. Welcome!' He was your typical smiley and efficient high-end travel rep, salt-of-the-middle-class-earth. 'Would you please follow me.' He took Mike through to a boot room, handed him some leather moccasins and led the way up a couple of flights of stairs, through a hallway and into the kitchen of a small apartment.

'Take a seat,' said Colza, waving Mike to the table. 'Some tea or coffee or something?'

'Tea would be good, thank you.'

'I should say straight away you are in safe hands – which I imagine is more than can be said for previous hosts?'

'I hope so,' said Mike.

'The people who snatched you are looking for you all over town so it is important that you don't leave this building. If you do try you will be forcibly restrained. That's for your good as well as ours. Everything will be explained to you shortly. Meanwhile we must just ask you to accept your circumstances and trust us. Can we do that?'

Mike nodded. He didn't really have a choice and at that moment he didn't even want one.

'Supper is at eight o'clock but can we offer you something to eat now? There is some quite nice cheese.'

After his high stress day, the warmth of the chalet and the simple offer of hospitality told his brain he suddenly felt overwhelmed with tiredness.

'I wouldn't say no to a bit of a kip.'

'Of course. I'll take you to your quarters. Why don't you bring your tea.'

Colza led him down to a basement room with its own shower room and a small, very shallow window just below the ceiling.

'Just bang on the door if you need anything.'

Mike kicked off his borrowed shoes, lay on the bed fully dressed and went out like a light.

When he awoke, his body was aching and his head felt muzzy. He looked at his watch; it was almost 6.50 p.m. Occasionally his right knee went into a tiny involuntary spasm as if it had a memory of its own. The facts of his situation started to arrive in his brain in an incoherent order. *I have been rescued in the forest. I have been kidnapped. I have lost the Team's video. I just have to bang on the door. The memory stick thief had a chrome syringe. There is some quite nice cheese. A very cold chisel is stroking my knee. I am a guest of a Non-Governmental Organisation.* Mike stared at his half-empty mug of tea; it seemed to be his only friend in the world.

I don't have to bang on any door. I am not a prisoner. He tried the handle. It wasn't locked and he stepped into the corridor. At that moment a figure came round the corner. It was Colza. He looked Mike up and down.

'Have we lost our shoes, Mike?' He sounded as if he was dealing with some dementia patient in an old people's home. 'Let's pop back in there and get them, shall we?' He ushered Mike back into his room. 'Then we can go up and meet the boss.'

43

Colza took Mike across the corridor and through a door into a large apartment with a double-height living room dominated a big stone fireplace. One wall consisted of tall partition doors, from beyond which came the clattering of cutlery.

'You can use this place at any time but you have to be ready to evacuate at a moment's notice. As you can see from the wall notice we are on Threat Level Orange. We have a range of emergency drills to test our readiness. More details later, but if you hear the alarm in the meantime you come up here pronto, okay? Supper is at 8.00 but tonight you'll be eating with our Director of Operations at around 7.30. On the comms front, we found your phone in the car and we'll be taking care of it. Okay? Let's go and see the Director then.'

Colza led the way up to the second floor and knocked on one of the doors leading off the small hall and without waiting for a reply, ushered Mike through a living room into a spacious bedroom with a desk and a sofa. There were four chairs around a table by the window. 'They never put the bloody plugs in the right place, do they? Colza, we're going to need another power-bar here.'

Mike traced the speaker to the owner of a pair of legs protruding from beneath the desk. He recognised the voice immediately and, sure enough, the short stocky figure that got up to greet him was, as Mike expected, the man who robbed him on the chairlift and gave him the dire warning in the bubble. Now that he had no goggles, Mike could see an impish face with an aggressive jaw; the skin below his eyes was dark with tiredness – combating tax evasion must be really hard work. He wore a T-shirt which announced, HOUSTON, WE HAVE AN ISSUE.

'I'm Clay,' he said, shaking Mike's hand vigorously.

'And I'm Mike Warne.'

'Indeed you are. Indeed. How are you, Mike? Are you recovered from your adventures?'

'Yes, thank you,' Mike lied.

'And are we looking after you properly?' This with a stern glance directed at Colza.

'Indeed.'

'One does one's best. Do you have everything you need?'

'I seem to be missing a Gideon bible.' Mike was struggling to retain some initiative.

'No problem. We'll get customer services on to that. Okay, Colza, thank you; that'll be all for the moment.'

Colza left and Clay sat down at the desk.

'Very good to have you on board, Mike. I need to explain a few things and bring you up to date. A certain amount has happened since we had our little chat.'

Mike looked around the room. On the table there were half a dozen cell phones in a neat row marked with different coloured tapes; on the desk sat an open laptop and a tray of papers.

Clay waved Mike to the sofa.

'First thing: your boy racer pals are all safe and well and staying with us at another location. They're in good spirits but getting a bit restless; like you they're confined to barracks.' He paused and looked hard at Mike for a moment.

'The thing is: where do we start?'

'Maybe the beginning?' said Mike.

'Good God, no!' Clay sounded genuinely appalled.

'I'm sorry.'

'Broader picture later but to put it at its simplest, our organisation has an interest in the recent comings and goings at Chalet Messigny.'

'What is your organisation?' Mike interrupted but Clay ignored him.

'Tell me about Messigny. Odd that your people turned up there of all places.'

'We were just passing through.'

'Very unhelpful.'

Mike shrugged. 'They weren't *trying* to be unhelpful.'

'We had a job to do and you fucked it up for us.'

'And we had a movie to make and you certainly fucked it up for us – big-time.'

'I know, I know.'

'This is about the man in white in the trees, isn't it?'

'Yes, him and Mr Kornelius Løvland who gate-crashed the coffee party on the terrace.' Mike detected a hint of amusement in his tone; a schoolmaster reprimanding a child but with grudging admiration for the impertinence of the offence.

'Those people did everything they could to meet in the utmost secrecy. So try, if you will, and imagine how unhappy they were when your long-haired lout appears out of nowhere, videos the entire proceedings and vanishes.

'And it gets worse. A few hours later the organisers of this ultra hush-hush gathering walk into town to find that they're all starring in a movie playing in high definition on 72-inch screens in the middle of town for all to see. You can understand their feelings. They're really very cross, you know.'

'Tell me about it. I had a bit of a chat with one of them this afternoon.'

Clay was beginning to learn that, as a conversational player, Harpenden Man was rather more dangerous than he had first suspected.

'Explain something to me, Mike. You must admit it was a remarkable coincidence?'

'Not really. If anyone was walking through the town centre they'd almost certainly pass by Bar X. A couple of the big screens face out onto the pavement. The Couloir Noir video was playing for quite a long time but it's only a short piece of footage on a continuous loop. The chances of them seeing the terrace scene were pretty high. In fact it would be a miracle if they'd missed it.'

'I was actually talking about the chances of your man pitching up at Chalet Messigny with his camera just as everyone comes out on the terrace?'

'We didn't know that. We didn't plan it, if that's what you mean. How would we know whether they were on the terrace or not? Or care?'

'You tell me.'

'That was just chance. We'd done our work at the Couloir Noir and we were skiing home. Messigny was on the route. It's as simple as that.'

'Oh come on.'

'I mean that.'

'But the guests had been in the Chalet all morning; you came by at the one time they were outside. Too good to be true, Mr Warne.' Mike noted that Clay had moved from Mike to Mister, which wasn't encouraging, but he had a good point: it did seem a bit unlikely.

'We had to shoot that day . . . this was the first decent break we'd had in days. Our director was obsessed with the weather. We all talked about it all the time because we were so dependent on it. Saul was always waiting for the sun; he'd hold everyone up for a shot if he thought there was so much as a glimmer coming. And that's what happened before Kornie and the others went by the Chalet. Everyone was tired but Saul made everyone wait. Then, when the sun did appear, he let us go.'

In the silence that followed Mike thought he had a brainwave.

'Maybe when the people in the Chalet saw the sun appear they decided to go outside to enjoy it?'

Occasionally Mike was convinced that he was cleverer than he thought.

All the time they'd been talking Mike noticed Clay's eyes constantly flicking towards the screen on the desk beside him. Now he suddenly got up, opened the door and shouted.

'Colza, this is crazy; someone needs to have a word with Amande and Aunée and put them in the picture quickly. Thank you.'

He came back and sat down again, his eyes fixed, staring disapprovingly at the floor as though the carpet was misbehaving or something.

Mike took advantage of the interruption to try to take the initiative. 'So why was our footage so important to you? Why did you steal it?'

At the word 'steal' Clay closed his eyes and shook his head in irritation.

'Not steal, just borrow.' The words had been spoken by a newcomer who had appeared in the open doorway.

The new arrival was thin: thin bony face, early thirties with an unmilitary demeanour which contrasted with Clay. To Mike he looked a bit academic. He was shy, in a confident sort of a way – perhaps on the edge of being pleased with himself.

'Mike, this is Ludo,' said Clay.

The new arrival extended a languid arm but the handshake on the end of it was firm.

'We needed your video for two reasons,' said Ludo. 'After your gala world premiere at Bar X we realised that your material was much better than anything we had. It had to be. Your man pitching up in the middle of the party with his Access-All-Areas pass and hosing down the guests with his head-cam had to get better stuff than our man in the trees buried in snow a hundred metres away.

'We also had to know if you had got anything of our photographer. We were trying to find you all afternoon.'

'We just went to have some lunch at Michel's.'

'We know that now but we didn't know who you were – let alone where you were – until the evening when we saw the video playing at Bar X. We tried again to get hold of your footage – with your help.'

'You mean with the help of Tyler's phone?'

Ludo nodded.

What kind of an organisation was this? Mike didn't believe Clay's explanation of the Messigny crowd; he could see no connection between the need for chisel-therapy on his knee and a gathering of specialists in serial high-end tax evasion. And Clay with his syringe and his rope trick did not convince as an employee of the Inland Revenue.

'This isn't about income tax at all, is it?' said Mike.

Ludo's slightly pained expression suggested Mike had committed a serious breach of etiquette.

'Not really.'

Ludo's distracted intensity made for a slight awkwardness.

'Well, we've got a lot to talk about, haven't we?' Clay now interrupted brightly.

'We certainly have,' said Mike.

'It's good to have Mike on board, isn't it, Ludo?'

'Indeed,' said Ludo, but he didn't sound too sure. 'Anyway, that'll do for now. Let's meet downstairs at seven o'clock for a drink before supper.'

Ludo and Clay were waiting for him in the living room when Mike appeared.

'First can we offer you a glass of something?' said Clay, gesturing to the fridge in the corner of the room. 'You just need to know you are permitted 175 millilitres of wine per day, so that's a glass, just in case you want to wait until supper and have your drink with your meal.'

'Are you being serious?'

'Yes.'

'I wasn't planning on driving anywhere.' Mike was beginning to wonder about the sanity of his hosts.

'It's a necessary precaution. Same for everyone.'

'I'll wait till supper then. But a glass of water would be most welcome if it doesn't infringe house rules.'

'Of course.' Clay peered into the fridge.

'Is Evian alright?' Mike nodded. 'Ludo?'

'The same, thank you, Clay.'

Mike was trying to come to terms with his situation. It was gone seven, he'd had one hell of a day and the three of them, grown men, were standing there holding glasses of water.

Clay, clearly the more outgoing of the two, led the conversation which was confined to small talk about the resort, the skiing conditions, Mike's favourite runs and so forth. At seven thirty his hosts led the way through the double doors into a large dining room with a long table which could have seated about twenty but was laid for just three at one end; Ludo sat at the head. Mike groaned inwardly as he tasted the grim, nondescript soup.

'Some water?'

Mike had to admit his host was generous with the water.

'Damn good soup, isn't it, eh?' Clay said. Mike didn't know if he was being serious or was just trying to stop him committing suicide. 'Brebis does us proud when he is duty chef. Taught himself.'

'Indeed,' said Ludo. 'I'd say these ingredients have been deceased for quite some time.'

'Oh come on, Ludo, this is good,' said Clay testily.

'As to the cause of death: dried, tinned or frozen? What do you think, Mike?'

'It's great,' Mike lied.

'Or maybe they just died of . . . despair.'

Clay ignored Ludo. He seemed reassured that at least soup-wise Mike was 'on board'.

Mike wondered if he'd have been better off at Ken Simmonds's place. He also kept thinking about Anne's text: R U HAVING A GOOD TIME?

44

'Well, I don't think he'll give us any problems,' said Clay after supper when Mike had retired to his room leaving him alone with Ludo.

'But we'll need to tell him stuff if we're going to get any help from him.'

Ludo agreed that they'd struck lucky with Mike. He seemed trustworthy and Clay, who was the more suspicious and secretive of the two of them, obviously thought so too. Actually Clay's reluctance to be entirely open was causing Ludo some irritation. For instance, he was being particularly uncommunicative about what he was up to down at Thermidor Two. Clay maintained that he was collecting more 'foot soldiers' as 'a precaution'. True, they'd proved their worth that very afternoon in rescuing Mike when he was being taken to Messigny, but this wasn't what Thermidor was about. Its job was to gather information, not to 'go kinetic' but Ludo sensed that going kinetic was all Clay really wanted to do.

'We'll have to keep Mike here,' said Ludo. 'It would be unhelpful if Cropper got him.'

'What are we going to tell him?' said Clay.

'Let me have a think,' said Ludo.

45

Colza: brassica rape, producing rapeseed oil, also
27th day of Thermidor in French Republican calendar.

Encyclopédie Décosse

Mike was woken the next morning by the muffled sound of children coming from the apartment below. He dozed while his brain tried to reassemble the events of the day before.

At 7.30 Colza arrived with a tray of breakfast.

'I must ask you to stay here in your room until ten,' he said. 'Then you can come across to the main living room where you'll be more comfortable. There'll be others around but not much in the way of company. They're all rather pushed at the moment.'

The living room was a thoroughfare linking the entrance corridor, several bedrooms, the dining room and kitchen which had a coffee machine, so Mike had a chance to take a look at the other occupants who came and went throughout the morning.

They were all youngish, mid-thirties at most, apart from an anxious-looking man, probably ten years older, who seemed to be in charge. A large girl with thick pink-framed glasses appeared from time to time, usually to have conversations which involved joshing but beady enquiries about various people's expenses. There was a kooky waif of a creature with a chopstick through her piled-up pale brown hair and a good-looking chestnut-haired City Professional-type. A couple of earnest young men came and went carrying thin files.

The enthusiastic buzz about the place made Mike feel he was in the offices of a charity or maybe a start-up with high hopes. They seemed to have been told to be polite to him but not to fraternise. Any phone calls he managed to overhear were uninformative.

Occasionally one or other of them would acknowledge Mike with a nod when they came into the room, others would courteously ignore him. Once he saw a girl carrying a big box of groceries through to the kitchen. She was a blondish, blue-eyed, chalet-girl type, mid-twenties. When she emerged she threw Mike a warm but controlled smile and said hello, which encouraged him to attempt a conversation.

'You must be Brebis,' he said. She looked puzzled.

'Brebis, the cook?' he added.

The girl put down the groceries, stared at Mike as if he was pond life and walked out without a word. Later Mike heard someone call her Candy. She turned out to be Clay's personal assistant and guard dog; what she most definitely wasn't was the cook.

In the absence of live human company, Mike checked out the bookshelves. Apart from Hoag's *Innocents on Ice*, which was to be found in every chalet in the Alps, it was a small and depressing collection. There were *Churches of the Western Alps* by E.J. Carlton, *Where the Serpents Do Not Tread: the Alps in Romantic Painting and Literature* by Maurice Shepherd, a handful of J.G. Tallon 'Inspector Byron' detective thrillers, a French encyclopaedia, an *Haute Savoie Cookbook* and a floppy book of French crosswords with novelty-shaped grids.

Mike flicked through the encyclopaedia and looked up 'Colza'.

46

That evening, as he sat drinking alone in the hotel
bar, Inspector Byron considered the snow's role
in the crime. It had acted as an accomplice not
only by hiding the corpse but also by covering the
culprit's fleeing footprints. So what else might it be
guilty of?

White Lies, *an Inspector Byron story by J.G. Tallon*

'How did this book get over here?' said Clay.

'I threw it,' said Mike.

Clay picked up the injured volume and looked at the cover.

'You no likee Inspector Byron?'

'Not my kind of thing,' said Mike.

'Hmm.' Clay put the book on the table and turned to Mike.

'We've got a problem.

'Apparently the mairie is hassling the gendarmerie to do more to catch the ski thieves; they've set up a road block and are searching every vehicle leaving town – trucks, cars the lot. Very thorough, apparently; they're checking everyone's ID. You're going to have to dig in here for a bit.'

'How long will this last?' asked Mike

'I don't know.'

'And how is a roadblock going to be any use – no one would be daft enough to try and get through with a load of stolen skis?'

'I know. It's probably only for show but the fact is they're doing it. Our real problem is that it gives the Messigny people a chance to scrutinise everyone as they're being checked.'

47

'Mike, we'd like to tell you a little bit about the work we're doing here,' said Ludo. 'But meanwhile this is something you need to read.' He was holding out a thin, bound A4 document. The title on the cover read *Triumph of the Gangster State*, beneath which was the name, Professor Glyn Owen.

'So who's Glyn Owen then?'

'An academic specialising in security working for the Government.'

Mike flipped through the pages.

'As you can see, it was meant to be a PowerPoint presentation but there was a power failure while Owen was speaking; they had to move to another room where there was no screen. Owen said what he always used to say when this happened: "No problem, I'll do it *a capella*."'

'*A capella?*' asked Mike.

Ludo emitted a thin, pleased smile.

'Voice without instrumental accompaniment.'

48

> In most countries it is the custom for organised
> crime to be organised by the police.
> *Prof. Glyn Owen,* Triumph of the Gangster State

'So, what did you think of it?' asked Ludo.

'Interesting.' No point in falling out with the management, thought Mike.

He had woken shortly after 7.00 a.m. and tried to bring the day ahead into focus as the various facets of his new situation re-formed in his mind. Anne: what was he going to tell her and when? More immediately, what was he going to say to Ludo and Clay about Glyn Owen, the tiresome Welsh Merchant of Doom? And how was he going to get out of here?

He showered, dressed and took *Triumph of the Gangster State* across to the living room. There was no one around. He helped himself to coffee and started re-reading bits of Owen's text. After a few minutes he stopped and sat staring at the document before chucking it on the table. His view hadn't changed since last night. These were the ramblings of a paranoid, self-proclaimed prophet who enjoyed frightening people. Mike was surprised that these skiing tax inspectors had been so impressed. It made him all the more worried, indebted to them though he was. He took his mug over to an armchair. While a portion of Mike's mind was trying to get his taste buds to find any evidence of coffee in the hot brown water, the rest of it was endeavouring to focus on this lunatic lecture.

There was nothing in this thing that amounted to anything. Owen made some wild assertions and created a rickety thesis, but where was the evidence? Yes, he supposed he could go along with the stuff about the country going a bit soft. And yes, he'd often speculated about those defence lawyers colluding with their crooked clients. He could even buy the idea of a few bent coppers and judges, some dodgy politicians and civil servants, but these could all be dealt with case by case. It didn't mean that the end of the world was nigh. People like Owen shouldn't be let loose in the community to play on the ignorance and insecurity of others. It was just scaremongering. We aren't in a crowded theatre and there isn't a fire.

Suddenly Mike felt claustrophobic. He wanted to be out of the apartment and up the mountains, not stuck in here contemplating the tacky world of crims with a couple of nutters. But what should he say to his hosts? He was still keen to be regarded as 'on board' – they were his protectors after all. He didn't want to get chucked out and find himself having non-elective knee surgery in some pop-up operating theatre in a cellar at Chalet Messigny.

Mike had been pondering all this when Ludo came into the room, helped himself to coffee and joined Mike at the table.

'But how interesting?' he asked.

'Interesting,' said Mike, 'but a bit over the top?' He was annoyed that he'd been unable to contain his criticism.

They sat there staring at the document in unison. Ludo broke the uneasy silence.

'Mike, you have to understand what Owen was doing here. He was talking at a seminar for civil servants. He'd been brought in to pep up the proceedings. They had spent hours in that room listening to people banging on about *Cloud Modelling in Cyber Insurgency, The Voluntary Sector in Aid of Civil Power, The Role of Non-State Actors in Piracy Interdiction and Associated Funds Retrieval*. Owen was the big finale. Send them home happy; it was sort of show business.'

'For this I pay my taxes?'

'You have to understand that it was for the benefit of a generalist audience. These weren't front line troops. His talks on terrorism or counter-insurgency at a military or police academy were more focused, more academically rigorous. I've got plenty you can read.'

Mike felt his heart sink.

'Excellent, I'd like to.' He wanted to sound obliging – to show them he was grateful for the hospitality, the soup and so on. But he also wanted to maintain his dignity in spite of his abject dependency.

'And what's the big deal with this Criminal Impunity stuff? Even I know that the Mafia have been bumping off police chiefs for years. It's hardly a new idea.'

'But it's a new idea *in the United Kingdom*,' insisted Ludo. 'And it has never been given a name before.'

'Okay,' said Mike sounding unconvinced. 'But the man's all over the place. He says organised crime is "a virus in the system"; it's "wounds in the bark"; it "wears a collar and tie"; it's a "canker"? What the hell isn't it?'

Ludo inclined his head in polite assent.

'Yes, I'll grant you it is something of . . .' Ludo allowed himself a self-satisfied smile '. . . a cocktail of metaphors.'

'Anyhow, whenever Owen says something, you have to take it seriously. He's produced a large and highly respected body of work. But if you look at all of his writing you'll find it full of contradictions. Sometimes he plays at being a sort of academic shock jock. He often urges his audience, his readers, to think ahead, to try to see what might be coming over the horizon.

'Owen believed that you have to consider crazy contingencies to make sure your thought processes retain their elasticity. And it was his job to consider worst-case scenarios. "Grey-sky thinking", he liked to call it; sometimes he'd describe himself as "a stand-up tragedian".

'This Hedley Coram stuff was directed at tomorrow's high fliers. He was inviting his audience to think about possibilities – in the Course Schedule his talk was billed as "an afternoon of entertaining speculation".'

'It certainly is that,' said Mike. 'I mean, is this chap on something? I think he's writing so much stuff about Charlie that some of it is going up his nose.'

'*Was* going up his nose,' said Ludo.

'Was . . . ?'

'His circumstances have drastically changed.'

'I don't understand.'

'He's dead, Mike.'

This new information stopped Mike in his tracks; Ludo was happy let the silence run and enjoy his discomfort before he eventually spoke.

'Owen was subjected to a brutal attack and died from his injuries. His death is why we're here. It's also why you're here, chum.'

49

Soon after Ludo had left the room Clay appeared.

'Had a good chat with Ludo, did you?'

'Yes, indeed.'

Clay now lowered his voice as if fearful of being overheard.

'What Ludo won't tell you, of course, is that he's a bit of a clever clogs.'

'Yes, I'd sort of formed that impression for myself,' said Mike.

'Knows lots of long words. Always catching me out. Before I knew him I thought a Manichaean struggle was when City played United. No, seriously, real brains. Got a scholarship to a bog-standard Oxford college, then got a bog-standard double first. He could have been anything, but he chose historian. Likes the forensics – finding out what really happened. Been enjoying himself on our little project to find out why Owen died; says it's interesting doing historical research when the people are still alive. Well, some of them.

'Owen reckoned Ludo was the brightest student he ever had. Absolutely trusted him. It was his background, d'you see. Father was a soldier with a helluva record – but "much undecorated" as they say of the deserving but neglected. Owen had a lot of time for that sort of thing. But he wouldn't trust anyone in the Village, only Ludo. Chose him as custodian of his work.'

'And how come Ludo chose you?'

'Owen told him to. He knew Ludo and I were connected and that I had worked in the Village. And he knew that Ludo could trust me.'

'Why's that?'

'Because I am the son of a friend of his family.'

'What kind of a friend of his family?'

Clay clasped his hands and looked down at them for a moment before staring at Mike, ready to savour his reaction to the answer.

'My father killed his father.'

50

It seemed to Mike that Clay was very anxious to emphasise that the people in the chalet were only a part of the Thermidor force.

'We have more people outside the perimeter fence down at Thermidor Two on the other side of town,' Clay had said. But when Mike asked what he meant by 'perimeter fence' he didn't get an answer, so he asked Ludo when he next found him on his own.

'It's a Chindit thing,' explained Ludo. 'Something he got from his grandfather, who fought in the guerrilla campaign behind the Japanese lines in Burma. When the enemy besieged one of their jungle camps they'd suddenly find themselves under attack from behind by a force that'd been turned loose to roam in the forest outside the fence. They could cause a lot of panic among the Japs at a critical moment and change the tide of a battle. That's what Clay thinks he has set up here.'

51

'We have an emergency notice from Armoise.' The announcement in what sounded like Candy's voice came across the PA system.

Ludo almost ran out of the room. Mike didn't know what was expected of him, so he went to his quarters and awaited developments. He'd only been there for a few minutes when there was a knock at the door. It was Colza.

'Mike, Fancy an outing? Ludo and Clay want to know if you'd like to join us on a little op.'

Twenty minutes later Mike was one of six passengers sitting in Count Fernando, with Colza at the wheel and Clay beside him, parked in a line of cars beside the road at the bottom of the hill. Mike didn't recognise any of the others and guessed they were from 'outside the perimeter fence'.

52

Every spring when the snow melts they find people. Usually it is within a year of their disappearance but it can be longer. When they found Ötzi the Iceman in the Austrian Alps in 1991 scientists concluded that he died in 3300 BC.

Matthew Gloag, Innocents on Ice

'What's happening?' Blake shouted, frightened, desperate.

'What's happening is drinks on the house,' a voice answered. Eastern European, cheerful, courteous.

Blake's failure to ski the Couloir had left him morose and isolated at the celebration party. His detachment from the others made him a promising target for Cropper, who had pulled him in for an interrogation that began affably enough over a drink but turned extremely unpleasant when Cropper abducted him and put him through some high-pressure treatment for a couple of days. He found that Blake was useless as a source of information – he clearly knew nothing of the white suit footage – and now they had compromised themselves by their treatment of him, their prisoner's fate was inevitable.

As they approached Blake could see they were both wearing bright yellow washing-up gloves. One held his jaws open while the other tipped half a bottle of schnapps down his throat. The effect was startling. His innards felt as though they'd burst into flames and now, as they dragged him out onto the balcony, the alcohol surged into his brain.

When his mind cleared a little he was aware that he was strapped to a chair by his chest, knees and ankles, unable to move. They had given him his suit back after taking it for a couple of hours but they'd unzipped the front, leaving him with nothing more than a polo shirt between his chest and the freezing night air.

No one would see or hear him, gagged as he was with a strip of duct tape and a tea towel featuring *Les Ponts de France*. *The fuckers are going to let me die.* After fifteen minutes he lost consciousness.

He wasn't as close as he had wanted but Brebis was already in position in the woods beside the road and was able to give Clay a running commentary on the radio link as he stared through his night vision binoculars.

'They've stopped at a gap in the trees . . . they're taking Blake out of the car . . . the car has driven off . . .' He saw two men holding Blake's wrists and ankles swing him to and fro a couple of times to gather momentum. When they let him go, the body flew in an arc out over the slope before dropping twenty metres and disappearing into the scrub of saplings and bushes. A couple of minutes later Brebis reported that the car, which had now done a U-turn, had picked up the two men and was heading back downhill.

Once it was out of sight, Clay started the engine and shot up the hill until he reached Brebis who was standing at the roadside marking the point of Blake's take-off and staring down the ravine.

As Clay drew the car to a halt he called out, 'Thank you, Jacques, you can let her go.'

The first thing that had restored Blake to semi-consciousness was the impact of his landing. After a few minutes he heard shouts that seemed to be getting closer. Now someone was wiping his face with a warm moist sponge and he found himself staring into a pair of dark brown eyes that looked at him with a mixture of reproach and concern. It was Hortense, Jacques' mountain rescue dog.

The rescue party set to administering primary revival procedures before strapping Blake to a short aluminium ladder. With the help of a hawser taken round the tow-bar pin of the SUV and all of them, Mike included, pulling and pushing like hell, they got him up the steep slope to the road.

*

'What was all that about?' Mike asked Clay as they drove back to the apartment.

'The idea was that if and when Blake's body was found a post mortem would reveal a massive intake of alcohol. That would tally with several reports that someone in a yellow ski jacket had been seen that evening with a couple of others, all three clearly drunk and fooling around in the middle of the road, chucking snowballs and shouting at passers-by.'

'But how did you know that they were going to do this?'

'Another time, Mike.'

53

'It just doesn't ring true.' Mike was having trouble believing Ludo's account.

'How come Owen's revelations in the Balmoral room were greeted with such indifference?' asked Mike.

'I know; it may seem odd but it's very understandable,' said Ludo. 'The director herself called Owen a controversialist which was her way of saying he wasn't universally admired. It wasn't just that people disagreed with some of his theories, but that they saw him as a showman who was prone to over-dramatise. But you have to understand that the business of speech is as much about music as words. That's particularly true of Owen. He's a Welshman so you have to let him be a bit Welsh. Inevitably some of his listeners found him over-florid and his style made them doubt his content. They would have found his dramatic claims that afternoon too gross and outlandish to be plausible. Also these people would have wanted to come across as cool and ungullible in front of each other. They would have reckoned that if Owen's assertions were true, the high-ups would know about it and be acting on it. The Hedley Coram crowd weren't to know they were getting first dibs on such shattering information.'

'I'm not sure I'm buying this,' said Mike, frowning at the sky beyond the window.

'The dissemination of a big idea is seldom percussive. It seeps rather than explodes into the public consciousness. People often don't get the point straight away. Churchill's wartime speeches made little impact at the time; Bizet's *Carmen* and the French impressionists got a right old tonking from the critics when they first appeared.'

Mike shrugged wearily. 'If you say so.'

'For ideas to gain any traction they need to be discussed. But Owen's assertions weren't subjected to that. He didn't stay to answer questions and apart from a perfunctory conversation in the hall as everyone was leaving there was no debate among the members of his audience. The only people who did talk about them properly were Rebecca and Terry. And as you know, that bore fruit.'

'For Owen, the significance of his appearance at Hedley Coram was not to pass on his information to the authorities for them to act on it. He would handle that himself in due course. No, the second iteration of the Gangster State was Owen putting down a marker so that when the information reached the public domain there would be enough witnesses around who would be able to testify that the credit was his, that Prof. Glyn Owen got their first.'

'But why didn't Owen do something sooner about sharing his knowledge?'

'He daren't,' said Ludo. 'He believed there were enemies of the state embedded in our national security apparatus and he didn't know who he could trust.'

'But hang on a mo, so he's found out all this stuff, why didn't the silly bugger just summarise it on a bit of paper, pop it in the post to you and save everyone a lot of trouble, instead of leaving you faffing about with a bunch of . . . of crossword clues?'

'You're right of course, but you have to understand that as often as not the central notion, the great big idea at the heart of something, is the one thing that never gets written down. It's too . . . obvious.'

'I don't understand.'

'Well, if you were to look on William Shakespeare's desk when he was halfway through say . . . *Coriolanus*, you'd maybe see some half-completed scenes, some bits of dialogue, phrases and notes on this and that, but nothing to tell you what it was about. There wouldn't be anything saying, "A victorious general spurned by the Roman mob seeks his bloody revenge . . . a tale of savage politics in the ancient world" and so on. That wouldn't happen until the publicity man from the Globe came round and asked, "So what's this one about, Will? Mr Burbage says we need to make a start on the posters." Owen might have been planning to provide a summary but he just didn't get round to it.'

'But why not?'

Ludo didn't answer immediately but walked across the room and peered at the fireplace, frowning as though the burning logs were a malfunctioning autocue. Eventually he spoke.

'My suspicion was that he felt he was always on the brink of finding out more and was waiting to include that. Research is addictive; hard to know when to stop. I also wonder if it was because he almost couldn't believe what he'd found – it was so . . . awesome. I can understand that. One would be assailed by doubt. Imagine what it's like being locked up all day alone with this sort of toxic information – the grand improbability of it. You'd begin to wonder if you've made it all up. Owen would have had that recurring fear that he'd turned into some kind of crazed conspiracy theorist of the kind he so despised.

'And something else. Vanity. He'd have wanted to be the sole author and was reluctant to let anyone else in on the glory. Socially he was a team player, but professionally he was a loner – quite selfish, actually. Understandable though: he'd worked on his own all his life. When you've done all the hard work by yourself you don't want to share the glory. So he delayed passing on his information – with near-catastrophic consequences.'

54

They sprang it on Mo without warning when she came into the living room one afternoon in Val shortly after the Messigny debacle.

The risk of Mo's exposure had reached its high point when Cropper arrived in Val de Ligne and found the white suit footage in the Couloir Noir video material. It told him that someone had betrayed the location of the meeting. Only a handful of people knew that it was to be at the Chalet Messigny, and although Cropper suspected that the leak came from one of the Board's people, Mo knew she would come under suspicion. When Crane had called for a break in the meeting at Messigny it was she who had suggested that people might like to take their coffee outside because the sun had just come out. They could suspect that she was less concerned with the welfare of the guests than setting up a group photo opportunity for Kornie. But in fact after the Board meeting broke up in panic, Crane told Cropper and Dubois that Mo should stay behind and help them because her special skill might yield something. So Mo was still in the clear, but she realised that the time must surely come when Cropper and Dubois would subject her to serious scrutiny again.

Now that time had come. It was Cropper who made the running.

'Who are you working for, love?' His tone was chillingly soft. Bad cop.

Mo knew this was it. The crucial seconds that would test her. She looked across at Cropper quizzically but said nothing.

'Why did you do it then, love?'

Again she looked nonplussed.

'Why did you tell them we'd be at Chalet Messigny?'

'Tell what? Tell who?'

Dubois helped her. Good cop.

'The people whose man was hiding in the trees.'

'Ah, that,' said Mo. 'Not me.' She expressed no surprise at being questioned and seemed to dismiss the idea as some minor matter that was nothing to do with her.

'Do you know what I do to anyone who spills on me?'

Mo remained blankly unfazed by Cropper's threat. No need to bother to deny the accusation: it was a nonsense. She gave him a slightly bored look of deep, doe-eyed pity. *I'm sad for you with your crazy little suspicions.* She stood there and held his gaze, not challenging but just waiting; it was for Cropper, her superior, to make the next move. When he looked away without saying anything she remained motionless for some moments and then, assuming she was dismissed, carried on with her work.

Beneath the cool, the terror. The moment she got the chance she raised the alarm, flicking the light in the empty bedroom on and off twice and placing a blue towel on the windowsill. Shin, Kang and Thermidor needed to be on full alert.

55

'Thermidor?' Mike asked Clay, who was trying to explain the intricacies of their funds acquisition strategy. 'Why Thermidor? Did you get the name from Companies House or something?'

'No, Mike. Not quite.'

'It's to do with the French Revolution, isn't it?'

'Very good,' said Ludo. 'It was name they gave to some summer months in the new revolutionary calendar; it marked the end of the Reign of Terror.'

'It's a privilege to be in the company of such educated people.'

'No problems, Mike,' said Ludo. It was one of many moments when Mike felt like thumping them both.

'The thing is we never really use the name,' said Clay. 'We don't run round leaving our signature everywhere.'

'Not like Zorro,' said Ludo, with his characteristic quietly-pleased-with-himself smirk.

Clay had agreed with Ludo's proposal to tell Mike a bit more about what they were doing. 'We need to if he is going to be our tethered goat.' So they sat Mike down and told him all about the birth of Thermidor and their investigation into Glyn Owen's death; how they funded the enquiry. They explained how they got on the trail of Parsons and Drake and how with the help of Rebecca and Terry they had discovered Crane and his burgeoning empire. And they described the operational characteristics of their most formidable enemies, Cropper and Tsanko.

'But what's poor old Val de Ligne done to get mixed up in this?' asked Mike.

'Crane decided he must confront his Board,' said Clay. 'Cropper and Dubois were tasked with finding a venue that was both secure and easily accessible. In the end they chose . . .' Clay paused and raised his eyebrows questioningly at Mike.

'The Chalet Messigny?'

Clay stared at Mike, raised his arm and did the pistol finger, aiming between his eyes and making a little clicking sound.

'You're a smart one, Mike.'

'Why have you told me so much?' asked Mike later in the day. 'You've rather compromised yourselves, haven't you?'

'I felt we owed you an explanation after what happened to you. We were grateful to you for not leading the Messigny people to our planned rendezvous in the car park' said Ludo. 'They could have bagged us and you'd have been off the hook.'

'My God, I wish I'd thought of that!'

56

The division of responsibilities between Ludo and Clay had remained unchanged from the beginning. Ludo was the CEO of

Thermidor, whose sole purpose was to prosecute the investigation into Owen's death. Ludo determined the direction and analysis of the intelligence; Clay oversaw the intelligence-gathering and the handling of Messidor. It was he who came up with the Tethered Goat proposal. It turned out to be a near catastrophe and diminished Ludo's faith in Clay at a time when that faith was already on the ebb.

Ever since Thermidor had recruited Mo, Clay was a changed man. At first he'd become less informative but now he was positively secretive. Ludo also noticed how Candy had become more distant and made it clear that her loyalty lay with Clay. Clay's relationship with Mo hadn't helped. Yes, Ludo didn't mind admitting to himself: there was an element of jealousy, but he was more concerned about the hideous security risks their trysts imposed on Thermidor.

Differences between the two men were growing. There was, for instance, the small but telling matter of the skiing. When they'd got on the slopes together for the first time it soon became apparent that Ludo was much the better skier. Clay, who turned every moment of life into a competition, found it galling to be beaten by Ludo in their occasional undeclared races. What made it worse was that Ludo skied without any apparent effort. Clay, the soldier, brave but unstylish, would attack the mountain with a manic ferocity while his relaxed and looser limbed, rival merely borrowed its gravity as casually as someone might cadge a cigarette.

Although Ludo knew that he like Clay was guilty of indulging in that kind of junior doctor's unfeeling black humour as a way of coping with their grisly task, he suspected that beneath Clay's callousness lay a thin seam of sadism. It became uncomfortably clear from an early stage that he was less interested in Thermidor's investigation than the punitive possibilities it might offer.

Ludo also found there was something unsettling about Clay's restlessness; it was like having a large child with Attention Deficit Disorder clumping about the place, while the speed of his verbal aggression and impetuousness contrasted with the slower pace of his guile. Ludo wasn't sure whether Clay was good, bad or barking mad, yet he was all too aware that his own judgement might be influenced by the peculiarly shocking experience that their fathers, in their very different ways, had shared. Ludo wondered how Clay might be affected; he guessed that Clay wasn't the sort of chap to give it much thought.

Ludo had become aware of his own capacity for paranoia ever since his career moved into the private sector. In spite of its secret and deceitful work, his time in the Service had been much less fraught with the sort of internecine loathing and treachery that he was encountering at A&G Oil. Reggie had warned him what to expect very early on: 'You have to understand, Ludo, everyone in this company is plotting to stab someone else in the guts. Corporate life is essentially the first act of *Julius Caesar* in modern dress.'

57

'So what's with the weirdo names?' said Mike.

'They're all the days of Thermidor from the Revolutionary calendar. Code names for security. Clay's idea.' Ludo was washing his hands of it.

'What about Candy? That doesn't sound very Thermidor.'

'I know. She was meant to be Carline but she refused; she's posh, you see, and she thought it sounded a bit common.'

And you two, you don't have special names?'

'Actually, yes. But don't use them.' Ludo seemed slightly embarrassed.

'Go on then,' said Mike, savouring that embarrassment, 'what are they?

'I'm Caprier and he's Moulin,' he said sheepishly.

*

At various stages Mike was introduced to Juniper's residents and visitors. For the most part he was told only their Thermidor names and Mike still found himself confused as to who was who. 'Don't worry about it,' Ludo had told him, 'once you're out of here you won't be seeing them again'.

Given the presence of Ludo and Clay and their lieutenants Colza and Candy, Juniper was the headquarters of the Thermidor operation in Val. Those working in the block were concerned with intelligence gathering and a miscellany of chores which Ludo would not specify. Mike established that older chap in charge was Salicor the Peacemaker. He was often in close conversation with Carthame, who Ludo described as 'an information specialist'. The cooky waif was Prêle, the big girl who chased the figures was Gentiane and the city lawyer type was known as Ecluse. The other two in what Ludo called 'the home team', a couple of keen fresh-faced young chaps, were Cotton and Lupin. They reminded Mike of the youngsters who volunteered to help in the parliamentary constituency office during elections. He overheard the name Stella Taplock mentioned occasionally but saw no sign of her.

Mike also learned that augmenting the Juniper contingent there were also, at any one time, always at least two soldierly types from 'security' who were apparently based in an apartment block in another part of town known as Thermidor Two. 'Juniper is clerical,' Ludo explained, 'the other place is more involved in the kinetic end of things.'

Some of the Thermidor Two people were already known to Mike; Ludo had told him about Abricot, who was the inspiration for Messidor's fundraising tactics. Basilic, who seemed to be Prêle's lover, was one of Clay's former brother officers. His mate, Bélier, was the operative who had come to Thermidor from several lucrative years in the unregulated sector of the maritime security industry, while Brebis was the former Special Forces trigger-happy trooper whose death-dealing mishaps so entertained Clay. There was a silent presence called Arrosoir who was said to be the group's fastest skier. A young man called Ivraie turned out to be the son of the judge found drowned off the Kent coast in circumstances which had aroused Owen's suspicions.

They were for the most part an engaging and affable bunch but cautious in their conversation. Any attempt by Mike to draw them on the subject of their current task was courteously ignored and steered back to the generalities of skiing and the joys of Val de Ligne.

'Maybe after all I've been through I should have a Thermidor name, too,' Mike had jokingly suggested to his hosts.

'I believe Panic is still available,' said Ludo.

58

Mike stared at the text. He had known several kinds of fear during his time as a guest of Thermidor, but this new variety clawed at his brain – and his conscience. The text that Ludo was showing to him was on his own phone. It was from Anne. SUSPICIOUS MEN SNOOPING NEAR HOUSE. POLICE VISITED BUT NOT HELPFUL. WHAT THE HELL ARE YOU UP TO? WE HAVE TO TALK.

'I know that this is not good news, Mike,' said Ludo as he took back the phone. 'But please understand we'll make sure she's safe. We have people there.'

Mike was as furious as he was fearful.

'You never said my family would be at risk. You've got to let me talk to her and explain. I can't do this by text for God's sake.'

'We can't let you speak to her. I'm sorry.'

'Why?'

'Because. Now, you need to reply to this quickly and reassure her.'

Ludo suggested a message which Mike slightly amended.

DARLING, I KNOW ABOUT THIS BUT CANNOT EXPLAIN. YOU ARE 100 PER CENT SAFE. YOU MUST BELIEVE ME. ALL MY LOVE, M

Mike waited to make certain that they actually sent the message.

It was Clay who had insisted that they needed to do more to divert any possible doubts that Cropper might have about Mo.

'She needs to do something proactive against Cropper's unseen enemies,' he told Ludo. 'She needs to play a convincing part in hunting us down. Any ideas?' Within an hour and a half they had a plan. When they revisited Mike a little later – when they deemed Mike had had enough time to get in a serious panic – they unfolded the demands of Tethered Goat.

'So what do I have to do?'

'Exactly as we ask. Clay, would you . . .?'

'So this is the deal,' said Clay, spreading out the Val de Ligne piste map on the table. 'The little charmer who's put the nasties outside your house is Kevin Cropper. He's in charge of the Messigny crowd now. We think he's brought extra people with him but we're not sure how many.

'We know Cropper often has someone watching from various points just on the off chance of seeing you. Les Trois Oiseaux is one of those places and we want the Messigny watcher there to see you and alert Cropper; he'll call out his posse and we'll be able to see how many people we're dealing with.'

'No way.'

'Quite understand. One sympathises. Damn difficult situation for you. Feel sorry for you.' Mike was discovering that even Clay's sympathy had a ballistic quality. 'Fact is you're the only one of us that the Messigny people know.'

'*I'm* not one of their enemies.'

'Ah, but they *think* you are. They want you very badly. So you're going to let them *see* you but we'll make sure they don't *get* you.'

'Oh yes?'

'Can't afford to let you fall into their hands,' said Clay. 'They'd tear everything you know about us out of your head. You need to understand that this is the one thing you can do to ensure the safety of your family. But this time you need to make sure you do exactly as you're effing told.'

Next morning Mike took up his position on the terrace of Les Trois Oiseaux, a restaurant a couple of hundred metres below the cable car station. Normally the terrace would have been busy but the weather had driven all the customers inside. Clay had told him he'd have protection but he certainly couldn't see it from where he sat on the corner of the terrace facing down the slope. Because he was 'the target' they wanted him to be easily visible, so they'd made him wear a black and yellow ski suit. He felt ridiculous.

As instructed he'd pushed his goggles high up his head and pulled down the muffler. *This is suicide.* Exposing his whole face was scary but also liberating. He was fed up with having to be wrapped up like an Egyptian mummy on the rare occasions he'd stepped out of the chalet. He basked in being unmasked in the fresh cold air.

Mike never saw the figure sitting inside the restaurant by a window. Cropper's people had photographed Mike after they'd snatched him and he was clearly recognisable to the watcher in the restaurant. Within seconds Dubois received a text reporting the sighting of Mike Warne and moments later Cropper was heading for the restaurant with Tsanko and a hunting party of four. Mike, meanwhile, received the order from Colza through the earpiece of his mobile that, as planned, he had been seen by the watcher from Messigny and Cropper's posse was on its way; he must get ready to leave.

Almost as soon as Cropper got out of the cable car he spotted Mike on the restaurant terrace a couple of hundred metres below in his distinctive black and yellow. His prey was putting on his skis.

'We follow him at a distance,' Cropper told Tsanko, 'until we find a quiet place to bag him.'

Mike edged onto the piste and waited for Colza's signal.

'Go!' shouted Colza and Mike went. His pursuers got there just in time to see him disappear around a bend; when they reached it they spotted him drop off the edge of the piste and disappear. Cropper ordered his men to follow. They were not to know that Mike was heading for some seriously steep and awkward terrain which few skiers could manage. This was only possible because it wasn't Mike but Tyler in an identical suit acting as a decoy, drawing his pursuers away from the restaurant while Mike himself had hid under the terrace. When Colza gave him the all clear he went into the bar and made for the gents' so he could change into another suit to disguise himself for his return to Juniper.

Up to that point everything had gone according to plan. Unfortunately Cropper, a middling skier at best, had decided not to follow but to wait until Tsanko told him that they'd caught their man. From his vantage point Colza could see that Cropper was heading for the restaurant and made a frantic call to warn Mike.

'Mike, you've got to stay out of the way. Cropper didn't go with the others. He's heading for the restaurant.'

'Christ! Where can I go?'

'I can't help you, Mike. You've just got to stay out of his way.'

Mike tried to control his panic, to focus. He wasn't exactly inconspicuous in his yellow and black ski suit. It would be difficult to disappear in the crowd looking like a giant wasp. The way to the gents would take him down a short corridor with windows facing the slopes. The merest flash of his bright yellow suit at the window would be enough to alert Cropper. He could see only one other option. He hurried into an adjoining dining room, which was deserted.

Through the gap between the door and its frame Mike was able to see Cropper come into the bar. He didn't order anything but just paced around deep in thought, phone in hand, seemingly waiting for a call. When it came, it looked like very bad news. Mike saw his whole body stiffen with rage.

Some loud guffawing broke among a group at the bar. Cropper looked up angrily; he was having trouble hearing and searched round for somewhere quieter. He saw the entrance to an empty room – the room in which Mike had taken refuge.

Mike stared around him desperately. The only possible hiding place was behind a sackcloth curtain covering an alcove that served as a general store cupboard. One can't really tiptoe in a pair of ski boots but Mike did the next best thing; he managed to reach the alcove and slip behind the curtain moments before Cropper appeared in the doorway.

Mike held his breath and stood very, very still as Cropper came in, still talking on the phone, pulled out a chair and sat down with his back to the alcove. Mike, who could clearly see him through the coarse sackcloth curtain, would never forget the words with which Cropper ended the phone call.

'You can tell your fucking crew that if they don't get him we'll do to them what we're going to do to Mr Mike fucking Warne: deliver him home to Mrs fucking Warne jointed up in freezer bags.'

Mike, his skin prickling with fire, his scalp growing cold, contemplated the back of Cropper's evil head with rising revulsion and terror. The silence was broken when one of the restaurant staff entered the room. She acknowledged Cropper with a nod and a smile which he ignored and went across to another alcove on Mike's side of the room and flicked a light switch. *No!* One of the lights that came on was a very bright bulb in Mike's store space. He stared through the cloth at the mirror on the other side of the room, which showed that now there was a light *behind* his curtain he could be clearly seen *through* it by anyone in the room. If Cropper was to get up and turn around . . . Mike, damp with the sweat of fear, could only stand as still as he could and wait.

After the waitress turned off the light and returned to the bar Cropper sat brooding and fiddling with his phone. Mike stood there frozen still, knowing that the slightest scuff of the giant wasp man-made fibre skin could be his undoing.

In his terror he began to attribute supernatural properties to the powers of Cropper's antennae. It was surely a matter of minutes before the ogre's ears would be deafened by the volume of Mike's heartbeat or a tiny whiff of the odour of his fear would alert Cropper to his presence. All the while the sweat driven from his overheated scalp ran in rivulets from his brow down to his collar where it cooled to a chill.

Cropper stayed there for several more long minutes before he slowly rose, stretched and clumped out of the room. Mike felt he'd aged several years. He waited for some fifteen minutes before going to change into his other outfit, collecting his skis and heading back to Juniper and where he was pathetically grateful to resume his confinement.

59

In Ludo's eyes it all looked so warm and inviting, so safe and untroubled. He had found himself standing by a window in Juniper, peering across at the neighbouring apartment blocks and chalets below and watching the people inside. He'd been on enough skiing holidays to be able to imagine the conversations that were taking place. Now that it was midweek the tentativeness of the first evening was past and everyone would feel as if they had known each other for years. Talk would be easy and noisy; doughy winter-white complexions burnished to glowing shades of red and brown from hours of exposure to Val's wind and cloud-filtered sun. Intense exercise would have infused a feeling of wellbeing and they'd be looking forward to their food with a sense of having earned it.

The idea of a travel company renting a chalet, subletting the rooms and providing flights, food and drink in an all-inclusive deal had proved one of the most successful business models the travel industry ever devised. Each season saw a 110,000-strong British invasion of the French Alps – around ten times as many as made the trip to Agincourt. Ludo and his family were invariably among them.

The companies shovelled a bunch of complete strangers into a house for a week, where they would have breakfast and dinner together every day bar one. For Ludo it was a high risk game of social roulette. However, although normally choosy about the company he kept, he found that the common bond of skiing with its anecdote-generating days in the mountains fuelled an easy camaraderie among people who had little else in common. His wife, Liz, thought the same and when she said she loved skiing so much because she got to meet a complete cross-section of society he understood, but with some qualification.

'You're quite right, darling,' Ludo told her. 'All human life is here except for the very old, the sick, the physically idle and anyone who isn't pretty well off.'

As he watched people taking their seats at the dinner table Ludo thought about the others in their group on their last family skiing trip. There'd been a flooring salesman, a professional golf caddy, an orthopaedic surgeon, a carpenter, a solicitor, a girl who described herself as a biscuit designer and one of those yummy mummies who'd taken leave of café society and gone all manic – doing tough-stuff Iron Woman triathlons, and generally going on like Superwoman on steroids instead of sitting around drinking lattes with the other mums and taking it in turns to bonk the tennis coach.

Ludo liked to use the evenings to test what his boss at A&G Oil, Reggie, called 'Peplow's First Theory of Conversation', which had it that 'Within twenty-seven minutes of first encountering each other, two or more members of the middle classes will have found that they know someone in common.' 'Peplow's Second Theory of Conversation' would also be vindicated. That one had it that 'Any social encounter of the kind in Peplow's First Theory will feature a minimum of one assertion to demonstrate the speaker's skill at the game of life.'

'You know the kind of thing,' Reggie had explained to Ludo: '"I suppose we've been quite clever. Margery's parents are on the road to Sam's school so in term time we can just go straight down to the cottage on Friday evenings . . . Kevin's mum lives very close so she can go in and turn on the heating which is brilliant . . . I guess I'm quite lucky really, my company seems to like what I do for them.'" Good old Reggie. If only he could be here in Juniper now, he'd certainly brighten things up a bit.

The other big subject in the last Ludo chalet had been the latest developments in *Fit*, 'now in its second body-funk-pumping year'. The astounding sexual and workplace antics of the staff and members of a health club in an unspecified Midlands city had gripped Middle England along with the rest of the country. Ludo suspected that *Fit* would still be on the conversational menu over there in that chalet tonight. And after dinner they'd amble through for coffee in the living room and the bards among them would take their turn to recite epic tales of edges caught, and last lifts missed, of face plants and cartwheels, of treacherous blacks masquerading as reds and of titanic struggles with merciless moguls and deceitful restaurant bills. All this declaimed as if they were veterans of a hoplite phalanx reminiscing around the campfire after battle on the blood-soaked plains of Thrace.

Ludo felt Mike hovering at his side; he didn't seem to have anything to say but the poor chap was clearly in a terrible state about his family.

'Are you okay, Mike? That tethered goat stuff must have given you a fright?'

'Yes it was scary outside, but I'm tired of being cooped up in this place. It's getting seriously claustrophobic. The people . . .'

'I know what you mean. I remember when I spent a fortnight sailing with university friends. The boat might have been alone in the empty ocean but you're never more than a few feet from the others, and they can really get on your nerves. My friend Reggie at work has this theory that all those solo yachtsmen you see being welcomed home by cheering crowds actually set off with a full crew but come to loathe them so much that, one by one, they dump them all overboard.'

'I can think of someone I'd like to chuck over the side,' said Mike.

'You mean Clay? Oh, he's harmless. Can't help himself. It's in his nature.'

'I'm not sure I quite trust him.'

'What do you mean?' said Ludo sharply.

'I don't know.'

'There must be some reason?'

Mike just shook his head. There was a long pause before he spoke again.

'He seems quite cross about everything. He's got the loathing, but where's the loving?'

Ludo didn't respond at first; Mike didn't let go. He kept the question hanging in the air.

'In his circumstances the loving is difficult.'

'I would have thought impossible.'

'No, not impossible, but difficult.'

'There is someone then?'

'Oh yes.'

'So where is she?'

'She's at work.' Ludo didn't seem to know what to say given that he couldn't, of course, tell him about Mo, so he just gave a slight shrug.

'Is she in the same line of business?' asked Mike.

'Pretty much.'

'In the same company?'

No answer.

'Christ, it's not Candy is it?

Ludo shook his head and smiled. He knew them both too well and the suggestion amused him.

'A bit of the old office romance, anyway?'

Ludo decided he needed to end this line of questioning.

'So, Mike, what do you think they're all talking about out there?'

Mike thought for a moment.

'I dunno. Usual stuff, I suppose,' said Mike. He thought for a moment. 'But I know what the chalet girls will be talking about – next week's Piste Bashers' Ball.'

'It's that time of the year already?' said Ludo.

The Piste Bashers' Ball! Ludo knew all about these fundraising parties organised by Brits simultaneously in resorts all over the Alps. Beginning late on a Wednesday, they ended in the small hours of Thursday, which, being a day off for staff, allowed time for recovery following the trail of damage to reputations, relationships, brains, livers and limbs. In an incorrect moment Ludo speculated that the beneficiaries of the charities would happily forego the restoration of their eyesight, access to fresh water and cures for fatal diseases if they realised the scale of human suffering inflicted for their sake upon the gilded youth of Val de Ligne by the annual Piste Bashers' Ball.

60

Doing nothing can have unintended consequences
so it's always worth a try.

Reggie Peplow

Ludo missed Liz and the girls. Thinking about them provided some succour in the small hours when the darkness of his situation nudged him into a terrible clear-headed wakefulness. He craved being with them in their trouble-free existence; he wanted to get out from under the gruesome threat that loomed over Juniper. He missed his old life with its peace, its absence of threat. In his unhappiness Ludo would also often think about his office colleague Reggie Peplow, who was always a source of solace and a valued guide to the world both inside and outside A&G Oil. Reggie belonged in that safer, nicer world where there was room for intransigence or laziness that did not result in some privately administered death penalty. Reggie represented a warmth and wry affability that were missing from Ludo's current existence.

Reggie, a former newspaperman, was not at ease with the orderliness of his corporate life; Ludo had once asked him why he didn't chuck it in and go freelance. 'I used to work for myself,' he had replied, 'but I fell out with my employer.' His younger colleagues would refer to Reggie's corner of the office it as 'the Galapagos' on the grounds that it was the habitat of a life form that had long been extinct on the rest of the earth's surface.

Reggie thought that corporate life was an as yet uncategorised form of insanity. He had a theory that they put something in the air-conditioning that made everyone go bananas. Nevertheless he revelled in it. Once when Ludo was grumbling about some deeply frightful colleagues Reggie counselled him, 'Ludo, you must learn to savour the nectar of their ghastliness!'

Many wondered how Reggie survived in the bleak no-nonsense corporate world of A&G but the fact was, Reggie was a valued asset. As he himself said, 'A demand to explain its actions in plain English is perhaps the greatest single challenge a large corporation can face,' and Reggie was a genius at this. When A&G needed its more contentious policies turned from obfuscating gibberish into plausible human-speak, it was to Reggie they turned. Sir James Filton himself, the CEO, would call often call him in. 'Reggie,' he would say, 'I'd like you to do this one please; you've got all the conversion tables.'

The HR department took a different view of Reggie and were always lecturing him about his 'un-corporate behaviours'. Reggie and HR had a longstanding feud rooted in his refusal to attend a two-day management course featuring role-play sessions because he said role-playing was what everyone in the office did all day anyway. Reggie was averse to any kind of corporate event. He had this theory that they were only organised so management could prance about in front of their troops and make out that they were inspiring leaders. He maintained that they were the corporate equivalent of a Nuremburg Rally.

It was Reggie's duty to wine and dine people in the cause of big oil and he did it with gusto. 'One of the pleasures of executive life,' he would say, 'is to have one's corporate duty perceived as personal generosity.' This duty was not without its hazards. In a tone that made them sound like war heroes, Reggie told Ludo that he had known two people who had died of lunch. This entertaining took its toll on Reggie himelf. Some afternoons Ludo would find him strewn over his desk fast asleep with a handwritten sign next to his head saying CLOSED FOR STAFF TRAINING. Once when he'd returned from some heavy-duty corporate lunching he inserted the words EXTRA VIRGIN between A&G and Oil on a prominent sign in the foyer.

Snatches of Reggie flickered through Ludo's mind: Reggie enquiring about 'the football outcomes'; Reggie summoning Ludo to join him in 're-tox' or 'to sally forth and make some poor lifestyle choices'; Reggie on his stool in the Recovery Position calling to Jolanta in his Wimbledon umpire voice for 'new balls please'; Reggie announcing that he had to visit 'the Department of Inhuman Resources' – a reference to Stationery and Stores where he went to court the pert-breasted Jacintha Coggley, with whom he had a showy but demure relationship. Reggie had designated Miss Coggley to be an Area of Outstanding Natural Beauty; in his eyes she could do no wrong, unlike his wretched son-in-law, a landscape gardener referred to as 'Capability Kevin' who had a calamity-prone business tending window boxes in Tufnell Park.

Reggie relied on mockery and wisdom to handle life's tricky patches. Ludo wondered how he would cope with the circumstances that he, Ludo, now faced. Suddenly the Peplow strand of thought ceased to comfort him. In his heart of hearts he knew the answer. Reggie would get pissed.

61

It was as good a time as any; Mike and Ludo and Clay were the only ones in the room.

'So what was all that about your father killing Ludo's father?'

'You'd like to know about that, would you?' said Clay.

Mike nodded. Ludo spoke first. He told how their fathers were serving together in 22 Squadron 'doing the usual' when rebellion was the contagion of the time. How doctrines forged in cold damp libraries fought it out in foetid foreign lands. The Regiment won battles that have never been forgotten because they were battles about which nobody knew – tiny needles of heat in a long cold world war, a war fought by proxies, a war of rebellions and counter-insurgency.

As Ludo spoke Mike suspected from his smooth delivery that he had clearly told this story many times before. He told how the Regiment was much in demand because fomenting rebellions or crushing them was what it did. Sometimes they fought around beleaguered villages, sometimes in tumbledown towns. Sometimes in clammy jungles; sometimes in the high dry mountains of desert kingdoms, lands of water-less wadis and roasting rocks where the sun cast shadows as sharp as a knife. This time they were in a dank and soaking forest, the largest on earth, in a land with a river fed by five countries, a river as long as an ocean is wide. The forest was home to wild people who had never been tamed and once-tame people who had gone to the wild; beside them the murderous fauna seemed a model of manners.

'So,' said Ludo, 'classic scenario in such a place at such a time: rebels rock up and force villagers to give food and information. Government soldiers in pursuit punish villagers for helping rebels. Rebels return and kill villagers for helping Government. And so the ghastly gavotte goes on: people, like the animals, dying together in perfect harmony in the darkness of the forest, parrots screeching, leeches leeching and poor bloody villagers silently shrieking, frightened to help anybody, frightened not to help anybody. You'd pity the civic leader in a place like this; he's called the village headman because that's the bit of him that ends up on a sharpened stick.'

Ludo looked over to Clay

'Doomed patrol,' said Clay, taking his cue and picking up the narrative. 'Duff intelligence, so what's new, eh? Everything tits-up from the off. That's the trouble when they hire you out to foreign governments. Find yourself working for unknown others. Never know what you're dealing with.

'Deep in the forest, halfway along a hostile valley. Contact. Rebel force four times larger than estimated. No air support. Shambles. Ludo's pa takes one in the chest and another in the gut. Bad. No way they'd get him out of the place – they'd have had to carry him seven kilometres in the midday heat to the evacuation point. Not an option. Also not an option: leaving him for the amusement of enemy tribesmen with bones through their noses.

'My father got him into some cover, told him he'd be alright – just needed more morphine for the trip back to base. Reminded him about some cricket match when Jean, his fiancée – that's Ludo's ma – had shown up and he'd been thrilled. Once he'd got his mind filled with that pleasant memory, father gave him the morphine, waited the few seconds for his eyes to close, then he shot him in the head.'

Mike didn't know what to say so they sat in silence until Clay spoke again.

'And that's why I'm the son of a friend of the family . . .'

Mike shook his head in silent distaste.

'. . . and you must admit,' said Clay, 'friendly fire doesn't get any friendlier than that.'

62

The reward for deceit and counterfeit in a struggle that
     nobody knows:
A medal that can't be worn and a silence that must
     be kept.
No freedom of the city, no marching through the town,
Lives lived in shadows that others may walk in the sun.

*Verses for a Silent Service by
Revd Marcus Willoughby, Chaplain to the
UK Secret Intelligence Service 1959-1973*

'Clay, you must come and see this,' said Colza, who was watching the TV news.

'What are they giving us now? *Celebrities on the Toilet*?'

'No, not quite. They're saying they've got Jerry Tremlett in the studio. He's just about to come on.'

'Old Jerry? Grief. Mike, do come here, you've got to see this.'

When a portly fellow in dark suit and regimental-type tie appeared on the screen Clay start to clap, wolf-whistle and shout.

'Come on, Jerry, tell it like it really is.'

Jerry Tremlett, dimly lit, standing in front of a breezeblock wall, was being interviewed about reports of a British diplomat who'd gone missing in Algeria.

'Now Mike, this is perfect. This is how the telly does spooks.'

It was indeed a near-classic set-up, from the sulphur bulb in the bulkhead lamp to the menacing shadows on a breezeblock wall adorned with bits of old pipe-work. It was trying to say, 'We are in the bowels of the Secret Service HQ, and just down the corridor there's the room with rusty wall hooks and uncertain stains on the concrete floor and the stainless-steel table where they do the waterboarding' – in fact they were in the TV station's boiler room.

It reminded Ludo of how A&G would get similar treatment when a TV crew came to do one of their Inside-the-Evil-Oil-Empire investigations and make their executives look like Count Dracula on Halloween Night. Reggie called this libel by lighting.

'Go, Jerry, go!' Clay was now perched on the edge of the sofa shouting at the screen as Jerry Tremlett started to talk. 'Come on, Jerry, *vee heff vays off maykink you tokk!*' Then in an aside to Mike, 'They all want to be on the telly now. Look at him. I am Jerry. I am a spook who's come out of the shadows. Am I cool or what?'

Tremlett, red-faced and jowly, was delivering his analysis of likely suspects. 'Well, intelligence insiders are telling me that all the indications point to the involvement of one of the terrorist groups operating in the country at this time.' Short of tapping the side of his nose while blinking very slowly, he couldn't have done much more to suggest that he was the-man-in-the-know.

'Behold a man who knows nothing tells us what he knows!' jeered Clay. 'Jerry, you are a ruddy genius, old boy!' He threw up his hands in mock despair. 'You rumbled it was terrorists while all along we poor fools suspected it was the East Grinstead chapter of the Townswomen's Guild.'

'. . . and the Intelligence Services will appreciate at this time that it is imperative their man is found and released as soon as possible.'

Clay now sprang from the sofa and, landing on all fours, prostrated himself in front of the screen.

'Oh Jerry, we bow before you,' said Clay in a tone of exaggerated awe. 'The man's a complete prat, of course. Ludo, did I ever tell you about the time when . . .?'

'Indeed, you did.'

'The thing was, Mike, we'd already heard that one of our people had been killed in the Yemen but Jerry clumps into the office all self-important and grave-faced and announces, "Gentlemen, I am afraid we have just lost . . . another wicket."

'If it hadn't been such a god-awful situation everyone would have thrown stuff at him, but all we could do was cringe. You can see what happens. He's not the only one. They've seen all the telly series and the poor sods think they're meant to go on like that.'

'I think it's called life imitating art,' said Ludo.

'They all go mad in the end, you know,' said Clay.

'Have you gone mad, Clay?' Mike asked.

For a moment Clay looked a little wounded.

'You can be quite childish sometimes, Mike.'

Mike reckoned that he was now ahead on points.

63

'We've just had some news,' announced Clay. '*Les druides* are now the chief suspects for the ski thefts.' Clay had invited Mike to join him, Ludo and Colza at lunch. 'Rumour has it that they have been seen selling skis over at Pentes du Paradis; they are running short of funds to buy food and fuel. The gendarmerie hasn't pulled any of them in yet, but they say it's only a matter of time.'

To Mike that seemed like a nonsense idea.

'It's a good rumour, though, because it's what people would like to believe, but it can't be true.'

'I'm sure most people don't really believe it,' said Colza, 'but if they want to that's good enough.'

'So that means the roadblocks are over and I can get out of here?'

'No, they are still in force, the little green folk are still only suspects.'

'How did they come to be suspects?'

'An anonymous tip-off, apparently.'

Mike saw a knowing smirk spread across Ludo's face and turned to Clay.

'You didn't!'

Clay shrugged.

'We needed to slow down the pace of the search for us . . . have the spotlight point in the wrong direction.'

'You bastards. The poor little sods haven't done anyone any harm.'

'You don't understand,' said Ludo. 'We've given them a chance to help save the environment that matters. The most toxic pollutants are the Cranes of this world. They're like Sarin nerve gas blowing in the breeze.'

64

'Why,' Mike asked Ludo later in the day, 'was it was called the "Thursday Country" – the column in the *Swanborne Riot*?'

'It puzzled me too,' said Ludo. 'It turned out to be Carling's little joke. Some hunts thought that the part of their territory which they hunted on Thursdays was inferior and thus considered it "not done" to hunt on that day – and so the phrase was used to suggest "not quite socially acceptable". Someone might say that a certain person had "married a girl from the Thursday country"; Carling, the grammar school boy who despised any class pretension, would have relished the irony of it as a title for his column. He knew most of his readers wouldn't have understood the reference but he was more interested in the handful that did.'

65

Even before the Gallic tribes found themselves facing
the terrible geometry of the Roman legions, successive
generations have said, 'But wars are not fought like this!'

Prof. Glyn Owen, The Path to Peak Terror

Clay, in his role as head of operations, insisted that everyone in
Juniper had to be fit for whatever lay ahead and must therefore
exercise every day; that included Ludo and Mike. So the next
morning found the three of them in the garage with Mike and
Ludo on the two exercise bikes while Clay poked around examin-
ing various cartons, crates and bits of equipment. Now they'd got
Mike trapped on the cross trainer, his hosts were taking the opportunity to explain themselves.

'It's para-judicial action,' said Clay. 'It's about trying to protect
democracy and the rule of law – that kind of thing. Just doing what
our chaps did on the Normandy beaches.'

'The Normandy beaches? Are you being serious?' asked Mike
who, listening to him explain the theory of Thermidor, thought
that Clay had a rather inflated view of their work.

'Sounds to me like an excuse for playing at vigilantes,' said
Mike. He found he was struggling with the intermittent hill climb
programme; he had set it an optimistic Level 14.

'Nothing wrong with that,' said Clay. 'If the state won't do the
operation you have to go private. What the hell is this?'

'Colza says it's a bouncy-ball trampoline combo,' said Ludo.
'Apparently Candy ordered it.'

'Always been a place for vigilantes in every culture: *Zorro*, *The
Seven Samurai*, *The Four Just Men*.'

'I don't think they were for real, Clay,' said Mike, gratified to
see him smarting at the jibe. 'Real vigilantes are the bad guys, the
knee-cappers, the lynch mobs, the Klan.'

'Only sometimes,' said Clay. 'What about the Guardian Angels or those girls in Middlesborough and their Pimp Choppers Co-operative. Scary for sure but you've got to admit it worked.'

Clay paused while he dragged the aluminium-framed contraption out of its corner.

'In the old American West they had to make their own law and order. That's where the vigilantes came in – took care of things until the Sherriff arrived. How much did this thing cost for God's sake?'

'But we aren't in the Wild West.' Mike was having a bit of a struggle with the next uphill phase and his breathlessness amplified his indignation. He noticed Ludo, untypically, was having no part in this argument, but sat slouched in his saddle reading his typescript, pedalling effortlessly, knees out, like a jaunty bike courier with time on his hands. *He* sure as hell wasn't at Level 14 of the hill climb programme.

'We've had a proper police force up and running for two hundred years,' insisted Mike.

'So what is one meant to do?' said Clay poking at his new-found toy. Mike had become aware that Clay was in the habit of asking colleagues questions to which he already knew the answer. It was some complicated mind game which involved seeking reassurance by exaggerating his own doubts.

'I think you're meant to bounce on it,' drawled Ludo without glancing up from his paper.

'Like this?'

'Maybe.'

'Okay, Things have moved ahead of the police. Justice system can't cope any more. We cut out the middle men.'

'You mean the judge and jury?'

'You've got it, Mike.'

'What if you get it wrong – if your targets are innocent?'

'Always been very careful,' said Clay. 'Insist on clear evidence before we nail the bad boy.'

'Nail? What does nail mean?'

'Whatever we decide it should mean.'

'I don't think I like the sound of that.'

'There is no sound, Mike.'

Mike wondered if Thermidor were just a bunch of retarded adults playing boys' games.

'We save the taxpayer a heap of money,' continued Clay, 'Prison Service too.'

'How come?'

'Non-custodial sentences.'

'Careful, Clay, it's not rigged up properly,' said Ludo in a tone of resigned concern. 'I think that's what the nets are for.'

'What nets?'

'It comes with special nets. They must be over there somewhere.'

'Look, I'm managing fine without.'

'What sort of non-custodial sentences?' asked Mike.

'Maybe we confiscate goods and cash . . . hand out a good smacking.'

'Robbery with violence then?'

Clay too was now fighting for breath.

'For Christ's sake, Mike, which button do I have to press to get you out of your predictive text?'

His answers are always bit too pat, thought Mike. Did Thermidor actually do this stuff? Or were they just fantasists – a bunch of hoorays swanning around with a trunk full of different-coloured ski jackets and a colourful line in tough talk?

'You're taking the law into your own hands,' said Mike.

Clay laughed derisively.

'Best place for it, chum, because, after all, it's ours.'

'But this is the road to anarchy,' said Mike.

'No,' insisted Clay, 'a road to law and order. Bad guys get what they deserve; people get their revenge. I think this will be good for the back. . . posture and so on. Look, you can get to quite a height.'

'People? What people? Anyway, you know what they say, "Beware of those who call for revenge".'

'In that case I say, "Beware of Thermidor".'

'For God's sake, this is Neighbourhood Watch on steroids.'

Clay cackled.

'Nice one, Mike, but . . .'

Clay was only slightly off the vertical as he came down on the trampoline, but it was enough. The stretched fabric catapulted him with considerable velocity at a sharp angle into a high arcing trajectory, its endpoint coinciding with a large stack of cardboard boxes filled with plastic water-cooler cups. Some had burst open on impact, leaving Clay spread-eagled in a snow drift of white polypropylene which cackled at him mockingly as he struggled to get up.

'Crikey, Clay, are you alright?' said Mike who had jumped off his bike and hurried over to the scene of the incident. Ludo slowly slid off his mount and strolled over to his stricken comrade whom he addressed in a softly patronising tone.

'Did we do a proper risk assessment here?'

Clay looked quiet sorry for himself as he stood clutching his wrist.

'Why the hell have we got this thing, anyway?'

'Candy absolutely insisted,' said Ludo. 'Said it was an essential piece of kit.'

'Nets,' said Clay. 'That's what this thing needs. It needs nets.'

66

'You must understand we're not the only ones in this field. Some people have begun to figure out that they don't need to put up with crap any more.'

Even though this was his special subject Ludo was having a hard time convincing a doubtful Mike of the benefits that flowed from what he called the PJIs or Private Justice Initiatives and what Mike called vigilantism. Part of Ludo's remit in the Unorthodox Threat Field Section when he was in the Service had been to research private judicial action. The subject was closely related to his unfinished thesis on Non-Violent Insurgency and, more obviously, Thermidor's own foray into freelance law enforcement. He was always more than happy to talk about it and in Mike he had a literally captive audience. Better still, Clay was *hors de combat* having his injury attended to, so Ludo, spared his tiresome interventions, had the floor to himself.

'Cultural conventions can be quite rigid. For instance an out-of-control vehicle in a movie car chase can crash into a fruit stall or a pile of cardboard boxes but it may not hit a single innocent passer-by let alone a party of nuns pushing children in wheel chairs. Today we are as reluctant to talk about the pervasiveness of organised crime as in the 1950s people were reluctant to admit and discuss the prevalence of paedophilia.

'But things are changing . . . the passion, aggression and ingenuity which used to be the monopoly of the animal rights campaigners are no longer confined to protecting small furry creatures; they are being deployed in the harassment of a more venomous two-legged species – members of the criminal fraternity. Organised Crime has provoked Organised Retribution.

'There's a mass of little outfits out there with names like Nemesis and Precium, some of them operating within the law, some without it. They're organising naming-and-shaming fly-posting campaigns, pop-up courts dealing out unorthodox sentencing tariffs, physical harassment, serious violence against the person, some really nice houses going up in flames. Only a fraction of this activity gets reported for what it is. That's why you are not aware of it but what you have here is a coherent movement growing rapidly.'

'Yes, well, I'm vaguely aware of some of the stuff that's been happening. But why now?' said Mike. 'What's new?'

'Of course the net. The research possibilities are so potent. So now you've got all these people – from loners to large groups – crawling around cyberspace, uncovering sin and hunting down the sinners. Some have a personal grievance, some are just hacking and dumping data on the pavement for others to sort through and use to take what action they choose – all of them volunteer keyboard cops taking down the bad hats one way or the other.'

Ludo began to offer some choice examples of the genre in a sort of note-form delivery which made Mike wonder if he was being fed morsels from the Power-Point briefing that Ludo used to give new arrivals in the weird world of Unorthodox Threat.

'Notorious Indonesian ferry owner kidnapped while holidaying in Europe is forced to instruct his people to pay out millions to the relatives of the hundreds who drown when one of his overcrowded rust-buckets goes down.

'Hundreds of thousands of rupees dropped from a hijacked crane in downtown Mumbai are scattered among the midday crowd. Event turns out to be an involuntary donation from family of one of the more egregiously corrupt politicians. When family refuses to negotiate, politico's toes start turning up in ones and twos at their home in Marine Drive. Family capitulates just before they start on the fingers.

'Inflatable found in middle of the Med with eleven men chained to each other, four of them still alive but looking poorly. All identified as fraudulent people-smugglers allegedly guilty of cheating and drowning hundreds.'

'Hang on a mo: allegedly?'

'Yes, but these people do their research quite carefully.

'Gulf Arab princeling is found tied to a tree in a London park, shirtless, back in shreds. Responsibility claimed by Papier Mensen, Antwerp-based Maoist group, who pronounce Prince Abdul Doo-Dah guilty of flogging a Filipino servant girl. Like all Maoists, they are really cross about everything all the time. Their USP? Won't use a mobile, laptop or any electronic device; it's all on paper, every damn thing, so they're tricky to catch.

'But it's not all lefties. Quite a lot of people come from aid organisations, NGOs who've just got pissed off. That's certainly true of the Angels, who operate at the high end of the sector. The evidence points to them having people in Monaco, the Cayman Islands and almost certainly in some of the other hidey holes where they gather intelligence on the unclean and pass it on to those who can work with it. Apparently it was the Angels who blew the whistle on the financial arrangements of Adeus Indios. Ever head of them, Mike?'

'Can't say I have.'

'Gang of former Brazilian army officers who were living high in Rio from proceeds of throwing Indians off their land and running illicit logging operations enforced by a small army of jungle thugs. All snatched by persons unknown and never seen again.

'Some are quite niche. Yacht Watch, which you will have heard about, are obviously part of this. They have ensured that even the open seas are no refuge for the ill-gotten rich. Boats get daubed and sabotaged or find their arrival at a pleasant Mediterranean port is spoilt by some unpleasant quayside demonstrations. There's another lot operating out of Luxembourg who like to "go in through the drains", which is to say they infiltrate the secretive private security firms. They get a lot of really good information from tracking bodyguards.

'Then we have the MMPKD – which stands for the Hindi, *Makaan Maalik Prakaash Ko Dekhane*; not sure I've got the pronunciation absolutely right, but that means 'Landowner See The Light'. Big bad landlord – they're never worse than in India – makes bad mistake of leaving his home territory for a bit of R&R in Thailand. Finds himself making a Caliphate-style video publicly regretting his actions and cancelling all the debts that hold scores of farmers in subjugation on his land. Epidemiology? Close contact with the Naxalites. The group are now also targeting bonded labourers, aka slaves and are having some interesting successes.

'Biggest PJI has to be the battalion of web soldiers in China who compiled a data base of all buildings sited on land stolen by thugs and government officials. A movement, not an organisation. They create registers listing 'in perpetuity' names and whereabouts of miscreants who profited from expulsions, also of their children, grandchildren and other vulnerable and sometimes innocent relatives, who are sometimes subject to blackmail, robbery or violence. This introduces the concept of 'blood debt' as opposed to blood feud. Scores of properties have been handed back, or big money paid out in compensation by those anxious to get their names removed from the register.

'Mexican drugs lord, unfamiliar with the concept of justice without borders, gets kidnapped while on his hols in Spain. Gang post a demand to leave mega spondulicks at a precise time in a shallow shaft in a remote wooded location back in Mexico. Family of Señor Nero Sombrero dutifully comply having hired off-duty special forces to survey whole area. But they never get the kidnappers because minutes after the sacks of cash are delivered an incendiary device goes off at the bottom of the shaft and every last peso goes up in flames. Poor old Sombrero never seen again. Brilliant! You could almost call it conceptual art!'

'I don't remember that being reported.'

'Well it wouldn't be, would it?'

Ludo, who had concluded his tales of retribution, went across to the window and stared out over the town. When he'd exhausted the dramatic potential of his I-am-a-visionary-having-important-thoughts pose, he turning to face Mike and pronounced.

'The inevitable consequence of citizen journalism is citizen justice.'

67

It happened late in the morning after she had made her usual call to her mother.

'Well, I think this has gone on for long enough, don't you?'

Mo hadn't even heard him come into the room. She swung round to see Cropper standing there, staring at her.

'Oh Mo, you'll never guess what's happened.' A strange mock alarm in his tone. Mo immediately sensed trouble.

'We've had some tree surgeons operating in Brompton Crescent. They found a lovely little camera on one of the branches.'

'What was that?' said Mo.

'Who are you working for, love?' said Cropper, his voice soft and kind.

'I thought I was working for you,' replied Mo.

'And so did I.' Both were motionless. 'But you're not, are you?'

'Why do you say that?'

'Oh Mo. It's time to sing for your supper.'

Mo said nothing but turned back to the window. At least she'd have time to do what she needed.

'But first thing, we need to change your accommodation. Put you somewhere safer. Don't want you coming to any harm. After all, Cropper Dubois has a duty of care to you and your little friend.'

'Friend?'

Cropper smiled and pulled open the half-closed door. Tsanko was standing there; his arms wrapped round the chest of Shin, holding him upright. His captive was tightly gagged and bound, his head lolling, chin on chest. Tsanko smirked triumphantly at Mo.

'What's all this about?' said Mo. She hadn't given up yet. 'Who's he?'

'Oh, give us a break, Mo. I've asked your good friend Tsanko to put himself at your disposal so you can both tell him what you've been up to.'

'I don't understand this but I will help Mr Tsanko in any way I can.'

'Oh you will, my love, you will.'

Mo fell unconscious to the floor.

68

Mike was suddenly wide awake. *Something is wrong; something is different.* He stared at the ceiling listening. Then he realised there was no sound of children in the apartment below; There had been no goodbyes from the family, but then there hadn't been any hellos either – Mike had never met them and now they'd gone. About time too. Mike guessed that Clay had finally decided that the advantage of the convincing cover provided by these friends of his was outweighed by the risk. How could anyone let their children be used like this? Clay was the sort of person who'd site a rocket launcher in a school playground.

It was day six in the Thermidor household and Mike was cabin-fever crazy. An emergency drill shortly after 2 a.m. hadn't helped his mood. It looked as though it was going to be a great day to be on the slopes but he was trapped indoors with a bunch of over-educated loonies. Mike wanted out. He wanted to be on his balcony, drinking coffee, enjoying his view of the mountains. He wanted to be down in Bar X trading gossip over a beer with Sandy or playing a game of chess with Yuri, the nastiest-looking of Oleg's bodyguards, who had become one of Mike's favourite chess partners. But most of all Mike wanted to be up on the mountain doing what he came here to do: skiing. He dreamt of being in that intoxicating air, looking down on the clouds as he was flipping turns on his flappy wands, to feel the snow hurrying back up the slope beneath his feet, to feel the mountain fall away from under him and let him fly.

Mike was sick to death of life day in and day out with Emil and his fucking Detectives and his rules and his keep-fit sessions and their god-awful coffee and the horrendous food. He'd thought about breaking the lock on the drinks cupboard and slaughtering the Scotch. He wanted to give Ludo a piece of his mind and find out when they'd let him go.

Ludo had apparently gone into town so Mike went to Clay's

office. Candy was duty guard dog. She looked at him with a pained smile as though he'd escaped from a facility for the mentally deranged and she needed to humour him while she reached under her chair for the Taser.

'How can we help you, Mike?'

How did she always manage to make his name sound like a troublesome medical condition? He tried to steady himself with some small talk.

'That's an unusual bracelet. Very nice. Where's it from?'

'It's from Nepal,' then added hurriedly, 'a trekking holiday. What can I do for you?'

'Nepal? When were you in Nepal, Ulrike?'

'Oh way back. Why are you calling me Ulrike, Mike?'

'Why do you think?'

'I don't know.'

'Baader Meinhof? Ulrike Meinhof?'

'Oh, I see. That's not very nice, Mike. But quite funny. Just one thing, though: we don't do jokes when it's Threat Level Orange or above.'

'You what? Of course, how foolish of me. So tell me, Ulrike, what are the jokey colours? Red with yellow spots, is it?'

'Blue, brown and green, actually. And it's Candy. But how can we help you, Mike?'

'I know it's Candy, Candy, but I want to talk to Brown Owl . . . NOW!' Mike barked.

She looked down at the two sets of his whitening knuckles resting on her desk as though they were muddy boots on her living-room carpet.

'Which one's Brown Owl, Mike?'

'You know exactly who I mean . . . or is he off somewhere saving mankind?'

'I'm sorry?'

'Clay.'

'He's usually around, Mike. He tends not to go very far.'

'Well would you tell him I'd like to see him please?'

'Of course.' She tapped in an extension number.

'Are you alright, Mike?' she asked, while she waited for an answer. "Would you like me to find you an aspirin?" She felt around in her desk drawer without taking her eyes off him. Blue eyes, fantastic eyes, he had to admit. Eyes that could captivate a tableful of subalterns. But he wasn't going to let them get in his way.

'You're not looking too good, Mike . . . Oh, Clay, I've got Hangonamo here in reception. He says he wants to see you."

Hangonamo? For a moment Mike was confused and then the penny dropped. Hang-on-a-mo. That's what they're calling him. He couldn't believe it . . . they'd got a bloody cheek.

Clay sensed trouble as soon as Mike walked in so he fired a burst of pre-emptive bonhomie.

'Mike, come on in. My goodness, you look well. How do you manage it stuck in here all day? You must give us all some lessons. Pull up a pew, won't you. Great, now how can I help?'

Mike's anger was slightly assuaged by seeing that Clay's arm was in a sling.

'How much longer is this going to go on? I'm fed up with this place. I'm fed up with your fucking wolf cubs. And I'm fed up with your god-awful coffee.'

It was the last item on the list that seemed to strike home; Clay looked quite wounded and turned unpleasantly cool.

'Try not to forget the reason you're stuck in here with us is because you fucked up.'

'I fucked up?'

'By leaving some of your footage behind of the man in the white suit.'

'How could I know where that footage was,' said Mike. 'And, another thing, what's all this crap about, "We don't do jokes when it's Threat Level Orange"? For God's sake! You guys are all off your trolleys.'

Clay looked startled. 'Who told you that?'

'Candy.'

'She did?' He considered this information and began to smile to himself. 'Candy told you that?'

'Yes, just now.'

'Oh, that's very good.'

'What?'

'That's really very good. She's quite something, isn't she, our Candy?'

'I'm sure, but . . .'

'She was just winding you up, Mike.'

'She . . . I'll kill her.'

'Go for it, Mike, but my money's on the girl.'

Clay's laptop bleeped. He went over to read it; then addressed Mike, now unsmiling and businesslike.

'So how exactly can I help?'

'How much longer do I have to be here?'

'If I knew I'd tell you, but I don't.'

'There's no reason why you couldn't just let me get the hell out of town. I can go to another resort for ten days or so and get on with my life . . . my work and so on.'

'There's every reason why we can't let you do that.'

'So why?'

'You'd better sit down.'

69

Now that Mike was seated, Clay rose and began to pace around the room.

'You don't seem to have taken on board what we – and you, Mike – are up against here. You need to do what I say. No exaggeration: make the wrong choice now and you'll regret it for the rest of your days . . . which won't be many – we're talking single figures here. You need to understand that your life insurance policy is with

Thermidor now. We're all that's between you and the people who took care of Maldini – and you saw what happened to him.'

'Maldini?'

'The stiff on the chairlift.'

'Him? What was that all about?'

'The work of one of the Italian Board members. When he found out that he was starring in a movie shown on giant screens at a downtown wine bar, he went ape and ordered the execution of his security man – that was Maldini.

'Crane went completely tonto over the incident. Maldini's bravura descent from the clouds in full view of the whole resort with the speakers blaring show tunes by Verdi wasn't his idea of keeping a low profile. And Cropper wasn't a happy bunny either. "These fucking Italians," was his reaction. "I swear to God, they'll do for us." He was right of course. Got to remember that these are the people who put the opera in operational.'

Mike wasn't listening. He was wondering how Ludo could possibly know what Cropper had said.

'Your friends have been a great help to us with that footage.' Clay pulled the laptop back towards him and hunted for a file in the video folder. 'Look at it, it's fantastic.'

Mike hadn't paid much attention to the Messigny faces on the footage, but he now realised that Kornie had reaped a rich harvest as he zipped through the throng. One or two faces would have been unrecognisable, but most of them were quite sharp. 'Look, there's our boy! Crane. Bingo, eh?' Mike recognised him even with sunglasses: the white hair, thin nose, thin lips.

'This saved our bacon. We needed to video everyone who was at the Chalet that day. Best chance was to put a man in the trees facing the main entrance and catch them coming and going. Although it was partly hidden by the building, he managed to video some of the guests coming out onto the terrace. Then your man Tyler comes blundering through the woods threatening to blow his cover to the Chalet security guards. As it happened they were distracted by the pandemonium from the terrace as Mr Kornie Løvland, may his name be praised, made his fleeting appearance at the party.

'As soon we saw what was showing on the screens at Bar X we had to have it. Unfortunately the Messigny crowd were already on your case before we could get to you. We could only sit and watch as they made their move. I realised you were up to something when you came up to the gallery. So we tracked you and for insurance we took Tyler into our care along with his cell phone.'

'I know about that bit.'

'Indeed. Which was how we knew what you were up to. When you left Bar X we followed at a discreet distance.'

'Hardly discreet; I saw your guy.'

'That wasn't our man. We didn't have to stay so close because we knew where you were going. You saw one of Cropper's people – and you shook him off. Good work, that. As soon as you'd got to the editing suite we sent you a text from Tyler telling you what to do and we sent you two other warning texts to tell you to get out of the chalet. Which you ignored. We lost you when you went up the hill into Chalet Mazot. You didn't help us by not going home. We tried to organise a rendezvous that night to get the stick off you but you went off air. Only option was send you a warning text saying bad people were looking for you and hope for the best.

'We asked around and discovered where you kept your skis; next morning we followed your pal when he came to collect them so we were able to have our little chat on the Morillon chair.

'But then the following day it became apparent that your situation had changed for the worse.'

'In what way?'

'When they first looked at the material from the edit suite they were searching for the terrace footage. Tyler's endless footage going through the woods seemed irrelevant so they didn't bother to check it properly. Sloppy. It was only when Cropper appeared and he went through every centimetre of the footage himself that they learned about our man hiding in the woods. They assumed he was linked to Kornie's intrusion so in their eyes you and the Team were no longer innocents who'd blundered into the gathering on the terrace but were part of a big operation working against them. You were in a very bad place.'

'How do you know all this? How do you know about Cropper discovering the white suit footage?'

'Another time, Mike. The point was that as soon as we heard about it, I followed you to the Pascal bubble to warn you of the danger you were in. I detailed someone to keep an eye on you while I organised for your Tyler and Co to be rounded up. I clearly told you not to make or take any calls, but you couldn't even manage that, so when Cropper's lot texted you from Blake's phone your minder had to watch helpless as you walked right into the trap – all because you just couldn't do what you were fucking well told. And that's why you're stuck with us and, more to the point, that's why we're stuck with you.'

Mike was now getting the picture and it wasn't pretty. He could see how his visit to Messigny had incriminated him – Dubois had already seen him snooping around the Chalet; he'd have assumed Mike was reconnoitring for Kornie's intrusion.

'By the way, our minder who kept tabs on you after you were snatched was Candy – so maybe some thanks from you are in order here – and we were able to con them into moving you out of the lift engine shed with a bogus warning of an imminent inspection.'

Mike remembered the call that ended his interrogation.

'You cut it a little fine.'

'We didn't have a lot of time to get organised.'

'You did well to recruit *les druides* so quickly.'

'Don't be daft, Mike. That was just our people in fancy dress.'

'What!

'To make Cropper's people think it was the little green folk.'

Mike wasn't sure if Clay's self-satisfied look was prompted by their own ingenuity or seeing him looking so shocked.

70

Armoise: Perennial herbaceous plant. 17th day of
the Republican Calendar month of Thermidor.

Encyclopédie Décosse

'Tell you what. How about we take a short walk? Some fresh air? Colza says the coast is clear at the moment.'

Clay was trying to placate poor Mike, who was still seething with indignation. He accepted the offer; anything to get out of that place, even if only for few minutes. They went down to the boot room, where Mike was given a maroon jacket, a muffler, deep-brimmed ski cap and wraparound sunglasses by little Prêle, the chopstick.

Mike felt weirdly disoriented by being out of doors. He turned to look back at his prison. The garage door was open; the kids' bikes and the purple space hopper were on view, with a picnic cold box and some old tarpaulins strewn across the floor. On the balconies duvets were airing. Toys cluttered the ground-floor windowsill of the apartment which had been occupied by the family whose children he had heard but never seen. Juniper was saying, 'We have nothing to hide.'

'So you've been coming here for a long time?' asked Clay after a few minutes.

'Yes,' said Mike unhelpfully.

'What brought you here in the first place? Why Val?'

Mike took a perverse pleasure in ignoring Clay's question and asking one of his own.

'Okay. Then how did you get the chairlift to stop the first time I met you? Also, what about that call to the wheelhouse of the cable car hut which ended my interrogation?'

'We have friends here.'

'How come?'

'The war tore this place apart,' replied Clay, 'and there's still a divide – not that you'd notice it.'

Mike knew all about Val de Ligne's war; he'd been coming here for more than twenty years. He knew how the town was divided, how some had become collaborators and how others had left their homes to join the Ferryman and his Resistance in the mountains. He also knew about the Battle of the Plateau and its traumatic consequences, about which families were still unreconciled. But he said nothing.

'The past is still present here,' said Clay. 'All over Europe descendants of Resistance families have kept in touch with the British and the others who helped them. Not just the annual ceremonies at the war memorial. There is still a living network. A couple of our people are part of that, so we've found locals here who've been happy to help. We haven't asked too much of them.'

Mike wasn't completely convinced.

Clay's cell phone chirruped.

'Yes, Colza, what is it?' Clay stopped dead in his tracks and seemed to sway on his feet for a moment as if he'd taken a really hard punch.

'Oh my Christ!'

71

Clay had said nothing. It was Ludo who told Mike the news.

'Two of our people have been caught by Cropper; they're being held in a chalet on the edge of town. We have to get them back. Clay and Colza are refining a plan. We'll need to account for a lot of comings and goings, so we're having a birthday party for one of our neighbour's kids.'

Juniper was suddenly buzzing with activity. Clay and Colza were scrutinising a blow-up of the piste map spread across the dining-room table. The living-room windows were bright with coloured balloons. Outside on the veranda two people were fixing a banner to the handrail. And beside the chalet there were now two life-size snowmen flanking a giant bright red polystyrene figure '11'. Nearby a small group were building a bonfire.

From one of the bedrooms Mike could hear three or four voices softly singing what sounded like a German drinking song. People were hurrying in and out with information for Colza. Ludo, aloof from it all, sat alone with a pile of papers on his lap in a corner.

Mike could overhear Clay interrogating Colza.

'What about Bélier and Abricot?'

'They're having their driving lesson.'

'And Sherman – they've given him a thorough once-over?'

'Of course, Clay.'

'I mean we don't want everything going wrong because of a flat tyre or something.'

'I don't think it's going to have a flat tyre, Clay.'

'So we're all sorted?'

'We're still trying to clarify the geography. The chalet where they're being held is called Ibex. There's nothing online so someone's gone to find a letting agency that has got it on its books. They'll say they're interested in renting it and would like to see the floor plans.'

'Let's hope that works – it's going to be a lot more difficult without them. And what about the wagons? You're sure you're happy with that idea?'

Clay was being doggedly uncertain in his search for reassurance; Colza was doing his best to give him some.

'It's a good solution and a lot less risky than the road option.'

Clay looked up and saw Mike.

'Mike, we've got a bit of an operation running this evening and we need your help.

Do you do fireworks?'

'Well, I always put on something for my son Paul . . .'

'Great, grab your jacket and boots. Colza will show you what to do.'

Colza led the way to the garage where someone was changing the front number plate on one of the two SUVs, the rear screen was being covered in garish stickers.

'Lady Alicia is having a bit of a makeover for tonight,' he explained. Lady Alicia! Mike despaired at the sheer childishness of Thermidor's people. To them it was all just some daft party game.

On one side of the garage half a dozen cardboard boxes had been stacked against the wall.

'Grab an armful of these,' said Colza, pointing to a stack of cardboard boxes. From the maker's labels Mike could see they were top-of-the-range fireworks. They carried them out to an open patch of snow well clear of the chalet, which now had, strung along the length of the first-floor balcony railing, the words 'HAPPY BIRTHDAY, TABITHA!'

'This'll do just here,' said Colza. 'I'll leave you to it, if that's okay. Got a lot on. You can set them up and let them off in any way you want – except for the twelve large rockets you'll find in here. These are very precious. You need to arrange them in three groups of four. That's how you'll end your display. Each of the four must go off at very short but regular intervals like this.' He demonstrated by clapping four times at short intervals. 'Have you got that?'

'Got it.'

'Then show me.'

Mike repeated the four claps.

'You understand what's happening here?

'Yes, I think I do.'

72

The four of them were sprawled around the living room, Tyler, Jean-Luc, Blake and Kornie who was wearing his I SKIED WITH THE DOLPHINS T-shirt. When Mike came in they stared at him as if he was a ghost, then rose to greet him like a long-lost brother. To

Mike's surprise Blake, although a little subdued, seemed none the worse for his ordeal.

After they had exchanged accounts of what had happened to them since they'd last seen each other, Blake went to his room, Jean-Luc went off to check his portfolio and Kornie moved to a quiet corner of the room to play Galactic Swamp Wars Two, giving Mike a chance to talk to Tyler alone; he wanted to ask him a question.

'Why did Blake stay away from you after the Couloir?'

'He felt humiliated.'

'How come?'

'Put yourself in his boots. You are just about to chuck yourself off the top of a mountain that wants to kill you when you hear a voice inside your head saying, "No, I don't think so. This is crazy." If you heard a voice like that you'd do what any sensible person would do and say, "You're quite right. I don't want to do this any more. Something inside me has changed. I'm going to go back down in the chopper and I'm going to get on with the rest of my life."'

'You mean he bottled it?'

'Yes.'

'That business with the binding was just an excuse?'

'Of course. You don't have faulty equipment in a situation like that. Everything had been checked by each of us the night before. The broken binding thing was just for the benefit of Saul and the crew. We knew what had happened and Blake knew we knew.

'And you should know that a couple of days before the Couloir Noir his girlfriend told him she was pregnant. That would have made him think twice about risking his life, which is why he bottled out.'

'Chemicals in the brain . . . they change when you get older,' said Mike, nodding in agreement. He was all too aware of how his own skiing had grown more cautious over the years.

'You don't need to feel sorry for him,' said Tyler. 'Remember, in his day he was fearless, one of the best. Nothing can change that.'

Later that afternoon a tall auburn-haired twenty-something girl arrived with a shorter, slightly older man. Mike noticed this good-looking couple were welcomed with a certain respect by Ludo and Clay. When he asked Colza about them he was told they were Amande and Aunée aka Rebecca and Terry. They spent almost an hour talking with Ludo in his room.

73

'Gentlemen, it's time for everyone to have their sweeties,' said Clay, gesturing to Mike and the Team to join him at the dining table. He produced a zip-top leather wallet from his pocket and emptied the contents onto his open palm – five small plastic tubes like miniature cigarettes, each waisted in the middle, one half red, one half black. Clay walked around the table placing one capsule in front of each of them, murmuring as he made his first delivery a soft but jaunty 'There you go,' like a waiter in a pizza restaurant. When Clay got to him, Mike heard himself murmuring, 'Thank you', which made him feel foolish; when Clay said, 'No worries', Mike wanted to throttle him.

Next Clay produced some cord lanyards, on each of which was threaded a small brass cylinder. 'And these are for you to put your capsules on, OK? From now on you wear these round your neck at all times. At *all* times. Is that clear?

'This is worst-case scenario,' he continued. 'When things go seriously wrong and there is no other way out, you have a choice. Bite into the black end of the capsule the contents will knock you out for three and a half to four hours. Or bite the red end and you'll be dead within a minute. Got that? Black for black-out and red rhymes with dead.'

'I get it,' said Tyler. 'This is the Kool-Aid, right?'

Clay conceded the point with a slight incline of his head and sat down. The uneasy silence that followed was eventually broken by

Kornie, who was ostentatiously sniffing his capsule and pulling a series of disapproving faces.

'Dooday cummin any udder flavuss?'

Clay remained expressionless.

'Good question, Kornie. We'll try and get an answer for you . . .' Clay suddenly rose in his seat, reached across and forced Kornie's hand down on the table like a parent with a misbehaving child. 'And keep that thing AWAY FROM YOUR MOUTH . . . there's a good chap. Any other questions?'

Clay chose to let the silence run for a bit before he continued.

'If you think this is an unnecessary measure, bear with me while I tell you a true story.'

And he told them the tale of Customs Officer Han while they all listened in a stunned silence.

When he'd finished he plucked some sheets of paper from the file in front of him and passed them round.

'These are the before and afters.'

'He's sort of smiling?' asked Jean-Luc as he stared at the second of the two pictures, puzzled.

'Not really. Look at the others – the close-ups.'

Jean-Luc looked as though he was going to vomit.

'These were taken in the Chronic Ward unit of the naval hospital outside Ping Pei – he's been there for over four years and he's still in a very bad way. As long as he lives he'll never be well enough to be a witness . . . or anything else.'

Mike looked at the others as the pictures were examined. Kornie had more or less adopted the foetal position. Tyler pushed the pages away from him, whispering, 'Okay, okay, okay!'

Clay looked around the table, his eyes engaging each of them in turn. 'I have been telling you this to emphasise the seriousness of our situation. The man who gave the order and the man who inflicted these things on Customs Officer Han are both within a kilometre or two of where we are sitting now. Their people are scouring the town for you; they want to talk to you very badly.

That's why I've given you these things. Remember if you get caught it's not the dying that you should be worried about as much as the staying alive. So just remember Customs Officer Han.'

Clay let them think about that for a few moments then suddenly became brusque and businesslike. 'Let's get the sweeties round our necks, yes?'

They did as they were told in silence.

'Gentlemen, perhaps you'd like to return to your quarters. We'll have a hot snack at 16.05 before we set off at 16.50.'

74

'Mike, it's show-time,' Colza announced, 'and here, just in case you'd forgotten to bring a box of matches . . .' He held out a cigarette lighter.

'I hadn't, actually.'

As he emerged from the boot room Mike saw Bélier, Abricot and Basilic loading boxes into Lady Alicia. Outside, a large party of children and adults were standing around the bonfire.

Mike launched a couple of mines from the mortars to get everyone's attention. It was as gratifying as ever to hear the spectators' *oooh*s and *aaah*s; as he darted around lighting the touch-paper fuses, he felt that for the first time in four days he was actually enjoying himself. As the Roman candles gave way to horsetails and cherry bombs he moved to the back of the display to be ready for the grand finale.

Mike set off the rockets in their groups of four as he had been instructed. It didn't seem to have any connection with Beethoven's Fifth; but Clay was sure that the captives in their agony, mental or physical, would recognise it as a signal; they would know that this was Thermidor saying, 'We are here. Have hope. Be strong. We will rescue you.' Mike wondered, though, if it might be a bit too late. Maybe they'd already taken their sweeties. The red ones.

ACT THREE

1

'Ludo, would you go with the decoy party,' said Clay. 'Decoy' had a whiff of the 'tethered goat' about it, but having volunteered Ludo felt he had to accept. He was assigned to one of three snowmobiles which took them to their position above the target site.

Clay pressed the button on the short wave radio. Somewhere in the background raucous voices were singing *Eisgekühlter Bommerlunder*. Ludo listened as Clay gave occasional orders and called for situation reports from his command post on the side of the piste some two kilometres above Ibex.

'Basilic, are you in position? Over.'

'Prêle, where have you got to? Over.' There was a long pause before some muffled cursing and a voice saying, 'Okay, we're on station.'

As they waited, Ludo thought about the plight of Mo. They owed her everything. She had spent almost two years working at the nerve centre of the Board as an assistant in the private office of Crane himself. The risk she had taken was unimaginable, but her presence had been like having a webcam hidden in the heart of the enemy's headquarters perpetually trained on Crane relaying a stream of crucial information. It was to Mo that Tsanko had confided the grisly story of his military service and given clues to his murderous past; it was she who warned of Cropper's plan to dispose of Blake and who had discovered the reason for Crane's unshakable hold over Drake and Parsons. And of course, it was Mo who had revealed that the location for the meeting of the Board was to be the Chalet Messigny and, crucially, warned Thermidor that Cropper had found the White Suit footage. Everyone in Thermidor owed her.

'The Beauregard lift has stopped.' Ludo didn't recognise the voice.

'Who's that?' he asked.

'Prêle,' said Clay.

There was only the sound of ambient crackling, then Clay's voice.

'Abricot, this is Clay. Where have we got to? Over.'

'We're good. Enough to raise complaints but not enough to bring out the gendarmerie. Over.'

'Christ, I hope not. So are you in position?'

'Yes, Clay.'

'What about Sherman?'

'He's on the way. You'll be able to hear him in a minute.'

'Okay everyone, it's a go. Basilic?'

'Affirmative.'

'Ivraie?'

'Affirmative.'

'Brebis?'

'Affirmative.'

For a moment Ludo couldn't help suspecting that these people were having a whale of a time.

'Okay,' shouted Clay. 'Roll Sherman!'

At the end of the day the closure of the mountain bars tips the late drinkers down the hill. Most are in reasonable order even if they do ski a bit more recklessly, but that evening the sounds of a group of three young, drunk Germans could be heard especially clearly as they came down Marmotte from Bar Normand, where they had been drinking for an hour and a half. As they came round the last bend just above the houses they stopped to hurl raucous abuse at each other and at brief intervals united in ragged song.

In a carefully phased programme the lifts were coming to a halt all over the resort, which was the cue for phalanxes of piste bashers to emerge from their sheds and fan out across the slopes to all quarters of the resort. One of them was grinding its way up Marmotte as the German drinkers were coming down on the other side of the run. It was only when they were within twenty metres of each other that one of the skiers swerved across the piste, spun round and collapsed in a tangle of limbs in the path of the machine. The driver stabbed the brake pedal and came to a halt just a few metres from the fallen skier. Intent on the figure struggling to his feet, the driver failed to notice that the other two skiers had moved round behind his machine. The next thing he knew was that his cabin door had burst open and a masked figure armed with a pistol was gesturing to him to get out.

'I am sorry about this but we need to borrow your vehicle.'

The gunman produced an envelope and pushed it into the pisteur's jacket.

'Here is a small gift by way of apology for the inconvenience. Please go quickly and report what has happened. No need to mention the envelope.'

The pisteur hurried off.

Bélier, now at the controls, put the machine into gear; it lurched forward with a roar and crawled noisily up the side of the piste. After four hundred metres, he swung the steering wheel hard to the left and opened the throttle; the machine clambered up a slight incline and headed straight for the first of a group of four chalets at almost 24 mph. Two people rushed out of the building, gesticulating frantically, but there was no arguing with nine tons of 450-horse-powered steel and they scurried out of the way. In the moment before the machine reached the building, Basilic sounded three short blasts on the klaxon followed by a long one.

The collision was spectacular. Later Jean-Luc, watching from the slope above with Tyler and Kornie, said that it reminded him of a croupier's rake pushing a pile of chips across the baize. The piste basher's curved blade, designed to shift nine tons of snow, struck the building at forty-five degrees, shattering and scattering timber and breezeblock. As planned, the entire corner of the structure was removed. Moments after the impact there was a shattering of glass on the other side of the building and the sound of sharp explosions from two stun grenades. When the renegade vehicle was brought to a standstill by the pyramid of debris it had created, Bélier eased the gear stick into neutral but left the engine running: Colza had said they would need the noise.

The scene in the ruins of Ibex was chaotic. Over the roaring of the engine there were sounds of German voices shouting. Abricot led Brebis and Bélier through the breach in the walls and immobilised two guards who, dazed by the stun grenades, offered no resistance. The assault party found Mo and Shin bound, gagged and semi-conscious in adjacent rooms; they appeared to have bitten the black end of their capsules. Shin in his groggy confusion was trying to convey something as he pointed at Basilic's headgear, possibly because it was one of those medieval court jester caps in bright red and yellow felt sprouting curved horns with bells on the end.

As they carried Mo and Shin from the chalet to the edge of the piste, Jean-Luc and Kornie appeared, each at the helm of a blood wagon, accompanied by Tyler. Moments later they sped off down the slope.

By this stage everyone from the neighbouring chalets had come outside to watch the mayhem, tut-tutting about this appalling bunch of drunks who had hijacked the piste basher for a prank; things had got out of control. Several people had rung the gendarmerie who said that officers who were on their way.

Although some in the Ibex contingent were in disarray, some were not. Cropper Dubois had learned the lesson from Kornie's intrusion at Messigny: two guards had their skis right by them and they were out on the piste soon after the piste basher struck, in time to see the prisoners whisked away in the blood wagons. They went off in hot pursuit and were soon gaining on Tyler, Kornie and Jean-Luc. The Team seemed badly hampered by their sledges and after a couple of hundred metres, they abandoned their cargoes to their fate and flew off down the slope.

While one of Cropper's two guards sped off after the Team the other went to recapture the escaped prisoners who had remained motionless in their sledges. It was soon clear why. The two blood wagons were occupied by nothing more than piles of blankets. In the confusion none of Cropper's contingent had noticed that the two captives, once removed from the shattered chalet, had been taken out of sight over the bank and onto the piste. There they were strapped to trailers behind two waiting snowmobiles, which, their engines drowned by the din of the piste basher, roared up the slope and into the safety of the night.

2

Kornie, Jean-Luc and Tyler had successfully carried out their diversion, which was designed to lure their pursuers well below their chalet so they wouldn't be able to get back up and rejoin any struggle at Ibex. The Team's orders were to ski down to town and rendezvous with Count Fernando on the edge of the piste by the Grand Hotel. But the immediate pursuit by Cropper's two guards had taken them by surprise and although Kornie and Jean-Luc had got well clear and were heading for the rendezvous, Tyler, some distance behind them, was being closely followed. He reckoned that the least he could do was lead his pursuer away from the rendezvous so he abandoned his planned route and headed towards the hamlet of Mazou.

Ludo sat waiting nervously at the controls of a snowmobile with the engine running. His was the first of four lined up at ten-metre intervals along the far side of the slope from Ibex ready to evacuate the assault party who were now running across the snow towards them, having emerged from the smokescreen which they'd laid to cover their retreat.

In the event, the assault party made for the first three snowmobiles and the whole convoy roared off as soon as the last man was aboard. The whole convoy, that is, except for Ludo and his machine, which had gone just a few metres before a lucky bullet smacked into the engine and cut it dead, bringing the machine to a halt. Ludo made one effort to restart it. Not a cough. The others had now disappeared up the hill, leaving Ludo to face the Cropper Dubois contingent alone. He abandoned his vehicle and, jinking left and right as he ran, reached the edge of the piste, scrabbled up the bank and flung himself over the top into the cover of the far side. It was quite a steep drop of some fifty metres and, completely out of control, he tumbled all the way to the bottom and lay there breathless. Although he could still hear the roar of the tireless Sherman trying to push the remnants of Chalet Ibex out of its way, it was quieter here and, more importantly, out of range. But that wouldn't last. The gunman would be crossing the slope now in pursuit.

Ludo knew he had to get off the open expanse of snow as quickly as possible, so he set off downhill towards the uncertain cover of some trees – a scrawny plantation rather than a wood. From there he would make his way to the village beyond. He didn't need to look behind him to know that he was leaving clear footprints in the moonlit virgin snow.

Twenty minutes later Ludo was crouching in the shelter of the log pile of an unoccupied house, checking that the road was clear before he made his dash for the middle of the village. There he'd find ample cover and his tracks would no longer be visible. He knew his armed pursuer would have seen where he rolled down the slope and followed his footprints. Now they were both in the village but neither knew where the other one was. He had just broken his cover and was trying to walk silently down the road when he heard a voice.

'Hello, my friend. I know you are there.'

Ludo froze. It couldn't have been more than a block away, somewhere between him and the piste. That voice!

Ludo knew instinctively that this must be the dreaded Georgi Tsanko.

'Stop and talk, my friend.'

He can't possibly see me; Tsanko is bluffing.

'We do business. It is better for you, I think!' No! The words seemed to be coming *towards* him. Ludo felt sick with terror. Tsanko wasn't bluffing; he knew exactly where Ludo was.

Ludo moved slowly up the road, trying not to make any noise.

'You don't talk to me, my friend?' The voice was definitely closer. Tsanko must be coming along the road towards the intersection ahead of him. He'd be spotted immediately; he needed to hide.

'I catch you. This making me happy. Then you talk. And I have way to make you smile . . .'

Ludo edged off the road into the entrance area of a chalet that had a small rubbish bin shed at the edge of the road, in the penumbra of the nearest sodium street light. He crouched down in its meagre cover.

'. . . then you find out things we can do to you.' The voice, now unmasked by buildings, was much clearer and closer. Tsanko must have turned the corner and was probably in the middle of the crossroads.

'I think you are scared, no?' Wrong. Ludo wasn't scared. He was terrified. But Tsanko had raised his voice, although he was now much closer. Ludo told himself, 'That means he *doesn't* know where I am.'

'You are scared, yes?'

The voice sounded so close and the questioner so genuinely concerned, that Ludo almost answered out loud. Moving with extreme caution, he peered around the edge of the bin shed. Tsanko was no more than twenty metres away; he was on his skis, poling a few yards, stopping, then poling again.

'Scared? You scared of losing your ears? Your eyes? Your balls? No problems; you are choosing.'

Ludo winced.

'Maybe you lose all!'

Ludo was enraged as much as he was terrified by the obscenity of this creature roaming the picturesque streets of this hamlet, shouting his depraved threats while beyond the cosy gingham curtains families were having their supper.

'My friend, I make special offer because you are my friend!'

Christ! Now he was looking in the direction of Ludo's hiding place.

'Is last chance for you.'

Remember he still hasn't seen you.

'We do deal. You come and talking with me; no harm to you. I make this promise.'

Ludo was trying not to panic, trying to keep very still. It was so quiet that he thought he could almost hear the snowflakes land.

'Stop for us, friend. Is better for you.' Tsanko moved forward, his head turning slowly, looking left and right, systematically scanning the space in front of him, with the precision of a security camera. A few metres, pause, search repeated, until he was out of sight. He was heading towards the piste.

'You have a bad time when we catch you!' And then the same voice but a little more faintly, 'You better working with us, my friend!'

As the threat receded, Ludo began to see an upside to his situation: after all they'd been through together, Tsanko still counted Ludo as his friend.

3

Tyler carried on down the slope, unaware that the other skier from Cropper's contingent was behind him and concealing the sound of his pursuit by synchronising the rasp of his turns with those of Tyler. When the distance seemed right, the pursuer stopped suddenly and raised his rifle, aiming between Tyler's zigzagging shoulder blades; they presented a needle-sharp dark target against the moonlit white slope.

Hearing the crunch of the gunman's skis as he braked, Tyler turned to see his pursuer; he did a violent jump-turn to get himself to the edge of the piste. Frantically jinking and swooping, now dropping into a low crouch to offer a smaller target, now rising and sinking in exaggerated movements to take more speed out of the ground, Tyler avoided all of the six shots loosed at him before he was able to get far enough ahead and out of the line of fire.

There was no way Tyler could shake the gunman off and get to the rendezvous; he needed to stop and contact Colza to make a new arrangement. He jinked into the woods, going far enough to be out of sight but not in so deep that he couldn't keep a clear view of the slope and escape quickly. The sudden exertion had been quite a shock and now that he had stopped moving he was feeling tired as well as scared.

He took his phone from his breast pocket. Although he didn't think his voice could be heard he wasn't taking any chances and texted the pre-loaded number. THINK HAVE LOST TAIL. IN TREES ABOVE NURSERY. CANT DO RV. PLAN B?

He got a reply within a couple of minutes.

GO CARPARK. LEAVE SKIS + BOOTS. THRU TOWN TO NEW RV IN TREES BY LAST BUS STOP.

Not a bad idea, thought Tyler. The new RV, accessible but out of the way, was also good. It would mean getting far enough ahead of Cropper's man to dump his skis and change into the hiking boots in his backpack, then he could get down to the river, which was shallow enough to wade cross. Once on the other side it would be ten minutes to the RV on the road on the edge of the woods. The run, if he could manage it, might be just enough to stop his wet feet from freezing.

Tyler replied OK and moved forward to the edge of the piste. He looked and listened carefully for several minutes. No sign of his pursuer but the expanse of pure smooth snow in front of him took on an air of deep menace. He forced himself to leave the safe cover of the trees. He bore right down a bank to pick up some speed before heading out across the open space. This area was hardly ever skied so he knew he was taking the risk of leaving clear tracks but his trail would disappear once he got into the town.

Tyler made it to the car park and was poling frantically through the cars when he heard a commotion behind him. His pursuer was back on his tail. No time to stop and shed his boots and skis; now he'd have to ski on through town. As it was early evening there were a lot of people around and as he shot down the main street he had to shout at groups dawdling along the middle of the street to get out of the way. Every now and then he heard a cheer go up behind him and some clapping. He realised why. On seeing a second skier, the onlookers assumed they were watching a race and were urging on the man in second place.

In the hope of shaking off his pursuer, Tyler took a sudden right.

Rue d'Allemagne was much quieter, with a reasonable incline, and he made fast progress; no sooner had he thought *I must have lost him now* than he heard an angry voice shouting at him. *This is no ordinary skier.* Tyler was now speeding down to the old town without a clue what he'd do when he got there. The revised rendezvous on the other side of the river was *kaput* – it depended on him having a decent lead over his pursuer and he didn't. Only hope: duck into some hiding place, wait until it seemed safe and then sneak down to the river. Easier thought than done. What hiding place?

Every metre that Tyler travelled narrowed his options. He'd had to cut his speed as he entered the old town, where houses were clustered close and higgledy-piggledy, flanking a maze of narrow streets and alleys which were only dimly lit if they were lit at all. Assailed by a mounting terror, he tried to tell himself that he'd skied his way out of trouble before. But it didn't help; that was different. This was not a technical problem that lay in the terrain beneath his skis; this threat was behind his back, chasing him, presenting a danger he'd been told about but didn't really comprehend. And if he needed to be reminded what the stakes were in this race he had only to think about the capsule on the lanyard round his neck. '*You are the better skier,*' he kept telling himself. But this is about more than skiing; this is about tactics. So think.

An idea. One way to lose his shadow which might work, but it was a risk. *Go up instead of down.* It might present new possibilities. And an opportunity did soon present itself: at the fork ahead of him one of the narrow tracks led upwards. He drove his weight down to generate every ounce of power and schussed up the path in a low crouch, letting his skis take him as far as they could. Then he stamped open his bindings, shouldered his skis and hurried up the zigzagging track. He could hear his pursuer below. He had slowed as he approached the fork, unsure which path Tyler had taken. By the time he'd decided, he had only a fraction of Tyler's impetus to get up the slope and had to walk most of the way. Tyler had increased his lead substantially.

Now it was a matter of turning off the path and negotiating an obstacle course of stumpy trees and saplings, near-snowless rocky terrain from which he could drop onto a chalet roof and then down to disappear from sight in another section of the old town. Skiing on and off chalet roofs was all in a day's work for Tyler: the Team had done several sequences of this for one of their pre-Saul-era movies. When he landed on the evenly sloping surface he did a half-turn and sprang onto the narrow roof of a woodpile and then down onto the road, following its slope, cutting through gardens between the chalets, side-stepping over small banks, getting back on the road and skating his skis. He even found a moment to regret that there'd be no video of his bravura rooftop performance.

In circumstances like this he knew that confidence was everything and Tyler fought to reassure himself. *Anything I can do he can do, but anything he can do I can do faster.* The problem was that Tyler was running out of terrain and with it his room for manoeuvre. He had come to the top of the flight of stairs that led through the trees down a steep rocky bank to the river, where the thick canopy of pine branches had kept out the snow. Hardly promising skiing terrain. He contemplated what he was going to have to do next. Ski the railing!

This wasn't going to be like one of the Team's movies where they shot the stunts in manageable sections and edited it all together in one glorious, apparently continuous sequence. This would be one long real-time shot. No cuts. No retakes. Also, it was a few years since he'd done something like this – as one of a bunch of teenagers fooling around, trying new stuff in the snow park at Pike's Rock in Utah. At least this time all he had to do was slide down. He didn't have to do a couple of sycamore spins on the way like he did back then when they were showing off to girls. But if it worked it would give him the time he needed to get clear away and make the rendezvous. If it didn't work, if he fell badly and injured himself – well, that would be that.

When he reached the steps, he sacrificed a few seconds to compose himself as he would if his ski tips were hanging over several hundred feet of rock-lined oblivion like the Couloir Noir. He had to cope with a new fear unconnected to his skiing, which was having a bad effect on the whole of his body. He'd never felt like this before. He had to relax. He stretched to loosen his fraught frame, worked to control his breathing and regain his focus, tapped his ski poles together twice like a lead guitarist counting in the band and sprang up onto the handrail.

There were three thirty-metre sections and he only wished he had the chance to enjoy it. It wasn't easy. As he crashed down on the stony path at the end of each section he winced for the suffering of his skis. He had planned to hide them in a snowdrift but now had second thoughts. *Never abandon your skis.* What if there was no one at the rendezvous and he had to get all the way down to Petit Ligne, the village below Val? So he resigned himself to clumping and stumbling in the dark across the boulder-strewn river bed, carrying his skis and poles while icy water was surging into his boots and freezing his feet. The upside of this situation: the noise of the river rushing through the sluices of a dam upstream and churning through the rocks in the river below was loud enough to drown the clacking of his skis and the crunk of his Schreibers on the rocks. It wasn't enough, though, to drown the shouts of his enraged pursuer.

When Tyler made it to the other side he stumbled up the rocky bank and hurriedly swapped his ski boots for the hiking boots in his backpack. He clamped his ski boots into their ski bindings, settled the bulky load onto his shoulder and managed a painful jog as he set off down the refreshingly level terrain of the road. Behind him one angry man wading in the water cursed as he searched the rocks and rehearsed how he'd explain his failure to Cropper.

Away from the river it was quiet. Tyler could see the bus stop and the trees. He was in no doubt that this was the rendezvous but there was no sign of his rescue party. He took out the torch they'd put in his kit and flashed it: three short ones then a long one. There was the sound of a car engine starting and moments later a black SUV drew up and stopped just long enough for hands to reach out from the rear door and haul Tyler aboard before it accelerated off and took a deliberately indirect route back to Juniper.

Keep going at all costs. Remember the capsule. Ludo's lungs felt as they'd never felt before. He heard a car coming down the road. In spite of all his efforts they'd caught up with him. The only possible escape was up and over one of the steep banks on either side of the road. Now he could see the lights swinging round the bend in the road behind him. He hurled himself at the bank and scrabbled up it but in his exhausted state he couldn't make it to the top and slid helplessly down, landing in an inert heap on the edge of the road just as the car drew up.

'Hey, meester,' said a foreign voice, 'you vont to valk . . . or ken vee geeve you a leeft?'

There was only one person Ludo knew who was so crap at foreign accents. And sure enough it was Clay who was staring down at him from the wheel of Count Fernando.

4

Anyone observing the scene outside Juniper as the main rescue party returned would have assumed from the stumbling about, the chucking of snowballs and the loudmouthed exchanges that this was a party of Brit revellers who had hit the bar early and were noisily considering the possibilities of a further expedition.

Once everyone was inside and seated around the dining-room table, Ludo asked Clay to take the debriefing on the evening's operation. It was a fairly perfunctory affair, after which Brebis appeared with a giant cauldron of what he called his 'special beef soup'. Ludo's heart sank; he wondered if they hadn't all suffered enough already. He noticed the expression on poor Mike's face as he cautiously sipped from his mug.

At eleven o'clock, as Brebis and Belier shovelled snow onto the embers of the bonfire, Mike went out onto the balcony to get some air and solitude. Through a neighbouring chalet window he could see the sated guests sunk in the sofas with their coffee cups, contentedly basking in the log fire's softly pulsating glow. From below him in the centre of town came a series of those jagged disjointed squealing sounds that brass players make when they are warming up. The Val de Ligne town band was preparing for its late-night concert in the square. Ludo could envisage the scene: the bandsmen standing round a burning brazier, their reflected faces grotesquely distorted in the curved surfaces of their instruments.

Now as the snow began to fall again, the band played a brisk polka, then some yodelly alpine stuff. Mike knew the repertoire and was ready for the moment when they launched into a thumping waltz. Although no musician himself, he had noticed that when his son practised the piano the black notes would often make a sort of sinister sound, which was why he always thought of this ominous tune as 'the Black Note Waltz'.

This piece never sounded more sinister than it did that night. The gloom-doom-doom of the tune caught the spirit of Thermidor's predicament: boom-pah-pah, boom-pah-pah, a three-time tattoo, insistent and menacing. This was the music the whole of Val was dancing to and he, Mike, was just one in the crowd, an innocent moving among the laughter and the brightly coloured costumes, while two goggled gangs of vengeful hearts waltzed their own wayward waltz, whirling in the swirling snow, murderous guests at a mad masked ball.

5

Thermidor's first proper contact with the enemy the previous night at Chalet Ibex had brought a sharp change in the atmosphere. In spite of the success of the operation everyone was much more nervy and tense. Clay and Colza were constantly on the prowl for any security infringement that might jeopardise them, while Ludo, Mike noticed, seemed quite unaffected, engrossed as always in his papers, thinking his important thoughts.

Ludo was actually contemplating, among other things, the new status that Thermidor must now have in the eyes of their enemies. The rescue of Shin and Mo forced Cropper to accept that he faced some effective opposition. Clay had already learnt from Mo that Cropper had called for reinforcements in his desperation to recover the Messigny footage and dispose of the culprits before his and Crane's reputations were completely destroyed in the eyes of the Board.

The new constraints of life in Chalet Thermidor were extremely difficult for everyone. With Mo, Kang and Shin plus the four members of the Team now in residence, Juniper was feeling crowded and claustrophobic. The Team were taking their confinement particularly badly. Any day not spent skiing was a day stolen from their lives. Accustomed to intense physical activity, they were trapped in the apartment and faced with hours of idleness. Normally they got on well, but now they were stuck with each other all day without the release of skiing their small quarrels began to last longer and became more bad-tempered. By the sixth day of Mike's captivity in Juniper they were all on edge; the chalet had become a wooden-walled pressure cooker.

Mike had retreated to his room with the chess board from the living room when there was a bang on the door. It was Colza.

'Need to let you know, Mike. Non-trivial development. We've just heard from one of our people that the police have started house to house searches. They've been getting stick for not catching the ski thieves. We're pretty certain Cropper's got people working with them.'

6

In his strange state of protective custody, Mike felt lonely, scared and homesick. He was missing his wife and his children. He would have dearly liked to get out of Juniper and visit some of his old haunts in Val. If he wanted company he usually went to Bar X, but if it was solitude that he was after, then he'd go to Maurice's, a little place in an alley running between the ski school assembly area and the market square. The place had a simple comfort about it with its L'Isle d'Abeau rugby team posters taped to the pine panelling, plastic flowers on the tables, terracotta floor tiles, newspaper racks and 'Bar Maurice' in pinkish-red neon in the window. Smokers, who were welcome here, gathered in the back half of the room, which was also the location of choice for Maurice's pale beige cat, unhelpfully also called Maurice. He spent most of his time snoozing under the staircase, but every now and then he would get slowly to his feet and do the rounds of the tables, pausing here and there to swap a reproachful stare for a pat on his haunches or a rub behind the ears.

Mike could find his peace here in this noisy calm, in the sounds of the growling coffee grinder, the clinking cups, clattering cutlery, the hissing of the espresso machine; he fancied he could even hear it dribbling its near-black blood. The coffee was served in tiny white cups, each of such a thickness and weight as to suggest that Maurice's high-roast Sétif Blend was so corrosive and potent that it could only be safely contained in industrial-grade crucibles like this. When the machine had done its work, Maurice, with priest-like devotion, would put cup and saucer down on the marble-topped counter that was his altar. The customer would take it and join the others sitting at their tables, puffed up by several layers of man-made fibre, their arms curved protectively around the little phials of liquid as they savoured their heat and scent like giant pachyderms with their newborn. Over these sensations were the sounds: the greetings, the chatter and the music – the current hits from some terrible Euro rock station (this year they were hearing a lot of *Ci-Ci Boom-Boom, allez-allez toutes!*) and the din of the chair legs scraping across the floor tiles which made a noise like the yelping of trodden-on dogs. And all the while Maurice's customers would come and go through the glass swing-door accompanied by gusts of cold air which had also come to seek a few minutes warmth before heading back out into the cold mountain town.

7

It was late morning and Ludo was in his room working on the Thermidor Report when Clay burst in.

'Confucius he say, "When pursued by enemy on roller skates the wise man takes to his stairs."'

'What are you on about?' said Ludo.

'We've got to get out – make a run for it to Pentes du Paradis. The game is up here.'

'What do you mean?'

'Cropper's people have been seen in the road outside. They're sniffing around. It's just a matter of time. We're safe only as long as it's daylight. But we have to get out ... tonight. We need to move down to Thermidor Two and from there we can head into the mountains and make our way to Pentes du Paradis.'

'You must be joking!' said Ludo. 'Have you noticed the weather outside? It's bad enough down here. The conditions will be impossible up there.'

'That's the point. Cropper would never believe we'd attempt it while it's like this. Anyway, it's the only way out. And once we've got to Pentes we can go anywhere.'

Ludo was far from convinced.

'We're a pretty mixed bag in terms of skiing ability and the route would call for everyone to be able to climb, abseil, traverse crevasse fields and the rest of it.'

Clay was dismissive.

'They'll all be fine.'

'What, even Mo? Can she ski?'

'It so happens she was educated at an expensive private girls' school and got taken to the Alps every year. Took to it like a duck to water, became captain of the school team. Went on to become a Korean National Champion.'

'Good Lord! I had no idea.'

'No, Ludo, of course she doesn't bloody ski! She spent all of half a day in her teens on the kiddies' slopes of the Yangji Pine Resort 40 minutes outside Seoul. Loathed every minute of it. It's a big problem.'

He'd suddenly become very angry and walked out of the room without a further word. The incident did nothing to boost Ludo's confidence in Clay or his plan.

8

Clay insisted that Mo should not be disturbed for a couple of days so she could recover from her traumatic experiences and be in a fit state to be questioned by Ludo, who urgently needed her to fill in some gaps in their intelligence about Crane's operation. He found her in Clay's suite curled up on a sofa reading a magazine. She was small, thin and Asian-neat with smooth features on a sharp frame. Her delicate eyebrows tapered and faded to nothing on the edge of her temples, her black bobbed hair brushing her cheekbones and the roll of her pale blue cashmere collar. She wore black leggings that disappeared into floppy black-suede ankle boots. Ludo guessed one of the girls must have been shopping in town for her. She lowered her magazine and sat up to greet him, unfurling in a single languorous feline movement. He was reminded of Kornie's remark when he saw her on the night of the rescue and had said quite loudly within her earshot, 'Hevyu seen de Asian babe? I mean what kinda cat izdat?' The whole of her body seemed to be anchored by her eyes, which stayed still even as she moved. Ludo couldn't make out if they were passively seeing or actively watching.

One thing that Ludo needed to clarify was the story of the tie. Crane, as part of the process of inducting his son into his affairs, had got Max to help him go through the contents of the safe in Brompton Crescent. Crane had not realised that Mo, standing at the photocopier, could see his face in the reflection of the framed print on the wall above the machine. As he held up a polythene bag she saw him say, 'And this is his school tie I was talking about. Looks like tea stains but there's enough DNA on this to put Drake and Parsons away for ever, so it doesn't want to be going to the dry cleaners, okay?'

When Thermidor researched it they pieced together the facts of a schoolmate's murder by Drake and Parsons, how Crane had helped them frame poor Tommy Ealey and how he had had them over a barrel ever since then because of the evidence in his safe.

This incident had securely locked into place a triangle of mutual loyalty.

Now Thermidor had the information too and Ludo was considering how to reveal it.

9

What will you do in the war, Son?

Caption on pastiche of First World War
recruitment poster, Kimbertown
Cartoon Syndication

'That's the great thing about double-glazing,' Ludo was saying, 'you can't hear the screams outside in the street. You certainly can't hear Piers.'

Mike guessed he was meant to ask, 'Who is Piers?'

'Who is Piers?' he asked.

'There's always a Piers,' said Clay. 'He's the chap who runs a little bistro in Chelsea doing fab seared tuna and super salads. But given the average life expectancy of a London restaurant, Piers is finding things tough and they get even tougher when he starts getting a weekly visit from an unpleasant gentleman who comes to collect a "subscription for security-related services".

'Of course, protection rackets in the Chinese, Turkish and the Kurdish restaurant business have been doing well for a long time but in the non-ethnic sector it's a bit of novelty. Anyway, Piers reasons that this protection is probably costing him less than the nation's nuclear deterrent and, given what will happen to him if he doesn't pay up, is probably better value.'

Ludo and Clay had invited Mike to join them to 'do a bit of a recce' for the break-out, which involved finding a sheltered spot for an overnight bivouac before making the escape to Pentes du Paradis.

Clay had said the risk was low.

'Okay, I'm up for it,' Mike said. Even as he spoke he cursed himself for agreeing.

A couple of hours later he found himself sitting on the Caribou chair in 20 degrees C and patchy visibility. The upside for Mike was that he was out of the chalet and heading into the mountains; the downside was being trapped on a chairlift between Clay and Ludo while they tried to convince him of the righteousness of their ways. Being preached at by the two of them was like having a pair of Jehovah's Witnesses glued to the doorstep.

'Owen argued that defeating organised crime would be a massive task,' Ludo was saying, 'It would need such a commitment of money and manpower, the application of so much force and the suspension of so many civil freedoms that it would constitute a war – albeit a new kind of war.'

Below them a crocodile of small children were snaking down the slope, following in their instructor's tracks. Mike watched as one of them lost control and shot off straight down the piste, gathering speed before executing a series of somersaults and bouncing back onto its feet quite unharmed. Mike thought it looked like a tiny wind-up toy that had been chucked down the slope.

'So how is this war fought?' Mike asked.

'Dirty,' said Ludo. 'Owen used to say, "When gangsters learn how to be soldiers, soldiers must learn how to be gangsters." Of course, our lot have done this before. In the Second World War Britain fuelled a swathe of terrorist resistance movements across Europe against the Nazi occupation. Trouble is that it gave everyone else ideas and we've been on the receiving end of our own methods ever since . . .'

'I see,' said Mike. 'So now it's the other side's turn to go in and bat and our job to try and bowl them out?'

'Yes, Mike,' said Ludo.

10

You will all experience drastic change in your
time, for the face of conflict changes quickly.
Winston Churchill ended his military career as a
commander in an alliance that dropped the atomic
bomb; he began it on horseback charging against
tribesmen wielding spears.

Glyn Owen, Triumph of the Gangster State

'Our new enemies,' said Ludo, 'have moved into another dimen-
sion of criminality. I'm not saying that these are the first people
on earth to have discovered the efficacy of extreme brutality but
they have learnt how to achieve a devastating effect by applying it
in the right places.

'Owen's dossier suggested that seventeen civil servants in a single
government department were implicated in aiding and abetting
criminal interests – those interests turned out to be Crane's of
course, among others. But it wasn't money that corrupted them,
it was fear. What we have here is criminal intent harnessed to
terrorist method.'

'What does that mean?'

'It means a judge found drowned in the rigging of his sailing
dinghy and a conscientious copper killed by a train as a warning to
their colleagues, it means a harmless civil servant threatened in a
dark car park when he gets off his commuter train.'

Mike looked across at the piste, where a group of four skiers
were zinging down the slope in some style. They looked so carefree;
he wanted to get down from the chair and join them. He'd jumped
out of his groove into a parallel universe. *How do I get back?*

'The threat of disfigurement, disablement or death is a great
recruitment model, very persuasive,' Ludo was saying. 'It can be
made to work on judges, jurors, lawyers, policemen, customs

officers, security personnel, prison officers. Call it Criminal Terrorism.

'The clever thing about it is that everyone stays *schtum*. Those who know what's going on are too scared to speak; those who don't know don't want to know. It is too terrible for the authorities to contemplate so they aren't keen discuss it. The ordinary public don't want to know. The chattering classes certainly can't bring themselves to chatter about it – bit of a downer at a dinner party; they're happy to leave it to the politicians they claim to despise. The politicians think it should be left to the police because it's a vermin control problem, so they certainly don't want to be told that Vermin Control is controlled by vermin. We have an all-round state of wilful denial: the converse of moral panic.'

The final part of the lift's journey passed above a picturesque restaurant. Mike pictured to himself the cheery crowd inside, enjoying beer and bowls of pasta, oblivious of the dark scenario Ludo was prescribing for them.

'To prosecute this new kind of war they'll have to take some quite unpopular measures.'

'Like what?' asked Mike.

'Anonymity for police officers and judges, for instance.'

'What? Secret police and secret courts? You're not being serious?'

'Absolutely. Today we put a number on every single police officer and you are shocked by the idea of removing them. You think that's sinister but in our new world, law and justice become targets and they have to be protected. If that means a few balaclavas and numberless uniforms for the police, so be it.'

'People won't buy it,' said Mike.

'They'll have no choice. We've been living through a decades-long summer; now that winter is here the protective clothing worn by free democracies is no longer fit for purpose. Our security forces will be given greater anonymity while members of the public will come under increased surveillance.

'Come on, Ludo, this is ludicrous. You need to get out more.'

'Just wait and see. These things change. Think of that painting of the haywain by Constable – you know the one?'

'I do.'

'If you'd told the driver of that cart that within little more than eighty years his and every other four-wheeled vehicle on the road would have to have its own number stuck on the back of it, he wouldn't have believed you.

'There's an almighty fuss at first but people adapt. Look at all the indignation caused by CCTV cameras. Incorruptible Police Constable Closed-Circuit Plod out there day and night in all weathers, watching from doorways and rooftops, taking notes, telling the truth as he sees it; never fabricating the evidence and never taking a backhander. And he is vilified as "the thin end of the wedge", "the apparatus of the police state" and "the slippery slope". But when there's some breaking and entering or a night of mass rioting, suddenly everybody's begging him to tell them everything he knows so they can bring the hoodlums to justice'.

'There's world of difference between a few CCTV cameras and Uzi-toting policemen in balaclavas running round the place,' ventured Mike.

'Any new security measure,' Ludo continued, 'unleashes an outbreak of sanctimony from the posturing classes. You can just see them on Sunday night's *Answer the Question*. Someone only has to say "We-must-not-descend-to-their-depths" or talk about "our long-cherished freedoms" and the entire studio audience has a synchronised orgasm.

'People glorify those who fight for freedom yet ignore all those other brave souls who dare suspend it. We need to thank God that when it came to war with the Axis we had some wise guys in charge who were happy to park those "long-cherished freedoms" until the unpleasantness was over. They brought in conscription and sent hundreds of thousands to their deaths on land, sea and air. They suspended elections, freedom of speech and movement, imprisoned thousands of citizens without trial, introduced curfews and forced labour. And were we stuck with all that? Not at all. As soon as the war was over all the freedoms were restored and the task of extending them continued. Yes, we went down "the slippery slope"; then we came back up again.'

'I'm really not sure about this,' said Mike.

'Believe me,' said Ludo, 'it's just as Owen put it: "We're being held prisoner by our freedoms; if we're not careful they'll destroy us."'

11

> The young should pay attention to the old because
> we have lived long enough to see the future.
>
> *Reggie Peplow*

Alone in his room that afternoon Ludo began to feel depressed and homesick again. He tried to be optimistic. Thermidor's achievement was remarkable. They had embarked on their quest with nothing more than a few small strands of evidence poking out of Glyn Owen's grave, which they had patiently drawn out to expose the Board and its appalling work. Then as he thought about it his view shifted. It was a crackpot project and they hadn't nearly finished the job yet. Who knew what the hell would happen next? Much of their fate was in Clay's hands and that made him nervous.

For comfort he again sought the virtual company of Reggie and wondered how he would cope in Ludo's perilous position.

'Only one possible answer, Ludo,' Reggie would say. 'We need to shift the paradigm.' This would be the cue for an evening of 'clubbing'. It would begin in the stately grandeur of Burke's in St James's, which Reggie used for entertaining politicos and civil servants, and would go steadily downhill, usually ending in the company of some hard-drinking Scots desperadoes in a seedy journo hangout in Holborn, which Reggie would refer to as 'The Toupee and Laptop'. It would conclude with him suddenly announcing that the proceedings were at an end and that he had to get back to 'The Projects', as he called the grandly shabby Victorian villa in the prosperous part of Godalming which he had defiantly named Sea View. Ludo would then find himself feeling befuddled and slightly hollow on the last coach to Winslow, contemplating the conversation he was going to have with what Reggie called 'the daughter of his mother-in-law'.

Reggie suffered from something called Pottley's Syndrome and maintained he was having 'proximity talks with the Grim Reaper'. Pottley's, like many of those unserious-sounding niche diseases, didn't win much sympathy but was extremely unpleasant. He refused to do anything to help himself and continued on his *kamikaze* course as a matter of honour, telling everyone that he had arranged to have the words OUT OF OFFICE on his tombstone. Ludo feared that Reggie who liked to market himself as 'Palpably clubbable, pubbable Peplow', was trapped in a self-caricature; he believed that unless he consumed two or three bottles a day he would disappoint his admirers and cease to remain 'a character'. It was a tragic example of brand management gone terribly wrong.

Ludo knew he would greatly miss Reggie and prayed that he would overcome his illness. In his own way Reggie represented so much of a world for which Ludo was now pining.

12

The planning of Thermidor's escape necessitated a visit from Jean-Claude, a local guide, who, Clay told Mike, was from one of the 'Plateau' families. He would be leading them across the mountains. Meanwhile there were lists of supplies and equipment to be drawn up and assembled – rations, food, fuel, sat phone batteries, firearms, personal luggage and ski gear, along with some steel containers which Mike suspected contained explosives. Because weather would be a crucial factor in the escape, Colza was constantly checking all the relevant websites. They were praying for snow to cover their tracks.

Early in the afternoon when Mike was nosing around the chalet, he went into one of the spare rooms and found Clay wearing surgical gloves, huddled over a table on which lay a pile of papers and a small green rucksack. He was surprised and not best pleased at Mike's intrusion.

13

Ludo had to admit that Colza's plan for the evacuation of Juniper was masterful. Everything was loaded into Count Fernando and taken to Thermidor Two. A larger than usual contingent set off for the ski lifts that morning at the usual time, which left just the Team, Mo, Shin, Kang and Mike.

Count Fernando returned in the afternoon with several pieces of furniture on its roof rack, which were unloaded outside the chalet close to the garage doors. This was to conceal the embarkation of Mike and the Team, who were packed like sardines on the floor of the vehicle and covered in baggage. Fernando returned half an hour later with more furniture and the routine was repeated for Mo, Shin and Kang. The arrival of the furniture suggesting Thermidor's continued occupation was actually a cover for its departure.

There were now just two Thermidor operatives left in the chalet to welcome a crowd from neighbouring apartment blocks who'd been invited 'to celebrate a lottery win' with promises of plenty of food and drink. In the early evening the hosts announced that the party was moving to Paddy's Bar, enabling the Thermidor duo to leave in the general confusion. There was a big show of shouting and waving farewell to unseen occupants at the first-floor window, from where the sound of music continued.

Thermidor Two was bedlam with everyone crammed into four apartments in a block close to the assembly area. The first thing that Mike noticed was that a number of people were missing. None of the girls were there except Candy, Rebecca and Mo; nor were most of the 'non-kinetics' such as Lupin, Cotton and Salicor.

'Don't worry, they're in another safe place,' said Clay breezily when Mike asked about him. 'They're slow skiers and will be coming by a different route.'

Fortunately they didn't have to be in Thermidor Two for long because Clay wanted everyone in position on top of the hill before the piste bashers started work. Freshly pisted snow would show up their snowmobile tracks.

After a light supper and a final briefing by Clay, Colza returned Mike and the Team's mobiles, with instructions to make sure they were all fully charged and each had key numbers programmed for speed dialling. Mike thought that was a bit excessive given that where they were going they wouldn't be able to get a signal. Then everyone dispersed to get their gear ready for the coming trek.

In the late evening they set off in twos and threes and made their way through the darkness towards an unlit patch on the edge of the piste where their snowmobiles were waiting. The wind had strengthened and the temperature was dropping. Blake was put at the helm of one with Mo sitting on the back, pulling Ludo and five others, all hanging on to a tow rope knotted at two-metre intervals. It took them a good hour and a half to get to the trees that marked the site of the bivouac. Five tents had already been put up and a small fire was burning in the hard cold of the night.

While flasks of hot soup were handed round and everyone else gossiped by the fire, Clay and Colza drew apart to talk through details of their trek to Pentes one more time. Meanwhile Ludo was wondering why several of the Juniper crowd were missing and that most were Clay's people from Thermidor Two.

14

In peace we show them how we can amaze
We send a gunboat bristling with canapés.
Then comes the band of the Royal Marines,
One ukulele and two tambourines.

'The Ploughsharer's Dream' by Morris Cole in Peaceable Kingdom,
an Anthology of Poetry for Peace, *edited by Martin Richards*

'Everyone's gone soft in the head,' Ludo was saying. 'They've all been PC-whipped. Our political activists are gutless. We take order and justice for granted; nobody likes to admit that it is achieved by an abiding threat of force – any more than they will admit that much of our prosperity rests on long-ago land grabs and slavery in distant places. They're pacifists who've blagged free tickets for the victory celebrations.'

Mike and Ludo were sitting half-listening in on the conversations of the others gathered round the fire. Mike now realised he'd made a big mistake by asking Ludo about his 'New War'.

'Why are you so pessimistic about it?'

'Because our people have no idea what they're up against. Gone are the days when the greatest danger anyone faced was being run over by a spinster cycling to evensong. But now? We're re-wilding our environment. Foreign crims sense opportunities in the UK like sharks scenting blood from the far end of the ocean. Our police are like the ushers at the Wigmore Hall facing a mob of football hooligans. These people are going to rearrange the *Titanic* under our deckchairs; soon it'll be *us* who are seeking asylum from *them*.'

Mike smiled to himself. Ludo's delivery may have sounded sober and measured but his words were just plain loopy. *Here we go again. This time it's sharks, football and deckchairs.* Ludo's spiel reminded him of those environmental doomsters who got a creepy pleasure in saying, 'You won't be able to say we didn't warn you.'

'So you don't think we've got much of a chance then?' said Mike.

Ludo's laugh was more like a sardonic cough.

'We've got about as much of a chance as a Morris dancer in a cage fight.'

At 10.30pm everyone turned in and Colza ordered a couple of people to cover the first watch. Ludo had never been a fan of sleeping under canvas, or even multi-ply, spun-bound polypropylene composite, and he was not enjoying himself. Apart from the cold, the layers of clothing and sleeping bag bunched lumpily in all the wrong places and the contours of the snow beneath the ground-sheet bore no relation to his frame. He lay wide awake as the little encampment fell silent. The last voice he heard was Clay's in the neighbouring tent asking Colza about the latest forecast.

'Temperature dropping; visibility worsening,' replied Colza. 'It's looking pretty bad.'

'Excellent,' said Clay.

15

Well, dead man!

You may not be looking at your best but there is still something imposing about you, some might say almost heroic. Certainly those gendarmes from the helicopter will recognise the face of a leader. You were a leader, of course; you had to persuade others to join you in your risky work. And you had to be brave as well as ruthless to do your job. But given the way things turned out, do you now regret you career choice? How did you rate it for job satisfaction?

You can't really complain about your present situation: you broke the law big-time! Once you were a figure in the community, a uniformed officer. Everything you have done is against everything you once stood for. Now that you're dead you're in a good position to explain how you managed to live with yourself?

And did you seriously think you could get away with it? Didn't you realise you were up against forces that were greater than yours? Forces you might scoff at but which, and I really don't mean to be pompous here, are sanctioned by the law that secures our civilisation?

Was it all about the exquisite pleasure of risk? That and being a free agent. You wouldn't lead the grey life so you had to be an outlaw – 'a lifestyle choice' as they say. It was also about the pleasure of secrecy and the power of secrets – secrets like the ones in that small green rucksack of yours.

You dead people are what's wrong with our society. You have it so easy and you contribute so little. Why not make yourselves a little useful: you are in a good position to tell us things we do not know. After all, doing the dying thing must have taught you so much about life?

16

'Look, Sergeant, there's your murderer,' said
Inspector Byron pointing to the window.
Braithwaite could see nothing but the gently falling
snow.

J.G. Tallon, White Lies

A vast expanse of ever-changing terrain. From the edge of the resort they had looked down on the glacier and seen a sea of level white; when they got down to it, it was cracked by a mass of crevasses through which their guide, Jean-Claude, cautiously led them, roped to each other. Sometimes the surface was as flat and level as a tabletop; sometimes it was covered in a chaotic jumble of hillocks the size of garden sheds.

At one stage they moved through a landscape formed from a rubble of ice, at another the snow lay in strange smooth shapes sculpted by the wind to look like the folds of a robe over which they crawled like mice. The day had brightened and darkened and brightened again. In the light moments they could see distant white peaks flecked with dark bare rock that the snow could not clothe. They encountered vistas of fabulous grandeur and some of the party spared a moment to recognise their good fortune in being among the few souls on earth who had ever passed this way in winter. Ludo was not among them.

Ludo wished he wasn't there. In this wide-open vista he felt confined. Smothered in multiple layers of several species of oil-based products, he was hot all over except for those areas of his face that weren't covered by his wraparound sunglasses, his hat clamped low over his head. The textile wizards couldn't stop his brain from sweating. He could hear the heaviness of his own breathing. Like everyone else he had fixed skins on his skis for traction on the uphill snow; likewise he had touring bindings that released the heels so he could 'walk' his skis on the level, but this trekking was still hard work and Ludo was tiring.

Some people would pay good money to do what they were doing now, but not Ludo; he wasn't a distance man. He liked skiing, but he liked it short and sharp; most of all he liked to do it in places where there was a lift to take you up to the top of a hill, where you didn't have to climb on foot like this in a seemingly endless, lung-thumping effort. They'd been going for three hours and there was a long way till dusk when, if Jean-Claude had got it right, they'd all reach the St Christophe refuge, a stone hut where they'd be spending a sheltered but Spartan night on wooden bunks.

'This is where we must decide,' said Clay. 'So, Jean-Claude, which is it to be?'

The wizened face turned to look at the sun and then the mountains as though he was reading lines of text.

'The western route will give you what you need.'

Ludo was puzzled. He'd put Clay in charge of getting them to Pentes du Paradis but he was going about it in an odd way. They had risen well before dawn when the snow was already falling from a windless sky. Ludo, cold and aching, discovered that the Team, accompanied by Thermidor's best skier, Arrosoir, had already been despatched. The Korean contingent or 'The Triads', as Clay insisted on calling them, had also disappeared.

After a hurried breakfast of porridge and coffee Clay had ordered everyone to 'saddle up' and file onto the piste. They'd climbed the last eighty metres and halted at the orange tape marking the end of the resort's ski area.

'So I guess we're the TA, isn't that right, Colza?' said Clay. The knowing smile that flitted across Colza's face had made Ludo and Mike think that it was private joke about them being Territorial Army-type amateur soldiers. Now, three hours after their departure, Ludo was wondering what was going on.

And so was Mike.

It was snowing lightly; the wind was moderate; the group was maintaining its steady pace. Colza's radio bleeped. He pressed the button.

'Colza here. Over.'

Ludo saw him tense as he listened.

'What! . . . Yes, but where? . . . How many? . . . But how far behind us?'

'What's happening?' said Clay.

'That was Brebis. Unwelcome development,' said Colza. 'Cropper seems to have found us. He's on our tail and he and Dubois have got people with them.'

'Jesus!' Ludo felt as though a lead weight had been dropped on his stomach. How could Cropper have possibly have found out where they were given all the precautions they'd taken.

'How many?' he asked.

'Not quite sure yet. But quite a few.'

'Better get going,' said Clay.

Colza set a goodish pace and they skied down, skinned up, and slid over the ever-changing terrain. At the top of a long climb he stopped and waved on the others until Ludo and Clay reached him.

'Take a look,' he said, passing Ludo his binoculars.

Ludo scanned the route they'd just taken and there they were, about a dozen of them, a sinister sight and not just because they had rifles slung on their backs.

'They're gaining on us,' Colza announced, matter-of-factly.

'Are we in range?'

'That's one thing we don't need to worry about,' said Clay. 'They want us alive.' Ludo, trying not to think about the capsule on his lanyard, looked anxiously at the rest of his group, who were standing with their heads bowed and leaning on their poles. They were very much a mixed-ability bunch and Ludo knew it was only a matter of time before Cropper caught up. Clay gave them a few minutes to recover before resuming their flight.

The snow was still falling.

Ludo saw that Clay had stopped and was looking back. Curious, Ludo stopped too. The visibility was down to fifty metres and the rest of the party soon disappeared from sight. Clay stared into the silent white nothingness; he seemed to be waiting for something.

As he peered through the dull light, Ludo saw the whiteness begin to fragment into darker patches. He felt he was hallucinating until he made out two vaguely human shapes moving towards him; as they got closer he saw they were swathed in white camouflage. It was Bélier and Brebis.

Clay greeted them.

'Ku Klux Klan is a good look for you,' he said.

'Thank you, Clay,' said Brebis.

'Are your bang-bangs in good order?'

'They're fine,' said Brebis.

'You make sure you get the right ones this time, okay?'

'Of course.'

'Good. You go on ahead.'

As they passed, Ludo could see they both had short stubby weapons slung over their shoulders.

'What's going on, Clay?'

'They're going to be minding our back, that's all.'

Ludo wondered what Clay was hiding from him.

Another half hour of painful retreat, the silence broken only by occasional words of encouragement as Clay and Colza urged on their flagging charges. As the visibility began to clear they could see all too clearly that their pursuers had gained on them. Colza's radio squawked and he relayed the message.

'Four hundred metres, Clay.'

Just then a snow-muffled *c-r-a-c-k!* And then another.

Colza's radio listened to the radio message and shouted over to Ludo.

'It's Brebis. They've got Cropper and Tsanko. Confirmed.'

Ludo couldn't believe it.

'For Christ's sake,' he muttered, 'they've just killed the only two people we needed to keep alive.'

'No problem,' said Clay.

'But the others are still with us,' said Colza, looking through his binoculars.

They came to a halt beside a long wide thirty-degree slope of what looked like heavy snow. When everyone had caught up, Colza led them across to the far side and waited until everyone was well clear. Clay had stayed behind, looking back at the point they had traversed. After a few minutes, Ludo saw him raise his arm and wave it slowly from side to side. It seemed to be a signal for Colza, who now spoke quietly into his radio:

'Okay, Tyler, now!'

A loud dull explosion thumped the air. Next a long pause followed by an awesome crescendo of deep thunderous rumbling, the sound of an ocean of snow rolling down the mountain accompanied by the shouts of those about to be drowned. When the din had subsided, Clay and Colza gave a whispering cheer and touched fists like a pair of doubles players who'd just taken the set.

'Are you thinking what we're thinking?' said Terry who with Rebecca had appeared at Ludo's side.

'I think so,' said Ludo.

'He sure fooled us.' They were as angry as Ludo and were cursing themselves for not realising before. Ever since the History of Britain Museum fiasco, which had been Clay's responsibility, Rebecca and Terry had preferred to deal with Ludo and in any arguments they almost always sided with him. The three of them were now forced to acknowledge that Clay had completely conned them. He had never had any intention of going to Pentes du Paradis. The news of Thermidor's bid to cross the glacier hadn't been betrayed to Cropper: it had been planted on him so he and his people would follow. Clay's game had been to draw Cropper into the mountains so his entire force would be spread out on this great white cloth, clearly visible and deployed for destruction. The plan wasn't about getting Thermidor to the Slopes of Paradise; it was about delivering Cropper and Company to the gates of Hell.

Ludo was aware that while he'd been absorbed in pursuing the investigation into Crane and the Board with his small band of non-combatants in Juniper he hadn't paid enough attention to Clay. He knew that Clay was recruiting from the ex-military to take care of the action stuff and, indeed, they'd proved their worth. It was Clay's contingent who'd carried out the risky rescue of Mike from the Messigny woods. Their quick action had saved Blake's life and the assault on Ibex and rescue of Mo and Shin had been a triumph. But Ludo now regretted his failure to monitor more closely what had been happening down in Thermidor Two. A bit late now, but Ludo decided the time had come for a Grand Remonstrance.

'We need to talk,' said Ludo.

'I know, I know,' said Clay. 'I can explain everything.'

'You'll fucking well need to.'

Colza, who had just taken a radio call, interrupted before the row could escalate.

'It's Brebis. He says they're waiting for us. They've got Cropper and Tsanko.'

Still unconscious, the two men had been laid out for inspection like dead game by Brebis and Bélier, who stood proprietarily on either side of their trophies.

'Just nerve shells...' Clay explained. 'Latest kit from the Czechs... large-calibre plastic bullets... toxin particles in the nose cone... all the rage with Special Forces. The absolute must-have for those tricky situations when you need a body but don't want a corpse.'

Clay leant down and tugged the goggles off their faces.

'Oh dear.'

'What's the problem?'

'What a fucking cock-up.'

'How come?' said Brebis defensively.

'Yes, that's Cropper alright,' said Clay, poking the body with his ski pole, 'but that's not Tsanko.'

'What! He fits the description we were given.'

'That may be,' said Clay. 'But you've got the wrong man. Not for the first time, eh, Captain Blue on Blue?'

Brebis scowled but said nothing.

'Well at least this time he's not one of your own chaps, which makes a change.'

'So where's Tsanko?' asked Ludo.

'He must be in that lot,' said Clay, nodding towards the avalanche field.

'I hope so,' said Ludo, who was peering at the inert form of Cropper. 'What are we going to do about these two?'

The answer came in the sound of snowmobile engines approaching.

'If we get a move on,' said Clay, 'we can have our chat with Cropper as soon as he comes round and be back at Juniper in time for din-dins.'

17

The temperature was dropping and the sky was a darkening grey. Eight of the posse had formed a circle around Cropper, who was so trussed up with cord he looked pretty much oven-ready.

'Sorry about the bits of string and everything,' Clay told him, 'but it's for your own good; we can't have you wandering off or anything.'

Given his circumstances Cropper wasn't as contrite as Ludo would have expected.

'I've got stuff on Crane you'd give anything for,' he said, 'so tell me what you want and let's see if we can cut a deal.'

'We're not really in the mood for deals, Cropper,' said Ludo.

Cropper seemed unfazed.

'Lay a finger on me and my people will make you seriously regret what's left of your life. There's nowhere on this earth you'll be able to hide.'

'Quite so, quite so,' said Ludo languidly. 'So here's the thing. You need to tell us everything we need to know. If you do that, you'll live. If you don't give it to us, we'll just tear it out of you anyway. We've got some great kit.' He turned to Ivraie.

'Now, Ivraie, have you got your bits and pieces ready?'

'Absolutely,' said Ivraie, keen as mustard, unzipping a small plastic case.

Cropper, apparently unimpressed by the psy-ops, spat back, 'Don't think you can mess with my mind; better people than you have tried and it doesn't work.'

You had to hand it to him, thought Ludo, he was going down with all guns blazing.

'And who are *you* working for anyway?' Cropper sneered.

'Oh we're just a small claims recovery service,' said Ludo. 'You wouldn't have heard of us but we're doing quite well for a recent start-up. Now we need to get going. If I may I'll just run through our terms and conditions so there's no misunderstanding. You get one crack at each question and if your testimony is inaccurate in any way we'll ask Ivraie here to take over. He's our duty acupuncturist today – still on work experience, so don't be too hard on him if he gets it wrong.'

'Thank you, sir,' said Ivraie.

'Good, but before we start the therapy, just a few questions about your health.' Ludo was enjoying himself. 'Just answer yes or no . . . Are you on any form of medication? . . . Any history of heart problems in your family? . . . Are you preg– oh, silly me – not that one!'

Cropper's fighting spirit was evaporating fast; now he was down to a murmur.

'Tell me what you want to know.'

Ivraie placed a small tape recorder on a glove on the snow and clipped the mic to Cropper's collar. The interrogation was led by Ludo, but some of the others in the circle now surrounding the prisoner joined in from time to time, so questions came at Cropper from every direction – questions prompted by Mo's information, questions about Owen's Swanborne File notes on the deaths of the police inspector, the judge and the police informer, questions about Cropper's work for Crane, questions probing the areas which Mo had never been able to get at. The approach was brisk and without any chronological structure. Cropper was given no time to conceal truths or construct lies; whenever he tried to slow the pace, Ludo gave the nod to Ivraie, who shuffled closer with his needles.

Bit by bit Cropper gave up the secrets of Crane's grisly empire, secrets that had evaded months of Mo's scrutiny and Thermidor's investigation – names of Cropper's former bent-copper colleagues, information about associates of Messrs Drake and Parsons and their work, the identity of Security Service collaborators including Mary Grigor and, crucially, Marian Close, Ricky Phibbs's collaborator at GCHQ. The only questions about which he genuinely seemed to know nothing concerned the framing of Tommy Ealey for Drake and Parsons' murder of their schoolmate.

'Now tell me, Cropper,' said Ludo, 'can you enlighten us on the matter of a very good friend of ours, a Mr Blake Bale? Seems to have vanished. Last thing we heard was that he was in your . . . possession.'

'We thought he would be useful but he wasn't and we let him go.'

'What do you mean, "let him go"?'

'We drove him into town and dropped him off in the car park.'

'So you didn't do him any harm?'

'Certainly not.'

'Oh it's good to know he's alright.'

Catching the sarcasm in Ludo's tone, Cropper smelled a rat, but it was too late.

'Clay, that's really good news, isn't it – Blake being alright?'

'I should say so.'

'Now,' said Ludo, turning back to the crouching Cropper, 'this is the point in the show when we bring on a mystery guest.' He nodded at Colza, who disappeared for half a minute and returned with a figure shrouded in white.

Cropper wriggled and shifted in his bonds.

The newcomer removed his head covering; Cropper immediately recognised Blake.

'"Drinks on the house", I seem to remember, wasn't it?' said Blake.

Cropper said nothing.

'Anything you'd like to say to Mr Bale?' said Ludo. 'Are, for instance, apologies perhaps in order? "Ever so sorry we tried to kill you", "We apologise for any inconvenience we may have caused", "*Je suis désolé*" sort of thing?'

'Whatever,' murmured Cropper.

'Perhaps,' Ludo suggested, '"My behaviour was entirely unacceptable and fell well below the standards expected of me"?'

Cropper's eyes were fixed on his knees which were a few inches from his nose.

'So Mr Cropper,' said Ludo, 'what we're all keen to hear is your take on events at Quay Number 17.'

'Crane's businesses use a lot of big dockyards. I'm not sure about Quay Number 17?'

'It's in the port of Busan. That's in South Korea.'

'Yes, Crane has dealings there.'

'Thank you; we know this. But why would we ask you about this particular quay? Any idea?'

'No idea.'

'Are you aware of what happened to a Korea Customs Service officer named Han Jin-Ho?'

'Not to my recollection. I mean, I don't even know who he is.'

'This is surprising because as it happens we have a relative of Customs Officer Han who's come all the way from Korea to be with us here in our audience today.'

Ludo signalled in the direction of a group of people standing some twenty metres away; one of them started to walk through the falling snow towards the folded form of Cropper.

As soon as he recognised Mo, Cropper let out a low groan of despair.

'Allow me to introduce Han's sister-in-law,' said Ludo.

Cropper began to rock to and fro like an asylum inmate.

'I know what you're thinking, Cropper – things have come to a pretty pass when you can't even trust your PA? Get her from an employment agency, did you? If I were you I'd ask for your money back.'

Mo sank gently to her haunches in front of the prisoner and addressed him softly.

'Time to pay, Mr Kevin. Take a look.'

She reached inside her jacket and drew out a photograph, which she held inches from Cropper's eyes. 'That's Han, my brother-in-law, dead alive. I want to know what you have to say. What is your *explanation*?'

Cropper, unable to stop rocking his wracked body, tried to turn away. Mo kept moving the picture so it was always right in front of his face.

'Don't shut your eyes; it offends. Look NOW!' yowled Mo. Some physiological process seemed to have drawn the skin of Cropper's skull so tightly that his anguish was visible in the pulsating of his temple.

'Tell me what you have to say,' persisted Mo, but Ludo intervened.

'Mo would like to give you a gift,' he said. 'She was wondering what would be appropriate and I suggested that you might like her to give you a nice smile – one just like Mr Tsanko makes. Then we can take some pictures for your mum to see, a nice picture of My Boy Kevin with a Kasrik Smile? Look good over the fireplace at Number 14, Glebe Terrace, Brackley? She'd be so *proud*!'

'Please . . .'

'Please? Maybe Han said "please". A simple question: did you order this?'

'No,' rasped Cropper.

'Who did?'

'Crane.'

'And who carried out the order?'

'Georgi Tsanko, the Bulgarian. She knows him.' He nodded towards Mo.

'We know all about Mr Georgi Tsanko, thank you very much," said Ludo. 'He's currently unavailable on account of being under several feet of snow along with the rest of your crew. So please explain how the order from Crane was passed to our Bulgarian friend?'

'Not through me.'

'That's not what Tsanko told me,' said Mo.

'I expect he said all kinds of things while you were in his bed.'

Ludo turned to Mo. Mo nodded.

'Okidoke,' said Ludo, 'come on, everyone, let's leave these two alone so they can have a chat and catch up.'

'This'll do fine,' Clay shouted as he signalled the party to halt. They were about two thirds of the way down a steepish slope. When Cropper was taken off the snowmobile he realised that he had reached the allotted place and indeed his allotted time.

'Hey!' he pleaded. 'What's going on here?'

They untied the prisoner but left his hands bound behind his back while they dug a pit a couple of feet deep in which he was made to stand; the snow was shovelled back and tamped down until he was firmly planted. Colza produced a screwdriver and rendered the bindings on Cropper's skis useless and left them with their poles a few metres away.

Clay unclipped a small green rucksack from his own backpack. When he was done he called out for everyone to move away before speaking quietly to Mo.

'He's all yours.'

With the help of Shin and Kang, Mo did what she had so long planned to do. The sound of Cropper's roaring and squealing had Ludo wondering if they were slaughtering a pig. Once the job was done Mo wiped her gloves in the snow while Shin took photographs of the nearly departed. From his distant viewpoint, Kornie, who so often failed to catch the spirit of an occasion, called out, 'Hey, can vee all be inder pickchaar?'

'Are we finished?' said Clay to Mo. She nodded. He called out to Colza.

'Colza, if you please.'

Colza pulled his hunting horn from his jacket, pressed it to his tightly pursed lips and blew a long mournful call.

A strange contorted sound emerged from Cropper's throat – recognisable as interrogatory but otherwise indecipherable on account of the state of the lower half of his face.

'It's the call to signal a kill,' said Clay to Cropper by way of explanation.

After they had gone a few hundred yards, Ludo stopped and looked back. He could just about make out the lone figure in its white graveyard. He wondered how long he had got.

18

'Why didn't you ask me? We could have talked about it?'

'No point. If I told you what I was planning to do you'd have tried to stop me.'

Ludo couldn't argue with that.

It was early afternoon and the weather was closing in on the weary but elated Thermidor contingent as it trekked back across the glacier to Val.

'We agreed what we'd do when we'd got the necessary evidence against Crane & Co,' insisted Ludo.

'I know.'

'We said we'd let the legal system take its course.'

'I've learnt that the rule of law is bollocks.'

'But you broke our agreement. I didn't sign up for this cowboys-and-Indians nonsense.'

'No, but admit it: but you seemed happy enough back there doing your vindictive little interrogation. No, we've done the right thing by your man Owen. We couldn't let these people get off. They had to be made to pay for what they'd done.'

'Since when did you decide that that was our job?' asked Ludo.

'I'll tell you when – when Mo told me what Crane and his people were doing and what they did to young Han, her brother-in-law. Changed my mind about things. I did what I did for her. Had to.'

'So you let her wind you round her little finger and put all of us at risk?'

'It was them or us.' Clay sounded exasperated. 'Face it, Ludo, Cropper and Tsanko wanted to eat our kidneys for breakfast. We'd have never been safe as long as they were still on this earth.'

That was a tough one to contradict so Ludo tried a different tack.

'We were always a cut above it all. We had justice on our side. You've brought us down to their level.' As soon as he said it he regretted that he might have come across as just a tad pompous.

'Justice? Give us a break,' Clay groaned. 'You think we could've counted on the courts to deliver justice? Cropper would never have even got to the dock. He'd say he was a double agent, acting in an unofficial capacity for the state or something. He'd be plausible. Confuse everyone like he did when he "resigned" from the police. If he was put on trial he'd suborn witnesses, arrange for Parsons or Drake to scare the shit out of the jury, likewise the judge. Think of the time and the cost of their abortive trials.'

'Oh, I see, it's all about cost-cutting?'

Clay paused before he said, 'Maybe,' as if he hadn't thought of a fiscal rationale for his actions but quite liked the idea.

'But Ludo, old chum, can't you grasp what Cropper has done? You could fill a lake with the blood and tears he's spilled, the suffering, pain and misery. So let's not get soppy, eh? God, you're all the same, you lot, you want your hamburger but you don't want to take your turn in the abattoir.'

That line of conversation ended there. Neither wanted the row to escalate and upset the troops, so by some mutual but unspoken agreement neither raised the matter of exactly what was to be done about Crane.

It was Clay who broke the long silence that followed.

'What are you going to do after all this?'

'Same as I was doing before,' replied Ludo. 'And you?'

'Me too, but I thought I might hook up with the Angels. Do a bit of work for them. They seem like a good bunch doing a decent job.'

'You like the revenge, don't you? Even Mike has spotted that.'

'Not really revenge, Ludo; just holding people to account. Anyhow, they've got a good track record, got some decent scalps. Why don't you give them a try? I'm sure they'd like to have you on board; they need people with brains.'

'No, Clay, it's not my scene, but thanks all the same. All I wanted to do was find out who killed my old friend and why. We've done that and I'm grateful for your help, but now Crane & Co should be handed over to be dealt with by the law. It's how things work.'

'But you're going to need something more than that now – after this lark – now you've tasted the *possibilities*? What about the rest of the stuff in the Swanborne File? We have only squeezed a fraction of the juice from that. You said yourself Owen had found evidence of other Cranes. A morass of other mysterious deaths, corporate resignations, disappearances and all the rest of it. We only scratched the surface.'

'Owen was keen for me to finish my thesis so I'm going to do that.'

'Oh come on. You can do that when you're shuffling around the place in your slippers. Right now you need something a little more pro-active . . . juicier!'

Ludo didn't answer but let the silence run. This time it was he who changed subject.

'I worry about Mike.'

'Worry? You mean you don't trust him?' Clay asked.

'No, not that. It's what we've put him through. The things we've told him.'

'You certainly scared him with your New War stuff,' said Clay. 'Heard him asking Colza about it.'

'I think I'd better go and have a word with him and come clean about his family.'

At that moment Mike, trudging along on his own twenty metres ahead of them, was thinking a lot less about Ludo's 'New War' theory than about the way Clay had misled him. He had worked out the reason behind the lies he'd been told. Ludo and Clay had to prevent him and the Team falling into Cropper's hands and revealing what they knew about Thermidor's surveillance of Messigny. That would have jeopardised Mo, who must have come under suspicion from the moment that Cropper saw the White Suit footage. Mo was their vital asset, a bug planted at the heart of Cropper's operation, transmitting every secret. Her existence was the one thing Ludo and Clay could never reveal to Mike. Clay had to stay in Val to maintain contact with Mo and be on hand to get her out of Cropper's clutches at a moment's notice. Mike had been conned into believing they couldn't move because of the roadblocks. *There were no roadblocks.* He had been trapped in Val by a big lie.

As Mike was untangling the machinations of Thermidor, Ludo appeared at his side. 'There's something you need to know, Mike.'

'There usually is,' said Mike.

'It's about your wife and children. And I'm really sorry about it.'

Mike stopped in his tracks.

'What!'

'No, no, they're fine. The truth is there was never any threat to them. The people outside your house were our people. I'm very sorry but we needed to . . .'

'You fucking bastards.'

The sky was clearing. The wind had dropped and so had the temperature.

19

'Oh bugger it!' Ludo wondered if Clay's response was quite adequate enough for the circumstances.

They were a tired bunch as they trudged up the slope that would take them back into the resort area, but their spirits were high. As they neared the crest they were cheered by the sight of a jovial party of pisteurs chatting and laughing as they repaired a section of the barrier marking the edge of the resort. Their red uniforms and the orange plastic netting told the Thermidor party that at last they'd made it home. Some of them burst into a chorus of the *Eisgekühlter Bommerlunder* and Colza gave them 'Blowing for Home' on his horn; the pisteurs waved back in cheery response. When they reached the barrier the pisteurs moved to let Thermidor through the gap in the mesh; in reality they were just getting into position so that when one of them, cop-style, shouted,

'Freeze!', the red jackets were perfectly placed to cover all of them with the semi-automatics they had produced from inside their jackets. Ludo recognised the man with the icy smile who had given the order. He was looking at Mo.

'Hi Miss Mo, good to see you again.'

Mo said, 'Hello Georgi.'

Clay said, 'Oh bugger it!'

Ludo couldn't believe Clay had led them into this trap; he certainly looked a bit sheepish.

'Who is boss here, Miss Mo, please?' Tsanko asked. Like Clay, he was a great one for the facetious courtesy.

'That's me,' said Clay, to his credit very quick off the mark.

'Where is Mr Cropper?'

'Who is Mr Cropper?'

'Maybe we call him, I think.' Tsanko pulled out his phone and pressed a preset. A few seconds later a ringtone sounded in Clay's breast pocket. Tsanko let it go on for quite a long time, which did nothing to improve the atmosphere.

'He lend you his phone then, this man you don't know?' said Tsanko.

'So it seems.'

'And Mr Dubois. Where is?'

'Sadly he couldn't be with us; he's a bit snowed under at the moment.'

'You tell me some more informations, but first we taking some pictures.'

Tsanko made them all stay on their skis while his henchmen forced everyone to form a long line standing at two metres apart from each other, with their wrists in the ski-pole loops and their ski poles across their shoulders behind their necks and in the crooks of their arms, which would slow down any attempt at a surprise attack. Tsanko did each of the mug shots himself, taking time and care. Then he added to his captives' humiliation by pulling their hats down over their eyes. Now as well as being encumbered by ski poles and shackled by their skis, they were blindfolded. Ludo appreciated that Clay's army didn't look too clever.

Ludo heard Tsanko get back on his skis and make a phone call. His voice receded as he moved back up the slope until eventually he was out of earshot. One of the 'pisteurs' searched each person, starting with Clay, relieving them of any weapons and chucking them into a pile a short distance up the slope. Another of Tsanko's men stood behind the person being searched to provide cover just in case anyone tried to resist while a third stood at some distance away at a point where everyone clearly visible and in range. He was the one who, at the sound of a loud crack, suddenly sat down in the snow with blood spouting out of his chest.

An explosion of chaos. Everyone wriggling out of their poles, pulling up their hats above their eyes and kicking off their skis so they could tackle the red suits. The hurried appearance of three armed skiers joining the fray from beyond the spur which had concealed them – three 'days of Thermidor' who had been watching over the main party at a distance from 'outside the perimeter fence'. As they were riding to the rescue, Colza grabbed the man who was searching him. Hampered by his skis, he couldn't stop him from breaking free and getting his hand on his firearm. He was about to shoot Colza in the chest when a banshee-like scream behind him made him turn in time to see Blake, his face contorted with fury, launch himself at him. They both went down in a heap; Blake, who was on top and apparently unhurt, began to pound his victim, while Colza, having freed himself of his skis, swung back his leg as if about to convert from the 23-metre line and let fly four kilos of ski boot at his opponent's skull. There was a nasty crunchy noise and the red-uniformed figure ceased to move.

While all around a clumsy, leaden-footed punch-and-grapple of a battle raged, Bélier and Brebis lumbered towards Tsanko. The Bulgar, who was still on his skis, realised that his men were completely outnumbered and the tables had turned. He began to pole frantically up the slope towards the top of the piste that would take him down towards town. Seeing Tsanko's bid to escape, Brebis, had retrieved a pistol from the pile and, not for the first time in his career, decided to risk some collateral damage. He loosed off a couple of rounds at the retreating form of Tsanko but the Bulgar made it to the top unharmed and, before either Bélier or Brebis could get to him, sped off down and round the curving piste and disappeared from sight.

'Get him! Get him!' Clay shouted. Then he saw Tyler.

'You lot have got the best chance. You *have* to follow him. If he gets down into town we'll never find him. And if he sends our mug shots to Crane we're all fucked.'

'But what do I do when I get to him?' said Tyler, who was already on the move.

'Phone your location. And just stick with him until we get to you.'

Tyler was gone.

A mêlée: some gathering up and handing out the firearms, some dealing with the injured, some securing the captives from Tsanko's contingent, some, as Clay urged them forward, shuffling towards the piste in the wake of Kornie, Blake and Jean-Luc, who were now in hot pursuit of Tyler.

'Fan out!' shouted Clay. 'We have to cover every inch between here and town. Colza, piste map? Quick, for Christ's sake.'

Colza, ever reliable, produced one; the two of them had a hurried council of war as they slid downhill. With dispositions agreed, Colza started giving orders to everyone. 'Brebis, you take a couple of people down the Vendôme run. Arro, you do Farandole. Try and fill in the gaps between; we want a thorough broad sweep all the way to town so if he jinks off course to avoid Tyler and co we'll still pick him up. Ludo, do you want to cover the extreme right and go down Forêt? And Mike, why don't you go with him?'

20

Because of the weather there were only a few people on the slopes, so Mike led at a brisk pace with Ludo following. Both of them knew that Clay had relegated them to an insignificant role way out on the flank of the chase – the equivalent of the cricket field's 'longstop'. They reckoned that Tsanko was by now probably at least two kilometres from where they were, so Mike was understandably astonished to come round a bend and see a figure in red standing at the edge of the piste a couple of hundred metres below him, facing downhill.

The pisteurs' uniforms had been a useful disguise to fool Thermidor, but the bright red was now a liability. The black headgear and distinctive white boots left Mike in no doubt: it was definitely Tsanko. He'd been quite clever. Instead of heading straight down to town, which would have put him at the mercy of the Team's superior speed, he'd cut right across to its very edge, the last place they'd think of checking.

The Bulgar was holding his phone to his ear, which was good because that meant he wasn't sending pictures to anyone. It was also fortunate that he was facing down the slope and hadn't seen Mike or Ludo. As soon as Mike recognised him he skied back across the piste to be out of Tsanko's sight and intercept Ludo. His companion wanted immediate action.

'We've got to get that cell phone off him NOW,' said Ludo. 'He thinks he's safe and he'll start sending our mug shots.'

'Maybe we should wait until we get some help,' said Mike

'No, we hit him now; we might not get another chance.'

Ludo tried to phone Colza but the line was busy so he texted Tsanko's position. Then from inside his jacket he pulled a pistol with a silencer screwed into the barrel and gave Mike his instructions. They waited until a small group of skiers appeared and tagged on behind to conceal their approach. It worked. When Tsanko looked back he saw a seemingly harmless bunch of adults and children;

having turned away he did not see Ludo peel off from the group and come speeding towards him.

Ludo didn't risk using his firearm but kept going until he slammed into Tsanko at full pelt, knocking him flat and sending his phone flying out of his hand. Mike, who was close behind, scooped it up, shoved it deep into his pocket and skied like hell straight down the slope.

Mike was all too aware that in abandoning his comrade to Tsanko's mercy he was taking the vegetarian option, but there was no point in tangling with the Bulgar in unarmed combat, firstly because he didn't do that sort of thing and secondly because he believed unarmed combat was never a good idea if the other guy is armed.

There was another selfish and more pressing reason for leaving Ludo alone with Tsanko: Mike's own mug shot was on the phone and he wanted to make damn sure that Tsanko didn't get it back. Yes, he felt bad about abandoning Ludo but he felt even worse when, after covering about 800 metres, he heard a shout behind him and saw Tsanko coming down the hill after him like an avenging red devil. With no sign of Ludo, Mike now had this unhappy psychopath all to himself. Instinctively, he dived off the exposed piste into the trees for cover and had to negotiate a choppy sea of tree trunks and fallen branches thinly topped with snow.

Mike's plan was to get in among the trees under the Malidon chair where he had skied a couple of times. Mike reckoned that his familiarity with this obstacle-strewn clearing should give him a chance of losing Tsanko, for whom this terrain would be completely unknown. As he skied for his life he couldn't help thinking that this was a dramatic reversal in their situation: Mike had been hunting Tsanko; now Tsanko was chasing Mike; for a moment the Swanborne Fox scurried across his mind. But only for a moment.

As he came out on Vasse, a red run flanked by a drag lift, Tsanko's taunts were unnervingly audible. He was much closer than Mike had imagined. *Think! If I stay on the piste, Tsanko will get me.* Time for desperate measures. And time for the counterintuitive. He'd go uphill instead of down and he'd do it by using the button lift beside the run. The problem was that the poles of each button are retracted when empty, lifting the button seat out of reach; Mike would have to find one that was in use and get rid of its occupant. However, all the poles within Mike's vision were empty and Tsanko was drawing closer. He inwardly groaned when he saw that the first person to appear over the crest was an elderly man. He wasn't proud of what he did next but it was either his button or Mike's life.

As the silver-haired gentleman came within earshot Mike shouted, 'There's a bad emergency at the top. I'm a doctor. I have got to get up there quickly. It's a matter of life or death.' At least the last bit was true, but there was no response.

'You've got to let me take your place,' shouted Mike. The man, who was drawing closer, smiled affably but showed no sign of getting off.

No choice then.

As soon as it came within his reach Mike seized the pole, yanking it downwards, and clung on. The pensioner didn't budge and they were both dragged up the slope; it was a seriously unstable arrangement. The old boy had an iron grip on the pole and only when Mike had pried his fingers free and given him a really hard shove did he manage to eject him and leave him bellowing with fury as he lay crumpled in the snow. It was then that he realised that the old man was speaking German and had probably not understood a word of what he'd said. But Mike faced another more immediate problem as he heard a commotion behind him and felt the cable above him bounce violently. To look straight back behind you on a drag lift is to court disaster, but he guessed Tsanko had come on board. Confirmation came soon enough. The chill of that flat cold voice struck terror in Mike.

'Still with you, my friend!' Tsanko yelled. 'One promise I make. Give me phone and you go free.'

It sounded like some sick parody of a supermarket special offer.

As soon as he'd got into a stable position on the button, Mike phoned Colza.

'Tell Clay it's his fucking longstop here and I need help quick. I've got Tsanko's phone and he's really keen to get it back. He can't be more than seventy metres behind me on the Vasse drag. I seem to have lost Ludo.' He heard Colza conferring with Clay before he came back on the line.

'If you can get to the Dorlay chair we'll have help waiting for you at the top. Well done and good luck.'

There was not much Mike could do. For the next few minutes at least this manhunt had a peculiar character. Predator and prey could get no closer or further apart; they could move only at a fixed speed separated by a fixed distance. Mike used the time to work out how to handle the next bit. He needed to get to the chair with enough of a lead so he'd be safe until he got to the top. Once he was there Clay's people would take over.

At the end of the drag lift Mike hung on to the pole as long as he could to get every bit of tension in the spring so he was catapulted as far forward as possible and given a flying start for the short run down to the Dorlay chair. There was a small queue; if he could get to the front he would put some decent space between himself and Tsanko. The doctor ploy had worked before so he used it again. Everyone was eager to let him pass and he got onto the two-seater chair. His fellow passenger was a teenage girl.

Mike turned to count the chairs behind him and saw a commotion in the now distant lift queue as Tsanko barged and fought his way to the front. Taking comfort from the fact that there was a healthy distance between them he phoned Colza to report his position.

Mike could hear Colza telling Clay, 'It's Hangonamo. He's made it to the Dorlay chair. Tsanko's still on his case.' Clay came on the line.

'Mike, really great stuff . . . two ears and the tail. You've done wonders. Now listen, we'll have some people at the top by the time you get there. When you get off the chair bear right as you leave the resort area and head for Cauchemar.'

'Cauchemar!' Mike felt a surge of panic overtaking him. Cauchemar was an off-piste run leading down to the glacier; the word meant nightmare and it was.

'Mike, you've told me you've skied it before, so no problem there.'

Yes, thought Mike, I did get down it once and, okay, I may have inadvertently made light of it in conversation. In fact it had been a near disaster. It was above Mike's ability and, humiliatingly, he had had to side-slip some of the way. It had taken bloody forever and he was a nervous wreck by the time he got to the bottom. Now he was being asked to go down it with Tsanko on his tail. It was quite clear to Mike that this was Clay's idea of payback time for who knows what conversational transgressions he may have committed in the course of his captivity.

'Not keen on that idea, Clay.'

'Nonsense. You'll be fine.'

'Oh great. That's alright then.'

Mike could see Clay's plan. His great worry was that Tsanko would catch up with Mike, retrieve his phone, and make his way back down to town before flying home to present Crane with all their mug shots. He needed to get Tsanko out of the resort area and below it with no lifts to take him back up. He'd be trapped like a spider in the bottom of a bath.

In a fit of displacement activity while he had nothing to do but wait, Mike started to check his texts. There was something from the secretary of the organising committee of the East Harpenden Tennis Club barn dance, a promise from Tony the plumber that he'd fix the broken shower pump in the spare room when he got back from New York, a cheeky note from Paul suggesting his father write an essay on *What I did in my holidays*, and a line from Anne sounding worried about Dahlia's paw which still wasn't healing.

When he returned to present reality he wondered what would happen when he got to the top; he hoped that the reinforcements from Thermidor would be there to rescue him from the clutches of that murdering lunatic who was screaming threats at him from a dozen or so chairs back.

'You waiting for me at top or you in big troubles!'

With fifty metres to go, Mike took a decision and prayed for forgiveness for what he was about to do. He looked across at his fellow passenger on the chair beside him. If it had been another one of those pensioners he would have a pile of matchwood on his hands but this girl was no more than fifteen or sixteen, which was good because they were still quite bendy at that age.

As the chair came in to land, Mike came off the seat with deliberate clumsiness and lurched across the girl's path, knocking her over. She went down with a shriek and a look of utter disbelief as Mike scooted off ignoring her plight, hell-bent on taking advantage of every second of the delay he was about to cause. The attendant hit the alarm button to bring the lifts to a halt and untangled the tearful teenage jumble of skis, sticks, earphones and limbs. Meanwhile, a hundred metres back, Tsanko was bouncing helplessly in mid-air, going nowhere and shouting Balkan obscenities into the Alpine sky.

Mike headed straight for the orange barrier and slipped under it, then paused, staring around in a frantic search for the help that Clay had promised. There was no one. He was on his own. *'Thank you, Clay, you bastard.'*

Few off-piste runs actually have names, but Cauchemar did, because it was a notorious obstacle course of special horribleness and of interest only to the intrepid. No one would ever attempt it unless they were pretty experienced, and even then you wouldn't do it on your own because you really would need someone around in case you came to grief.

For Mike the worst thing about Cauchemar was that from the departure point you could see the whole horror of it in one glance as it dropped away under the tips of your skis. It was basically a slightly sloping cliff. Tired and paralysed with terror, he stood poised to slip over the edge into the abyss. Or not. He remembered Tyler's vivid picture of poor Blake's agony at the couloir. Now Mike too was hearing contradictory voices. There was the wise one repeating louder and louder, *Don't do it!* while another voice, prompted by the menacing taunts of an approaching Tsanko, was telling him: *You must do it; you have no choice.*

Strangely, it wasn't as bad as he'd expected. Mike had vowed to ignore the bigger, more horrible picture, hang on to his technique and focus only on the few metres immediately in front of him. The fact that he survived those first few desperate turns gave him a measure of confidence. But the early part of the run was not the most difficult section. Pretty soon it started to change from steep moguls to slim, rock-lined alleys. He forced himself to ski instead of side-slipping as he had before, even if it did mean doing it in small sections and braking violently at the end of each.

He began to gain in confidence but he knew what was yet to come. 'This would not be a good place to fall,' his guide had told him when he talked him down an equally difficult run some years back. Although this was true it wasn't what he wanted to hear. There was no other route: only a narrow strip of snow which led straight down a steep slope to a sheer drop of a couple of hundred feet. It meant having to shoot straight down the slope and jink sharp left at the very edge of the precipice. If he fluffed it and went over that edge there was no deep snow to land in, just jagged rock. Curtains.

As he approached it, Mike's fear seemed to bring alive all the senses in his body, which groaned with aches, exhaustion. He might have stopped at the top of the section to collect himself, gather his concentration, but he didn't want to allow any time for his fear to build, so he kept flying towards the cliff edge where, with just a few feet remaining, he rose to un-weight his skis, sank down on his outside ski and let his body swing away from the mountain to take him into the turn. There was a long and hideous moment in the middle of the manoeuvre when he felt that the tails of his skis were hanging over the void. But eventually they came in to land.

Elated with relief, Mike tackled the next phase of very steep clear snow, picking up a rhythm again with gathering confidence at each turn. This glimmer of optimism was soured by a bloodcurdling cry from Tsanko; he sounded much closer than Mike would have thought possible. It had the desired effect. Mike began to crack up. His technique fell to pieces, his body felt hopelessly stressed and exhausted, and his injured knee was agony. Mike was losing it.

Then he heard a strange thin sound cutting through the darkening air. His spirits lifted. It was the sound of Colza's horn. Unfortunately he'd left it a bit too late because as Mike made a turn, he saw out of the corner of his eye the red shape of Tsanko no more than thirty metres above him, poised to shoot. Then he did. It all suddenly seemed so unfair, Mike thought to himself as he felt a sharp hard smack on his right arm. The shock of the impact overrode the pain. The mountain began to wriggle and slide beneath the soles of his boots, the sky went muzzy, then he was down.

'I'm helpless; I'll be carrion for Tsanko. It is time to take my sweetie but I'm not even sure I can be bothered. It is time to stop all this and take a rest. *I've had enough.*'

Mike stared back up the slope at his nemesis, but saw that Tsanko seemed to have had enough too because instead of taking another shot at him – and God knows he was an easy target – Tsanko let his pistol arm fall to his side, dropped down on his knees and studied the surface of the snow in front of him quite intently for some time as if he had just found something of considerable importance – maybe an abstract truth? Or a contact lens?

'Yes,' concluded Mike's rambling mind, 'this is how it is for us warriors. There comes a time when, sated by the blood we have shed, our minds call out for truce and say enough is enough. My enemy has proved himself worthy and even though he is at my mercy he and I may now go free.'

Certainly Tsanko had lost all interest in Mike. He was leaning forward, resting on his knuckles and prostrating himself in the attitude of a Moslem at prayer, his face almost touching the snow. For some moments he was motionless before he toppled over onto his side. Mike guessed he too was really tired after what had been quite a day and now he needed to get some sleep.

Mike, though, unlike Tsanko, was awake enough to see another figure forty metres up the slope lower a pistol, which made him reassess Tsanko's behaviour. The bang had occurred somewhere around the time that Tsanko keeled over. From the gunman came a voice, powerful, clear, cutting through the air, a female voice.

'Hang on a mo, Hangonamo, we're coming down.' It was Candy and when she got close enough, Mike could see she was all smiles.

Candy and Colza helped Mike down to the bottom of Cauchemar, where they were joined by Clay, Tyler and the Team and various members of Thermidor. Among them Mike was relieved to see Ludo who was mercifully none the worse for his encounter with Tsanko. Their brief struggle had ended with Ludo being knocked unconscious. The Bulgarian had left it at that because he was desperate to go after Mike and retrieve his mobile.

'Enjoy the old rough and tumble, did you, Mike?' said Clay. 'Now, have you got Tsanko's phone? Excellent. Oh my, oh my, we can have a bit of sport with this. Thank you. Good man.' As Mike passed him the phone Clay saw his injured arm.

'Good Lord, Mike, you're leaking. You appear to have been slightly shot.'

Mike looked down. Clay was quite right. Blood was seeping from his upper arm and dripping onto the snow, where he observed it turning from shocking red into the rusty pink of strawberries mashed into cream.

'Colza, have we got coping strategies in place for this?'

'Yes, Clay,' said Colza, who like Mike wondered wearily if Clay would ever stop taking the piss. 'We'll get him cleaned up.'

'Jolly good. Anyway, Mike, you did a grand job. Well done.'

'One does one's best,' replied Mike with a knowing glance at Ludo.

'Colza, how's our chum Tsanko? Need him to wake up for a bit of a chat before we say our goodbyes.'

'He'll have come round by the time we get him to a suitable location.'

'Excellent,' said Clay. As he moved off, Kornie made an announcement.

'And here is coming de Empress of China!'

It was a fair description of Mo arriving into the middle of their ragged group, serene on her snowmobile, surrounded by a gaggle of courtiers including her loyal Imperial Guards, Shin and Kang.

21

It would have been wrong to call it a funeral cortège because Tsanko wasn't dead yet, but the procession looked a bit like one. Colza led the way, followed by Thermidor operatives fore and aft of a snowmobile towing a platform on which a much-trussed and partly bandaged Bulgar lay semi-conscious. Mo rode in the second snowmobile, flanked by Shin and Kang. Ludo and Clay brought up the rear and were speculating on how Tsanko had escaped the avalanche.

'My guess,' said Clay, 'is that he became suspicious, suspected some kind of a trap and slipped away on the pretext of going back to check on Cropper who had fallen behind, leaving Dubois to lead his posse into the avalanche. When he heard our explosion he would have thought the worst and written off Dubois and the others as dead meat. He'd have lost any remaining faith in Cropper and decided to hook up with the reinforcements – the pros the Board had sent. Somehow we didn't see him. Maybe his mobile tells us something?'

Clay fished it out of his pocket and swiped up the log.

'Yes. Tsanko spoke to Crane before he caught us. Crane would have ordered him to get the identity of their pursuers at all costs – he had to know who was on his trail. So that's what Tsanko did first. Anyway, you'll be able to ask him in a minute.'

They halted at the edge of a deep crevasse. Then Colza came over and asked everyone to move away back up the hill.

'Mo and her friends would like to have some quality time alone with Tsanko,' he explained.

Brebis lifted Tsanko off his snowmobile and laid him out on the snow. Next he slipped the noose of a climbing rope over the captive's head and shoulders and drew it tight under his arms. All this was watched at close quarters by the Korean contingent, with Shin videoing every moment. After about twenty minutes Clay emerged from the group and went over to Ludo.

'Do you want to come down and ask our friend anything before he goes?'

There was a lot Ludo wanted to ask Tsanko, but he had no intention of being part of Clay's repellent charade. He shook his head and moved further away. He had his back turned to the proceedings but it didn't stop him hearing a horrible snapping sound, followed by the most terrible explosive groan from Tsanko that seemed to hang in the air. Then the sequence was repeated. A few minutes after that came a scream and then a series of terrible deep despairing moans.

When Ludo turned to face the scene, they were lowering Tsanko into the crevasse while Shin video-ed him until he was out of sight. When he'd got to the bottom, Clay came forward and passed Mo the remaining coil of rope. She went to the edge, looked down, shouted something in Korean and threw the rope down into the void. She turned to Clay and nodded. Clay gave a signal and for the second time that day Colza raised his horn to his lips and blew 'The Kill'.

Ludo was disgusted at the atrocity, ashamed with himself for not preventing it and angry at his own sanctimony in pretending to himself that he could have stopped it. He was even angrier that part of him applauded Tsanko's treatment. Ludo tried to assuage this guilt by calling up the image of Han in his hospital bed. So he just glowered at Clay when he came up to tell him what Tsanko had told them in his final interrogation. After he'd finished Ludo waited some time before he broke the silence.

'What about the cardboard boxes?'

'Yes, I asked him about that,' said Clay. 'Seems they were a bit of a signature item for him; used it to good effect in New Zealand and other places. Idea was that a man carrying a heavy bulky load doesn't walk normally. Although witnesses saw him arriving and leaving various crime scenes none of them reported a limp.'

'You still shouldn't have done what you did,' said Ludo, returning to his grievance.

'Had to be done,' said Clay. 'He won't last long now.'

'What if he climbs out of there?'

'Difficult with two broken arms and a bullet in his ribs.'

'For God's sake, Clay, what's happened to you?' Of course Ludo knew the answer. Mo had happened to him.

'Oh come on,' said Clay cheerily. 'I know you think we've been a bit hard on poor old Tsanko but at least we made sure he got some decent skiing in on his last day.'

Everyone was now close to exhaustion and the long climb back up into the resort was hard for them. Occasionally Ludo could hear Colza conferring with Clay before he spoke to someone on his radio and guessed that Clay still had some people 'outside the perimeter fence'.

At one point Mike came alongside Ludo; he was in a state of agitation.

'You know why Clay and Colza called our group the TA?'

'Territorial Army?' said Ludo.

'No. Towed Array. And I've just found out what that is.'

'And?'

'A disposable vessel used to provide target practice for naval gunners.'

Ludo smiled. It was a pretty good description of their function.

Ludo wanted to talk to Tyler while he was on his own. He wanted to express his regret at what he and the Team had had to go through and thank them for what they'd all done. He was particularly grateful for Blake's courageous attack during the battle with Tsanko's men.

'Sort of makes sense,' said Tyler. 'Blake's courage in that situation came from the same instinct that made him bottle out at the top of the couloir. It was all about surviving for the sake of his unborn child.'

'So what happens now?' Ludo asked Clay. 'You've changed the plan. We always said we'd hand over the evidence to the media and let the judicial system do its stuff.'

'No need. It's going to be better and easier. Kornie's Chalet Messigny video footage has changed all that. Podesti, Pivic and friends hold Crane responsible for the security fiasco; it was his show, he organised it and now they'll make him pay. They'll do our work for us, only they'll be more thorough and they'll work *pro bono*.'

'So what's going to happen to Crane?' asked Ludo.

'If they go by the form book they won't touch him until they've killed his son Max, 'cos they'll want him to know they've done that. It's a Balkan thing.' Clay made it all sound like regional cookery.

'And then they'll go for Frank Crane himself. He's very vulnerable – no Cropper, no Tsanko and most of his palace guard vanished on the glacier; he'll be easy meat for any rival who wants to come along and bite chunks out of his empire – Pivic and Co will come hopping in like crows. Meanwhile, until their bodies are found, Crane will believe that Cropper and Dubois are just hiding from him while they're plotting with Parsons and Drake to take control.'

'Why would he think that?'

'Because the last text he gets from Tsanko will tell him so.'

'How do you know?'

Ludo stared at Clay, whose efforts to look nonchalant couldn't conceal that he was pretty pleased with himself.

'Oh I get it,' said Ludo. 'You're sending it.'

Clay nodded.

'And what about Parsons and Drake?' he asked.

'Well, they'll be trying to convince Crane that Tsanko's information was wrong, but the fun will really start when the snow melts and they find Cropper's body and read the contents of that green rucksack.'

The rucksack had been Colza's idea. They had, without telling Ludo, filled it with compromising evidence against the two villains, notably material implicating them and Crane in the murder of their schoolmate Tommy Ealey – the original sin which Mo had uncovered.

'And Ricky Phibbs and his accomplice at GCHQ?'

'We tell the authorities what we know, but I doubt they'll give them much of a punishment, at worst a year or two in a gated community. But my guess is they'll get a suspended sentence and be kept in place: they're both talented operatives whose training cost a lot of money. They'll just need to teach them to piss out of the tent instead of into it. They'll be totally in hock to the Service for the rest of their careers.'

With everyone now close to exhaustion, Colza worked tirelessly to boost their spirits, moving from one group to another, cajoling, conferring and encouraging. By the time they re-entered the ski area it was completely dark and they had to rely on head-torches and a quarter moon. When they came round the shoulder of Mont Gaffe, Ludo felt he had the refuge of a familiar harbour after surviving a terrible storm. It was a glorious sight – Val spread out below them defined only by its lights.

22

A great cauldron of *Boeuf Bourguignon* was waiting for everyone when they got back to Juniper. It had been prepared by various non-combatants including Prêle and Guimauve who'd repopulated the abandoned apartments. Dinner was a high-spirited affair; they'd done what they had set out to do and they could afford a little self-congratulation. So they thought.

The main course had just been cleared away when there were two loud bangs on the apartment door as though it had been kicked very hard. Everybody froze.

'What the hell!' said Clay, rising to his feet. 'I'll get that.' Everyone sat in silence as he disappeared down the corridor. They could hear him open the door. The sound Clay made was almost a scream.

'Tsanko!'

The Team were the first to leave Val; they were already late for their next project in Canada and they set off a couple of days later. Before they went, Mike joined them for a farewell drink at Sandy's; it was a desultory affair; they had much to say but in the end said little. Ludo, Clay and most of the Thermidor people left over the next three days. Ludo fell into a depression which wasn't helped by an email from Reggie reporting that the results of his tests had come through. 'I stand,' he said, 'in the coldest expectation.' Ludo smiled grimly. Their colleagues at A&G would often mock Reggie for the odd way he put things.

Mike stayed on in Val for rather longer than he had planned. He had been in a hurry to get back to England, but Anne's father had fallen seriously ill in Vancouver and she had flown out to be with him, so Mike decided to prolong his stay. His injured arm caused him little discomfort but when it did it would remind him of Clay's irritatingly dismissive words. 'You must realise, Mike, that Tsanko needed you alive. He was only ever going to shoot you a little bit.'

Mike had been badly troubled by the horrors of recent days and sought comfort in some manic skiing. It had become a craving; each morning would find him on the slopes waiting for the lifts to open, like a drunk at the doors of a bar. Some evenings, when, just as he felt at peace with himself and was enjoying a beer on his balcony, he would hear the Val town band in the distance playing the Black Note Waltz and a dark tide of nightmarish memories would surge back into his mind. His scalp would tingle even at the thought of Tsanko turning up at the door of Juniper – so typical of Clay's idea of a joke. He had arranged for Colza to slip out earlier and bang on the door.

Ludo felt sorry for Mike. It was he who had precipitated the whole drama with his mischievous but apparently harmless suggestion that the Team should ski by the Chalet Messigny. He couldn't have got it more wrong. The poor chap had come to Val with hopes for a winter as blissful as a Blandings summer and, courtesy of Thermidor, instead of Bertie Wooster for company he'd got Georgi Tsanko. All hell had broken out in his own private paradise. Ludo pictured him on his return trying to explain to his wife over mugs of tea in the tidy kitchen of their Harpenden home his mysterious behaviour over the nine days. That night she'd see his war wound so he'd have to tell her all about that too.

Ludo fell sorry for himself too. He was now a troubled being. The days of unwanted proximity to some of the vilest men on the earth, the obscenities visited upon Glyn Owen in Tsanko's van and on Customs Officer Han in Quay Number 17 had taken their toll. He felt unclean carrying these things around in his mind yet could not get rid of them.

When he got home he found that his fear had given way to a gruelling anxiety. Being reunited with Liz and the girls gave him great comfort but back at the office he felt like a stranger. Reggie, Ludo's great source of solace, had had to go into hospital which made A&G a less pleasing place. Meanwhile he was constantly aware that Thermidor was still a work in progress; he wanted to talk things through with Clay who, irritatingly, was not answering emails or returning calls.

There were some days when Ludo took to drink in an attempt to delete his unpleasant memories. *Yes, Reggie, I too am trying to shift the paradigm.* Sometimes in his imagination he found himself hectoring the dead but still dreaded Cropper. *Wake up, dead man, it's time to move.* Ludo continued to wear his capsule round his neck because of the terrible truth that would not leave his mind: Crane was still at large.

But at least Tsanko had been removed from the face of the earth. *I bet Tsanko thought that hell would be hot.* How wrong he was. Ludo struggled to understand: how did Tsanko *happen*? Was he a finely crafted piece of evil from his childhood? His various employers were hardly a positive influence – that was a terrible thing they did when they broke him with a rock. Was it his experience of war that forever destined him to be among the cursed who work in rubber aprons, to serve the piteous guests at some eternal Gagro Hotel, to choose a ringtone made of screams? Anyway, as Clay said, although Tsanko may not have been much good at making people laugh he certainly knew how to make them smile.

When Ludo considered the problem presented by creatures like Tsanko he began to wonder if perhaps Clay was right: there was a job to be done and he was in a position to help do it. He ought to follow Clay's example and do battle with the bad hats. It would mean forsaking the comforts of the theoretical implicit in finishing his thesis and instead facing the risks of the practical which signing up with a Private Justice Initiative would entail. Ludo had already made tentative contact with St Leonards who specialised in the European people-trafficking sector. He was offering to do some research and analysis – maybe some target identification. He'd been very frank with them; he didn't want anything too onerous, nothing that would jeopardise his day job and his pension. Then, when he'd done his bit, he'd get back to his thesis. Yes, definitely; but meanwhile *Non-violent Insurgency* would have to wait.

Ludo certainly never expected the situation to develop as rapidly as it did. Early one afternoon he received a text from Clay: IF U R FEELING PECKISH + FANCY A KEBAB U SHOULD SWING BY MO'S PLACE. That could only mean one thing. He took a cab to the end of Brompton Crescent and walked towards Crane's house. They'd sealed the road with emergency tape patrolled by two constables who were holding back a small group of onlookers. Beyond was a small fire service vehicle, two ambulances and a police car. A squad of paramedics were working amid a clutter of saline and blood drips, stretchers, cutting equipment and rubber sheeting.

23

It was impossible to see the object of all the attention but one of the onlookers, a Brazilian female domestic from a neighbouring house, was only too keen to tell Ludo what had happened. Two men had been found impaled on the iron spikes of the railings after falling from the first-floor balcony. They were believed to be the owner of the house and his son.

'Maybe both drinking fighting and fall over.'

Or maybe not. From talking to others in the crowd Ludo learned that a Latvian nanny who had first come across the grisly scene and raised the alarm had noticed the tips of the railings which were protruding through the two bodies.

'Both still alive. Maybe only just!'

'Are you sure?'

'Yes, yes, making lot of noise. Very painful, I think.'

'Yes, I imagine it would be.'

No, thought Ludo, they didn't fall, those bodies were *arranged* like that. It was important that Crane and Max stayed alive – for a little while, anyway.

Scanning the crowd standing on the far side of the tape that had been strung across the road on the other side of the house, Ludo noticed right at the front a small man with familiar Asian features who was videoing the scene; rather than a mobile like the rest of the ghouls were using he had a serious bit of kit with a large telephoto lens.

One lunchtime Ludo was sitting in the early spring sunshine at an outside table at a restaurant near his office. He found himself watching the birds stealing crumbs from the tables and saw how to answer a question that had been troubling him. Was the capsule round his neck another of Clay's ruses? He felt he no longer needed it so now was the time to find out. He pulled the lanyard over his head, placed the capsule on the table in front of him. After contemplating it for a minute, he carefully broke open the 'red for dead' end with a knife, letting the thin syrup drip onto a piece of bread which he pushed over to the far side of the table. He didn't have long to wait before a sturdy sparrow landed beside it and, after a couple of exploratory jabs, nudged it around the tabletop, stabbing and pecking at it until half was gone. The bird, its appetite momentarily satisfied, remained on its feet quite unaffected. Ludo's fingers tightened on the table's edge in slow-burning fury. Either Clay had been conned by whoever supplied the so-called poison, or he had fooled them all into feeling safer with some kind of placebo? This train of thought was interrupted by some unseen force that seemed suddenly to swipe the bird sideways off its feet; it convulsed gently for a few seconds and lay still.

Occasionally Ludo wondered what would become of the Thermidor crowd. Candy, for instance? He imagined some day in the distant future when he'd bump into her in the supermarket by the breakfast cereals. She'd have a small baby in the trolley and a toddler beside her. They'd both do a double take and he would say, 'Hello, you're Candy, aren't you? I remember you from Juniper . . . in Val de Ligne.' And she'd stare at him and say, 'Good Lord! It's Ludo! Fancy that. Yes, Juniper! We certainly had a few odd types in there. Do you remember the Oriental Princess who couldn't ski and wanted to be driven everywhere? She had a mega downer on that chap Georgi – the one who went round cutting everybody's lips off – was that weird or what!' Then Candy would yell an ear-splitting 'Harry!' and tell Ludo, 'I'd better get these two home. Lovely to see you, Ludo!' before chasing after her boy, who'd be halfway down the aisle cantering past the savoury biscuits.

One evening Ludo came across the curious headline on a UK news site: PHANTOM FOXHUNTER MOVES NORTH. It was a report about residents of several neighbourhoods in Northeast London being woken by the sound of a hunting horn in the early hours of the morning. There'd been similar incidents south of the river one week earlier. The culprit was reckoned to move around by bike. Ludo knew who it was immediately. Colza! What was he up to, Colza the one-time hunt saboteur turned huntsman's ghost, plaguing the city-dwellers' sleep?

In response to an email from Mike, Tyler reported that the fortunes of the Team were riding high but they were 'having serious issues with Saul'. Apparently he had agreed to direct some movies with a new young group of free riders and might well just dump the Team. Anyway, in their never-ending search for the forever snow Tyler said they had plans to do Alaska again in the next season and then the Urals. Often, when reading some report about global warming, an image would form in Ludo's mind of Tyler, Jean-Luc and Kornie huddled together on their skis on the tip of a melting iceberg in an empty sea like the last polar bears in the world.

Ludo was, of course, curious to know how the CEO of Crane & Son ended up on the railings along with his boy. Clay had told Ludo to go to Brompton Crescent so he must have known what was going to happen, and Shin was there on hand to record the happy event, but no way was this Clay's own work. He was much more inclined to enlist the wrath of victims, because he believed that retribution should have the best possible pedigree. Ludo's guess was that Clay along with Mo had managed to get in touch with Pivic or maybe Pallengro – they would see themselves as victims of Crane's incompetence – and offered them details of the layout, routines and staffing of Number 27. Poor old Crane's security arrangements had fallen to pieces. Ludo reckoned that his regular staff of minders would have disappeared after being threatened into desertion or physically removed by Pivic. Cropper had always taken care of things but Crane had received what purported to be a selfie from Mo showing her sitting in the snow next to a Cropper who'd clearly undergone some drastic facial surgery. He was clearly in no position to help. Without Cropper there was little protection against the intruders who came to impale Crane and Max. Adele Crane, along with two domestic staff and a single security guard, had been found bound and gagged in the panic room in the lower basement.

So that just left Drake and Parsons to be pulled in; their slow-burn fate sealed in a small green rucksack that would soon emerge from the melting snow.

They certainly picked their moment. One weekday evening back in the UK Ludo was in the pub with some of the cricket team after indoor nets practice. As he made his way through the crowded bar with a full tray of drinks, a young woman, pale, dark-haired and unsmiling, came up beside him holding an envelope and said, 'I think you may have dropped this.' She tucked it under his arm, pressed his elbow firmly to his side as if to secure it and disappeared into the crowd. Ludo was helpless: there was nowhere he could put the tray down and he couldn't follow her; he felt a bit idiotic being held prisoner by three pints of Tilfords and a couple of lagers. As soon as he had delivered the drinks he went outside and opened the envelope. Inside was a single sheet of paper with a couple of typewritten lines. 'Sir, we thank you for your interest. Please call the number below to make an appointment. St Leonards.'

Ludo wouldn't give up his job, of course; he couldn't afford to, but he still hadn't completely decided on how he should spend his spare time and energy? When he thought about helping out in the PJI sector he found that Glyn Owen's reproachful stare kept intruding from beyond the grave. *I nurtured your promise, now you must acquit your debt to me. Retribution may seem appealing but your thesis has a grander purpose.* Owen had expressed so much faith in him and his notion of a significant and civilising mutation in the evolution of conflict. It was grand stuff. He'd more or less done the research; he just had to write the damn thing.

Ludo had taken his final decision in a moment of clarity that came to him in the cable car on one of his last days in Val. On the way up the cabin came to a halt and swung softly in the silent void. The awareness that his life was hanging by a thread had the effect of concentrating Ludo's mind. He had the distinct feeling that this delay was designed to nudge him into confronting the big question about his future and make his decision.

From his vantage point at the large rear window of the cabin he stared down to the valley floor and across to the mountains on the far side, a scene symphonic in its grandeur. As he looked he came to the sudden conclusion that places like this would always be eloquent enough to secure protection, but that there were other environments which cried out for help, hard and ugly places, cruel cities where the wretched of the streets cowered from debt and threat.

And so it was that Ludo had decided. He would forsake the vague possibilities of his Non-Violent Insurgency theory for the immediate and practical promise of the Private Justice sector. NVI would have its day, but not just yet.

The cabin seemed to divine that Ludo had reached his decision and with a slight nod of approval resumed its ascent.

Events outside the Crane house fulfilled a promise that Clay had given him when they parted after Thermidor's farewell lunch in Val. The day had been sunny and clear. Ludo had invited everyone to lunch at Jerome's at the end of the morning spent skiing together before they headed off in their various directions.

When the time came to part, everyone had assembled on their skis outside the restaurant.

Ludo said a few words of thanks. Then Clay, the old showman, stepped forward and raised his arms with his palms upturned like a bandleader calling for his musicians to take a bow.

'And so we say farewell to the days of Thermidor. We say farewell to Salicor . . . to Guimauve and to Armoise . . . to Bélier and Brebis.' Ludo, inwardly cringing at Clay's laboured theatricality, gave a shy smile in benign but embarrassed acknowledgement.

'Bid goodbye to Ivraie and Prêle . . . to Abricot and Basilic, to Colza and to Candy!'

When Clay had finished with his roll-call Ludo said his own individual goodbyes to everyone. After Mo, Shin and Kang had gone down in the chairlift, the rest of the party jostled for position on the edge of the piste. Colza blew a jubilant 'Gone Away' on his horn and they all surged forward in a raucous race down the slope.

Ludo and Clay watched them go like proud parents. When they were out of sight and Colza's horn had faded into nothing, Clay turned to Ludo.

'Well, old chap, must press on. Unfinished business.'

'So see you on Remembrance Day?'

'Yes . . . circumstances permitting. And don't worry about Crane. I give you my word that Mo and I will take care of him.'

'If you say so. Anyway, I've been grateful for your help, Clay. Thank you.'

'One does one's best.'

Clay pointed his skis down the hill, looked back at Ludo, shrugged his shoulders up to his ears and said with an impish smile, 'That's all, folks!' and slipped over the lip of the slope.

Whatever else he had to do, Mike made sure that he paid a visit to the clinic every day. Sandy was going to be fine but it would take time. Cropper and Dubois had been wrongly convinced that the Bar X proprietor knew where Mike was hiding and ordered Tsanko to reel him in and get him to talk. Fortunately, before he had done irreparable damage he very soon realised that his prisoner knew nothing and abandoned the project. Sandy was a robust old stick and the medical consensus was that, as long as he took it gently, he might be back on the slopes for the next season, if not, certainly the one after. Mike's visits to the clinic were clouded with a resurgence of guilt: they reminded him that it was his trespass at Messigny and his mischievous suggestion to Saul that someone should ski by the chalet that had started all the nonsense in the first place.

The events of the past weeks made it hard for Ludo to be at peace with himself. The terrible truth that Glyn Owen had divined and that Thermidor had disinterred was that the devil's agents could strut around as confident as peacocks in a rich man's park, committing their obscene brutalities without fear of retribution.

Most of his fellow citizens didn't know what was happening and didn't want to know; there were those who suspected but didn't want their suspicions confirmed, and there were those very few who, like Ludo himself, knew because it was their job to know. He sometimes found it hard to accept the appalling truth. He tried to reassure himself. *We live under the rule of law. We are too sophisticated to tolerate this nonsense.* But he saw his self-delusion for what it was; the facts told him otherwise. This thing is in our own house – down there in the far corner of that dark cellar where no one wants to go. Anyone *could* see it, but few *would* care or dare to face this icy truth for it was too cold, too terrible for the fingers of the mind to grasp.

For Mike, still in Val de Ligne, the moment he dreaded was coming. The weather was warming and the snow was melting fast.

Soon the streets of the town and the lower slopes would be almost clear and from a distance the mountains would look like a beautiful white wedding dress with a torn and muddy hem. Every second of sunshine uncovered more grass lying pale and limp after enduring months of winter darkness. Still Mike clung on like a guest staying too long at a party, making excuses that tested the patience of his colleagues until finally the day came when he settled his bills and made his way to the cable car for the last time.

When he stepped out of the cabin onto the platform at the top of Diabolo he winced in the white light of a near 180-degree mountain panorama brightened by the pale sun. He was on top of the world in a Garden of Eden where no tree could grow and where the serpents could not tread. Here the clear air brought a disturbing clarity of vision. Now he could see the world as the gods did. 'The mountains make us pure not because we are nearer to the gods but because we are further from man.' Who said that? Probably some philosopher. Or was it Kornie Løvland?

Mike felt the cold air rush at him, buffeting him all over, snatching at his anxieties and whisking them away to flap and snap like a piste map in the wind. He clumped down the steel steps, the quickening drumbeat of his heart sending urgent calls for extra oxygen. He let his skis fall to the snow with a muffled rattle and thump, tapped and scraped his soles and clicked his boots into the bindings. He poled over to the run marked Aigle, paused for a few moments to let his breathing settle and then eased himself over the edge.

As he dropped through the air he felt the pressure of all the days of unrelenting fear fall away from his shoulders. Weightless and free, he caught the power of the mountain, which flung him down its smooth surface of sparkling, softly rasping powder. He rose and sank, revelling in the movement which took him to the edge of flight. The fresh pure air flooded his lungs, blew through his brain and made his whole frame sing. He sped through the air as if on a curling wave, no other soul in sight.

Alone in his own white heaven.

Also by Mark Law:

THE PYJAMA GAME
A JOURNEY INTO JUDO

It is a sport of balletic beauty and extraordinary violence – where else are you allowed to strangle an opponent unconscious? But while its aim is to inflict symbolic death, judo is a form of combat which also rigorously insists on the most formal courtesies.

When Mark Law joined his local judo club he was able to observe at close quarters the sport practised at its highest level. He even found himself having to face some of its finest fighters – World Champions and Olympic medallists. His journey into judo took him to Osaka, Japan to see the World Championships and to Athens for the Olympics. With journalistic zeal he delved into the sport's history, exploring everything from its origins in the 17th-century Samurai warrior culture to its legendary proponents past and present.

The Pyjama Game, in which Law weaves his own experiences as judoka working his way through the coloured belts, is a fascinating account of this most enigmatic of sports which, in its own ferocious but highly codified regime, feeds man's immutable warrior instinct for combat. It tells the story of how judo conquered the world, and how the world has tried to conquer Japan. We are taken behind the scenes of the international tournament circuit populated by some of the most fearsomely single-minded and self-denying competitors of all time – men and women who have arrived at the apex of a sport from thousands of ordinary judo clubs all over the world. Through a series of colourful encounters – sublime, grotesque, comic and tragic – we experience the irresistible drama of tournament judo as fighters grapple, whirl and fly through the air or struggle on the ground for armlocks and chokes, each contest culminating in that symbolic death.

Funny, alarming and mesmerising, *The Pyjama Game* is one of the best sports books of recent years.

'Approaching his 50th birthday, Mark Law decides to take up judo and his initial interest becomes an obsession, then a book. The result is a fascinating journey in which he unravels this most opaque of sports with humour, verve and style. Part travelogue, part history, part chronicle of midlife discovery, *The Pyjama Game* is an illuminating exposition of an enigmatic and marginal sport'

James Corbett, *Observer*

'This is a must-read for every judo enthusiast'

Jimmy Pedro, World Champion and Olympic medallist

'Excellent . . . a classic in its genre'

Robert Twigger, *Sunday Times*

'Beautifully written, and no interest in the martial arts is required to find it absolutely riveting'

Independent

'If you really want to be bowled over by a book about a martial art then you really must read this extraordinary book. It is absolutely hilarious in parts, extremely well researched throughout and totally absorbing. I couldn't put it down and read it twice. Next year I will read it again'

David Finch, Judophotos

'A book that will be riveting to those who practice martial arts and those who don't. As a 49-year old who never did sport, the author took up judo. The book is partly his story, mostly that of the people who made the discipline. It's beautifully written and very funny'

John Meaney, *Cognitive Resonance*

'One of the year's most entertaining sporting books, and the best one to be written about a martial art since Robert Twigger's *Angry White Pyjamas*. It's lively, it's witty and, above all, so persuasively enthusiastic that by the end you'll find yourself feeling an intense urge to try it for yourself'

James Delingpole, *Mail on Sunday*

'I loved *The Pyjama Game*. It is one of the few books that makes judo understandable to a non-judo audience. It transmits some of the beauty and magic of judo while explaining the rigors of training and heartbreak of competition'

Judo Information Site

'Through his own observation of the sport and as a spectator, he is able to capture the *feeling* of an elite competitor. I know this feeling too well and it never lessens with experience'

Kylie Koenig, Australian Judo Squad

'At last someone has written a book that examines every facet of the sport. *The Pyjama Game* is by turns hilarious, intriguing and even horrifying'

Yogi Marlon, sports writer

'It is a fantastic read for all judokas, but unlike some sport books it is a mesmerising read for a wider audience . . . a book judo will be proud of'

Matside Magazine

'*The Pyjama Game*: a fantastic voyage, beautifully written, through this most challenging of sports'

Independent on Sunday

'This is damn fine stuff, and will entertain and enlighten an audience far beyond the confines of the dojo'

Andrew Baker, *Daily Telegraph*

'A brilliant exploration of judo'

Matthew D'Ancona, *Spectator*

Published by Aurum Press

www.thepyjamagame.com

20681759R00234

Printed in Great Britain
by Amazon